Doris Lessing was born in Persia in 1919 but moved to Southern Rhodesia, where her father went to farm, at the age of five. In 1949 she came to London, where she still lives.

Her first novel, *The Grass Is Singing*, was published in 1950, and she made her début as an accomplished writer of short stories with *This Was the Old Chief's Country* in 1951. 1956 saw her last visit to the country where she grew up and which provides the setting for so much of her fiction (the Southern Rhodesian authorities declared her a Prohibited Immigrant after her return to England). Her experiences there produced *Going Home*, a bitter, prophetic and often bleakly funny account of white settler society and its victims. Between 1952 and 1969 her famous novel-sequence, 'Children of Violence', appeared, and in 1962 what is perhaps her most well-known and haunting work, *The Golden Notebook*, was published.

Doris Lessing has been honoured with the Society of Authors' Somerset Maugham Award and is also a winner of the Prix Medici. As a novelist, she ranks among the most distinguished writing in English today, and, in an age when the short story seems to be in sad decline, she is one of the few authors whose writings in this form find both critical acclaim and popular success.

'Mrs Lessing has captured the sight and sound and smell of Africa and put it down on paper so that it may become real and tangible to those who have never set foot on African soil. This perhaps is her greatest achievement.'
Sunday Times

'It is her peculiar gift to write with the kind of honesty and generosity that suggests to the reader he is privileged to be a friend, to feel he knows something of the true ideals, the private agonies and delights that have inspired her writing.'
Times Literary Supplement

Also by Doris Lessing

NOVELS

The Grass Is Singing
Retreat to Innocence
The Golden Notebook
Briefing for a Descent into Hell
Memoirs of a Survivor

In the novel-sequence 'Children of Violence'

Martha Quest
A Proper Marriage
A Ripple from the Storm
Landlocked
The Four-Gated City

NON-FICTION

In Pursuit of the English
Particularly Cats
Going Home

SHORT STORIES

This Was the Old Chief's Country
Five
The Habit of Loving
A Man and Two Women
African Stories
The Story of a Non-marrying Man and Other Stories
Winter in July
The Black Madonna
This Was the Old Chief's Country (Collected African
    Stories Vol. 1)
To Room Nineteen (Collected Stories Vol. 1)
The Temptation of Jack Orkney (Collected Stories Vol. 2)

PLAYS

Play with a Tiger

Doris Lessing

The Sun
Between Their Feet

VOLUME TWO

of Doris Lessing's
Collected African Stories

TRIAD PANTHER

Published in 1979 by Triad/Panther Books
Frogmore, St Albans, Herts AL2 2NF

ISBN 0 586 04601 1

Triad Paperbacks Ltd is an imprint of
Chatto, Bodley Head & Jonathan Cape Ltd
and Granada Publishing Ltd

First published in Great Britain by
Michael Joseph Ltd 1973
Copyright © Doris Lessing 1954, 1957, 1958, 1962, 1963,
1964, 1972, 1973

Made and printed in Great Britain by
Richard Clay (The Chaucer Press) Ltd
Bungay, Suffolk
Set in Linotype Plantin

BIBLIOGRAPHICAL NOTE

This second volume of Doris Lessing's Collected African Stories was published in hardcover by Michael Joseph in 1973. Of these, 'The Black Madonna', 'The Trinket Box', 'The Pig', 'Traitors', and 'Hunger' appeared in *African Stories* (Michael Joseph, 1964), 'Hunger' originally appearing in *Five* (Michael Joseph, 1953). 'The Story of Two Dogs', 'The Sun Between Their Feet', 'A Letter From Home' and 'The New Man' appeared in the 1963 MacGibbon & Kee collection, *A Man and Two Women*; 'The Story of a Non-Marrying Man' in the collection of that name (Cape, 1972) together with 'Spies I Have Known'; and the rest of the stories in *The Habit of Loving* (MacGibbon & Kee, 1957).

These stories have also appeared previously in paperback in the following editions. 'The Black Madonna', 'The Trinket Box', 'The Pig' and 'Traitors' have appeared in *The Black Madonna*; the short novel 'Hunger' is also in *Five*; the stories 'A Letter From Home' 'The Sun Between Their Feet,' 'The Story of Two Dogs' and 'The New Man' have been published as part of the collection *A Man and Two Women*. All the remaining stories except 'Spies I Have Known' and 'A Story of a Non-Marrying Man' are included in *The Habit of Loving*. These collections are all published in Panther Books.

CONTENTS

PREFACE

This collection has in it some of the stories I like best. One of them is the title story to this volume, *The Sun Between Their Feet*. It was written out of memories of a part of Rhodesia that was very different from the part I was brought up in, which was Banket, in Mashonaland, not far from Sinoia. But I used to visit around the Marandellas and Macheke districts, which are mostly sandveld, and scattered all over with clumps of granite boulders piled on each other in a way I haven't seen anywhere else. These piles appear to be so arbitrary, so casual, that sometimes it seems as if a perched boulder may topple with a puff of wind. I spent hours, days, weeks sitting around, walking about, on that pale crusty soil, so different from the heavy dark soil of the district my father's farm was in, examining the vegetation and the insects.

Here, too, is *The Story of Two Dogs*, which I think is as good as any I have done. And it is a 'true' story: at least, there were two pairs of dogs in my childhood, the first called Lion and Tiger, and the second Jock and Bill. I don't know now which incidents belong to which pair of dogs; but it is true that Bill, or the 'stupid' dog, rescued Jock, the 'clever' dog, by gnawing through a strand of wire in which he was trapped – thus wearing his teeth down to stubs and shortening his life.

A Letter from Home seems to me to have in it the stuff of present-day South Africa. What sparked it off was hearing the account of a white friend, living in Cape Town with another – two bachelors in a small house – looked after, or nannied, by a large Zulu woman who treated them both like small boys. And then, as food for the same story, was my thinking about another friend, a marvellous poet, so I am told – but I don't understand his own language – and he writes his poetry in one of the very many languages of the world which 'no one speaks'. Except the million or so people born into it. Which leads one on to the thought that if a poet is born into one of the common languages he can be a world-poet; but if he is, for instance, Afrikaans, he can be as great as any poet in the world but it would be hard for this fact to cross the language barriers.

Of the five long stories, or short novels in *Five, Hunger* which is reprinted here is the failure and, it seems, the most liked.

It came to be written like this. I was in Moscow with a delegation of writers, back in 1952. It was striking that while the members of the British team differed very much politically, we agreed with each other on certain assumptions about literature – in brief, that writing had to be a product of the individual conscience, or soul. Whereas the Russians did not agree at all – not at all. Our debates, many and long, were on this theme.

Stalin was still alive. One day we were taken to see a building full of presents for Stalin, rooms full of every kind of object – pictures, photographs, carpets, clothes, etc., all gifts from his grateful subjects and exhibited by the State to show other subjects and visitors from abroad. It was a hot day. I left the others touring the stuffy building and sat outside to rest. I was thinking about what Russians were demanding in literature – greater simplicity, simple judgments of right and wrong. We, the British, had argued against it, and we felt we were *right* and the Russians *wrong*. But after all, there was Dickens, and such a short time ago, and his characters were all good or bad – unbelievably Good, monstrously Bad, but that didn't stop him from being a great writer. Well, there I was, with my years in Southern Africa behind me, a society as startlingly unjust as Dickens's England. Why, then, could I not write a story of simple good and bad, with clear-cut choices, set in Africa? The plot? Only one possible plot – that a poor black boy or girl should come from a village to the white man's rich town and ... there he would encounter, as occurs in life, good and bad, and after much trouble and many tears he would follow the path of ...

I tried, but it failed. It wasn't true. Sometimes one writes things that don't come off, and feels more affectionate towards them than towards those that worked.

Flight is, I think, a good story. But do I like it because I remember a very old man in a suburb in Africa, in a small house crammed with half-grown girls, all his life in his shelf of birds under jacaranda trees well away from that explosive house? In a green lacy shade he would sit and croon to his birds, or watch them wheel and speed and then come dropping back through the sky to his hand. The memory has something in it of a nostalgic dream.

I am addicted to *The Black Madonna* which is full of the bile that is produced in me by the thought of 'white' society in Southern Rhodesia as I knew and hated it.

Traitors is about two little girls. Why? It should have been a boy and a girl: the children were my brother and myself. I remember there was a short period when I longed for a sister: perhaps this tale records that time.

I have only recently written *Spies I have Known* and *The Non-marrying Man*.

Which brings me to a question raised often by people who write to me, usually from universities. In what order has one written this or that?

This seems to be a question of much interest to scholars. I don't see why. No one who understands anything about how artists work – and there is surely no excuse not to, since artists of all kinds write so plentifully about our creative processes – could ask such a question at all. You can think about a story for years and then write it down in an hour. You may work out the shape of a novel for decades, before spending a few months working on it.

As for the stories like these – which I always think of under the heading of *This Was the Old Chief's Country*, the title of my first collection of stories – when I write one, it is as if I open a gate into a landscape which is always there. Time has nothing to do with it. A certain kind of pulse starts beating, and I recognize it: it is time I wrote another story from that landscape, external and internal at the same time, which was once the Old Chief's Country.

Doris Lessing
January 1972

SPIES I HAVE KNOWN

I don't want you to imagine that I am drawing any sort of comparison between Salisbury, Rhodesia, of thirty years ago, a one-horse town then, if not now, and more august sites. God forbid. But it does no harm to lead into a weighty subject by way of the minuscule.

It was in the middle of the Second World War. A couple of dozen people ran a dozen or so organizations, of varying degrees of leftwingedness. The town, though a capital city, was still in that condition when 'everybody knows everybody else'. The white population was about ten thousand; the number of black people, then as now, only guessed at. There was a Central Post Office, a rather handsome building, and one of the mail sorters attended the meetings of The Left Club. It was he who explained to us the system of censorship operated by the Secret Police. All the incoming mail for the above dozen organizations was first put into a central box marked CENSOR and was read – at their leisure, by certain trusted citizens. Of course all this was as to be expected, and what we knew must be happening. But there were other proscribed organizations, like the Watchtower, a religious sect for some reason suspected by governments up and down Africa (perhaps because they prophesied the imminent end of the world?) and some Fascist organizations – reasonably enough in a war against Fascism. There were organizations of obscure aims and perhaps five members and a capital of five pounds, and also individuals whose mail had first to go through the process, as it were, of decontamination, or defusing. It was this last list of a hundred or so people which was the most baffling. What did they have in common, these sinister ones whose opinions were such a threat to the budding Southern Rhodesian State, then still in the Lord Malvern phase of the Huggins/Lord Malvern/Welenski/Garfield Todd/Winston Field/Smith succession? After months, indeed, years, of trying to understand what could unite them, we had simply to give up. Of course, half were on the left, kaffir lovers and so on, but what of the others? It was when a man wrote a letter to the *Rhodesia Herald* in solemn parody of Soviet official style – as heavy then as now, urging immediate extermination by firing squad of our government, in favour of a team from the Labour Opposition, and we heard from our contact in the Post Office that his name was now on the Black List, that we began to suspect the truth.

Throughout the war, this convenient arrangement continued. Our Man in the Post Office – by then several men, but it doesn't sound so well, kept us informed of what and who was on the Black List. And if our mail was being held up longer than we considered reasonable, the censors being on holiday, or lazy, authority would be gently prodded to hurry things up a little.

This was my first experience of Espionage.

Next was when I knew someone who knew someone who had told him of how a certain Communist Party Secretary had been approached by the man whose occupation it was to tap communist telephones – we are now in Europe. Of course, the machinery for tapping was much more primitive then. Probably by now they have dispensed with human intervention altogether, and a machine judges the degree of a suspicious person's disaffection by the tones of his voice. Then, and in that country, they simply played back records of conversation. This professional had been in the most intimate contact with communism and communists for years, becoming involved with shopping expeditions, husbands late from the office, love affairs, a divorce or so, children's excursions. He had been sucked into active revolutionary politics through the keyhole.

'I don't think you ought to let little Jackie go at all. He'll be in bed much too late, and you know how bad tempered he gets when he is overtired.'

'She said to me No, she said. That's final. If you want to do a thing like that, then you must do it yourself. You shouldn't expect other people to pull your chestnuts out of the fire, she said. If he was rude to you, then it's your place to tell him so.'

He got frustrated, like an intimate friend or lover with paralysis of the tongue. And there was another thing, his involvement was always at a remove. He was listening to events, emotions, several hours old. Sometimes weeks old, as for instance when he went on leave and had to catch up with a month's dangerous material all in one exhausting twenty-four hours. He found that he was getting possessive about certain of his charges, resented his colleagues listening in to 'my suspects'. Once he had to wrestle with temptation because he longed to seek out a certain woman on the point of leaving her husband for another man. Due to his advantageous position he knew the other man was not what she believed. He imagined how he would trail her to the café which he knew she frequented, sit near her, then lean over and ask: 'May I join you? I have something of importance to divulge.' He knew she would agree: he knew her character well. She was unconventional, perhaps not as responsible as she ought to be, careless for instance about the regularity of meals, but fundamentally, he was sure, a good girl with the potentiality of good wifehood. He would say to her: 'Don't do it, my dear! No, don't ask me how I know, I can't tell you that. But if you leave your husband for that man, you'll regret it!' He would press her hands in his, looking deeply into her eyes – he was sure they were brown, for her voice was definitely the voice of a brown-eyed blonde – and then stride for ever out of her life. Afterwards he could check on the success of his intervention through the tapes.

To cut a process short that took some years, he at last went secretly to a communist bookshop, bought some pamphlets, attended a meeting or two, and discovered that he would certainly become a Party Member if it were not that his job, and a very well paid one with good prospects, was to spy on the Communist Party. He felt in a false position. What to do? He turned up at the offices of the Communist Party, asked to see the Secretary, and confessed his dilemma. Roars of laughter from the Secretary.

These roars are absolutely obligatory in this convention, which insists on a greater degree of sophisticated understanding between professionals, even if on opposing sides, even if at war – Party officials, government officials, top ranking soldiers and the like – than the governed, ever a foolish, trusting and sentimental lot.

First, then, the roar. Then a soupçon of whimsicality: alas for this badly-ordered world where men so well-equipped to be friends must be enemies. Finally, the hard offer.

Our friend the telephone-tapper was offered a retaining fee by the Communist Party, and their provisional trust, on condition that he stayed where he was, working for the other side. Of course, what else had he expected? Nor should he have felt insulted, for in such ways are the double agents born, those rare men at an altogether higher level in the hierarchies of espionage than he could ever aspire to reach. But his finer feelings had been hurt by the offer of money, and he refused. He went off and suffered for a week or so, deciding that he really did have to leave his job with the Secret Police – an accurate name for what he was working for, though of course the name it went under was much blander. He returned to the Secretary in order to ask for the second time to become just a rank and file Communist Party member. This time there was no roar of laughter, not even a chuckle, but the frank (and equally obligatory) I-am-concealing-nothing statement of the position. Which was that he surely must be able to see their point of view – The Communist Party's. With a toehold in the enemy camp (a delicate way of describing his salary and his way of life) he could be of real use. To stay where he was could be regarded as a real desire to serve the People's Cause. To leave altogether, becoming just honest John Smith might satisfy his conscience (a subjective and conditioned organ as he must surely know by now if he had read those pamphlets properly) but would leave behind him an image of the capricious, or even the unreliable. What had he planned to tell his employers? 'I am tired of tapping telephones, it offends me!' Or: 'I regard this as an immoral occupation!' – when he had done nothing else for years? Come, come, he hadn't thought it out. He would certainly be under suspicion for ever more by his ex-employers. And of course he could not be so innocent, after so long spent in that atmosphere of vigilance and watchfulness not to expect the communists to keep watch on himself? No, his best course would be to stay exactly where he was, working even harder at tapping telephones. If not, then his frank advice (the Secretary's) could only be that he must become an ordinary citizen, as far from any sort of politics as possible, for his own sake, the sake of the Service he had left, and the sake of the Communist Party – which of *course* they believed he now found his spiritual home.

But the trouble was that he did want to join it. He wanted nothing more than to become part of the world of stern necessities he had followed for so long, but as it were from behind a one-way pane of glass. Integrity had disenfranchised him. From now on he could not hope to serve humanity except through the use of the vote.

His life was empty. His resignation had cut off his involvement, like turning off the television on a soap opera, with the deathless real-life dramas of the tapes.

He felt that he was useless. He considered suicide, but thought better of it. Then, having weathered a fairly routine and unremarkable nervous breakdown, became a contemplative monk – high Church of England.

Another spy I met at a cocktail party, said in the course of chat about this or that – it was in London, in the late Fifties – that at the outbreak of the Second World War he had been in Greece, or perhaps it was Turkey, where at another cocktail party, over the canapés, an official from the British Embassy invited him to spy for his country.

'But I can't,' said this man. 'You must know that perfectly well.'

'But why ever not?' enquired the official. A second Secretary, I think he was.

'Because, as of course you must know, I am a Communist Party member.'

'Indeed? How interesting! But surely that is not going to stand in the way of your desire to serve your country?' said the official, matching ferocious honesty with bland interest.

Cutting this anecdote short – it comes, after all, from a pretty petty level in the affairs of men, this man went home, and spent a sleepless night weighing his allegiances, and decided by morning that of course the Second Secretary was right. He would like to serve his country, which was after all engaged in a war against Fascism. He explained his decision to his superiors in the Communist Party, who agreed with him, and to his wife and his comrades. Then, meeting the Second Secretary at another cocktail party, he informed him of the decision he had taken. He was then invited to attach himself to a certain Army Unit, in some capacity to do with the Ministry of Information. He was to await orders. In due course they came, and he discovered that it was his task to spy on the Navy, or rather, that portion of it operating near him. Our Navy, of course. He was always unable to work out the ideology of this. That a communist should not be set to spy on, let's say, Russia, seemed to him fair and reasonable, but why was he deemed suitable material to spy on his own side? He found it all baffling, and indeed rather lowering. Then, at a cocktail party, he happened to meet a naval officer with whom

he proceeded to get drunk, and they both suddenly understood on a wild hunch that they were engaged on spying on
each other, one for the Navy, and one for the Army. Both found
this work without much uplift, they were simply not able to
put their hearts into it, apart from the fact that they had been
in the same class at prep school and had many other social
ties. Not even the fact that they weren't being paid, since it
was assumed by their superiors – quite correctly of course –
that they would be happy to serve their countries for nothing,
made them feel any better. They developed the habit of meeting regularly in a café where they drank wine and coffee and
played chess in a vine-covered arbour overlooking a particularly fine bit of the Mediterranean where, without going
through all the tedious effort of spying on each other, they
simply gave each other relevant information. They were found
out. Their excuse that they were fighting the war on the same
side was deemed inadequate. They were both given the sack
as spies, and transferred to less demanding work. But until
D-Day and beyond, the British Army spied on the British
Navy, and vice versa. They probably all still do.

The fact that human beings, given half a chance, start seeing
each other's point of view seems to me the only ray of hope
there is for humanity, but obviously this tendency must be one
to cause anguish to seniors in the diplomatic corps and the
employers of your common or garden spy – not the high level
spies, but of that in a moment. Diplomats, until they have
understood why, always complain that as soon as they understand a country and its language really well, hey presto, off
they are whisked to another country. But diplomacy could not
continue if the opposing factotums lost a proper sense of
national hostility. Some diplomatic corps insist that their
employees must only visit among each other, and never frater-
nize with the locals, obviously believing that understanding
with others is inculcated by a sort of osmosis. And of course,
any diplomat that shows signs of going native, that is to say
really enjoying the manners and morals of a place, must be
withdrawn at once.

Not so the masters among the spies: one dedicated to his
country's deepest interests must be worse than useless. The
rarest spirits must be those able to entertain two or three
allegiances at once; the counter spies, the double and triple
agents. Such people are not born. It can't be that they wake up

one morning at the age of thirteen crying: Eureka, I've got it,
I want to be a double agent! That's what I was born to do!
Nor can there be a training school for multiple spies, a kind
of top class that promising pupils graduate towards. Yet that
capacity which might retard a diplomat's career, or mean
death to the small fry among spies, must be precisely the one
watched out for by the Spymasters who watch and manipulate
in the high levels of the world's thriving espionage systems.
What probably happens is that a man drifts, even unwillingly,
into serving his country as a spy – like my acquaintance of the
cocktail party who then found himself spying on the Senior
Service of his own side. Then, whether there through a deep
sense of vocation or without enthusiasm, he must begin by
making mistakes, sometimes pleased with himself and sometimes not; he goes through a phase of wondering whether he
would not have done better to go into the Stock Exchange, or
whatever his alternative was – then suddenly there comes that
moment, fatal to punier men but a sign of his own future
greatness, when he is invaded by sympathy for the enemy.
Long dwelling on what X is doing, likely to be doing, or thinking, or planning, makes X's thoughts as familiar and as likeable
as his own. The points of view of the nation he spends all his
time trying to undo, are comfortably at home in a mind once
tuned only to those of his own dear Fatherland. He is thinking the thoughts of those he used to call enemies before he
understands that he is already psychologically a double agent,
and before he guesses that those men who must always be on
the watch for such precious material have noticed, perhaps
even prognosticated, his condition.

On those levels where the really great spies move, whose
names we never hear, but whose existence we have to deduce,
what fantastic feats of global understanding must be reached,
what metaphysical heights of international brotherhood!

It is of course not possible to do more than take the humblest
flights into speculation, while making do with those so fre-
quent and highly publicized spy dramas, for some reason or
other so very near to farce, that do leave obscurity for our
attention.

It can't be possible that the high reaches of espionage can
have anything in common with, for instance, this small happening.

A communist living in a small town in England, who had

been openly and undramatically a communist for years, and
for whom the state of being a communist had become rather
like the practice of an undemanding religion – this man looked
out of his window one fine summer afternoon to see standing
in the street outside his house a car of such foreignness and
such opulence that he was embarrassed, and at once began to
work out what excuses he could use to his working-class
neighbours whose cars, if any, would be dust in comparison.
Out of this monster of a car came two large smiling Russians,
carrying a teddy bear the size of a sofa, a bottle of vodka, a
long and very heavy roll, which later turned out to be a vast
carpet with a picture of the Kremlin on it, and a box of chocolates of British make, with a pretty lady and a pretty dog.

Every window in the street already had heads packed behind
the curtains.

'Come in,' said he, 'but I don't think I have the pleasure of
knowing who ...'

The roll of carpet was propped in the hall, the three children sent off to play with the teddy bear in the kitchen, and the
box of chocolates set aside for the lady of the house, who was
out doing the week's shopping in the High Street. The vodka
was opened at once.

It turned out that it was his wife they wanted: they were
interested in him only as a go-between. They wished him to
ask his wife, who was an employee of the town council, to get
hold of the records of the Council's meetings, and to pass
these records on to them. Now, this wasn't London, or even
Edinburgh. It was a small unimportant North of England
town, in which it would be hard to imagine anything ever
happening that could be of interest to anyone outside it, let
alone the agents of a Foreign Power. But, said he, these records
are open, anyone could go and get copies – you, for instance –
'Comrades, I shall be delighted to take you to the Town Hall
myself.'

No, what they had been instructed to do was to ask his wife
to procure them minutes and records, nothing less would do.

A long discussion ensued. It was all no use. The Russians
could not be made to see that what they asked was unnecessary.
Nor could they understand that to arrive in a small suburban
street in a small English town in a car the length of a battle-
ship, was to draw the wrong sort of attention.

'But why is that?' they enquired. 'Representatives of the

country where the workers hold power should use a good car. Of course, comrade. You have not thought it out from a class position!'

The climax came when, despairing of the effect of rational argument, they said: 'And comrade, these presents, the bear, the carpet, the chocolates, the vodka, are only a small token in appreciation of your work for our common cause. Of course you will be properly recompensed.'

At which point he was swept by, indeed taken over entirely by, atavistic feelings he had no idea were in him at all. He stood up and pointed a finger shaking with rage at the door: 'How dare you imagine,' he shouted, 'that my wife and I would take money? If I were going to spy, I'd spy for the love of mankind, for duty, and for international socialism. Take those bloody things out of here, wait I'll get that teddy bear from the kids. And you can take your bloody car out of here too.'

His wife, when she came back from the supermarket and heard the story, was even more insulted than he was.

But emotions like these are surely possible only in the lowest possible levels of spy material – in this case so low they didn't qualify for the first step, entrance into the brotherhood.

Full circle back to Our Man in the Post Office, or rather, the first of three.

After sedulous attendance at a lot of left-wing meetings, semi-private and public – for above all Tom was a methodical man who, if engaged in a thing, always gave it full value – he put his hand up one evening in the middle of a discussion about Agrarian Reform in Venezuela, and said: 'I must ask permission to ask a question.'

Everyone always laughed at him when he did this, put up his hand to ask for permission to speak, or to leave, or to have opinions about something. Little did we realize that we were seeing here not just a surface mannerism, or habit, but his strongest characteristic.

It was late in the meeting, at that stage when the floor is well-loaded with empty coffee cups, beer glasses, and full ash trays. Some people had already left.

He wanted to know what he ought to do: 'I want to have the benefit of your expert advice.' As it happened he had already taken the decision he was asking about.

After some two years of a life not so much double – the word implies secrecy – as dual, his boss in the Central Post Office called him to ask how he was enjoying his life with the Left. Tom was as doggedly informative with him as he was with us, and said that we were interesting people, well-informed, and full of a high-class brand of idealism which he found inspiring.

'I always feel good after going to one of their meetings,' he reported he had said. 'It takes you right out of yourself and makes you think.'

His chief said that he, for his part, always enjoyed hearing about idealism and forward-looking thought, and invited Tom to turn in reports about our activities, our discussions, and most particularly our plans for the future, as well in advance as possible.

Tom told us that he said to his boss that 'he didn't like the idea of doing that sort of thing behind our backs, because say what you like about the reds, they are very hospitable'.

The chief had said that it would be for the good of his country.

Tom came to us to say that he had told his boss that he had agreed, because he wanted to be of assistance to the national war effort.

It was clear to everyone that having told us that he had agreed to spy on us, he would, since that was his nature, most certainly go back to his boss and tell him that he had told us that he had agreed to spy. After which he would come back to us to tell us that he had told his boss that ... and so on. Indefinitely, if his boss didn't get tired of it. Tom could not see that his chief would shortly find him unsuitable material for espionage, and might even dismiss him from being a sorter in the Post Office altogether – a nuisance for us. After which he, the chief, would probably look for someone else to give him information.

It was Harry, one of the other two Post Office employees attending Left Club meetings, who suggested that it would probably be himself who would next be invited to spy on us, now that Tom had 'told'. Tom was upset, when everybody began speculating about his probable supercession by Harry or even Dick. The way he saw it was that his complete frankness with both us and his chief was surely deserving of reward. He ought to be left in the job. God knows how he saw the future. Probably that both his boss and ourselves would continue to employ him. We would use him to find out how our letters were slowly moving through the toils of censorship, and to hurry them on, if possible; his chief would use him to spy on us. When I say employ, I don't want anyone to imagine this implies payment. Or at least, certainly not from our side. Ideology had to be his spur, sincerity his reward.

It will by now have been noticed that our Tom was not as bright as he might have been. But he was a pleasant enough youth. He was rather good-looking too, about twenty-two. His physical characteristic was neatness. His clothes were always just so; he had a small alert dark moustache; he had glossy dark well-brushed hair. His rather small hands were well-manicured – the latter trait bound to be found offensive by good colonials, whose eye for such anti-masculine evidence – as they were bound to see it, then if not now – was acute. But he was a fairly recent immigrant, from just before the war, and had not yet absorbed the mores. He probably had not noticed that real Rhodesians, in those days at least, did not like men who went in for a careful appearance.

Tom, in spite of our humorous forecast that he would be bound to tell his boss that he had told us, and his stiff and wounded denials that such a thing was possible, found himself impelled to do just that. He reported back that his chief had 'lost his rag with him'.

But that was not the end. He was offered the job of learning how to censor letters. He had said to his boss that he felt in honour bound to tell us, and his boss said: 'Oh for Christ's sake. Tell them anything you damned well like. You won't be choosing what is to be censored.'

As I said, this was an unsophisticated town in those days, and the condition of 'everybody knowing everybody else' was bound to lead to such warm human situations.

He accepted the offer because: 'My mother always told me that she wanted me to do well for myself, and I'll increase my rating into Schedule Three as soon as I start work on censoring, and that means an increment of £50 a year.'

We congratulated him, and urged him to keep us informed about how people were trained as censors, and he agreed to do this. Shortly after that the war ended, and all the wartime camaraderie of wartime ended as the Cold War began. The ferment of Left activity ended too.

We saw Tom no more, but followed his progress, steady if slow, up the Civil Service. The last I heard he was heading a Department among whose duties is censorship. I imagine him, a man in his fifties, husband and no doubt a father, looking down the avenues of lost time of those dizzy days when he was a member of a dangerous revolutionary organization. 'Yes,' he must often say, 'you can't tell me anything about them. They are idealistic, I can grant you so much, but they are dangerous. Dangerous and wrong-headed! I left them as soon as I understood what they really were.'

But of our three Post Office spies Harry was the one whose career, for a while at least, was the most rewarding for humanist idealists.

He was a silent, desperately shy schoolboy who came to a public meeting and fell madly in love for a week or so with the speaker, a girl giving her first public speech and as shy as he was. His father had died and his mother, as the psychiatrists and welfare workers would say, was 'inadequate'. That is to say, she was not good at being a widow, and was frail in health. What little energy she had went into earning enough money for her two younger sons to live on. She nagged at Harry for not having ambition, and for not studying for the examinations which would take him up the ladder into the next grade in the Post Office – and for wasting time with the reds. He longed to be of use. For three years he devoted all his spare time to organization on the Left, putting up exhibitions, hiring halls and rooms, decorating ballrooms for fund-raising dances, getting advertisements for our socialist magazine – circulation two thousand, and laying it out and selling it. He argued principle with town councillors: 'But it's not *fair* not to let us have the hall, this is a democratic country, isn't it?' – and spent at least three nights a week discussing world affairs in smoke-filled rooms.

At the time we would have dismissed as beyond redemption anyone who suggested it, but I daresay now that the main function of those gatherings was social. Southern Rhodesia was never exactly a hospitable country for those interested in anything but sport and the sundowner, and the fifty or so people who came to the meetings were all, whether in the Forces, or refugees from Europe, or simply Rhodesians, souls in need of congenial company. And they were friendly occasions, those meetings, sometimes going on till dawn.

A girl none of us had seen before came to a public meeting. She saw Harry, a handsome, confident, loquacious, energetic, efficient young man. Everyone relied on him.

She fell in love, took him home, and her father, recognizing one of the world's born organizers, made him manager in his hardware shop.

Which leaves the third, Dick. Now there are some people who should not be allowed anywhere near meetings, debates, or similar intellect-fermenting agencies. He came to two meetings. Harry brought him, describing him as 'keen'. It was Harry who was keen. Dick sat on the floor on a cushion. Wild bohemian ways, these, for well-brought-up young whites. His forehead puckered like a puppy's while he tried to follow wild unRhodesian thought. He, like Tom, was a neat, well-set-up youth. Perhaps the Post Office, or at least in Rhodesia, is an institution that attracts the well-ordered? I remember he reminded me of a boiled sweet, bland sugar with a chemical tang. Or perhaps he was like a bulldog, all sleek latent ferocity, with its little bulging eyes, its little snarl. Like Tom, he was one for extracting exact information. 'I take it you people believe that human nature can be changed?'

At the second meeting he attended, he sat and listened as before. At the end he enquired whether we thought socialism was a good thing in this country where there was the white man's burden to consider.

He did not come to another meeting. Harry said that he had found us seditious and unRhodesian. Also insincere. We asked Harry to go and ask Dick why he thought we were insincere, and to come back and tell us. It turned out that Dick wanted to know why The Left Club did not take over the government of the country and run it, if we thought the place ill run. But we forgot Dick, particularly as Harry, at the zenith of his efficiency and general usefulness, was drifting off with his future wife to become a hardware store manager. And by then Tom was lost to us.

Suddenly we heard that 'The Party for Democracy, Liberty, and Freedom' was about to hold a preliminary mass meeting. One of us was delegated to go along and find out what was happening. This turned out to be me.

The public meeting was in a sideroom off a ballroom in one of the town's three hotels. It was furnished with a sideboard to hold the extra supplies of beer and sausage rolls and peanuts consumed so plentifully during the weekly dances, a palm in a pot so tall the top fronds were being pressed down by the ceiling, and a dozen stiff dining-room chairs ranged one by one along the walls. There were eleven men and women in the room, including Dick. Unable to understand immediately why this gathering struck me as so different from the ones in which I spent so much of my time, I then saw it was because there were elderly people present. Our gatherings loved only the young.

Dick was wearing his best suit in dark grey flannel. It was a very hot evening. His face was scarlet with endeavour and covered with sweat, which he kept sweeping off his forehead with impatient fingers. He was reading an impassioned document in tone rather like the Communist Manifesto, which began: 'Fellow Citizens of Rhodesia! Sincere Men and Women! This is the Time for Action! Arise and look about you and enter into your Inheritance! Put the forces of International Capital to flight!'

He was standing in front of the chairs, his well-brushed little head bent over his notes, which were handwritten and in places hard to read, so that these inflammatory sentiments were being stammered and stumbled out, while he kept correcting himself, wiping off sweat, and then stopping with an appealing circular glance around the room at the others. Towards him were lifted ten earnest faces, as if at a saviour or a Party leader.

The programme of this nascent Party was simple. It was to 'take over by democratic means but as fast as possible' all the land and the industry of the country 'but to cause as little inconvenience as possible' and 'as soon as it was feasible' to institute a régime of true equality and fairness in this 'land of Cecil Rhodes'.

He was intoxicated by the emanations of admiration from his audience. Burning, passionate faces like these (alas, and I saw how far we had sunk away from fervour) were no longer to be seen at our Left Club meetings, which long ago had sailed away on the agreeable tides of debate and intellectual speculation.

The faces belonged to a man of fifty or so, rather grey and beaten, who described himself as a teacher 'planning the total reform of the entire educational system'; a woman of middle age, a widow, badly dressed and smoking incessantly, who looked as if she had long since gone beyond what she was strong enough to bear from life; an old man with an angelic pink face fringed with white tufts who said he was named after Keir Hardie; three schoolboys, the son of the widow and his two friends; the woman attendant from the ladies' cloakroom who had unlocked this room to set out the chairs and then had stayed out of interest, since it was her afternoon off; two aircraftsmen from the RAF; Dick the convener; and a beautiful young woman no one had ever seen before who, as soon as Dick had finished his manifesto, stood up to make a plea for vegetarianism. She was ruled out of order. 'We have to get power first, and then we'll simply do what the majority wants.' As for me, I was set apart from them by my lack of fervour, and by Dick's hostility.

This was in the middle of the Second World War, whose aim it was to defeat the hordes of National Socialism. The Union of Socialist Soviet Republics was thirty years old. It was more than a hundred and fifty years after the French Revolution, and rather more than that after the American Revolution which overthrew the tyrannies of Britain. The Independence of India would shortly be celebrated. It was twenty years after the death of Lenin. Trotsky still lived.

One of the schoolboys, a friend of the widow's son, put up his hand to say timidly, instantly to be shut up, that 'he believed there might be books which we could read about socialism and that sort of thing'.

'Indeed there are,' said the namesake of Keir Hardie, nodding his white locks, 'but we needn't follow the writ that runs in other old countries, when we have got a brand new one here.'

(It must be explained that the whites of Rhodesia, then as now, are always referring to 'this new country'.)

'As for books,' said Dick, eyeing me with all the scornful self-command he had acquired since leaving his cushion weeks before on the floor of our living-room, 'books don't seem to do some people any good, so why do we need them? It is all perfectly simple. It isn't right for a few people to own all the wealth of a country. It isn't fair. It should be shared out among everybody, equally, and then that would be a democracy.'

'Well, obviously,' said the beautiful girl.

'Ah yes,' sighed the poor tired woman, emphatically crushing out her cigarette and lighting a new one.

'Perhaps it would be better if I moved that palm a little,'

said the cloakroom attendant, 'it does seem to be a little in your way perhaps.' But Dick did not let her show her agreement in this way.

'Never mind about the palm,' he said. 'It's not important.'

And this was the point when someone asked: 'Excuse me, but where do the Natives come in?' (In those days, the black inhabitants of Rhodesia were referred to as the Natives.)

This was felt to be in extremely bad taste.

'I don't really think that is applicable,' said Dick hotly. 'I simply don't see the point of bringing it up at all unless it is to make trouble.'

'They do live here,' said one of the RAF.

'Well, I must withdraw altogether if there's any likelihood of us getting mixed up with kaffir trouble,' said the widow.

'You can be assured that there will be nothing of that,' said Dick, firmly in control, in the saddle, leader of all, after only half an hour of standing up in front of his mass meeting.

'I don't see that,' said the beautiful girl. 'I simply don't see that at all! We must have a policy for the Natives.'

Even twelve people in one small room, whether starting a mass Party or not, meant twelve different, defined, passionately held viewpoints. The meeting at last had to be postponed for a week to allow those who had not had a chance to air their views to have their say. I attended this second meeting. There were fifteen people present. The two RAF were not there, but there were six white trade unionists from the railways who, hearing of the new party, had come to get a resolution passed. 'In the opinion of this meeting, the Native is being advanced too fast towards civilization and in his own interests the pace should be slowed.'

This resolution was always being passed in those days, on every possible occasion. It probably still is.

But the nine from the week before were already able to form a solid block against this influx of alien thought – not as champions of the Natives, of course not, but because it was necessary to attend to first things first. 'We have to take over the country first, by democratic methods. That won't take long, because it is obvious our programme is only fair, and after that we can decide what to do about the Natives.' The six railway workers then left, leaving the nine from last week, who proceeded to form their Party for Democracy, Liberty and Freedom. A steering committee of three was appointed to draft a constitution.

And that was the last anyone ever heard of it, except for one cyclostyled pamphlet which was called 'Capitalism is Unfair! Let's Join Together to Abolish it! This Means You!'

The war was over. Intellectual ferments of this sort occurred no more. Employees of the Post Office, all once again good citizens properly employed in sport and similar endeavours, no longer told the citizens in what ways they were censored and when.

Dick did not stay in the Post Office. That virus, politics, was in his veins for good. From being a spokesman for socialism for the whites, he became, as a result of gibes that he couldn't have socialism that excluded most of the population, an exponent of the view that Natives must not be advanced too fast in their own interests, and from there he developed into a Town Councillor, and from there into a Member of Parliament. And that is what he still is, a gentleman of distinguished middle age, an indefatigable server on Parliamentary Committees and Commissions, particularly those to do with the Natives, on whom he is considered an authority.

An elderly bulldog of the bulldog breed he is, every inch of him.

THE STORY OF A NON-MARRYING MAN

I met Johnny Blakeworthy at the end of his life. I was at the beginning of mine, about ten or twelve years old. This was in the early Thirties, when the Slump had spread from America even to us, in the middle of Africa. The very first sign of the Slump was the increase in the number of people who lived by their wits, or as vagrants.

Our house was on a hill, the highest point of our farm. Through the farm went the only road, a dirt track, from the railway station seven miles away, our shopping and mail centre, to the farms farther on. Our nearest neighbours were three, four, and seven miles away. We could see their roofs flash in the sunlight, or gleam in the moonlight across all those trees, ridges, and valleys.

From the hill we could see the clouds of dust that marked the passage of cars or wagons along the track. We would say: 'That must be so-and-so going in to fetch his mail.' Or: 'Cyril said he had to get a spare for the plough, his broke down, that must be him now.'

If the cloud of dust turned off the main road and moved up through the trees towards us, we had time to build up the fire and put on the kettle. At busy times for the farmers, this happened seldom. Even at slack times, there might be no more than three or four cars a week, and as many wagons. It was mostly a white man's road, for the Africans moving on foot used their own quicker, short-cutting paths. White men coming to the house on foot were rare, though less rare as the Slump set in. More and more often, coming through the trees up the hill, we saw walking towards us a man with a bundle of blankets over his shoulder, a rifle swinging in his hand. In the blanket-roll were always a frying pan and a can of water, sometimes a couple of tins of bully beef, or a Bible, matches, a twist of dried meat. Sometimes this man had an African servant walking with him. These men always called themselves Prospectors, for that was a respectable occupation. Many did prospect, and nearly always for gold.

One evening, as the sun was going down, up the track to our

house came a tall stooped man in shabby khaki with a rifle and
a bundle over one shoulder. We knew we had company for
the night. The rules of hospitality were that no one coming to
our homes in the bush could be refused; every man was fed,
and asked to stay as long as he wanted.

Johnny Blakeworthy was burned by the suns of Africa to a
dark brown, and his eyes in a dried wrinkled face were grey,
the whites much inflamed by the glare. He kept screwing up
his eyes, as if in sunlight, and then, in a remembered effort of
will, letting loose his muscles, so that his face kept clenching
and unclenching like a fist. He was thin: he spoke of having
had malaria recently. He was old: it was not only the sun
that had so deeply lined his face. In his blanket-roll he had, as
well as the inevitable frying pan, an enamel one-pint saucepan,
a pound of tea, some dried milk, and a change of clothing. He
wore long, heavy khaki trousers for protection against lashing
grasses and grass-seeds, and a khaki bush-shirt. He also owned
a washed-out grey sweater for frosty nights. Among these
items was a corner of a sack full of maize-meal. The presence of
the maize-flour was a statement, and probably unambiguous,
for the Africans ate maize-meal porridge as their staple food.
It was cheap, easily obtainable, quickly cooked, nourishing,
but white men did not eat it, at least, not as the basis of their
diet, because they did not wish to be put on the same level as
Africans. The fact that this man carried it, was why my father,
discussing him later with my mother, said: 'He's probably
gone native.'

This was not criticism. Or rather, while with one part of
the collective ethos the white men might say, He's gone
native! and in anger; with a different part of their minds, or
at different times it could be said in bitter envy. But that is
another story . . .

Johnny Blakeworthy was of course asked to stay for supper
and for the night. At the lamplit table, which was covered
with every sort of food, he kept saying how good it was to see
so much real food again, but it was in a vaguely polite way,
as if he was having to remind himself that this was how he
should feel. His plate was loaded with food, and he ate, but
kept forgetting to eat, so that my mother had to remind him,
putting a little bit more of nice undercut, a splash of gravy,
helpings of carrots and spinach from the garden. But by the
end he had eaten very little, and hadn't spoken much either,

though the meal gave an impression of much conversation and interest and eating, like a feast, so great was our hunger for company, so many were our questions. Particularly the two children questioned and demanded, for the life of such a man, walking quietly by himself through the bush, sometimes twenty miles or more a day, sleeping by himself under the stars, or the moon, or whatever weather the seasons sent him, prospecting when he wished, stopping to rest when he needed – such a life, it goes without saying, set us restlessly dreaming of lives different from those we were set towards by school and by parents.

We did learn that he had been on the road for 'some time, yes, some time now, yes'. That he was sixty. That he had been born in England, in the South, near Canterbury. That he had been adventuring up and down and around Southern Africa all his life – but adventure was not the word he used, it was the word we children repeated until we saw that it made him uncomfortable. He had mined: had indeed owned his own mine. Had farmed, but had not done well. Had done all kinds of work, but 'I like to be my own master.' He had owned a store, but 'I get restless, and I must be on the move.'

Now there was nothing in this we hadn't heard before – every time, indeed, that such a wanderer came to our door. There was nothing out of the ordinary in his extraordinariness, except, perhaps, as we remembered later, sucking all the stimulation we could out of the visit, discussing it for days, he did not have a prospector's pan, nor had he asked my father for permission to prospect on this farm. We could not remember a prospector who had failed to become excited by the farm, for it was full of chipped rocks and reefs, trenches and shafts, which some people said went back to the Phoenicians. You couldn't walk a hundred yards without seeing signs ancient and modern of the search for gold. The district was called 'Banket' because it had running through it reefs of the same formation as reefs on the Rand called Banket. The name alone was like a signpost.

But Johnny said he liked to be on his way by the time the sun was up. I saw him leave, down the track that was sun-flushed, the trees all rosy on one side. He shambled away out of sight, a tall, much too thin, rather stooping man in washed-out khaki and soft hide shoes.

Some months later, another man, out of work and occupying himself with prospecting, was asked if he had ever met up with Johnny Blakeworthy, and he said yes, he had indeed! He went on with indignation to say that 'he had gone native' in the Valley. The indignation was false, and we assumed that this man too might have 'gone native', or that he wished he had, or could. But Johnny's lack of a prospecting pan, his maize meal, his look at the supper table of being out of place and unfamiliar – all was explained. 'Going native' implied that a man would have a 'bush wife', but it seemed Johnny did not.

'He said he's had enough of the womenfolk, he's gone to get out of their way,' said this visitor.

I did not describe, in its place, the thing about Johnny's visit that struck us most, because at the time it did not strike us as more than agreeably quaint. It was only much later that the letter he wrote us matched up with others, and made a pattern.

Three days after Johnny's visit to us, a letter arrived from him. I remember my father expected to find that it would ask, after all, for permission to prospect. But any sort of letter was odd. Letter-writing equipment did not form part of a tramp's gear. The letter was on blue Croxley writing paper, and in a blue Croxley envelope, and the writing was as neat as a child's. It was a 'bread and butter' letter. He said that he had very much enjoyed our kind hospitality, and the fine cooking of the lady of the house. He was grateful for the opportunity of making our acquaintance. 'With my best wishes, yours very truly, Johnny Blakeworthy.'

Once he had been a well-brought-up little boy from a small English country town. 'You must always write and say thank you after enjoying hospitality, Johnny.'

We talked about the letter for a long time. He must have dropped in at the nearest store after leaving our farm. It was twenty miles away. He probably bought a single sheet of paper and a lone envelope. This meant that he had got them from the African part of the store, where such small retailing went on – at vast profit, of course, to the storekeeper. He must have bought one stamp, and walked across to the post office to hand the letter over the counter. Then, due having been paid to his upbringing, he moved back to the African tribe where he lived beyond post offices, letter writing, and other impedimenta that went with being a white man.

The next glimpse I had of the man, I still have no idea where to fit into the pattern I was at last able to make.

It was years later. I was a young woman at a morning tea party. This one, like all the others of its kind, was an excuse for gossip, and most of that was – of course, since we were young married women, about men and marriage. A girl, married not more than a year, much in love, and unwilling to sacrifice her husband to the collective, talked instead about her aunt from the Orange Free State. 'She was married for years to a real bad one, and then up he got and walked out. All she heard from him was a nice letter, you know, like a letter after a party or something. It said Thank you very much for the nice time. Can you beat that? And later still she found she had never been married to him because all the time he was married to someone else.'

'Was she happy?' one of us asked, and the girl said, 'She was nuts all right, she said it was the best time of her life.'

'Then what was she complaining about?'

'What got her was, having to say Spinster, when she was as good as married all those years. And that letter got her goat, I feel I must write and thank you for ... something like that.'

'What was his name?' I asked, suddenly understanding what was itching at the back of my mind.

'I don't remember. Johnny something or other.'

That was all that came out of that most typical of South African scenes, the morning tea party on the deep shady veranda, the trays covered with every kind of cake and biscuit, the gossiping young women, watching their offspring at play under the trees, filling in a morning of their lazy lives before going back to their respective homes where they would find their meals cooked for them, the table laid, and their husbands waiting. That tea party was thirty years ago, and still that town has not grown so wide that the men can't drive home to take their midday meals with their families. I am talking of white families, of course.

The next bit of the puzzle came in the shape of a story which I read in a local paper, of the kind that gets itself printed in the spare hours of presses responsible for much more renowned newspapers. This one was called the *Valley Advertiser*, and its circulation might have been ten thousand. The story was headed: Our Prize-winning story, The Fragrant Black Aloe. By our new Discovery, Alan McGinnery.

'When I have nothing better to do, I like to stroll down the Main Street, to see the day's news being created, to catch fragments of talk, and to make up stories about what I hear. Most people enjoy coincidences, it gives them something to talk about. But when there are too many, it makes an unpleasant feeling that the long arm of coincidence is pointing to a region where a rational person is likely to feel uncomfortable. This morning was like that. It began in a flower shop. There a woman with a shopping list was saying to the salesman: "Do you sell black aloes?" It sounded like something to eat.

' "Never heard of them," said he. "But I have a fine range of succulents. I can sell you a miniature rock garden on a tray."

' "No, no, no. I don't want the ordinary aloes. I've got all those. I want the Scented Black Aloe."

'Ten minutes later, waiting to buy a toothbrush at the cosmetic counter at our chemist, Harry's Pharmacy, I heard a woman ask for a bottle of Black Aloe.

'Hello, I thought, black aloes have suddenly come into my life!

' "We don't stock anything like that," said the salesgirl, offering rose, honeysuckle, lilac, white violets and jasmine, while obviously reflecting that black aloes must make a bitter kind of perfume.

'Half an hour later I was in a seedshop, and when I heard a petulant female voice ask: "Do you stock succulents?" then I knew what was coming. This had happened to me before, but I couldn't remember where or when. Never before had I heard of the Scented Black Aloe, and there it was, three times in an hour.

'When she had gone I asked the salesman, "Tell me, is there such a thing as the Scented Black Aloe?"

' "Your guess is as good as mine," he said. "But people always want what's difficult to find."

'And at that moment I remembered where I had heard that querulous, sad, insistent hungry note in a voice before (voices, as it turned out!), the note that means that the Scented Black Aloe represents, for that time, all the heart's desire.

'It was before the war. I was in the Cape and I had to get to Nairobi. I had driven the route before, and I wanted to get it over. Every couple of hours or so you pass through some little dorp, and they are all the same. They are hot, and dusty. In the tearoom there is a crowd of youngsters eating ice-cream

and talking about motor cycles and film stars. In the bars men
stand drinking beer. The restaurant, if there is one, is bad, or
pretentious. The waitress longs only for the day when she can
get to the big city, and she says the name of the city as if it
was Paris, or London, but when you reach it, two hundred or
five hundred miles on, it is a slightly larger dorp, with the
same dusty trees, the same tearoom, the same bar, and five
thousand people instead of a hundred.

'On the evening of the third day I was in the Northern
Transvaal, and when I wanted to stop for the night, the sun
was blood-red through a haze of dust, and the main street was
full of cattle and people. There was the yearly Farmers' Show
in progress, and the hotel was full. The proprietor said there
was a woman who took in people in emergencies.

'The house was by itself at the end of a straggling dust
street, under a large jacaranda tree. It was small, with chocolate-
coloured trellis-work along the veranda, and the roof was
sagging under scarlet bougainvillaea. The woman who came
to the door was a plump, dark-haired creature in a pink apron,
her hands floury with cooking.

'She said the room was not ready. I said that I had come all
the way from Bloemfontein that morning, and she said, "Come
in, my second husband was from there when he came here in
the beginning."

'Outside the house was all dust, and the glare was bad, but
inside it was cosy, with flowers and ribbons and cushions and
china behind glass. In every conceivable place were pictures
of the same man. You couldn't get away from them. He
smiled down from the bathroom wall, and if you opened a
cupboard door, there he was, stuck up among the dishes.

'She spent two hours cooking a meal, said over and over
again how a woman has to spend all her day cooking a meal
that is eaten in five minutes, enquired after my tastes in food,
offered second helpings. In between, she talked about her
husband. It seemed that four years ago a man had arrived in
the week of the Show, asking for a bed. She never liked taking
in single men, for she was a widow living alone, but she did
like the look of him, and a week later they were married. For
eleven months they lived in a dream of happiness. Then he
walked out and she hadn't heard of him since, except for one
letter, thanking her for all her kindness. That letter was like a
slap in the face, she said. You don't thank a wife for being

kind, like a hostess, do you? Nor do you send her Christmas cards. But he had sent her one the Christmas after he left, and there it was, on the mantelpiece, With Best Wishes for a Happy Christmas. But he was so good to me, she said. He gave me every penny he ever earned, and I didn't need it, because my first hubby left me provided for. He got a job as a ganger on the railways. She could never look at another man after him. No woman who knew anything about life would. He had his faults of course, like everyone. He was restless and moody, but he loved her honestly, she could see that, and underneath it all, he was a family man.

'That went on until the cocks began to crow and my face ached with yawning.

'Next morning I continued my drive North, and that night, in Southern Rhodesia, I drove into a small town full of dust and people standing about in their best clothes among milling cattle. The hotel was full. It was Show time.

'When I saw the house, I thought time had turned back twenty-four hours, for there were the creepers weighing down the roof, and the trellised veranda, and the red dust heaped all around it. The attractive woman who came to the door was fair-haired. Behind her, through the door, I saw a picture on the wall of the same handsome blond man with his hard grey eyes that had sunmarks raying out from around them into the sunburn. On the floor was playing a small child, obviously his.

'I said where I had come from that morning, and she said wistfully that her husband had come from there three years before. It was all just the same. Even the inside of the house was like the other, comfortable and frilly and full. But it needed a man's attention. All kinds of things needed attention. We had supper and she talked about her "husband" – he had lasted until the birth of the baby and a few weeks beyond it – in the same impatient, yearning, bitter, urgent voice of her sister of the evening before. As I sat there listening, I had the ridiculous feeling that in hearing her out so sympathetically I was being disloyal to the other deserted "wife" four hundred miles South. Of course he had his faults, she said. He drank too much sometimes, but men couldn't help being men. And sometimes he went into a daydream for weeks at a stretch and didn't hear what you said. But he was a good husband, for all that. He had got a job in the Sales Department of the Agricultural Machinery Store, and he had worked hard. When the little boy was born he was so pleased ... and then he left. Yes, he did write once, he wrote a long letter saying he would never forget her "affectionate kindness". That letter really upset her. It was a funny thing to say, wasn't it?

'Long after midnight I went to sleep under such a large tinted picture of the man that it made me uncomfortable. It was like having someone watching you sleep.

'Next evening, when I was about to drive out of Southern Rhodesia into Northern Rhodesia, I was half looking for a little town full of clouds of reddish dust and crowding cattle, the small house, the waiting woman. There seemed no reason why this shouldn't go on all the way to Nairobi.

'But it was not until the day after that, on the Copper Belt in Northern Rhodesia, that I came to a town full of cars and people. There was going to be a dance that evening. The big hotels were full. The lady whose house I was directed to was plump, red-haired, voluble. She said she loved putting people up for the night, though there was no need for her to do it since while her husband might have his faults (she said this with what seemed like hatred) he made good money at the garage where he was a mechanic. Before she was married, she had earned her living by letting rooms to travellers, which was how she had met her husband. She talked about him while we waited for him to come in to supper. "He does this every night, every night of my life! You'd think it wasn't much to ask, to come in for meals at the right time, instead of letting everything spoil, but once he gets into the bar with the men, there is no getting him out."

'There wasn't a hint in her voice of what I had heard in the voices of the other two women. And I have often wondered since if in her case too absence would make the heart grow fonder. She sighed often and deeply, and said that when you were single you wanted to be married, and when you were married, you wanted to be single, but what got her was, she had been married before, and she ought to have known better. Not that this one wasn't a big improvement on the last, whom she had divorced.

'He didn't come in until the bar closed, after ten. He was not as good-looking as in his photographs, but that was because his overalls were stiff with grease, and there was oil on his face. She scolded him for being late, and for not having washed, but

all he said was: "Don't try to housetrain me." At the end of
the meal she wondered aloud why she spent her life cooking
and slaving for a man who didn't notice what he ate, and he
said she shouldn't bother, because it was true, he didn't care
what he ate. He nodded at me, and went out again. It was
after midnight when he came back, with a stardazed look,
bringing a cold draught of night air into the hot lamplit room.
' "So you've decided to come in?" she complained.
' "I walked out into the veld a bit. The moon is strong
enough to read by. There's rain on the wind." He put his arm
around her waist and smiled at her. She smiled back, her
bitterness forgotten. The wanderer had come home.'

I wrote to Alan McGinnery and asked him if there had been
a model for his story. I told him why I wanted to know, told
him of the old man who had walked up to our house through
the bush, fifteen years before. There was no reason to think
it was the same man, except for that one detail, the letters he
wrote, like 'bread and butter' letters after a party or a visit.

I got this reply: 'I am indebted to you for your interesting
and informative letter. You are right in thinking my little
story had its start in real life. But in most ways it is far from
fact. I took liberties with the time of the story, moving it
forward by years, no, decades, and placing it in a modern setting. For the times when Johnny Blakeworthy was loving
and leaving so many young women – I'm afraid he was a
very bad lot! – are now out of the memory of all but the
elderly among us. Everything is so soft and easy now. "Civilization" so-called has overtaken us. But I was afraid if I put
my "hero" into his real setting, it would seem so exotic to
present-day readers that they would read my little tale for
the sake of the background, finding that more interesting than
my "hero".

'It was just after the Boer War. I had volunteered for it, as a
young man does, for the excitement, not knowing what sort
of war it really was. Afterwards I decided not to return to
England. I thought I would try the mines, so I went to Johannesburg, and there I met my wife, Lena. She was the cook
and housekeeper in a men's boarding-house, a rough job, in
rough days. She had a child by Johnny, and believed herself
to be married to him. So did I. When I made enquiries, I

found she had never been married, the papers he had produced at the office were all false. This made things easy for us in the practical sense, but made them worse in some ways. For she was bitter and I am afraid never really got over the wrong done to her. But we married, and I became the child's father. She was the original of the second woman in my story. I describe her as home-loving, and dainty in her ways. Even when she was cooking for all those miners, and keeping herself and the boy on bad wages, living in a room not much larger than a dog's kennel, it was all so neat and pretty. That was what took my fancy first. I daresay it was what took Johnny's too, to begin with, at any rate.

'Much later – very much later, the child was almost grown, so it was after the Great War, I happened to hear someone speak of Johnny Blakeworthy. It was a woman who had been "married" to him. It never crossed our minds to think – Lena and me – that he had betrayed more than one woman. After careful thought, I decided never to tell her. But I had to know. By then I had done some careful field work. The trail began, or at least, began for me, in Cape Province, with a woman I had heard spoken of, and had then tracked down. She was the first woman in my story, a little plump pretty thing. At the time Johnny married her, she was the daughter of a Boer farmer, a rich one. I don't have to tell you that this marriage was unpopular. It took place just before the Boer War, that nasty time was to come, but she was a brave girl to marry an Englishman, a *roinek*. Her parents were angry, but later they were kind and took her back when he left her. He did really marry her, in Church, everything correct and legal. I believe that she was his first love. Later she divorced him. It was a terrible thing, a divorce for those simple people. Now things have changed so much, and people wouldn't believe how narrow and churchbound they were then. That divorce hurt her whole life. She did not marry again. It was not because she did not want to! She had fought with her parents, saying she must get a divorce, because she wanted to be married. But no one married her. In that old-fashioned rural community, in those days, she was a Scarlet Woman. A sad thing, for she was a really nice woman. What struck me was that she spoke of Johnny with no bitterness at all. Even twenty years later, she loved him.

'From her, I followed up other clues. With my own wife, I found four women in all. I made it three in my little story: life is always much more lavish with coincidence and drama than any fiction writer dares to be. The red-headed woman I described was a barmaid in a hotel. She hated Johnny. But there was little doubt in my mind what would happen if he walked in through that door.

'I told my wife that I had been big game hunting. I did not want to stir up old unhappiness. After she died I wrote the story of the journey from one woman to another, all now of middle age, all of whom had been "married" to Johnny. But I had to alter the settings of the story. How fast everything has changed! I would have had to describe the Boer family on their farm, such simple and old-fashioned, good and bigoted people. And their oldest daughter – the "bad" one. There are no girls like that now, not even in convents. Where in the world now would you find girls brought up as strictly and as narrowly as those on those Boer farms, fifty years ago? And *still* she had the courage to marry her Englishman, that is the marvellous thing. Then I would have had to describe the mining camps of Johannesburg. Then the life of a woman married to a storekeeper in the bush. Her nearest neighbour was fifty miles away and they didn't have cars in those days. Finally, the early days of Bulawayo, when it was more like a shanty town than a city. No, it was Johnny that interested me, so I decided to make the story modern, and in that way the reader would not be distracted by what is past and gone.'

It was from an African friend who had known the village in which Johnny died that I heard of his last years. Johnny walked into the village, asked to see the Chief, and when the Chief assembled with his elders, asked formally for permission to live in the village, as an African, not as a white man. All this was quite correct, and polite, but the elders did not like it. This village was a long way from the centres of white power, up towards the Zambesi. The traditional life was still comparatively unchanged, unlike the tribes near the white cities, whose structure had been smashed for ever. The people of this tribe cherished their distance from the white man, and feared his influence. At least, the older ones did. While they had nothing against this white man as a man – on the contrary, he seemed more human than most – they did not want a white man in their life. But what could they do? Their traditions of hospitality were strong: strangers, visitors, travellers, must be sheltered and fed. And they were democratic: a man was as good as his behaviour, it was against their beliefs to throw a person out for a collective fault. And perhaps they were, too, a little curious. The white men these people had seen were the tax-collectors, the policemen, the Native Commissioners, all coldly official or arbitrary. This white man behaved like a suppliant, sitting quietly on the outskirts of the village, beyond the huts, under a tree, waiting for the council to make up its mind. Finally they let him stay, on condition that he shared the life of the village in every way. This proviso they probably thought would get rid of him. But he lived there until he died, six years, with short trips away to remind himself, perhaps, of the strident life he had left. It was on such a trip that he had walked up to our house and stayed the night.

The Africans called him Angry Face. This name implied that it was only the face which was angry. It was because of his habit of screwing up then letting loose his facial muscles. They also called him Man Without a Home, and The Man Who Has no Woman.

The women found him intriguing, in spite of his sixty years. They hung about his hut, gossiped about him, brought him presents. Several made offers, even young girls.

The Chief and his elders conferred again, under the great tree in the centre of the village, and then called him to hear their verdict.

'You need a woman,' they said, and in spite of all his protests, made it a condition of his staying with them, for the sake of the tribe's harmony.

They chose for him a woman of middle age whose husband had died of the blackwater fever, and who had had no children. They said that a man of his age could not be expected to give the patience and attention that small children need. According to my friend, who as a small boy had heard much talk of this white man who had preferred their way of life to his own, Johnny and his new woman 'lived together in kindness'.

It was while I was writing this story that I remembered something else. When I was at school in Salisbury there was a girl called Alicia Blakeworthy. She was fifteen, a 'big girl' to me. She lived with her mother on the fringes of the town. Her step-father had left them. He had walked out.

Her mother had a small house, in a large garden, and she took in paying guests. One of these guests had been Johnny. He had been working as a game warden up towards the Zambesi river, and had had malaria badly. She nursed him. He married her and took a job as a counter hand in the local store. He was a bad husband to Mom, said Alicia. Terrible. Yes, he brought in money, it wasn't that. But he was a cold hardhearted man. He was no company for them. He would just sit and read, or listen to the radio, or walk around by himself all night. And he never appreciated what was done for him.

Oh how we schoolgirls all hated this monster! What a heartless beast he was.

But the way *he* saw it, he had stayed for four long years in a suffocating town house surrounded by a domesticated garden. He had worked from eight to four selling groceries to lazy women. When he came home, this money, the gold he had earned by his slavery, was spent on chocolates, magazines, dresses, hair-ribbons for his townified step-daughter. He was invited, three times a day, to sit down at a table crammed with roast beef and chickens and puddings and cakes and biscuits.

He used to try and share his philosophy of living.

'I used to feed myself for ten shillings a week!'

'But why? What for? What's the point?'

'Because I was free, that's the point! If you don't spend a lot of money then you don't have to earn it and you are free. Why do you have to spend money on all this rubbish? You can buy a piece of rolled brisket for three shillings, and you boil it with an onion and you can live off it for four days! You can live off mealiemeal well enough. I often did, in the bush.'

'Mealiemeal! I'm not going to eat native food!'

'Why not? What's wrong with it?'

'If you can't see why not, then I'm afraid I can't help you.'

Perhaps it was here, with Alicia's mother, that the idea of 'going native' had first come into his head.

'For crying out aloud, why cake all the time, why all these new dresses, why do you have to have new curtains, why do we have to have curtains at all, what's wrong with the sunlight? What's wrong with the starlight? Why do you want to shut them out? Why?'

That 'marriage' lasted four years, a fight all the way.

Then he drifted North, out of the white man's towns, and up into those parts that had not been 'opened up to white settlement', and where the Africans were still living, though not for long, in their traditional ways. And there at last he found a life that suited him, and a woman with whom he lived in kindness.

THE BLACK MADONNA

There are some countries in which the arts, let alone Art, cannot be said to flourish. Why this should be so it is hard to say, although of course we all have our theories about it. For sometimes it is the most barren soil that sends up gardens of those flowers which we all agree are the crown and justification of life, and it is this fact which makes it hard to say, finally, why the soil of Zambesia should produce such reluctant plants.

Zambesia is a tough, sunburnt, virile, positive country contemptuous of subtleties and sensibility: yet there have been States with these qualities which have produced art, though perhaps with the left hand. Zambesia is, to put it mildly, unsympathetic to those ideas so long taken for granted in other parts of the world, to do with liberty, fraternity and the rest. Yet there are those, and some of the finest souls among them, who maintain that art is impossible without a minority whose leisure is guaranteed by a hard-working majority. And whatever Zambesia's comfortable minority may lack, it is not leisure.

Zambesia — but enough; out of respect for ourselves and for scientific accuracy, we should refrain from jumping to conclusions. Particularly when one remembers the almost wistful respect Zambesians show when an artist does appear in their midst.

Consider, for instance, the case of Michele.

He came out of the internment camp at the time when Italy was made a sort of honorary ally, during the Second World War. It was a time of strain for the authorities, because it is one thing to be responsible for thousands of prisoners of war whom one must treat according to certain recognized standards; it is another to be faced, and from one day to the next, with these same thousands transformed by some international legerdemain into comrades in arms. Some of the thousands stayed where they were in the camps; they were fed and housed there at least. Others went as farm labourers, though not many; for while the farmers were as always short of labour, they did not know how to handle farm labourers who were also white men: such a phenomenon had never happened in Zambesia before. Some did odd jobs around the towns, keeping a sharp eye out for the trade unions, who would neither admit them as members nor agree to their working.

Hard, hard, the lot of these men, but fortunately not for long, for soon the war ended and they were able to go home.

Hard, too, the lot of the authorities, as has been pointed out; and for that reason they were doubly willing to take what advantages they could from the situation; and that Michele was such an advantage there could be no doubt.

His talents were first discovered when he was still a prisoner of war. A church was built in the camp, and Michele decorated its interior. It became a show-place, that little tin-roofed church in the prisoners' camp, with its whitewashed walls covered all over with frescoes depicting swarthy peasants gathering grapes for the vintage, beautiful Italian girls dancing, plump dark-eyed children. Amid crowded scenes of Italian life appeared the Virgin and her Child, smiling and beneficent, happy to move familiarly among her people.

Culture-loving ladies who had bribed the authorities to be taken inside the camp would say, 'Poor thing, how homesick he must be.' And they would beg to be allowed to leave half a crown for the artist. Some were indignant. He was a prisoner, after all, captured in the very act of fighting against justice and democracy, and what right had he to protest? – for they felt these paintings as a sort of protest. What was there in Italy that we did not have right here in Westonville, which was the capital and hub of Zambesia? Were there not sunshine and mountains and fat babies and pretty girls here? Did we not grow – if not grapes, at least lemons and oranges and flowers in plenty?

People were upset – the desperation of nostalgia came from the painted white walls of that simple church, and affected everyone according to his temperament.

But when Michele was free, his talent was remembered. He was spoken of as 'that Italian artist'. As a matter of fact, he was a bricklayer. And the virtues of those frescoes might very well have been exaggerated. It is possible they would have been overlooked altogether in a country where picture-covered walls were more common.

When one of the visiting ladies came rushing out to the camp in her own car, to ask him to paint her children, he said he was not qualified to do so. But at last he agreed. He took a room in the town and made some nice likenesses of the children. Then he painted the children of a great number of the first lady's friends. He charged ten shillings a time. Then one of the ladies wanted a portrait of herself. He asked ten pounds for it; it had taken him a month to do. She was annoyed, but paid.

And Michele went off to his room with a friend and stayed there drinking red wine from the Cape and talking about home. While the money lasted he could not be persuaded to do any more portraits.

There was a good deal of talk among the ladies about the dignity of labour, a subject in which they were well versed; and one felt they might almost go so far as to compare a white man with a kaffir, who did not understand the dignity of labour either.

He was felt to lack gratitude. One of the ladies tracked him down, found him lying on a camp-bed under a tree with a bottle of wine, and spoke to him severely about the barbarity of Mussolini and the fecklessness of the Italian temperament. Then she demanded that he should instantly paint a picture of herself in her new evening dress. He refused, and she went home very angry.

It happened that she was the wife of one of our most important citizens, a General or something of that kind, who was at that time engaged in planning a military tattoo or show for the benefit of the civilian population. The whole of Weston-ville had been discussing this show for weeks. We were all bored to extinction by dances, fancy-dress balls, fairs, lotteries and other charitable entertainments. It is not too much to say that while some were dying for freedom, others were dancing for it. There comes a limit to everything. Though, of course, when the end of the war actually came and the thousands of troops stationed in the country had to go home – in short, when enjoying themselves would no longer be a duty, many were heard to exclaim that life would never be the same again.

In the meantime, the Tattoo would make a nice change for us all. The military gentlemen responsible for the idea did not think of it in these terms. They thought to improve morale by giving us some idea of what war was really like. Headlines in the newspaper were not enough. And in order to bring it all home to us, they planned to destroy a village by shell-fire before our very eyes.

First, the village had to be built.

It appears that the General and his subordinates stood around in the red dust of the parade-ground under a burning sun for the whole of one day, surrounded by building materials, while hordes of African labourers ran around with boards and nails, trying to make something that looked like a village. It became evident that they would have to build a proper village in order to destroy it; and this would cost more than was allowed for the whole entertainment. The General went home in a bad temper, and his wife said what they needed was an artist, they needed Michele. This was not because she wanted to do Michele a good turn; she could not endure the thought of him lying around singing while there was work to be done. She refused to undertake any delicate diplomatic missions when her husband said he would be damned if he would ask favours of any little Wop. She solved the problem for him in her own way: a certain Captain Stocker was sent out to fetch him.

The Captain found him on the same camp-bed under the same tree, in rolled-up trousers, and an uncollared shirt; unshaven, mildly drunk, with a bottle of wine standing beside him on the earth. He was singing an air so wild, so sad, that the Captain was uneasy. He stood at ten paces from the disreputable fellow and felt the indignities of his position. A year ago, this man had been a mortal enemy to be shot on sight. Six months ago, he had been an enemy prisoner. Now he lay with his knees up, in an untidy shirt that had certainly once been military. For the Captain, the situation crystallized in a desire that Michele should salute him.

'Piselli!' he said sharply.

Michele turned his head and looked at the Captain from the horizontal. 'Good morning,' he said affably.

'You are wanted,' said the Captain.

'Who?' said Michele. He sat up, a fattish, olive-skinned little man. His eyes were resentful.

'The authorities.'

'The war is over?'

The Captain, who was already stiff and shiny enough in his laundered khaki, jerked his head back, frowning, chin out. He was a large man, blond, and wherever his flesh showed, it was brick-red. His eyes were small and blue and angry. His red hands, covered all over with fine yellow bristles, clenched by his side. Then he saw the disappointment in Michele's eyes, and the hands unclenched. 'No, it is not over,' he said. 'Your assistance is required.'

'For the war?'

'For the war effort. I take it you are interested in defeating the Germans?'

Michele looked at the Captain. The little dark-eyed artisan looked at the great blond officer with his cold blue eyes, his narrow mouth, his hands like bristle-covered steaks. He looked and said: 'I am very interested in the end of the war.'

'*Well?*' said the Captain between his teeth.

'The pay?' said Michele.

'You will be paid.'

Michele stood up. He lifted the bottle against the sun, then took a gulp. He rinsed his mouth out with wine and spat. Then he poured what was left on to the red earth, where it made a bubbling purple stain.

'I am ready,' he said. He went with the Captain to the waiting lorry, where he climbed in beside the driver's seat and not, as the Captain had expected, into the back of the lorry. When they had arrived at the parade-ground the officers had left a message that the Captain would be personally responsible for Michele and for the village. Also for the hundred or so labourers who were sitting around on the grass verges waiting for orders.

The Captain explained what was wanted. Michele nodded. Then he waved his hand at the Africans. 'I do not want these,' he said.

'You will do it yourself – a village?'

'Yes.'

'With no help?'

Michele smiled for the first time. 'I will do it.'

The Captain hesitated. He disapproved on principle of white men doing heavy manual labour. He said: 'I will keep six to do the heavy work.'

Michele shrugged; and the Captain went over and dismissed all but six of the Africans. He came back with them to Michele.

'It is hot,' said Michele.

'Very,' said the Captain. They were standing in the middle

of the parade-ground. Around its edge trees, grass, gulfs of shadow. Here, nothing but reddish dust, drifting and lifting in a low hot breeze.

'I am thirsty,' said Michele. He grinned. The Captain felt his stiff lips loosen unwillingly in reply. The two pairs of eyes met. It was a moment of understanding. For the Captain, the little Italian had suddenly become human. 'I will arrange it,' he said, and went off down-town. By the time he had explained the position to the right people, filled in forms and made arrangements, it was late afternoon. He returned to the parade-ground with a case of Cape brandy, to find Michele and the six black men seated together under a tree. Michele was singing an Italian song to them, and they were harmonizing with him. The sight affected the Captain like an attack of nausea. He came up, and the Africans stood to attention. Michele continued to sit.

'You said you would do the work yourself?'

'Yes, I said so.'

The Captain then dismissed the Africans. They departed, with friendly looks towards Michele, who waved at them. The Captain was beef-red with anger. 'You have not started yet?'

'How long have I?'

'Three weeks.'

'Then there is plenty of time,' said Michele, looking at the bottle of brandy in the Captain's hand. In the other were two glasses. 'It is evening,' he pointed out. The Captain stood frowning for a moment. Then he sat down on the grass, and poured out two brandies.

'Ciao,' said Michele.

'Cheers,' said the Captain. Three weeks, he was thinking. Three weeks with this damned little Itie! He drained his glass and refilled it, and set it in the grass. The grass was cool and soft. A tree was flowering somewhere close – hot waves of perfume came on the breeze.

'It is nice here,' said Michele. 'We will have a good time together. Even in a war, there are times of happiness. And of friendship. I drink to the end of the war.'

Next day, the Captain did not arrive at the parade-ground until after lunch. He found Michele under the trees with a bottle. Sheets of ceiling board had been erected at one end of the parade-ground in such a way that they formed two walls and part of a third, and a slant of steep roof supported on struts.

'What's that?' said the Captain, furious.

'The church,' said Michele.

'Wha-at?'

'You will see. Later. It is very hot.' He looked at the brandy bottle that lay on its side on the ground. The Captain went to the lorry and returned with the case of brandy. They drank. Time passed. It was a long time since the Captain had sat on grass under a tree. It was a long time, for that matter, since he had drunk so much. He always drank a great deal, but it was regulated to the times and seasons. He was a disciplined man. Here, sitting on the grass beside this little man whom he still could not help thinking of as an enemy, it was not that he let his self-discipline go, but that he felt himself to be something different: he was temporarily set outside his normal behaviour. Michele did not count. He listened to Michele talking about Italy, and it seemed to him he was listening to a savage speaking: as if he heard tales from the mythical South Sea islands where a man like himself might very well go just once in his life. He found himself saying he would like to make a trip to Italy after the war. Actually, he was attracted only by the North and the Northern people. He had visited Germany, under Hitler, and though it was not the time to say so, had found it very satisfactory. Then Michele sang him some Italian songs. He sang Michele some English songs. Then Michele took out photographs of his wife and children, who lived in a village in the mountains of North Italy. He asked the Captain if he were married. The Captain never spoke about his private affairs.

He had spent all his life in one or other of the African colonies as a policeman, magistrate, native commissioner, or in some other useful capacity. When the war started, military life came easily to him. But he hated city life, and had his own reasons for wishing the war over. Mostly, he had been in bush-stations with one or two other white men, or by himself, far from the rigours of civilization. He had relations with native women; and from time to time visited the city where his wife lived with her parents and the children. He was always tormented by the idea that she was unfaithful to him. Recently he had even appointed a private detective to watch her; he was convinced the detective was inefficient. Army friends coming from L—— where his wife was, spoke of her at parties, enjoying herself. When the war ended, she would not find it so easy to have a good time. And why did he not simply live with her and be done with it? The fact was, he could not. And his long exile to remote bush-stations was because he needed the excuse not to. He could not bear to think of his wife for too long; she was that part of his life he had never been able, so to speak, to bring to heel.

Yet he spoke of her now to Michele, and of his favourite bush-wife, Nadya. He told Michele the story of his life, until he realized that the shadows from the trees they sat under had stretched right across the parade-ground to the grandstand. He got unsteadily to his feet, and said: 'There is work to be done. You are being paid to work.'

'I will show you my church when the light goes.'

The sun dropped, darkness fell, and Michele made the Captain drive his lorry on to the parade-ground a couple of hundred yards away and switch on his lights. Instantly, a white church sprang up from the shapes and shadows of the bits of board.

'Tomorrow, some houses,' said Michele cheerfully.

At the end of the week, the space at the end of the parade-ground had crazy gawky constructions of lath and board over it, that looked in the sunlight like nothing on this earth. Privately, it upset the Captain; it was like a nightmare that these skeleton-like shapes should be able to persuade him, with the illusions of light and dark, that they were a village. At night, the Captain drove up his lorry, switched on the lights, and there it was, the village, solid and real against a background of full green trees. Then, in the morning sunlight, there was nothing there, just bits of board stuck in the sand.

'It is finished,' said Michele.

'You were engaged for three weeks,' said the Captain. He did not want it to end, this holiday from himself.

Michele shrugged. 'The army is rich,' he said. Now, to avoid curious eyes, they sat inside the shade of the church, with the case of brandy between them. The Captain talked endlessly, about his wife, about women. He could not stop talking.

Michele listened. Once he said: 'When I go home – when I go home – I shall open my arms ...' He opened them, wide. He closed his eyes. Tears ran down his cheeks. 'I shall take my wife in my arms, and I shall ask nothing, nothing. I do not care. It is enough, it is enough. I shall ask no questions and I shall be happy.'

The Captain stared before him, suffering. He thought how he dreaded his wife. She was a scornful creature, gay and hard, who laughed at him. She had been laughing at him ever since they married. Since the war, she had taken to calling him names like Little Hitler, and Storm-trooper. 'Go ahead, my Little Hitler,' she had cried last time they met. 'Go ahead, my Storm-trooper. If you want to waste your money on private detectives, go ahead. But don't think I don't know what *you* do when you're in the bush. I don't care what you do, but remember that I know it . . .'

The Captain remembered her saying it. And there sat Michele on his packing-case, saying: 'It's a pleasure for the rich, my friend, detectives and the law. Even jealousy is a pleasure I don't want any more. Ah, my friend, to be together with my wife again, and the children, that is all I ask of life. That and wine and food and singing in the evening.' And the tears wetted his cheeks and splashed on to his shirt.

That a man should cry, good Lord! thought the Captain. And without shame! He seized the bottle and drank.

Three days before the great occasion, some high-ranking officers came strolling through the dust, and found Michele and the Captain sitting together on the packing-case, singing. The Captain's shirt was open down the front, and there were stains on it.

The Captain stood to attention with the bottle in his hand, and Michele stood to attention too, out of sympathy with his friend. Then the officers drew the Captain aside – they were all cronies of his – and said, what the hell did he think he was doing? And why wasn't the village finished?

Then they went away.

'Tell them it is finished,' said Michele. 'Tell them I want to go.'

'No,' said the Captain, 'no. Michele, what would you do if your wife . . .'

'This world is a good place. We should be happy – that is all.'

'Michele . . .'

'I want to go. There is nothing to do. They paid me yesterday.'

'Sit down, Michele. Three more days and then it's finished.'

'Then I shall paint the inside of the church as I painted the one in the camp.'

The Captain laid himself down on some boards and went to sleep. When he woke, Michele was surrounded by the pots of paint he had used on the outside of the village. Just in front of the Captain was a picture of a black girl. She was young and plump. She wore a patterned blue dress and her shoulders came soft and bare out of it. On her back was a baby slung in a band of red stuff. Her face was turned towards the Captain and she was smiling.

'That's Nadya,' said the Captain. 'Nadya ...' He groaned loudly. He looked at the black child and shut his eyes. He opened them, and mother and child were still there. Michele was very carefully drawing thin yellow circles around the heads of the black girl and her child.

'Good God,' said the Captain, 'you can't do that.'

'Why not?'

'You can't have a black Madonna.'

'She was a peasant. This is a peasant. Black peasant Madonna for black country.'

'This is a German village,' said the Captain.

'This is my Madonna,' said Michele angrily. 'Your German village and my Madonna. I paint this picture as an offering to the Madonna. She is pleased – I feel it.'

The Captain lay down again. He was feeling ill. He went back to sleep. When he woke for the second time, it was dark. Michele had brought in a flaring paraffin lamp, and by its light was working on the long wall. A bottle of brandy stood beside him. He painted until long after midnight, and the Captain lay on his side and watched, as passive as a man suffering a dream. Then they both went to sleep on the boards. The whole of the next day Michele stood painting black Madonnas, black saints, black angels. Outside, troops were practising in the sunlight, bands were blaring and motor cyclists roared up and down. But Michele painted on, drunk and oblivious. The Captain lay on his back, drinking and muttering about his wife. Then he would say 'Nadya, Nadya', and burst into sobs.

Towards nightfall the troops went away. The officers came back, and the Captain went off with them to show how the village sprang into being when the great lights at the end of the parade-ground were switched on. They all looked at the village in silence. They switched the lights off, and there were only tall angular boards leaning like gravestones in the moonlight. On went the lights – and there was the village. They were silent, as if suspicious. Like the Captain, they seemed to feel it was not right. Uncanny it certainly was, but *that* was not it. Unfair – that was the word. It was cheating. And profoundly disturbing.

'Clever chap, that Italian of yours,' said the General.

The Captain, who had been woodenly correct until this moment, suddenly came rocking up to the General, and steadied himself by laying his hands on the august shoulder. 'Bloody Wops,' he said. 'Bloody kaffirs. Bloody … Tell you what, though, there's one Itie that's some good. Yes, there is. I'm telling you. He's a friend of mine, actually.'

The General looked at him. Then he nodded at his underlings. The Captain was taken away for disciplinary purposes. It was decided, however, that he must be ill, nothing else could account for such behaviour. He was put to bed in his own room with a nurse to watch him.

He woke twenty-four hours later, sober for the first time in weeks. He slowly remembered what had happened. Then he sprang out of bed and rushed into his clothes. The nurse was just in time to see him run down the path and leap into his lorry.

He drove at top speed to the parade-ground, which was flooded with light in such a way that the village did not exist. Everything was in full swing. The cars were three deep around the square, with people on the running-boards and even the roofs. The grandstand was packed. Women dressed up as gipsies, country girls, Elizabethan court dames, and so on, wandered about with trays of ginger beer and sausage-rolls and programmes at five shillings each in aid of the war effort. On the square, troops deployed, obsolete machine-guns were being dragged up and down, bands played, and motor cyclists roared through flames.

As the Captain parked the lorry, all this activity ceased, and the lights went out. The Captain began running around the outside of the square to reach the place where the guns were hidden in a mess of net and branches. He was sobbing with the effort. He was a big man, and unused to exercise, and sodden with brandy. He had only one idea in his mind – to stop the guns firing, to stop them at all costs.

Luckily, there seemed to be a hitch. The lights were still out. The unearthly graveyard at the end of the square glittered white in the moonlight. Then the lights briefly switched on, and the village sprang into existence for just long enough to show large red crosses all over a white building beside the church. Then moonlight flooded everything again, and the crosses vanished. 'Oh, the bloody fool!' sobbed the Captain, running, running as if for his life. He was no longer trying to reach the guns. He was cutting across a corner of the square direct to the church. He could hear some officers cursing behind him: 'Who put those red crosses there? Who? We can't fire on the Red Cross.'

The Captain reached the church as the searchlights burst on. Inside, Michele was kneeling on the earth looking at his first Madonna. 'They are going to kill my Madonna,' he said miserably.

'Come away, Michele, come away.'

'They're going to . . .'

The Captain grabbed his arm and pulled. Michele wrenched himself free and grabbed a saw. He began hacking at the ceiling board. There was a dead silence outside. They heard a voice booming through the loudspeakers: 'The village that is about to be shelled is an English village, not as represented on the programme, a German village. Repeat, the village that is about to be shelled is . . .'

Michele had cut through two sides of a square around the Madonna.

'Michele,' sobbed the Captain, '*get out of here.*'

Michele dropped the saw, took hold of the raw edges of the board and tugged. As he did so, the church began to quiver and lean. An irregular patch of board ripped out and Michele staggered back into the Captain's arms. There was a roar. The church seemed to dissolve around them into flame. Then they were running away from it, the Captain holding Michele tight by the arm. 'Get down,' he shouted suddenly, and threw Michele to the earth. He flung himself down beside him. Looking from under the crook of his arm, he heard the explosion, saw a great pillar of smoke and flame, and the village disintegrated in a mass of debris. Michele was on his knees gazing at his Madonna in the light from the flames. She was unrecognizable, blotted out with dust. He looked horrible, quite white, and a trickle of blood soaked from his hair down one cheek.

'They shelled my Madonna,' he said.

'Oh, damn it, you can paint another one,' said the Captain. His own voice seemed to him strange, like a dream voice. He was certainly crazy, as mad as Michele himself ... He got up, pulled Michele to his feet, and marched him towards the edge of the field. There they were met by the ambulance people. Michele was taken off to hospital, and the Captain was sent back to bed.

A week passed. The Captain was in a darkened room. That he was having some kind of a breakdown was clear, and two nurses stood guard over him. Sometimes he lay quiet. Sometimes he muttered to himself. Sometimes he sang in a thick clumsy voice bits out of opera, fragments from Italian songs, and – over and over again – There's a Long Long Trail. He was not thinking of anything at all. He shied away from the thought of Michele as if it were dangerous. When, therefore, a cheerful female voice announced that a friend had come to cheer him up, and it would do him good to have some company, and he saw a white bandage moving towards him in the gloom, he turned sharp over on to his side, face to the wall.

'Go away,' he said. 'Go away, Michele.'

'I have come to see you,' said Michele. 'I have brought you a present.'

The Captain slowly turned over. There was Michele, a cheerful ghost in the dark room. 'You fool,' he said. 'You messed everything up. What did you paint those crosses for?'

'It was a hospital,' said Michele. 'In a village there is a hospital, and on the hospital the Red Cross, the beautiful Red Cross – no?'

'I was nearly court-martialled.'

'It was my fault,' said Michele. 'I was drunk.'

'I was responsible.'

'How could you be responsible when I did it? But it is all over. Are you better?'

'Well, I suppose those crosses saved your life.'

'I did not think,' said Michele. 'I was remembering the kindness of the Red Cross people when we were prisoners.'

'Oh shut up, shut up, shut up.'

'I have brought you a present.'

The Captain peered through the dark. Michele was holding up a picture. It was of a native woman with a baby on her back, smiling sideways out of the frame.

Michele said: 'You did not like the haloes. So this time, no haloes. For the Captain – no Madonna.' He laughed. 'You like it? It is for you. I painted it for you.'

'God damn you!' said the Captain.

'You do not like it?' said Michele, very hurt.

The Captain closed his eyes. 'What are you going to do next?' he asked tiredly.

Michele laughed again. 'Mrs Pannerhurst, the lady of the General, she wants me to paint her picture in her white dress. So I paint it.'

'You should be proud to.'

'Silly bitch. She thinks I am good. They know nothing – savages. Barbarians. Not you, Captain, you are my friend. But these people, they know nothing.'

The Captain lay quiet. Fury was gathering in him. He thought of the General's wife. He disliked her, but he had known her well enough.

'These people,' said Michele. 'They do not know a good picture from a bad picture. I paint, I paint, this way, that way. There is the picture – I look at it and laugh inside myself.' Michele laughed out loud. 'They say, he is a Michelangelo, this one, and try to cheat me out of my price. Michele – Michelangelo – that is a joke, no?'

The Captain said nothing.

'But for you I painted this picture to remind you of our good times with the village. You are my friend. I will always remember you.'

The Captain turned his eyes sideways in his head and stared at the black girl. Her smile at him was half innocence, half malice.

'Get out,' he said suddenly.

Michele came closer and bent to see the Captain's face. 'You wish me to go?' He sounded unhappy. 'You saved my life. I was a fool that night. But I was thinking of my offering to the Madonna – I was a fool, I say it myself. I was drunk, we are fools when we are drunk.'

'Get out of here,' said the Captain again.

For a moment the white bandage remained motionless. Then it swept downwards in a bow.

Michele turned towards the door.

'And take that bloody picture with you.'

Silence. Then, in the dim light, the Captain saw Michele reach out for the picture, his white head bowed in profound obeisance. He straightened himself and stood to attention, holding the picture with one hand, and keeping the other stiff down his side. Then he saluted the Captain.

'Yes, *sir*,' he said, and he turned and went out of the door with the picture.

The Captain lay still. He felt – what did he feel? There was a pain under his ribs. It hurt to breathe. He realized he was unhappy. Yes, a terrible unhappiness was filling him, slowly, slowly. He was unhappy because Michele had gone. Nothing had ever hurt the Captain in all his life as much as that mocking *Yes, sir*. Nothing. He turned his face to the wall and wept. But silently. Not a sound escaped him, for the fear the nurses might hear.

THE TRINKET BOX

Yes, but it was only recently, when it became clear that Aunt Maud really could not last much longer, that people began to ask all those questions which should have been asked, it seems now, so long ago.

Or perhaps it is the other way about: Aunt Maud, suddenly finding that innumerable nieces and nephews and cousins were beginning to take an interest in her, asking her to meet interesting people, was so disturbed to find herself pushed into the centre of the stage where she felt herself to be out of place, that she took to her bed where she could tactfully die?

Even here, lying on massed pillows, like a small twig that has been washed up against banks of smooth white sand, she is not left in peace. Distant relations who have done no more than send her Christmas cards once a year come in to see her, sit by her bed for hours at a time, send her flowers. But why? It is not merely that they want to know what London in the 'nineties was like for a young woman with plenty of money, although they wake her to ask: 'Do tell us, do you remember the Oscar Wilde affair?' Her face puckers in a worried look, and she says: 'Oscar Wilde? What? Oh yes, I read such an interesting book, it is in the library.'

Perhaps Aunt Maud herself sees that pretty vivacious girl (there is a photograph of her in an album somewhere) as a character in a historical play. But what is that question which it seems everyone comes to ask, but does not ask, leaving at length rather subdued, even a little exasperated – perhaps because it is not like Aunt Maud to suggest unanswerable questions?

Where did it all begin? Some relation returned from a long holiday, and asking casually after the family, said: 'What! Aunt Maud still alive? Isn't she gone yet?' Is that how people began asking: 'Well, but how old is she? Eighty? Ninety?'

'Nonsense, she can't be ninety.'

'But she says she remembers ...' And the names of old 'incidents' crop up, the sort of thing one finds in dusty books of memoirs. They were another world. It seems impossible that living people can remember them, especially someone we know so well.

'She remembers earlier than that. She told me once – it must be twenty years ago now – of having left home years before the Boer War started. You can work that out for yourself.'

'Even that only makes her seventy – eighty perhaps. Eighty is not old enough to get excited about.'

'The Crimean War ...' But now they laugh. 'Come, come, she's not a hundred!'

No, she cannot be as much as that, but thirty years ago, no less, an old frail lady climbed stiffly but jauntily up the bank of a dried-up African river, where she was looking after a crowd of other people's children on a picnic, and remarked: 'My old bones are getting creaky.' Then she bought herself an ancient car. It was one of the first Ford models, and she went rattling in it over bad corrugated roads and even over the veld, if there were no roads. And no one thought it extraordinary. Just as one did not think of her as an old maid, or a spinster, so one did not think of her as an old lady.

And then there was the way she used to move from continent to continent, from family to family, as a kind of unpaid servant. For she had no money at all by then: her brother the black sheep died and she insisted on giving up all her tiny capital to pay his debts. It was useless of course; he owed thousands, but no one could persuade her against it. 'There are some things one has to do,' she said. Now, lying in bed she says: 'One doesn't want to be a nuisance,' in her small faded voice; the same voice in which she used to announce, and not so very long ago: 'I am going to South America as companion to Mrs Fripp – she is so very very kind.' For six months, then, she was prepared to wait hand and foot on an old lady years younger than herself simply for the sake of seeing South America? No, we can no longer believe it. We are forced to know that the thought of her aches and pains put warmth into Mrs Fripp's voice when she asked Aunt Maud to go with her.

And from the Andes or the Christmas Islands, or some place as distant and preposterous as the Russian-Japanese war or the Morocco scramble seem to be in time, came those long long letters beginning: 'That white dressing-jacket you gave me was so useful when I went to the mountains.' She got so many presents from us all that now we feel foolish. They were not what she wanted after all.

Then, before we expected it, someone would write and say: 'By the way, did you know I have had Aunt Maud with me since Easter?' She had come back from the Andes, or wherever it was? But why had she gone *there*? Was Anne having another baby perhaps?

Sitting up in bed surrounded by the cushions and photographs that framed her in the way other people's furniture frames them, always very early in the morning – she wrote letters from five to seven every day of her life – she answered in her tiny precise handwriting: 'Jacko's leg is not quite healed yet, although I think he is well on the way to recovery. And then I shall be delighted to avail myself of your kind offer. I will be with you by the middle of ...' Punctually to the hour she would arrive; the perfect guest. And when she left, because of the arrival of a baby or a sudden illness perhaps five hundred miles away or in another country, with what affectionate heart-warming gratitude she thanked us, until it was easy to forget the piles of mending, the delicious cooking, the nights and nights of nursing. A week after she had left would arrive the inevitable parcel, containing presents so apt that it was with an uneasy feeling that we sat down to write thanks. How did she come to know our most secret wants? And, imperceptibly, the unease would grow to resentment. She had no right, no right at all, to give such expensive presents when she was dependent on relations for her support.

So it was that after every visit a residue of spite and irritation remained. And perhaps she intended that the people she served should never have to feel the embarrassment of gratitude? Perhaps she intended us – who knows? – to think as we sat writing our thank-yous: But after all, she has to live on us, it is after all a kindness to feed and house her for a few weeks.

It is all intolerable, intolerable; and it seems now that we must march into that bedroom to ask: 'Aunt Maud, how did you bear it? How could you stand, year in and year out, pouring out your treasures of affection to people who hardly noticed you? Do you realize, Aunt Maud, that now, thirty years or more after you became our servant, it is the first time that we are really aware you were ever alive? What do you say to that, Aunt Maud? *Or did you know it all the time ...*' For that is what we want to be sure of: that she did not know it, that she never will.

We wander restlessly in and out of her room, watching that expression on her face which – now that she is too ill to hide what she feels – makes us so uneasy. She looks impatient when she sees us; she wishes we would go away. Yesterday she said: 'One does not care for this kind of attention.'

All the time, all over the house, people sit about, talking, talking, in low urgent anxious voices, as if something vital and precious is leaking away as they wait.

'She *can't* be exactly the same, it is impossible!'

'But I tell you, I remember her on the day the war started – the old war, you know. On the platform, waving good-bye to my son. She was the same, wrinkle for wrinkle. That little patch of yellow on her cheek – like an egg-stain. And those little mauvish eyes, and that funny voice. People don't talk like that now, each syllable sounding separately.'

'Her eyes have changed though.' We sneak in to have a look at her. She turns them on us, peering over the puffs of a pink bedjacket – eyes where a white film is gathering. Unable to see us clearly, afraid – she who has sat by so many death-beds – of distressing us by her unsightliness, she turns away her head, lies back, folds her hands, is silent.

When other people die, it is a thing of horror, swellings, gross flesh, smells, sickness. But Aunt Maud dies as a leaf shrivels. It seems that a little dryish gasp, a little shiver, and the papery flesh will crumble and leave beneath the bedclothes she scarcely disturbs a tiny white skeleton. That is how she is dying, giving the least trouble to the niece who waited sharp-sightedly for someone else to use the phrase 'a happy release' before she used it herself. 'She might not eat anything, but one has to prepare the tray all the same. And then, there are all these people in the house.'

'Before she retired, what did she do?'

'Taught, didn't you know? She was forty when her father married again, and she went out and took a post in a school. He never spoke one word to her afterwards.'

'But why, why?'

'He was in the wrong of course. She didn't marry so as to look after him.'

'Oh, so she might have married? Who was he?'

'Old John Jordan, do you remember?'

'But he died before I left school – such a funny old man!'

Impossible to ask why she never married. But someone asks it. A great-niece, very young, stands beside the bed and looks down with shivering distaste at such age, such death: 'Aunt Maud, why did you never marry?'

'Marry! Marry! Who is talking about marrying?' she sounds angered and sullen; then the small eyes film over and she says: 'Who did you say is getting married?'

The niece is banished and there are no more questions.

No more visitors either, the doctor says. A question of hours. A few hours, and that casket of memories and sensations will have vanished. It is monstrous that a human being who has survived miraculously and precariously so many decades of wars, illnesses and accidents should die at last, leaving behind nothing.

Now we sit about the bed where she lies and wait for her to die. There is nothing to do. No one stirs. We are all sitting, looking, thinking, surreptitiously touching the things that belonged to her, trying to catch a glimpse, even for a moment, of the truth that will vanish in such a little while.

And if we think of the things that interested her, the enthusiasms we used to laugh at, because it seemed so odd that such an old lady should feel strongly about these great matters, what answer do we get? She was a feminist, first and foremost. The Pankhursts, she said, 'were so devoted'. She was a socialist; she had letters from Keir Hardie. There had been no one like him since he died. She defended vegetarians, but would not be one herself, because it gave people so much trouble in the kitchen. Madame Curie, Charles Lindbergh, Marie Corelli, Lenin, Clara Butt – these were her Idols, and she spoke of them in agitated defiance as if they were always in need of defence. Inside that tiny shrivelled skull what an extraordinary gallery of heroes and heroines. But there is no answer there. No matter how hard we try, fingering her handkerchief sachet, thinking of the funny flat hats she wore, draped with bits of Liberty cottons, remembering how she walked, as if at any moment she might be called upon to scale a high wall, she eludes us. Let us resign ourselves to it and allow her to die.

Then she speaks after such long hours of waiting it is as if a woman already dead were speaking. Now, now!! We lean forward, waiting for her to say that one thing, the perfect word of forgiveness that will leave us healed and whole.

She has made her will, she says, and it is with the lawyer 'who has always been so kind' to her. She has nothing to leave but a few personal trinkets ... The small precise voice is breathless, and she keeps her eyes tight shut. 'I have told my lawyer that my possessions, such as they are, are kept in my black trinket box in the cupboard there. He knows. Everything is in order. I put everything right when people became so kind and I knew I was ill.'

And that is the last thing she will ever say. We wait intently, shifting our feet and avoiding each other's eyes for fear that our guilty glances may imprint upon our memories of her the terrible knowledge let slip in the order of the words of that final sentence. We do not want to remember her with guilt, oh no! But although we wait, straining, nothing else comes; she seems to be asleep, and slowly we let our limbs loosen and think of the black box. In it we will find the diaries, or the bundle of letters which will say what she refuses to say. Oh most certainly we will find something of that sort. She cannot die like this, leaving nothing. There will be evidence of a consumed sorrow, at the least, something that will put substance into this barrenness. And when at last we look up, glancing at our watches, we see there is a stillness in the tiny white face which means she is dead.

We get up, rather stiffly, because of the hours of sitting, and then after a decent interval open the black box. It is full to the brim with bits of lace and ribbon, scraps of flowery stuffs, buckles, braid, brooches, cheap glass necklaces. Each has a bit of paper pinned to it. 'These buttons I thought would do for the frock Alice was making when I was there last month.' And: 'To little Robin with my fond love. I bought this glass peacock in Cape Town in 1914 for another little boy.' And so on, each of us has something. And when we come to the end and search for the diaries and letters there is nothing! Secretively each of us taps at the wood of the bottom – but no, it is solid. And we put back the things and we feel for the first time that Aunt Maud is dead. We want to cry. We would, if it were not absurd to cry for an old woman whom none of us wanted. What would she say if she saw those tears? 'One cannot help feeling it would have been more useful to feel for me when I was still alive'? No, she would never say a thing like that; but we can have no illusions now, after that last remark of hers, which revealed the Aunt Maud she had been so carefully concealing all these years. And she would know we were not weeping for her at all.

We cannot leave the black box. We finger the laces, stroke the wood. We come back to it again and again, where it lies on the table in the room in which she is waiting for the funeral people. We do not look at her, who is now no more than a tiny bundle under the clothes. And slowly, slowly, in each of us, an emotion hardens which is painful because it can never be released. Protest, is that what we are feeling? But certainly a protest without bitterness, for she was never bitter. And without pity, for one cannot imagine Aunt Maud pitying herself. What, then, is left? Are we expected to go on, for the rest of our lives (which we hope will be as long as hers) feeling this intolerable ache, a dull and sorrowful rage? And if we all feel, suddenly, that it is not to be borne, and we must leap up from our chairs and bang our fists against the wall, screaming: 'No, no! It can't all be for nothing!' – then we must restrain ourselves and remain quietly seated; for we can positively hear the scrupulous little voice saying: 'There are some things one does not do.'

Slowly, slowly, we become still before the box, and now it seems we hold Aunt Maud in the hollow of our palms. That was what she was; now we know her.

So it comes to this: we are grown proud and honest out of the knowledge of her honesty and pride and, measuring ourselves against her we allow ourselves to feel only the small, persistent, but gently humorous anger she must have felt. Only anger, that is permissible, she would allow that. But against what? Against what?

THE PIG

The farmer paid his labourers on a Saturday evening, when the sun went down. By the time he had finished it was always quite dark, and from the kitchen door where the lantern hung, bars of yellow light lay down the steps, across the path, and lit up the trees and the dark faces under them.

This Saturday, instead of dispersing as usual when they took their money, they retired a little way into the dark under the foliage, talking among themselves to pass the time. When the last one had been paid, the farmer said: 'Call the women and the children. Everybody in the compound must be here.' The boss-boy, who had been standing beside the table calling out names, stood forward and repeated the order. But in an indifferent voice, as a matter of form, for all this had happened before, every year for years past. Already there was a subdued moving at the back of the crowd as the women came in from under the trees where they had been waiting; and the light caught a bunched skirt, a copper armlet, or a bright headcloth.

Now all the dimly-lit faces showed hope that soon this ritual would be over, and they could get back to their huts and their fires. They crowded closer without being ordered.

The farmer began to speak, thinking as he did so of his lands that lay all about him, invisible in the darkness, but sending on the wind a faint rushing noise like the sea; and although he had done this before so often, and was doing it now half-cynically, knowing it was a waste of time, the memory of how good those fields of strong young plants looked when the sun shone on them put urgency and even anger into his voice.

The trouble was that every year black hands stripped the cobs from the stems in the night, sacks of cobs; and he could never catch the thieves. Next morning he would see the prints of bare feet in the dust between the rows. He had tried everything; had warned, threatened, docked rations, even fined the whole compound collectively – it made no difference. The lands lying next to the compound would be cheated of their yield, and when the harvesters brought in their loads, everyone knew there would be less than what had been expected.

And if everyone knew it, why put on this display for the tenth time? That was the question the farmer saw on the faces in front of him; polite faces turning this way and that over impatient bodies and shifting feet. They were thinking only of the huts and the warm meal waiting for them. The philosophic politeness, almost condescension, with which he was being treated infuriated the farmer; and he stopped in the middle of a sentence, banging on the table with his fist, so that the faces centred on him and the feet stilled.

'Jonas,' said the farmer. Out on to the lit space stepped a tall elderly man with a mild face. But now he looked sombre. The farmer saw that look and braced himself for a fight. This man had been on the farm for several years. An old scoundrel, the farmer called him, but affectionately: he was fond of him, for they had been together for so long. Jonas did odd jobs for half the year; he drew water for the garden, cured hides, cut grass. But when the growing season came he was an important man.

'Come here, Jonas,' the farmer said again; and picked up the .33 rifle that he had been leaning against his chair until now. During the rainy season, Jonas slept out his days in his hut, and spent his nights till the cold dawns came guarding the fields from the buck and the pigs that attacked the young plants. They could lay waste whole acres in one night, a herd of pigs. He took the rifle, greeting it, feeling its familiar weight on his arm. But he looked reluctant nevertheless.

'This year, Jonas, you will shoot everything you see – understand?'

'Yes, baas.'

'Everything, buck, baboons, pig. And everything you hear. You will not stop to look. If you hear a noise, you will shoot.'

There was a movement among the listening people, and soft protesting noises.

'And if it turns out to be a human pig, then so much the worse. My lands are no place for pigs of any kind.'

Jonas said nothing, but he turned towards the others, holding the rifle uncomfortably on his arm, appealing that they should not judge him.

'You can go,' said the farmer. After a moment the space in front of him was empty, and he could hear the sound of bare feet feeling their way along dark paths, the sound of loudening angry talk. Jonas remained beside him.

'Well, Jonas?'

'I do not want to shoot this year.'

The farmer waited for an explanation. He was not disturbed at the order he had given. In all the years he had worked this farm no one had been shot, although every season the thieves moved at night along the mealie rows, and every night Jonas was out with a gun. For he would shout, or fire the gun into the air, to frighten intruders. It was only when dawn came that he fired at something he could see. All this was a bluff. The threat might scare off a few of the more timid; but both sides knew, as usual, that it was a bluff. The cobs would disappear; nothing could prevent it.

'And why not?' asked the farmer at last.

'It's my wife. I wanted to see you about it before,' said Jonas, in dialect.

'Oh, your wife!' The farmer had remembered. Jonas was old-fashioned. He had two wives, an old one who had borne him several children, and a young one who gave him a good deal of trouble. Last year, when this wife was new, he had not wanted to take on this job which meant being out all night.

'And what is the matter with the day-time?' asked the farmer with waggish good-humour, exactly as he had the year before. He got up, and prepared to go inside.

Jonas did not reply. He did not like being appointed official guardian against theft by his own people, but even that did not matter so much, for it never once occurred to him to take the order literally. This was only the last straw. He was getting on in years now, and he wanted to spend his nights in peace in his own hut, instead of roaming the bush. He had disliked it very much last year, but now it was even worse. A younger man visited his pretty young wife when he was away.

Once he had snatched up a stick, in despair, to beat her with; then he had thrown it down. He was old, and the other man was young, and beating her could not cure his heartache. Once he had come up to his master to talk over the situation, as man to man; but the farmer had refused to do anything. And, indeed, what could he do? Now, repeating what he had said then, the farmer spoke from the kitchen steps, holding the lamp high in one hand above his shoulder as he turned to go in, so that it sent beams of light swinging across the bush: 'I don't want to hear anything about your wife, Jonas. You should look after her yourself. And if you are not too old to take a young wife, then you aren't too old to shoot. You will take the gun as usual this year. Good night.' And he went inside, leaving the garden black and pathless. Jonas stood quite still, waiting for his eyes to accustom themselves to the dark; then he started off down the path, finding his way by the feel of the loose stones under his feet.

He had not yet eaten, but when he came to within sight of the compound, he felt he could not go farther. He halted, looking at the little huts silhouetted black against cooking fires that sent up great drifting clouds of illuminated smoke. There was his hut, he could see it, a small conical shape. There his wives were, waiting with his food prepared and ready.

But he did not want to eat. He felt he could not bear to go in and face his old wife, who mocked him with her tongue, and his young wife, who answered him submissively but mocked him with her actions. He was sick and tormented, cut off from his friends who were preparing for an evening by the fires, because he could see the knowledge of his betrayal in their eyes. The cold pain of jealousy that had been gnawing at him for so long, felt now like an old wound, aching as an old wound aches before the rains set in.

He did not want to go into the fields, either to perch until he was stiff in one of the little cabins on high stilts that were built at the corners of each land as shooting platforms, or to walk in the dark through the hostile bush. But that night, without going for his food, he set off as usual on his long vigil.

The next night, however, he did not go; nor the next, nor the nights following. He lay all day dozing in the sun on his blanket, turning himself over and over in the sun, as if its rays could cauterize the ache from his heart. When evening came, he ate his meal early before going off with the gun. And then he stood with his back to a tree, within sight of the compound; indeed, within a stone's throw of his own hut, for hours, watching silently. He felt numb and heavy. He was there without purpose. It was as if his legs had refused an order to march away from the place. All that week the lands lay unguarded, and if the wild animals were raiding the young plants, he did not care. He seemed to exist only in order to stand at night watching his hut. He did not allow himself to think of what was happening inside. He merely watched; until the fires burned down, and the bush grew cold and he was so stiff that when he went home, at sunrise, he had the appearance of one exhausted after a night's walking.

The following Saturday there was a beer drink. He could have got leave to attend it, had he wanted; but at sundown he took himself off as usual and saw that his wife was pleased when he left.

As he leaned his back to the tree trunk that gave him its support each night, and held the rifle lengthwise to his chest, he fixed his eyes steadily on the dark shape that was his hut, and remembered that look on his young wife's face. He allowed himself to think steadily of it, and of many similar things. He remembered the young man, as he had seen him only a few days before, bending over the girl as she knelt to grind meal, laughing with her; then the way they both looked up, startled, at his approach, their faces growing blank.

He could feel his muscles tautening against the rifle as he pictured that scene, so that he set it down on the ground, for relief, letting his arms fall. But in spite of the pain, he continued to think; for tonight things were changed in him, and he no longer felt numb and purposeless. He stood erect and vigilant, letting the long cold barrel slide between his fingers, the hardness of the tree at his back like a second spine. And as he thought of the young man another picture crept into his mind again and again, that of a young waterbuck he had shot last year, lying soft as his feet, its tongue slipping out into the dust as he picked it up, so newly dead that he imagined he felt the blood still pulsing under the warm skin. And from the small wet place under its neck a few sticky drops rolled over glistening fur. Suddenly, as he stood there thinking of the blood, and the limp body of the buck, and the young man laughing with his wife, his mind grew clear and cool and the oppression on him lifted.

He sighed deeply, and picked up the rifle again, holding it close, like a friend, against him, while he gazed in through the trees at the compound.

It was early, and the flush from sunset had not yet quite gone from the sky, although where he stood among the undergrowth it was night. In the clear spaces between the huts groups of figures took shape, talking and laughing and getting ready for the dance. Small cooking fires were being lit; and

a big central fire blazed, sending up showers of sparks into
the clouds of smoke. The tom-toms were beating softly; soon
the dance would begin. Visitors were coming in through the
bush from the other compounds miles away: it would be
a long wait.

Three times he heard steps along the path close to him
before he drew back and turned his head to watch the young
man pass, as he had passed every night that week, with a
jaunty eager tread and eyes directed towards Jonas's hut. Jonas
stood as quiet as a tree struck by lightning, holding his breath,
although he could not be seen, because the thick shadows from
the trees were black around him. He watched the young man
thread his way through the huts into the circle of firelight,
and pass cautiously to one side of the groups of waiting people,
like someone uncertain of his welcome, before going in through
the door of his own hut.

Hours passed, and he watched the leaping dancing people,
and listened to the drums as the stars swung over his head and
the night birds talked in the bush around him. He thought
steadily now, as he had not previously allowed himself to
think, of what was happening inside the small dark hut that
gradually became invisible as the fires died and the dancers
went to their blankets. When the moon was small and high and
cold behind his back, and the trees threw sharp black windows
on the path, and he could smell morning on the wind, he saw
the young man coming towards him again. Now Jonas shifted
his feet a little, to ease the stiffness out of them, and moved
the rifle along his arm, feeling for the curve of the trigger on
his finger.

As the young man lurched past, for he was tired, and moved
carelessly, Jonas slipped out into the smooth dusty path a few
paces behind, shrinking back as the released branches swung
wet into his face and scattered large drops of dew on to his
legs. It was cold; his breath misted into a thin pearly steam
dissolving into the moonlight.

He was so close to the man in front that he could have
touched him with the raised rifle; had he turned there would
have been no concealment; but Jonas walked confidently,
though carefully, and thought all the time of how he had shot
down from ten paces away that swift young buck as it started
with a crash out of a bush into a cold moony field.

When they reached the edge of the land where acres of mealies sloped away, dimly green under a dome of stars, Jonas began to walk like a cat. He wanted now to be sure; and he was only fifty yards from the shooting platform in the corner of the field, that looked in this light like a crazy fowl-house on stilts. The young man was staggering with tiredness and drink, making a crashing noise at each step as he snapped the sap-full mealies under heavy feet.

But the buck had shot like a spear from the bush, had caught the lead in its chest as it leaped, had fallen as a spear curves to earth; it had not blundered and lurched and swayed. Jonas began to feel a disgust for this man, and the admiration and fascination he felt for his young rival vanished. The tall slim youth who had laughed down at his wife had nothing to do with the ungainly figure crashing along before him, making so much noise that there could be no game left unstartled for miles.

When they reached the shooting platform, Jonas stopped dead, and let the youth move on. He lifted the rifle to his cheek and saw the long barrel slant against the stars, which sent a glint of light back down the steel. He waited, quite still, watching the man's back sway above the mealies. Then, at the right moment, he squeezed his finger close, holding the rifle steady to fire again.

As the sound of the shot reverberated, the round dark head jerked oddly, blotting out fields of stars; the body seemed to crouch, one hand went out as if he were going to lean sideways to the ground. Then he disappeared into the mealies with a startled thick cry. Jonas lowered the rifle and listened. There was a threshing noise, a horrible grunting, and half-words muttered, like someone talking in sleep.

Jonas picked his way along the rows, feeling the sharp leaf edges scything his legs, until he stood above the body that now jerked softly among the stems. He waited until it stilled, then bent to look, parting the chilled, moon-green leaves so that he could see clearly.

It was no clean small hole : raw flesh gaped, blood poured black to the earth, the limbs were huddled together shapeless and without beauty, the face was pressed into the soil.

'A pig,' said Jonas aloud to the listening moon, as he kicked the side gently with his foot, 'nothing but a pig.'

He wanted to hear how it would sound when he said it again, telling how he had shot blind into the grunting, invisible herd.

TRAITORS

We had discovered the Thompsons' old house long before their first visit.

At the back of our house the ground sloped up to where the bush began, an acre of trailing pumpkin vines, ash-heaps where pawpaw trees sprouted, and lines draped with washing where the wind slapped and jiggled. The bush was dense and frightening, and the grass there higher than a tall man. There were not even paths.

When we had tired of our familiar acre we explored the rest of the farm: but this particular stretch of bush was avoided. Sometimes we stood at its edge, and peered in at the tangled granite outcrops and great ant-heaps curtained with Christmas fern. Sometimes we pushed our way a few feet, till the grass closed behind us, leaving overhead a small space of blue. Then we lost our heads and ran back again.

Later, when we were given our first rifle and a new sense of bravery, we realized we had to challenge that bush. For several days we hesitated, listening to the guinea-fowl calling only a hundred yards away, and making excuses for cowardice. Then, one morning, at sunrise, when the trees were pink and gold, and the grass-stems were running bright drops of dew, we looked at each other, smiling weakly, and slipped into the bushes with our hearts beating.

At once we were alone, closed in by grass, and we had to reach out for the other's dress and cling together. Slowly, heads down, eyes half closed against the sharp grass-seeds, two small girls pushed their way past ant-heap and outcrop, past thorn and gully and thick clumps of cactus where any wild animal might lurk.

Suddenly, after only five minutes of terror, we emerged in a space where the red earth was scored with cattle tracks. The guinea-fowl were clinking ahead of us in the grass, and we caught a glimpse of a shapely dark bird speeding along a path. We followed, shouting with joy because the forbidding patch of bush was as easily conquered and made our own as the rest of the farm.

We were stopped again where the ground dropped suddenly to the vlei, a twenty-foot shelf of flattened grass where the cattle went to water. Sitting, we lifted our dresses and coasted down-hill on the slippery swathes, landing with torn knickers and scratched knees in a donga of red dust scattered with dried cow-pats and bits of glistening quartz. The guinea-fowl stood in a file and watched us, their heads tilted with apprehension; but my sister said with bravado: 'I am going to shoot a buck!'

She waved her arms at the birds and they scuttled off. We looked at each other and laughed, feeling too grown-up for guinea-fowl now.

Here, down on the verges of the vlei, it was a different kind of bush. The grass was thinned by cattle, and red dust spurted as we walked. There were sparse thorn trees, and everywhere the poison-apple bush, covered with small fruit like yellow plums. Patches of wild marigold filled the air with a rank, hot smell.

Moving with exaggerated care, our bodies tensed, our eyes fixed half a mile off, we did not notice that a duiker stood watching us, ten paces away. We yelled with excitement and the buck vanished. Then we ran like maniacs, screaming at the tops of our voices, while the bushes whipped our faces and the thorns tore our legs.

Ten minutes later we came slap up against a barbed fence. 'The boundary,' we whispered, awed. This was a legend; we had imagined it as a sort of Wall of China, for beyond were thousands and thousands of miles of unused Government land where there were leopards and baboons and herds of koodoo. But we were disappointed: even the famous boundary was only a bit of wire after all, and the duiker was nowhere in sight.

Whistling casually to show we didn't care, we marched along by the wire, twanging it so that it reverberated half a mile away down in the vlei. Around us the bush was strange; this part of the farm was quite new to us. There was still nothing but thorn trees and grass; and fat wood-pigeons cooed from every branch. We swung on the fence stanchions and wished that Father would suddenly appear and take us home to breakfast. We were hopelessly lost.

It was then that I saw the pawpaw tree. I must have been staring at it for some minutes before it grew in on my sight;

for it was such an odd place for a pawpaw tree to be. On it were three heavy yellow pawpaws.

'There's our breakfast,' I said.

We shook them down, sat on the ground, and ate. The insipid creamy flesh soon filled us, and we lay down, staring at the sky, half asleep. The sun blared down; we were melted through with heat and tiredness. But it was very hard. Turning over, staring, we saw worn bricks set into the ground. All round us were stretches of brick, stretches of cement.

'The old Thompson house,' we whispered.

And all at once the pigeons seemed to grow still and the bush became hostile. We sat up, frightened. How was it we hadn't noticed it before? There was a double file of pawpaws among the thorns; a purple bougainvillaea tumbled over the bushes; a rose tree scattered white petals at our feet; and our shoes were scrunching in broken glass.

It was desolate, lonely, despairing; and we remembered the way our parents had talked about Mr Thompson who had lived here for years before he married. Their hushed, disapproving voices seemed to echo out of the trees; and in a violent panic we picked up the gun and fled back in the direction of the house. We had imagined we were lost; but we were back in the gully in no time, climbed up it, half sobbing with breathlessness, and fled through that barrier of bush so fast we hardly noticed it was there.

It was not even breakfast-time.

'We found the Thompsons' old house,' we said at last, feeling hurt that no one had noticed from our proud faces that we had found a whole new world that morning.

'Did you?' said Father absently. 'Can't be much left of it now.'

Our fear vanished. We hardly dared look at each other for shame. And later that day we went back and counted the pawpaws and trailed the bougainvillaea over a tree and staked the white rosebush.

In a week we had made the place entirely our own. We were there all day, sweeping the debris from the floor and carrying away loose bricks into the bush. We were not surprised to find dozens of empty bottles scattered in the grass. We washed them in a pothole in the vlei, dried them in the wind, and marked out the rooms of the house with them, making walls of shining bottles. In our imagination the Thompson house was built again, a small brick-walled place with a thatched roof.

We sat under a blazing sun, and said in our Mother's voice: 'It is always cool under thatch, no matter how hot it is outside.' And then, when the walls and the roof had grown into our minds and we took them for granted, we played other games, taking it in turn to be Mr Thompson.

Whoever was Mr Thompson had to stagger in from the bush, with a bottle in her hand, tripping over the lintel and falling on the floor. There she lay and groaned, while the other fanned her and put handkerchiefs soaked in vlei water on her head. Or she reeled about among the bottles, shouting abusive gibberish at an invisible audience of natives.

It was while we were engaged thus, one day, that a black woman came out of the thorn trees and stood watching us. We waited for her to go, drawing together; but she came close and stared in a way that made us afraid. She was old and fat, and she wore a red print dress from the store. She said in a soft, wheedling voice: 'When is Boss Thompson coming back?'

'Go away!' we shouted. And then she began to laugh. She sauntered off into the bush, swinging her hips and looking back over her shoulder and laughing. We heard that taunting laugh away among the trees; and that was the second time we ran away from the ruined house, though we made ourselves walk slowly and with dignity until we knew she could no longer see us.

For a few days we didn't go back to the house. When we did we stopped playing Mr Thompson. We no longer knew him: that laugh, that slow, insulting stare had meant something outside our knowledge and experience. The house was not ours now. It was some broken bricks on the ground marked out with bottles. We couldn't pretend to ourselves we were not afraid of the place; and we continually glanced over our shoulders to see if the old black woman was standing silently there, watching us.

Idling along the fence, we threw stones at the pawpaws fifteen feet over our heads till they squashed at our feet. Then we kicked them into the bush.

'Why have you stopped going to the old house?' asked Mother cautiously, thinking that we didn't know how pleased she was. She had instinctively disliked our being there so much.

'Oh, I dunno ...'

A few days later we heard that the Thompsons were coming to see us; and we knew, without anyone saying, that this was no ordinary visit. It was the first time; they wouldn't be coming after all these years without some reason. Besides, our parents didn't like them coming. They were at odds with each other over it.

Mr Thompson had lived on our farm for ten years before we had it, when there was no one else near for miles and miles. Then, suddenly, he went home to England and brought a wife back with him. The wife never came to this farm. Mr Thompson sold the farm to us and bought another one. People said: 'Poor girl! Just out from home, too.' She was angry about the house burning down, because it meant she had to live with friends for nearly a year while Mr Thompson built a new house on his new farm.

The night before they came, Mother said several times in a strange, sorrowful voice, 'Poor little thing; poor, poor little thing.'

Father said: 'Oh, I don't know. After all, be just. He was here alone all those years.'

It was no good; she disliked not only Mr Thompson but Father too, that evening; and we were on her side. She put her arms round us, and looked accusingly at Father. 'Women get all the worst of everything,' she said.

He said angrily: 'Look here, it's not my fault these people are coming.'

'Who said it was?' she answered.

Next day, when the car came in sight, we vanished into the bush. We felt guilty, not because we were running away, a thing we often did when visitors came we didn't like, but because we had made Mr Thompson's house our own, and because we were afraid if he saw our faces he would know we were letting Mother down by going.

We climbed into the tree that was our refuge on these occasions, and lay along branches twenty feet from the ground, and played at Mowgli, thinking all the time about the Thompsons.

As usual, we lost all sense of time; and when we eventually

returned, thinking the coast must be clear, the car was still there. Curiosity got the better of us.

We slunk on to the veranda, smiling bashfully, while Mother gave us a reproachful look. Then, at last, we lifted our heads and looked at Mrs Thompson. I don't know how we had imagined her; but we had felt for her a passionate, protective pity.

She was a large, blonde, brilliantly coloured lady with a voice like a go-away bird's. It was a horrible voice. Father, who could not stand loud voices, was holding the arms of his chair, and gazing at her with exasperated dislike.

As for Mr Thompson, that villain whom we had hated and feared, he was a shaggy and shambling man, who looked at the ground while his wife talked, with a small apologetic smile. He was not in the least as we had pictured him. He looked like our old dog. For a moment we were confused; then, in a rush, our allegiance shifted. The profound and dangerous pity, aroused in us earlier than we could remember by the worlds of loneliness inhabited by our parents, which they could not share with each other but which each shared with us, settled now on Mr Thompson. Now we hated Mrs Thompson. The outward sign of it was that we left Mother's chair and went to Father's.

'Don't fidget, there's good kids,' he said.

Mrs Thompson was asking to be shown the old house. We understood, from the insistent sound of her voice, that she had been talking about nothing else all afternoon; or that, at any rate, if she had, it was only with the intention of getting round to the house as soon as she could. She kept saying, smiling ferociously at Mr Thompson: 'I have heard such *interesting* things about that old place. I really must see for myself where it was that my husband lived before I came out . . .' And she looked at Mother for approval.

But Mother said dubiously: 'It will soon be dark. And there is no path.'

As for Father, he said bluntly: 'There's nothing to be seen. There's nothing left.'

'Yes, I heard it had been burnt down,' said Mrs Thompson with another look at her husband.

'It was a hurricane lamp . . .' he muttered.

'I want to see for myself.'

At this point my sister slipped off the arm of my Father's chair, and said, with a bright, false smile at Mrs Thompson, 'We know where it is. We'll take you.' She dug me in the ribs and sped off before anyone could speak.

At last they all decided to come. I took them the hardest, longest way I knew. We had made a path of our own long ago, but that would have been too quick. I made Mrs Thompson climb over rocks, push through grass, bend under bushes. I made her scramble down the gully so that she fell on her knees in the sharp pebbles and the dust. I walked her so fast, finally, in a wide circle through the thorn trees that I could hear her panting behind me. But she wasn't complaining: she wanted to see the place too badly.

When we came to where the house had been it was nearly dark and the tufts of long grass were shivering in the night breeze, and the pawpaw trees were silhouetted high and dark against a red sky. Guinea-fowl were clinking softly all around us.

My sister leaned against a tree, breathing hard, trying to look natural. Mrs Thompson had lost her confidence. She stood quite still, looking about her, and we knew the silence and the desolation had got her, as it got us that first morning.

'But *where* is the house?' she asked at last, unconsciously softening her voice, staring as if she expected to see it rise out of the ground in front of her.

'I told you, it was burnt down. *Now* will you believe me?' said Mr Thompson.

'I *know* it was burnt down ... Well, where was it then?' She sounded as if she were going to cry. This was not at all what she had expected.

Mr Thompson pointed at the bricks on the ground. He did not move. He stood staring over the fence down to the vlei, where the mist was gathering in long white folds. The light faded out of the sky, and it began to get cold. For a while no one spoke.

'What a god-forsaken place for a house,' said Mrs Thompson, very irritably, at last. 'Just as well it was burnt down. Do you mean to say you kids play here?'

That was our cue. 'We like it,' we said dutifully, knowing very well that the two of us standing on the bricks, hand in hand, beside the ghostly rosebush, made a picture that took all the harm out of the place for her. 'We play here all day,' we lied.

'Odd taste you've got,' she said, speaking at us, but meaning Mr Thompson.

Mr Thompson did not hear her. He was looking around with a lost, remembering expression. 'Ten years,' he said at last. 'Ten years I was here.'

'More fool you,' she snapped. And that closed the subject as far as she was concerned.

We began to trail home. Now the two women went in front; then came Father and Mr Thompson; we followed at the back. As we passed a small donga under a cactus tree, my sister called in a whisper, 'Mr Thompson, Mr Thompson, look here.'

Father and Mr Thompson came back. 'Look,' we said, pointing to the hole that was filled to the brim with empty bottles.

'I came quickly by a way of my own and hid them,' said my sister proudly, looking at the two men like a conspirator.

Father was very uncomfortable. 'I wonder how they got down here?' he said politely at last.

'We found them. They were at the house. We hid them for you,' said my sister, dancing with excitement.

Mr Thompson looked at us sharply and uneasily. 'You are an odd pair of kids,' he said.

That was all the thanks we got from him; for then we heard Mother calling from ahead: 'What are you all doing there?' And at once we went forward.

After the Thompsons had left we hung around Father, waiting for him to say something.

At last, when Mother wasn't there, he scratched his head in an irritable way and said: 'What in the world did you do that for?'

We were bitterly hurt. '*She* might have seen them,' I said.

'Nothing would make much difference to that lady,' he said at last. 'Still, I suppose you meant well.'

In the corner of the veranda, in the dark, sat Mother, gazing into the dark bush. On her face was a grim look of disapproval, and distaste and unhappiness. We were included in it, we knew that.

She looked at us crossly and said, 'I don't like you wandering over the farm the way you do. Even with a gun.'

But she had said that so often, and it wasn't what we were waiting for. At last it came.

'My two little girls,' she said, 'out in the bush by themselves, with no one to play with . . .'

It wasn't the bush she minded. We flung ourselves on her. Once again we were swung dizzily from one camp to the other. 'Poor Mother,' we said. 'Poor, poor Mother.'

That was what she needed. 'It's no life for a woman, this,' she said, her voice breaking, gathering us close.

But she sounded comforted.

THE WORDS HE SAID

On the morning of the braavleis, Dad kept saying to Moira, as if he thought it was a joke, 'Moy, it's going to rain.' First she did not hear him, then she turned her head slow and deliberate and looked at him so that he remembered what she said the day before, and he got red in the face and went indoors out of her way. The day before, he said to her, speaking to me, 'What's Moy got into her head? Is the braavleis for her engagement or what?'

It was because Moira spent all morning cooking her lemon cake for the braavleis, and she went over to Sam the butcher's to order the best ribs of beef and best rump steak.

All the cold season she was not cooking, she was not helping Mom in the house at all, she was not taking an interest in life, and Dad was saying to Mom: 'Oh get the girl to town or something, don't let her moon about here, who does she think she is?'

Mom just said, quiet and calm, the way she was with Dad when they did not agree: 'Oh let her alone, Dickson.' When Mom and Dad were agreeing, they called each other, Mom and Dad; when they were against each other, it was Marion and Dickson, and that is how it was for the whole of the dry season, and Moira was pale and moony and would not talk to me, and it was no fun for me, I can tell you.

'What's this *for*?' Dad said once about half-way through the season, when Moira stayed in bed three days and Mom let her. 'Has he said anything to her or hasn't he?'

Mom just said: 'She's sick, Dickson.'

But I could see what he said had gone into her, because I was in our bedroom when Mom came to Moira.

Mom sat down on the bed, but at the bottom of it, and she was worried. 'Listen, girl,' said Mom, 'I don't want to interfere, I don't want to do that, but what did Greg say?'

Moira was not properly in bed, but in her old pink dressing-gown that used to be Mom's, and she was lying under the quilt. She lay there, not reading anything, watching out of the window over at the big water-tanks across the railway lines.

Her face looked bad, and she said: 'Oh, leave me alone, Mom.'

Mom said: 'Listen, girlie, just let me say something, you don't have to follow what I say, do you?'

But Moira said nothing.

'Sometimes boys say a thing, and they don't mean it the way we think. They feel they have to say it. It's not they don't mean it, but they mean it different.'

'He didn't say anything at all,' said Moira. 'Why should he?'

'Why don't you go into town and stay with Auntie Nora a while? You can come back for the holidays when Greg comes back.'

'Oh let me alone,' said Moira, and she began to cry. That was the first time she cried. At least, in front of Mom. I used to hear her cry at night when she thought I was asleep.

Mom's face was tight and patient, and she put her hand on Moira's shoulder, and she was worried I could see. I was sitting on my bed pretending to do my stamps, and she looked over at me, and seemed to be thinking hard.

'He didn't say anything, Mom,' I said. 'But I know what happened.'

Moira jerked her head up and she said: 'Get that kid *away* from me.'

They could not get me away from Moira, because there were only two bedrooms, and I always slept with Moira. But she would not speak to me that night at all; and Mom said to me, 'Little pitchers have big ears.'

It was the last year's braavleis it happened. Moira was not keen on Greg then, I know for a fact, because she was sweet on Jordan. Greg was mostly at the Cape in college, but he came back for the first time in a year, and I saw him looking at Moira. She was pretty then, because she had finished her matric and spent all her time making herself pretty. She was eighteen, and her hair was wavy, because the rains had started. Greg was on the other side of the bonfire, and he came walking around it through the sparks and the white smoke, and up to Moira. Moira smiled out of politeness, because she wanted Jordan to sit by her, and she was afraid he wouldn't if he saw her occupied by Greg.

'Moira Hughes?' he said. Moira smiled, and he said: 'I wouldn't have known you.'

'Go on,' I said, 'you've known us always.'

They did not hear me. They were just looking. It was peculiar. I knew it was one of the peculiar moments of life because my skin was tingling all over, and that is how I always know.

Because of how she was looking at him, I looked at him too, but I did not think he was handsome. The holidays before, when I was sweet on Greg Jackson, I naturally thought he was handsome, but now he was just ordinary. He was very thin, always, and his hair was ginger, and his freckles were thick, because naturally the sun is no good for people with white skin and freckles.

But he wasn't bad, particularly because he was in his sensible mood. Since he went to college he had two moods, one noisy and sarcastic; and then Moira used to say, all lofty and superior: 'Medical students are always rowdy, it stands to reason because of the hard life they have afterwards.' His other mood was when he was quiet and grown-up, and some of the gang didn't like it, because he was better than us, he was the only one of the gang to go to university at the Cape.

After they had finished looking, he just sat down in the grass in the place Moira was keeping for Jordan, and Moira did not once look around for Jordan. They did not say anything else, just went on sitting, and when the big dance began holding hands around the bonfire, they stood at one side watching.

That was all that happened at the braavleis, and that was all the words he said. Next day, Greg went on a shooting trip with his father who was the man at the garage, and they went right up the Zambesi valley, and Greg did not come back to our station that holidays or the holidays after.

I knew Moira was thinking of a letter, because she bought some of Croxley's best blue at the store, and she always went herself to the post office on mail days. But there was no letter. But after that she said to Jordan, 'No thanks, I don't feel like it,' when he asked her to go into town to the flicks.

She did not take any notice of any of the gang after that, though before she was leader of the gang, even over the boys.

That was when she stopped being pretty again; she looked as she did before she left school and was working hard for her matric. She was too thin, and the curl went out of her hair, and she didn't bother to curl it either.

All that dry season she did nothing, and hardly spoke, and did not sing; and I knew it was because of that minute when Greg and she looked at each other; that was all; and when I thought of it, I could feel the cold-hot down my back.

Well, on the day before the braavleis, like I said, Moira was on the veranda, and she had on her the dress she wore last year to the braavleis. Greg had come back for the holidays the night before, we knew he had, because his mother said so when Mom met her at the store. But he did not come to our house. I did not like to see Moira's face, but I had to keep on looking at it, it was so sad, and her eyes were sore. Mom kissed her, putting both her arms around her, but Moira gave a hitch of her shoulders like a horse with a fly bothering it.

Mom sighed, and then I saw Dad looking at her, and the look they gave each other was most peculiar, it made me feel very peculiar again. And then Moira started in on the lemon cake, and went to the butcher's, and that was when Dad said that about the braavleis being for the engagement. Moira looked at him, with her eyes all black and sad, and said: 'Why have you got it in for me, Dad, what have I done?'

Dad said: 'Greg's not going to marry you. Now he's got to college, and going to be a doctor, he won't be after you.'

Moira was smiling, her lips small and angry.

Mom said: 'Why Dickson, Moira's got her matric and she's educated, what's got into your head?'

Dad said: 'I'm telling you, that's all.'

Moira said, very grown-up and quiet: 'Why are you trying to spoil it for me, Dad? I haven't said anything about marrying, have I? And what have I done to *you*, anyway?'

Dad didn't like that. He went red, and he laughed, but he didn't like it. And he was quiet for a bit at least.

After lunch, when she'd finished with the cake, she was sitting on the veranda when Jordan went past across to the store, and she called out: 'Hi, Jordan, come and talk to me.'

Now I know for a fact that Jordan wasn't sweet on Moira any more, he was sweet on Beth from the store, because I know for a fact he kissed her at the last station dance, I saw him. And he shouted out, 'Thanks, Moy, but I'm on my way.'

'Oh, please yourself then,' said Moira, friendly and nice, but I knew she was cross, because she was set on it.

Anyway, he came in, and I've never seen Moira so nice to anyone, not even when she was sweet on him, and certainly never to Greg. Well, and Jordan was embarrassed, because Moira was not pretty that season, and all the station was saying she had gone off. She took Jordan into the kitchen to see the lemon cake and dough all folded ready for the sausage rolls, and she said slow and surprised, 'But we haven't got enough bread for the sandwiches, Mom, what are you thinking of?'

Mom said, quick and cross, because she was proud of her kitchen, 'What do you mean? And no one's going to eat sandwiches with all that meat you've ordered. And it'll be stale by tomorrow.'

'I think we need more bread,' said Moira. And she said to me in the same voice, slow and lazy, 'Just run over to the Jacksons' and see if they can let us have some bread.'

At this I didn't say anything, and Mom did not say anything either, and it was lucky Dad didn't hear. I looked at Mom, and she made no sign, so I went out across the railway lines to the garage, and at the back of the garage was the Jacksons' house, and there was Greg Jackson reading a book about the body because he was going to be a doctor.

'Mom says,' I said, 'can you let us have some bread for the braavleis?'

He put down the book, and said, 'Oh, hullo, Betty.'

'Hullo,' I said.

'But the store will be open tomorrow,' he said. 'Isn't the braavleis tomorrow?'

'It's Sunday tomorrow,' I said.

'But the store's open now.'

'We want some stale bread,' I said, 'Moy's making some stuffing for the chicken, our bread's all fresh.'

'Mom's at the store,' he said, 'but help yourself.'

So I went into the pantry and got half a stale loaf, and came out and said 'Thanks,' and walked past him.

He said, 'Don't mench.' Then, when I was nearly gone, he said, 'And how's Moy?' And I said, 'Fine, thanks, but I haven't seen much of her this hols because she's busy with Jordan.' And I went away, and I could feel my back tingling, and sure enough there he was coming up behind me, and then he was beside me, and my side was tingling.

'I'll drop over and say hullo,' said Greg, and I felt peculiar I can tell you, because what I was thinking was: *Well! If this is love.*

When we got near our house, Moira and Jordan were side

by side on the veranda wall, and Moy was laughing, and I knew she had seen Greg coming because of the way she laughed.

Dad was not on the veranda, so I could see Mom had got him to stay indoors.

'I've brought you the bread, Moy,' I said, and with this I went into the kitchen, and there was Mom, and she was looking more peculiar than I've ever seen her. I could have bet she wanted to laugh; but she was sighing all the time. Because of the sighing I knew she had quarrelled with Dad. 'Well, I don't *know*,' she said, and she threw the bread I'd fetched into the waste-bucket.

There sat Mom and I in the kitchen, smiling at each other off and on in a peculiar way, and Dad was rattling his paper in the bedroom where she had made him go. He was not at the station that day, because the train had come at nine o'clock and there wasn't another one coming. When we looked out on the veranda in about half an hour Jordan was gone, and Greg and Moira were sitting on the veranda wall. And I can tell you she looked so pretty again, it was peculiar her getting pretty like that so sudden.

That was about five, and Greg went back to supper at home, and Moira did not eat anything, she was in our room curling her hair, because she and Greg were going for a walk.

'Don't go too far, it's going to rain,' Mom said, but Moira said, sweet and dainty, 'Don't worry, Mom, I can look after myself.'

Mom and Dad said nothing to each other all the evening.

I went to bed early for a change, so I'd be there when Moy got in, although I was thirteen that season and now my bed-time was up to ten o'clock.

Mom and Dad went to bed, although I could see Mom was worried, because there was a storm blowing up, the dry season was due to end, and the lightning kept spurting all over the sky.

And I lay awake saying to myself, Sleep sleep go away, come again another day, but I went to sleep, and when I woke up, the room was full of the smell of rain, of the earth wet with rain, the light was on and Moira was in the room.

'Have the rains come?' I said, and then I woke right up and saw of course they hadn't, because the air was as dry as sand, and Moira said, 'Oh shut up and go to sleep.'

She did not look pretty as much as being different from how I'd seen her, her face was soft and smiling, and her eyes were different. She had blue eyes most of the time, but now they seemed quite black. And now her hair was all curled and brushed, it looked pretty, like golden syrup. And she even looked a bit fatter. Usually when she wasn't too thin, she was rather fat, and when she was one of the gang we used to call her Pudding. That is, until she passed her J.C., and then she fought everyone, and the boys too, so that she could be called Moy. So no one had called her Pudding for years now except Dad to make her cross. He used to say, 'You're going to make a fine figure of a woman like your mother.' That always made Moy cross, I can tell you, because Mom was very fat, and she wore proper corsets these days, except just before the rains when it was so hot. I remember the first time the corsets came from the store, and she put them on, Moy had to lace her in, and Mom laughed so much Moy couldn't do the laces, and anyway she was cross because Mom laughed, and she said to me afterwards, 'It's disgusting, letting yourself *go* – I'm not going to let myself *go*.'

So it would have been more than my life was worth to tell her she was looking a bit fatter already, or to tell her anything at all, because she sat smiling on the edge of her bed, and when I said, 'What did he say, Moy?' she just turned her head and made her eyes thin and black at me, and I saw I'd better go to sleep. But I knew something she didn't know I knew, because she had some dead jacaranda flowers in her hair, so that meant she and Greg were at the water-tanks. There were only two jacaranda trees at our station, and they were at the big water-tanks for the engines, so if they were at the water-tanks, they must have been kissing, because it was romantic at the tanks. It was the end of October, and the jacarandas were shedding, and the tanks looked as if they were standing in pools of blue water.

Well next morning Moy was already up when I woke, and she was singing, and she began ironing her muslin dress that she made for last Christmas, even before breakfast.

Mom said nothing; Dad kept rustling his newspaper; and I wouldn't have dared open my mouth. Besides, I wanted to find out what Greg said. After breakfast, we sat around, because of its being Sunday, and Dad didn't have to be at the station office because there weren't any trains on Sundays.

And Dad kept grinning at Moira and saying: 'I think it's going to rain,' and she pretended she didn't know what he meant, until at last she jumped when he said it and turned herself and looked at him just the way she did the day before, and that was when he got red in the face, and said: 'Can't you take a joke these days?' and Moira looked away from him with her eyebrows up, and Mom sighed, and then he said, very cross, 'I'll leave you all to it, just tell me when you're in a better temper,' and with this he took the newspaper inside to the bedroom.

Anybody could see it wasn't going to rain properly that day, because the clouds weren't thunder-heads, but great big white ones, all silver and hardly any black in them.

Moy didn't eat any dinner, but went on sitting on the veranda, wearing her dress that was muslin, white with red spots, and big puffed sleeves, and a red sash around her waist.

After dinner, time was very slow, and it was a long time before Greg came down off the Jacksons' veranda, and came walking slowly along the gum-tree avenue. I was watching Moy's face, and she couldn't keep the smile off it. She got paler and paler until he got underneath our veranda, and she looking at him so that I had goose-flesh all over.

Then he gave a jump up our steps to the veranda, and said: 'Hoy, Moy, how's it?' I thought she was going to fall right off the veranda wall, and her face had gone all different again.

'How are you, Gregory?' said Moira, all calm and proud.

'Oh, skidding along,' he said, and I could see he felt awkward, because he hadn't looked at her once, and his skin was all red around the freckles. And she didn't say anything, and she was looking at him as if she couldn't believe it was him.

'I hope the rain will keep off for the braavleis,' said Mom, in her visiting voice, and she looked hard at me, and I had to get up and go inside with her. But I could see Greg didn't want us to go at all, and I could see Moy knew it; her eyes were blue again, a pale thin blue, and her mouth was small.

Well Mom went into the kitchen to finally make the sausage rolls, and I went into our bedroom, because I could see what went on on the veranda from behind the curtains.

Greg sat on the veranda wall, and whistled, he was whistling, I love you, yes I do; and Moira was gazing at him as if he were a Christmas beetle she had just noticed; and then he began whistling. Three little words, and suddenly Moira got down off the wall, and stretched herself like a cat when it's going to walk off somewhere, and Greg said, 'Skinny!'

At this she made her eyebrows go up, and I've never seen such a look.

And he was getting redder in the face, and he said: 'You'd better not wear that dress to the braavleis, it's going to rain.'

Moira didn't say a word for what seemed about half an hour, and then she said, in that lazy sort of voice, 'Well, Greg Jackson, if you've changed your mind it's okay with me.'

'Changed my mind?' he said, very quick, and he looked scared; and she looked scared, and she asked: 'What did you say all those things for last night?'

'Say what?' he asked, scareder than ever, and I could see he was trying to remember what he'd said.

Moira was just looking at him, and I wouldn't have liked to be Greg Jackson just then, I can tell you. Then she walked off the veranda, letting her skirt swish slowly, and through the kitchen, and into our room, and then she sat on the bed.

'I'm not going to the braavleis, Mom,' she said, in that sweet slow voice like Mom when she's got visitors and she wishes they'd go.

Mom just sighed, and slapped the dough about on the kitchen table. Dad made the springs of the bed creak, and he said half aloud: 'Oh my God preserve me!'

Mom left the pastry, and gave a glare through the door of their bedroom at Dad, and then came into our room. There was Moira sitting all lumped up on her bed as if she'd got the stitch, and her face was like pastry dough. Mom said nothing to Moira, but went on to the veranda. Greg was still sitting there looking sick.

'Well, son,' Mom said, in her easy voice, the voice she had when she was tired of everything, but keeping up, 'Well, son, I think Moy's got a bit of a headache from the heat.'

As I've said, I wasn't sweet on Greg that holidays but if I was Moy I would have been, the way he looked just then, all sad but grown-up, like a man, when he said: 'Mrs Hughes, I don't know what I've done.' Mom just smiled, and sighed. 'I can't marry, Mrs Hughes, I've got five years' training ahead of me.'

Mom smiled and said, 'Of course, son, of course.'

I was lying on my bed with my stamps, and Moira was

on her bed, listening, and the way *she* smiled gave me a bad shiver.

'Listen to him,' she said, in a loud voice, '*Marry?* Why does everyone go on about marrying? They're nuts. I wouldn't marry Greg Jackson anyway if he was the last man on a desert island.'

Outside, I could hear Mom sigh hard, then her voice quick and low, and then the sound of Greg's feet crunching off over the cinders of the path.

Then Mom came back into our room, and Moira said, all despairing, 'Mom, what made you say that about marrying?'

'He said it, my girl, I didn't.'

'Marrying!' said Moira, laughing hard.

Mom said: 'What did he *say* then, you talked about him saying something?'

'Oh you all make me sick,' said Moira, and lay down on her bed, turned away from us. Mom hitched her head at me, and we went out. By then it was five in the afternoon and the cars would be leaving at six, so Mom finished the sausage rolls in the oven, and packed the food, and then she took off her apron and went across to Jordan's house. Moira did not see her go, because she was still lost to the world in her pillow.

Soon Mom came back and put the food into the car. Then Jordan came over with Beth from the store and said to me, 'Betty, my Mom says, will you and Moy come in our car to the braavleis, because your car's full of food.'

'I will,' I said, 'but Moira's got a headache.'

But at this moment Moira called out from our room, 'Thanks, Jordan, I'd like to come.'

So Mom called to Pop, and they went off in our car together and I could see she was talking to him all the time, and he was just pulling the gears about and looking resigned to life.

I and Moira went with Jordan and Beth in their car. I could see Jordan was cross because he wanted to be with Beth, and Beth kept smiling at Moira with her eyebrows up, to tell her she knew what was going on, and Moira smiled back, and talked a lot in her visiting voice.

At the braavleis it was a high place at the end of a vlei, where it rose into a small hill full of big boulders. The grass had been cut that morning by natives of the farmer who always let us use his farm for the braavleis. It was pretty, with the hill behind and the moon coming up over it, and then the cleared space, and the vlei sweeping down to the river, and the trees on either side. The moon was just over the trees when we got there, so the trees looked black and big, and the boulders were big and looked as if they might topple over, and the grass was silvery, but the great bonfire was roaring up twenty feet, and in the space around the fire it was all hot and red. The trench of embers where the spits were for the meat was on one side, and Moira went there as soon as she arrived, and helped with the cooking.

Greg was not there, and I thought he wouldn't come, but much later, when we were all eating the meat, and laughing because it burned our fingers it was so hot, I saw him on the other side of the fire talking to Mom. Moira saw him talking, and she didn't like it, but she pretended not to see.

By then we were seated in a half-circle on the side of the fire the wind was blowing, so that the red flames were sweeping off away from us. There were about fifty people from the station and some farmers from round about. Moira sat by me, quiet, eating grilled ribs and sausage rolls, and she was pleased I was there for once, so that she wouldn't seem to be by herself. She had changed her dress back again, and it was the dress she had last year for the braavleis, it was blue with pleats, and it was the dress she had for best the last year at school, so it wasn't very modern any more. Across the fire, I could see Greg. He did not look at Moira and she did not look at him. Except that this year Jordan did not want to sit by Moira but by Beth, I kept feeling peculiar, as if this year was really last year, and in a minute Greg would walk across past the fire, and say: 'Moira Hughes? I wouldn't have known you.'

But he stayed where he was. He was sitting on his legs, with his hands on his knees. I could see his legs and knees and his big hands all red from the fire and the yellow hair glinting on the red. His face was red too and wet with the heat.

Then everyone began singing. We were singing *Sarie Marais*, and *Sugar Bush*, and *Henrietta's Wedding* and *We don't want to go home*. Moira and Greg were both singing as hard as they could.

It began to get late. The natives were damping down the cooking trench with earth, and looking for scraps of meat and bits of sausage roll, and the big fire was sinking down. It would be time in a minute for the big dance in a circle around the fire.

Moira was just sitting. Her legs were tucked under sideways, and they had got scratched from the grass, I could see the white dry scratches across the sunburn, and I can tell you it was a good thing she didn't wear her best muslin because there wouldn't have been much left of it. Her hair, that she had curled yesterday, was tied back in a ribbon, so that her face looked small and thin.

I said: 'Here, Moy, don't look like your own funeral,' and she said: 'I will if I like.' Then she gave me a bit of a grin, and she said: 'Let me give you a word of warning for when you're grown-up, don't believe a word men say, I'm telling you.'

But I could see she was feeling better just then.

At that very moment the red light of the fire on the grass just in front of us went out, and someone sat down, and I hoped it was Greg and it was. They were looking at each other again, but my skin didn't tingle at all, so I looked at his face and at her face, and they were both quiet and sensible.

Then Moira reached out for a piece of grass, pulled it clean and neat out of the socket, and began nibbling at the soft piece at the end; and it was just the way Mom reached out for her knitting when she was against Dad. But of course Greg did not know the resemblance.

'Moy,' he said, 'I want to talk to you.'

'My name is Moira,' said Moira, looking him in the eyes.

'Oh heck, Moira,' he said, sounding exasperated just like Dad.

I wriggled back away from the two of them into the crowd that was still singing softly *Sarie Marais*, and looking at the way the fire was glowing low and soft, ebbing red and then dark as the wind came up from the river. The moon was half-covered with the big soft silvery clouds, and the red light was strong on our faces.

I could just hear what they said, I wasn't going to move too far off, I can tell you.

'I don't know what I've said,' said Greg.

'It doesn't matter in the slightest,' said Moira.

'Moira, for crying out aloud!'

'Why did you say that about marrying?' said Moira, and her voice was shaky. She was going to cry if she didn't watch out.

'I thought you thought I meant . . .'

'You think too much,' said Moira, tossing her head carefully so that her long tail of hair should come forward and lie on her shoulder. She put up her hand, and stroked the curls smooth.

'Moira, I've got another five years at university. I couldn't say to you, let's be engaged for five years.'

'I never said you should,' said Moira, calm and lofty, examining the scratches on her legs.

The way she was sitting, curled up sideways, with her hair lying forward like syrup on her shoulder, it was pretty, it was as pretty as I've ever seen, and I could see his face, sad and almost sick.

'You're so pretty, Moy,' he said, jerking it out.

Moira seemed not to be able to move. Then she turned her head slowly and looked at him. I could see the beginning of something terrible on her face. The shiver had begun under my hair at the back of my neck, and was slowly moving down to the small of my back.

'You're so beautiful,' he said, sounding angry, leaning right forward with his eyes almost into her face.

And now she looked the way she had last night, when I was not awake and said, was it raining outside.

'When you look like that,' he said, quite desperate about everything, 'it makes me feel . . .'

People were getting up now all around us, the fire had burned right down, it was a low wave of red heat coming out at us. The redness was on our shoulders and legs, but our faces were having a chance to cool off. The moon had come out again full and bright, and the cloud had rolled on, and it was funny the way the light was red to their shoulders, and the white of the moon on their faces, and their eyes glistening. I didn't like it; I was shivering; it was the most peculiar moment of all my life.

'Well,' said Moira, and she sounded just too tired even to try to understand, 'that's what you said last night, wasn't it?'

'Don't you see,' he said, trying to explain, his tongue all mixed up, 'I can't help – I love you, I don't know . . .'

Now she smiled, and I knew the smile at once, it was the

way Mom smiled at Dad when if he had any sense he'd shut up. It was sweet and loving, but it was sad, and as if she was saying, Lord, you're a fool, Dickson Hughes!

Moira went on smiling like that at Greg, and he was sick and angry and not understanding a thing.

'I love you,' he said again.

'Well I love you and what of it?' said Moira.

'But it will be five years.'

'And what has that got to do with anything?' At this she began to laugh.

'But Moy . . .'

'My name is Moira,' she said, once and for all.

For a moment they were both white and angry, their eyes glimmering with the big white moon over them.

There was a shout and a hustle, and suddenly all the people were in the big circle around the big low heap of fire, and they were whirling around and around, yelling and screaming. Greg and Moira stayed where they were, just outside the range of the feet, and they didn't hear a thing.

'You're so pretty,' he was saying, in that rough, cross, helpless voice, 'I love you, Moira, there couldn't ever be anyone but you.'

She was smiling, and he went on saying: 'I love you, I see your face all the time, I see your hair and your face and your eyes.'

And I wished he'd go on, the poor sap, just saying it, for every minute, it was more like last night when I woke up and I thought it had rained, the feeling of the dry earth with the rain just on it, that was how she was, and she looked as if she would sit there and listen for ever to the words he said, and she didn't want to hear him saying, Why don't you say something Moy, you don't say anything, you do understand don't you? – it's not fair, it isn't right to bind you when we're so young. But he started on saying it in just a minute, and then she smiled her visiting smile, and she said: Gregory Jackson, you're a fool.

Then she got herself off the grass and went across to Mom to help load the car up, and she never once looked at Greg again, not for the rest of the holidays.

LUCY GRANGE

The farm was fifty miles from the nearest town, in a maize-growing district. The mealie lands began at a stone's throw from the front door of the farm house. At the back were several acres of energetic and colourful domestic growth: chicken runs, vegetables, pumpkins. Even on the veranda were sacks of grain and bundles of hoes. The life on the farm, her husband's life, washed around the house leaving old scraps of iron on the front step where the children played wagon-and-driver, or a bottle of medicine for a sick animal on her dressing-table among the bottles of Elizabeth Arden.

One walked straight from the veranda of this gaunt, iron-roofed, brick-barracks of a house into a wide drawing-room that was shaded in green and orange Liberty linens.

'Stylish?' said the farmers' wives, when they came on formal calls, asking the question of themselves while they discussed with Lucy Grange the price of butter and servants' aprons and their husbands discussed the farm with George Grange. They never 'dropped over' to see Lucy Grange; they never rang her up with invitations to 'spend the day'. They would finger the books on child psychology, politics, art; gaze guiltily at the pictures on her walls, which they felt they ought to be able to recognize, and say: 'I can see you are a great reader, Mrs Grange.'

There were years of discussing her among themselves before their voices held the good-natured amusement of acceptance: 'I found Lucy in the vegetable patch wearing gloves full of cold cream.' 'Lucy has ordered another dress pattern from town.' And later still, with self-consciously straightened shoulders, eyes directed primly before them, discreet non-committal voices: 'Lucy is very attractive to men.'

One can imagine her, when they left at the end of those mercifully so-short visits, standing on the veranda and smiling bitterly after the satisfactory solid women with their straight 'tailored' dresses, made by the Dutchwoman at the store at seven-and-six a time, buttoned loosely across their well-used breasts, with their untidy hair permed every six months in town, with their femininity which was asserted once and for all by a clumsy scrawl of red across the mouth. One can imagine her clenching her fists and saying fiercely to the mealie fields which rippled greenly all around her, cream-topped like the sea: 'I won't. I simply won't. He needn't imagine that I will!'

'Do you like my new dress, George?'

'You're the best-looking woman in the district, Lucy.' So it seemed, on the face of it, that he didn't expect, or even want, that she should . . .

Meanwhile she continued to order cook-books from town, made new recipes of pumpkin and green mealies and chicken, put skin-food on her face at night; constructed attractive nursery furniture out of packing cases enamelled white – the farm wasn't doing too well; and discussed with George how little Betty's cough was probably psychological.

'I'm sure you're right, my dear.'

Then the rich, over-controlled voice: 'Yes, darling. No, my sweetheart. Yes, of course, I'll play bricks with you, but you must have your lunch first.' Then it broke, hard and shrill: '*Don't* make all that noise, darling. I can't stand it. Go on, go and play in the garden and leave me in peace.'

Sometimes, storms of tears. Afterwards: 'Really, George, didn't your mother ever tell you that all women cry sometimes? It's as good as a tonic. Or a holiday.' And a lot of high laughter and gay explanations at which George hastened to guffaw. He liked her gay. She usually was. For instance, she was a good mimic. She would 'take off', deliberately trying to relieve his mind of farm worries, the visiting policemen, who toured the district once a month to see if the natives were behaving themselves, or the Government agricultural officials.

'Do you want to see my husband?'

That was what they had come for, but they seldom pressed the point. They sat far longer than they had intended, drinking tea, talking about themselves. They would go away and say at the bar in the village: 'Mrs Grange is a smart woman, isn't she?'

And Lucy would be acting, for George's benefit, how a khaki-clad, sun-raw youth had bent into her room, looking around him with comical surprise, had taken a cup of tea thanking her three times, had knocked over an ashtray, stayed for lunch and afternoon tea, and left saying with awkward gallantry: 'It's a real treat to meet a lady like you who is interested in things.'

'You shouldn't be so hard on us poor Colonials, Lucy.'

Finally one can imagine how one day, when the houseboy came to her in the chicken-runs to say that there was a baas waiting to see her at the house, it was no sweating police-man, thirsty after fifteen dusty miles on a motor-cycle, to whom she must be gracious.

He was a city man, of perhaps forty or forty-five, dressed in city clothes. At first glance she felt a shudder of repulsion. It was a coarse face, and sensual; and he looked like a patient vul-ture as the keen heavy-lidded eyes travelled up and down her body.

'Are you looking for my husband perhaps? He's in the cow-sheds this morning.'

'No, I don't think I am. I was.'

She laughed. It was as if he had started playing a record she had not heard for a long time, and which began her feet tapping. It was years since she had played this game. 'I'll get you some tea,' she said hurriedly and left him in her pretty drawing-room.

Collecting the cups, her hands were clumsy. 'Why, Lucy!' she said to herself, archly. She came back very serious and responsible to find him standing in front of the picture which filled half the wall at one end of the room. 'I should have thought you had sunflowers enough here,' he said, in his heavy over-emphasized voice, which made her listen for meanings behind his words. And when he turned away from the wall and came to sit down, leaning forward, examining her, she sup-pressed an impulse to apologize for the picture: 'Van Gogh *is* obvious, but he's rather effective,' she might have said; and felt that the whole room was that: effective but obvious. But she was pleasantly conscious of how she looked: graceful and cool in her green linen dress, with her corn-coloured hair knotted demurely in her neck. She lifted wide serious eyes to his face and asked: 'Milk? Sugar?' and knew that the corners of her mouth were tight with self-consciousness.

When he left, three hours later, he turned her hand over and lightly kissed the palm. She looked down at the greasy dark head, the red folded neck, and stood rigid, thinking of the raw creased necks of vultures.

Then he straightened up and said with simple kindliness:

'You must be lonely here, my dear,' and she was astounded to find her eyes full of tears.

'One does what one can to make a show of it.' She kept her lids lowered and her voice light. Inside she was weeping with gratitude. Embarrassed, she said quickly: 'You know, you haven't yet said what you came for.'

'I sell insurance. And besides, I've heard people talk of you.'

She imagined the talk and smiled stiffly. 'You don't seem to take your work very seriously.'

'If I may I'll come back another time and try again?'

She did not reply. He said: 'My dear, I'll tell you a secret: one of the reasons I chose this district was because of you. Surely there aren't so many people in this country one can really talk to that we can afford not to take each other seriously?'

He touched her cheek with his hand, smiled, and went.

She heard the last thing he had said like a parody of the things she often said and felt a violent revulsion.

She went to her bedroom, where she found herself in front of the mirror. Her hands went to her cheeks and she drew in her breath with the shock. 'Why, Lucy, whatever is the matter with you?' Her eyes were dancing, her mouth smiled irresistibly. Yet she heard the archness of her *Why, Lucy* and thought: I'm going to pieces. I must have gone to pieces without knowing it.

Later she found herself singing in the pantry as she made a cake, stopped herself; made herself look at the insurance salesman's face against her closed eyelids, and instinctively wiped the palms of her hands against her skirt.

He came three days later. Again, in the first shock of seeing him stand at the door, smiling familiarly, she thought: 'It's the face of an old animal. He probably chose this kind of work because of the opportunities it gives him.'

He talked of London, where he had lately been on leave; about the art galleries and the theatres.

She could not help warming, because of her hunger for this kind of talk. She could not help an apologetic note in her voice, because she knew that after so many years in this exile she must seem provincial. She liked him because he associated himself with her abdication from her standards by saying: 'Yes, yes, my dear, in a country like this we all learn to accept the second-rate.'

While he talked his eyes were roving. He was listening. Outside the window in the dust the turkeys were scraping and gobbling. In the next room the houseboy was moving; then there was silence because he had gone to get his midday meal. The children had had their lunch and gone off to the garden with the nurse.

No, she said to herself. No, no, no.

'Does your husband come back for lunch?'

'He takes it on the lands at this time of the year, he's so busy.'

He came over and sat beside her. 'Well, shall we console each other?' She was crying in his arms. She could feel their impatient and irritable tightening.

In the bedroom she kept her eyes shut. His hand travelled up and down her back. 'What's the matter, little one? What's the matter?'

His voice was a sedative. She could have fallen asleep and lain there for a week inside the anonymous comforting arms. But he was looking at his watch over her shoulder. 'We'd better get dressed, hadn't we?'

'Of course.'

She sat naked on the bed, covering herself with her arms, looking at his white hairy body in loathing, and then at the creased red neck. She became extremely gay, and in the living-room they sat side by side on the big sofa, being ironical. Then he put his arm around her, and she curled up inside it, and cried again. She clung to him and felt him going away from her, and in a few minutes he stood up saying: 'Wouldn't do for your old man to come in and find us like this, would it?' Even while she was hating him for the 'old man' she put her arms around him and said: 'You'll come back soon.'

'I couldn't keep away.' The voice purred caressingly over her head, and she said: 'You know, I'm very lonely.'

'Darling, I'll come as soon as I can. I've a living to make, you know.'

She let her arms drop, and smiled, and watched him drive away down the rutted red-rust farm road, between the rippling sea-coloured mealies.

She knew he would come again, and next time she would not cry; she would stand again like this watching him go, hating him, thinking of how he had said: In this country we learn to accept the second-rate; and he would come again and again and again; and she would stand here, watching him go and hating him.

A MILD ATTACK OF LOCUSTS

The rains that year were good, they were coming nicely just as the crops needed them – or so Margaret gathered when the men said they were not too bad. She never had an opinion of her own on matters like the weather, because even to know about what seems a simple thing like the weather needs experience. Which Margaret had not got. The men were Richard her husband, and old Stephen, Richard's father, a farmer from way back, and these two might argue for hours whether the rains were ruinous, or just ordinarily exasperating. Margaret had been on the farm three years. She still did not understand how they did not go bankrupt altogether, when the men never had a good word for the weather, or the soil, or the Government. But she was getting to learn the language. Farmer's language. And they neither went bankrupt nor got very rich. They jogged along, doing comfortably.

Their crop was maize. Their farm was three thousand acres on the ridges that rise up towards the Zambesi escarpment, high, dry windswept country, cold and dusty in winter, but now, being the wet season, steamy with the heat rising in wet soft waves off miles of green foliage. Beautiful it was, with the sky blue and brilliant halls of air, and the bright green folds and hollows of country beneath, and the mountains lying sharp and bare twenty miles off across the river. The sky made her eyes ache, she was not used to it. One does not look so much at the sky in the city she came from. So that evening when Richard said: 'The Government is sending out warnings that locusts are expected, coming down from the breeding grounds up North,' her instinct was to look about her at the trees. Insects – swarms of them – horrible! But Richard and the old man had raised their eyes and were looking up over the mountains. 'We haven't had locusts in seven years,' they said. 'They go in cycles, locusts do.' And then: 'There goes our crop for this season!'

But they went on with the work of the farm just as usual, until one day they were coming up the road to the homestead for the midday break, when old Stephen stopped, raised his finger and pointed: 'Look, look, there they are!'

Out ran Margaret to join them, looking at the hills. Out came the servants from the kitchen. They all stood and gazed. Over the rocky levels of the mountain was a streak of rust-coloured air. Locusts. There they came.

At once Richard shouted at the cook-boy. Old Stephen yelled at the house-boy. The cook-boy ran to beat the old ploughshare hanging from a tree-branch, which was used to summon the labourers at moments of crisis. The house-boy ran off to the store to collect tin cans, any old bit of metal. The farm was ringing with the clamour of the gong, and they could see the labourers come pouring out of the compound, pointing at the hills and shouting excitedly. Soon they had all come up to the house, and Richard and old Stephen were giving them orders – Hurry, hurry, hurry.

And off they ran again, the two white men with them, and in a few minutes Margaret could see the smoke of fires rising from all around the farm-lands. Piles of wood and grass had been prepared there. There were seven patches of bared soil, yellow and ox-blood colour, and pink, where the new mealies were just showing, making a film of bright green, and around each drifted up thick clouds of smoke. They were throwing wet leaves on to the fires now, to make it acrid and black. Margaret was watching the hills. Now there was a long low cloud advancing, rust-colour still, swelling forwards and out as she looked. The telephone was ringing. Neighbours – quick, quick, there come the locusts. Old Smith had had his crop eaten to the ground. Quick, get your fires started. For of course, while every farmer hoped the locusts would over-look his farm and go on to the next, it was only fair to warn each other, one must play fair. Everywhere, fifty miles over the countryside, the smoke was rising from myriads of fires. Margaret answered the telephone calls, and between stood watching the locusts. The air was darkening. A strange dark-ness, for the sun was blazing – it was like the darkness of a veld fire, when the air gets thick with smoke. The sunlight comes down distorted, a thick hot orange. Oppressive it was, too, with the heaviness of a storm. The locusts were coming fast. Now half the sky was darkened. Behind the reddish veils in front which were the advance guards of the swarm, the main swarm showed in dense black cloud, reaching almost to the sun itself.

Margaret was wondering what she could do to help. She did not know. Then up came old Stephen from the lands. 'We're finished, Margaret, finished! These beggars can eat every leaf and blade off the farm in half an hour! And it is only early afternoon – if we can make enough smoke, make enough noise till the sun goes down, they'll settle somewhere else perhaps ...' And then: 'Get the kettle going. It's thirsty work, this.'

So Margaret went to the kitchen, and stoked up the fire, and boiled the water. Now, on the tin roof of the kitchen she could hear the thuds and bangs of falling locusts, or a scratching slither as one skidded down. Here were the first of them. From down on the lands came the beating and banging and clanging of a hundred petrol tins and bits of metal. Stephen impatiently waited while one petrol tin was filled with tea, hot, sweet and orange-coloured, and the other with water. In the meantime, he told Margaret about how twenty years back he was eaten out, made bankrupt by the locust armies. And then, still talking, he hoisted up the petrol cans, one in each hand, by the wood pieces set corner-wise each, and jogged off down to the road to the thirsty labourers. By now the locusts were falling like hail on to the roof of the kitchen. It sounded like a heavy storm. Margaret looked out and saw the air dark with a criss-cross of the insects, and she set her teeth and ran out into it – what men could do, she could. Overhead the air was thick, locusts everywhere. The locusts were flopping against her, and she brushed them off, heavy red-brown creatures, looking at her with their beady old-men's eyes while they clung with hard serrated legs. She held her breath with disgust and ran into the house. There it was even more like being in a heavy storm. The iron roof was reverberating, and the clamour of iron from the lands was like thunder. Looking out, all the trees were queer and still, clotted with insects, their boughs weighed to the ground. The earth seemed to be moving, locusts crawling everywhere, she could not see the lands at all, so thick was the swarm. Towards the mountains it was like looking into driving rain – even as she watched, the sun was blotted out with a fresh onrush of them. It was a half-night, a perverted blackness. Then came a sharp crack from the bush – a branch had snapped off. Then another. A tree down the slope leaned over and settled heavily to the ground. Through the hail of insects a man came running. More tea, more water was needed. She supplied them. She kept the fires stoked and filled tins with liquid, and then it was four in the afternoon, and the locusts had been pouring across overhead for a couple of hours. Up came old Stephen again, crunching locusts underfoot with every step, locusts clinging all over him, cursing and swearing, banging with his old hat at the air. At the doorway he stopped briefly, hastily pulling at the clinging insects and throwing them off, then he plunged into the locust-free living-room.

'All the crops finished. Nothing left,' he said.

But the gongs were still beating, the men still shouting, and Margaret asked: 'Why do you go on with it, then?'

'The main swarm isn't settling. They are heavy with eggs. They are looking for a place to settle and lay. If we can stop the main body settling on our farm, that's everything. If they get a chance to lay their eggs, we are going to have every-thing eaten flat with hoppers later on.' He picked a stray locust off his shirt, and split it down his thumbnail – it was clotted inside with eggs. 'Imagine that multiplied by millions. You ever seen a hopper swarm on the march? Well, you're lucky.'

Margaret thought an adult swarm was bad enough. Outside now the light on the earth was a pale thin yellow, clotted with moving shadow, the clouds of moving insects thickened and lightened like driving rain. Old Stephen said: 'They've got the wind behind them, that's something.'

'Is it very bad?' asked Margaret fearfully, and the old man said emphatically: 'We're finished. This swarm may pass over, but once they've started, they'll be coming down from the North now one after another. And then there are the hoppers – it might go on for two or three years.'

Margaret sat down helplessly, and thought: Well, if it's the end, it's the end. What now? We'll all three have to go back to town ... But at this, she took a quick look at Stephen, the old man who had farmed forty years in this country, been bankrupt twice, and she knew nothing would make him go and become a clerk in the city. Yet her heart ached for him, he looked so tired, the worry-lines deep from nose to mouth. Poor old man ... He had lifted up a locust that had got itself some-how into his pocket, holding it in the air by one leg. 'You've got the strength of a steel-spring in those legs of yours,' he was telling the locust, good-humouredly. Then, although he had been fighting locusts, squashing locusts, yelling at locusts, sweeping them in great mounds into the fires to burn for the last three hours, nevertheless he took this one to the door, and carefully threw it out to join its fellows as if he would rather not harm a hair of its head. This comforted Margaret, all at once she felt irrationally cheered. She remembered it was not the first time in the last three years the men had announced their final and irremediable ruin.

'Get me a drink, lass,' he then said, and she set the bottle of whisky by him.

In the meantime, out in the pelting storm of insects, her husband was banging the gong, feeding the fires with leaves, the insects clinging to him all over – she shuddered. 'How can you bear to let them touch you?' she asked. He looked at her, disapproving. She felt suitably humble – just as she had when he had first taken a good look at her city self, hair waved and golden, nails red and pointed. Now she was a proper farmer's wife, in sensible shoes and a solid skirt. She might even get to letting locusts settle on her – in time.

Having tossed back a whisky or two, old Stephen went back into the battle, wading now through glistening brown waves of locusts.

Five o'clock. The sun would set in an hour. Then the swarm would settle. It was as thick overhead as ever. The trees were ragged mounds of glistening brown.

Margaret began to cry. It was all so hopeless – if it wasn't a bad season, it was locusts, if it wasn't locusts, it was army-worm, or veld fires. Always something. The rustling of the locust armies was like a big forest in the storm, their settling on the roof was like the beating of the rain, the ground was invisible in a sleek brown surging tide – it was like being drowned in locusts, submerged by the loathsome brown flood. It seemed as if the roof might sink in under the weight of them, as if the door might give in under their pressure and these rooms fill with them – and it was getting so dark ... she looked up. The air was thinner, gaps of blue showed in the dark moving clouds. The blue spaces were cold and thin: the sun must be setting. Through the fog of insects she saw figures approaching. First old Stephen, marching bravely along, then her husband, drawn and haggard with weariness. Behind them the servants. All were crawling all over with insects. The sound of the gongs had stopped. She could hear nothing but the ceaseless rustle of a myriad wings.

The two men slapped off the insects and came in.

'Well,' said Richard, kissing her on the cheek, 'the main swarm has gone over.'

'For the Lord's sake,' said Margaret angrily, still half-crying, 'what's here is bad enough, isn't it?' For although the evening air was no longer black and thick, but a clear blue, with a pattern of insects whizzing this way and that across it, everything else – trees, buildings, bushes, earth, was gone under the moving brown masses.

'If it doesn't rain in the night and keep them here – if it doesn't rain and weight them down with water, they'll be off in the morning at sunrise.'

'We're bound to have some hoppers. But not the main swarm, that's something.'

Margaret roused herself, wiped her eyes, pretended she had not been crying, and fetched them some supper, for the servants were too exhausted to move. She sent them down to the compound to rest.

She served the supper and sat listening. There is not one maize-plant left, she heard. Not one. The men would get the planters out the moment the locusts had gone. They must start all over again.

'But what's the use of that?' Margaret wondered, if the whole farm was going to be crawling with hoppers? But she listened while they discussed the new Government pamphlet which said how to defeat the hoppers. You must have men out all the time moving over the farm to watch for movement in the grass. When you find a patch of hoppers, small lively black things, like crickets, then you dig trenches around the patch, or spray them with poison from pumps supplied by the Government. The Government wanted them to co-operate in a world plan for eliminating this plague for ever. You should attack locusts at the source. Hoppers, in short. The men were talking as if they were planning a war, and Margaret listened, amazed.

In the night it was quiet, no sign of the settled armies outside, except sometimes a branch snapped, or a tree could be heard crashing down.

Margaret slept badly in the bed beside Richard, who was sleeping like the dead, exhausted with the afternoon's fight. In the morning she woke to yellow sunshine lying across the bed, clear sunshine, with an occasional blotch of shadow moving over it. She went to the window. Old Stephen was ahead of her. There he stood outside, gazing down over the bush. And she gazed, astounded – and entranced, much against her will. For it looked as if every tree, every bush, all the earth, were lit with pale flames. The locusts were fanning their wings to free them of the night dews. There was a shimmer of red-tinged gold light everywhere.

She went out to join the old man, stepping carefully among the insects. They stood and watched. Overhead the sky was blue, blue and clear.

'Pretty,' said old Stephen, with satisfaction.

Well, thought Margaret, we may be ruined, we may be bankrupt, but not everyone has seen an army of locusts fanning their wings at dawn.

Over the slopes, in the distance, a faint red smear showed in the sky, thickened and spread. 'There they go,' said old Stephen. 'There goes the main army, off South.'

And now from the trees, from the earth all round them, the locusts were taking wing. They were like small aircraft, manoeuvring for the take-off, trying their wings to see if they were dry enough. Off they went. A reddish brown steam was rising off the miles of bush, off the lands, the earth. Again the sunlight darkened.

And as the clotted branches lifted, the weight on them lightening, there was nothing but the black spines of branches, trees. No green left, nothing. All morning they watched, the three of them, as the brown crust thinned and broke and dissolved, flying up to mass with the main army, now a brownish-red smear in the Southern sky. The lands which had been filmed with green, the new tender mealie plants, were stark and bare. All the trees stripped. A devastated landscape. No green, no green anywhere.

By midday the reddish cloud had gone. Only an occasional locust flopped down. On the ground were the corpses and the wounded. The African labourers were sweeping these up with branches and collecting them in tins.

'Ever eaten sun-dried locust?' asked old Stephen. 'That time twenty years ago, when I went broke, I lived on mealie-meal and dried locusts for three months. They aren't bad at all – rather like smoked fish, if you come to think of it.'

But Margaret preferred not even to think of it.

After the midday meal the men went off to the lands. Everything was to be replanted. With a bit of luck another swarm would not come travelling down just this way. But they hoped it would rain very soon, to spring some new grass, because the cattle would die otherwise – there was not a blade of grass left on the farm. As for Margaret, she was trying to get used to the idea of three or four years of locusts. Locusts were going to be like bad weather, from now on, always imminent. She felt like a survivor after war – if this devastated and mangled countryside was not ruin, well, what then was ruin?

But the men ate their supper with good appetites.

'It could have been worse,' was what they said. 'It could be much worse.'

FLAVOURS OF EXILE

At the foot of the hill, near the well, was the vegetable garden, an acre fenced off from the Big Field whose earth was so rich that mealies grew there year after year ten feet tall. Nursed from that fabulous soil, carrots, lettuces, beets, tasting as I have never found vegetables taste since, loaded our table and the tables of our neighbours. Sometimes, if the garden boy was late with the supply for lunch, I would run down the steep pebbly path through the trees at the back of the hill, and along the red dust of the wagon road until I could see the windlass under its shed of thatch. There I stopped. The smell of manure, of sun on foliage, of evaporating water, rose to my head: two steps farther, and I could look down into the vegetable garden enclosed within its tall pale of reeds, rich chocolate earth studded emerald green, frothed with the white of cauliflowers, jewelled with the purple globes of eggplant and the scarlet wealth of tomatoes. Around the fence grew lemons, pawpaws, bananas, shapes of gold and yellow in their patterns of green.

In another five minutes I would be dragging from the earth carrots ten inches long, and so succulent they snapped between two fingers. I ate my allowance of these before the cook could boil them and drown them in the white flour sauce without which – and unless they were served in the large china vegetable dishes brought from that old house in London – they were not carrots to my mother.

For her, that garden represented a defeat.

When the family first came to the farm, she built vegetable beds on the kopje near the house. She had in her mind, perhaps, a vision of the farmhouse surrounded by outbuildings and gardens like a hen sheltering its chicks.

The kopje was all stone. As soon as the grass was cleared off its crown where the house stood, the fierce rains beat the soil away. Those first vegetable beds were thin sifted earth walled by pebbles. The water was brought up from the well in the water-cart.

'Water is gold,' grumbled my father, eating peas which he

reckoned must cost a shilling a mouthful. 'Water is gold!' he came to shout at last, as my mother toiled and bent over those reluctant beds. But she got more pleasure from them than she ever did from the exhaustless plenty of the garden under the hill.

At last, the spaces in the bush where the old beds had been were seeded by wild or vagrant plants, and we children played there. Someone must have thrown away gooseberries, for soon the low-spreading bushes covered the earth. We used to creep under them, William MacGregor and I, lie flat on our backs, and look through the leaves at the brilliant sky, reaching around us for the tiny sharp-sweet yellow fruits in their jackets of papery white. The smell of the leaves was spicy. It intoxicated us. We would laugh and shout, then quarrel; and William, to make up, shelled a double handful of the fruit and poured it into my skirt, and we ate together, pressing the biggest berries on each other. When we could eat no more, we filled baskets and took them to the kitchen to be made into that rich jam which – if allowed to burn just the right amount on the pan – is the best jam in the world, clear sweet amber, with lumps of sticky sharpness in it, as if the stings of bees were preserved in honey.

But my mother did not like it. 'Cape gooseberries!' she said bitterly. 'They aren't gooseberries at all. Oh, if I could let you taste a pie made of real English gooseberries.'

In due course, the marvels of civilization made this possible; she found a tin of gooseberries in the Greek store at the station, and made us a pie.

My parents and William's ate the pie with a truly religious emotion.

It was this experience with the gooseberries that made me cautious when it came to brussels sprouts. Year after year my mother yearned for brussels sprouts, whose name came to represent to me something exotic and for ever unattainable. When at last she managed to grow half a dozen spikes of this plant, in one cold winter which offered us sufficient frost, she of course sent a note to the MacGregors, so that they might share the treat. They came from Glasgow, they came from Home, and they could share the language of nostalgia. At the table the four grown-ups ate the bitter little cabbages and agreed that the soil of Africa was unable to grow food that had any taste at all. I said scornfully that I couldn't see what all the fuss was about. But William, three years older than myself, passed his plate up and said he found them delicious. It was like a betrayal; and afterwards I demanded how he could like such flavourless stuff. He smiled at me and said it cost us nothing to pretend, did it?

That smile, so gentle, a little whimsical, was a lesson to me and I remembered it when it came to the affair of the cherries. She found a tin of cherries at the store, we ate them with cream; and while she sighed over memories of barrows loaded with cherries in the streets of London, I sighed with her, ate fervently, and was careful not to meet her eyes.

And when she said: 'The pomegranates will be fruiting soon,' I would offer to run down and see how they progressed; and returned from the examination saying: 'It won't be long now, really it won't – perhaps next year.'

The truth was, my emotion over the pomegranates was not entirely due to the beautiful lesson in courtesy given me by William. Brussels sprouts, cherries, English gooseberries – they were my mother's; they recurred in her talk as often as 'a real London pea-souper', or 'chestnuts by the fire', or 'cherry blossom at Kew'. I no longer grudged these to her; I listened and was careful not to show that my thoughts were on my own inheritance of veld and sun. But pomegranates were an exotic for my mother; and therefore more easily shared with her. She had been in Persia, where, one understood, pomegranate juice ran in rivers. The wife of a minor official, she had lived in a vast stone house cooled by water trickling down a thousand stone channels from the mountains, she had lived among roses and jasmine, walnut trees and pomegranates. But, unfortunately, for too short a time.

Why not pomegranates here, in Africa? Why not?

The four trees had been planted at the same time as the first vegetable beds; and almost at once two of them died. A third lingered on for a couple of seasons and then succumbed to the white ants. The fourth stood lonely among the Cape gooseberry bushes, bore no fruit, and at last was forgotten.

Then one day my mother was showing Mrs MacGregor her chickens and as they returned through tangles of grass and weed, their skirts lifted high in both hands, my mother exclaimed: 'Why, I do believe the pomegranate is fruiting at last. Look, look, it is!' She called to us, the children, and we went running, and stood around a small thorny tree, and looked at a rusty-red fruit the size of a child's fist. 'It's ripe,' said my mother, and pulled it off.

Inside the house we were each given a dozen seeds on saucers. They were bitter, but we did not like to ask for sugar. Mrs MacGregor said gently: 'It's wonderful. How you must miss all that!'

'The roses!' said my mother. 'And sacks of walnuts ... and we used to drink pomegranate juice with the melted snow water ... nothing here tastes like that. The soil is no good.'

I looked at William, sitting opposite me. He turned his head and smiled. I fell in love.

He was then fifteen, home for the holidays. He was a silent boy, thoughtful; and the quietness in his deep grey eyes seemed to me like a promise of warmth and understanding I had never known. There was a tightness in my chest, because it hurt to be shut out from the world of simple kindness he lived in. I sat there, opposite to him, and said to myself that I had known him all my life and yet until this moment had never understood what he was. I looked at those extra-ordinarily clear eyes, that were like water over grey pebbles, I gazed and gazed, until he gave me a slow direct look which showed he knew I had been staring. It was like a warning, as if a door had been shut.

After the MacGregors had gone, I went through the bushes to the pomegranate tree. It was about my height, a tough, obstinate-looking thing; and there was a round yellow ball the size of a walnut hanging from a twig.

I looked at the ugly little tree and thought Pomegranates! Breasts like pomegranates and a belly like a heap of wheat! The golden pomegranates of the sun, I thought ... pome-granates like the red of blood.

I was in a fever, more than a little mad. The space of thick grass and gooseberry bushes between the trees was haunted by William, and his deep grey eyes looked at me across the pomegranate tree.

Next day I sat under the tree. It gave no shade, but the acrid sunlight was barred and splotched under it. There was hard cracked red earth beneath a covering of silvery dead grass. Under the grass I saw grains of red, and half a hard brown shell. It seemed that a fruit had ripened and burst without our knowing – yes, everywhere in the soft old grass lay the tiny crimson seeds. I tasted one; warm sweet juice flooded my tongue. I gathered them up and ate them until my mouth was full of dry seeds. I spat them out and thought that a score of pomegranate trees would grow from that mouthful.

As I watched, tiny black ants came scurrying along the roots of the grass, scrambling over the fissures in the earth, to snatch away the seeds. I lay on my elbow and watched. A dozen of them were levering at a still unbroken seed. Suddenly the frail tissue split as they bumped it over a splinter, and they were caught in a sticky red ooze.

The ants would carry these seeds for hundreds of yards; there would be an orchard of pomegranates. William Mac-Gregor would come visiting with his parents, and find me among the pomegranate trees; I could hear the sound of his grave voice, mingled with the tinkle of camel bells and the splashing of falling water.

I went to the tree every day and lay under it, watching the single yellow fruit ripening on its twig. There would come a moment when it must burst and scatter crimson seeds; I must be there when it did; it seemed as if my whole life was concentrated, and ripening with that single fruit.

It was very hot under the tree. My head ached. My flesh was painful with the sun. Yet there I sat all day, watching the tiny ants at their work, letting them run over my legs, waiting for the pomegranate fruit to ripen. It swelled slowly; it seemed set on reaching perfection, for when it was the size that the other had been picked, it was still a bronzing yellow, and the rind was soft. It was going to be a big fruit, the size of both my fists.

Then something terrifying happened. One day I saw that the twig it hung from was splitting off the branch. The wizened, dry little tree could not sustain the weight of the fruit it had produced. I went to the house, brought down bandages from the medicine chest, and strapped the twig firm and tight to the branch, in such a way that the weight was supported. Then I wet the bandage, tenderly, and thought of William, William, William. I wet the bandage daily, and thought of him.

What I thought of William had become a world, stronger than anything around me. Yet, since I was mad, so weak, it vanished at a touch. Once, for instance, I saw him driving with his father on the wagon along the road to the station. I remember I was ashamed that that marvellous feverish world should depend on a half-grown boy in dusty khaki, gripping a piece of grass between his teeth as he stared ahead of him. It came to this – that in order to preserve the dream, I must not see William. And it seemed he felt something of the sort himself, for in all those weeks he never came near me, whereas once he used to come every day. And yet I was convinced it must happen that William and the moment when the pomegranate split open would coincide.

I imagined it in a thousand ways, as the fruit continued to grow. Now, it was a clear bronze yellow with faint rust-coloured streaks. The rind was thin, so soft that the swelling seeds within were shaping it. The fruit looked lumpy and veined, like a nursing breast. The small crown where the stem fastened on it, which had been the sheath of the flower, was still green. It began to harden and turn back into iron-grey thorns.

Soon, soon, it would be ripe. Very swiftly, the skin lost its smooth thinness. It took on a tough pored look, like the skin of an old weatherbeaten countryman. It was a ruddy scarlet now, and hot to the touch. A small crack appeared, which in a day had widened so that the packed red seeds within were visible, almost bursting out. I did not dare leave the tree. I was there from six in the morning until the sun went down. I even crept down with the candle at night, although I argued it could not burst at night, not in the cool of the night, it must be the final unbearable thrust of the hot sun which would break it.

For three days nothing happened. The crack remained the same. Ants swarmed up the trunk, along the branches and into the fruit. The scar oozed red juice in which black ants swam and struggled. At any moment it might happen. And William did not come. I was sure he would: I watched the empty road helplessly, watching for him to come striding along, a piece of grass between his teeth, to me and the pomegranate tree. Yet he did not. In one night, the crack split another half-inch, I saw a red seed push itself out of the crack and fall. Instantly it was borne off by the ants into the grass.

I went up to the house and asked my mother when the Mac-Gregors were coming to tea.

'I don't know, dear. Why?'

'Because. I just thought . . .'

She looked at me. Her eyes were critical. In one moment, she would say the name *William*. I struck first. To have William and the moment together, I must pay fee to the family gods. 'There's a pomegranate nearly ripe, and you know how interested Mrs MacGregor is . . .'

She looked sharply at me. 'Pick it, and we'll make a drink of it.'

'Oh no, it's not quite ready. Not altogether . . .'

'Silly child,' she said at last. She went to the telephone and said: 'Mrs MacGregor, this daughter of mine, she's got it into her head – you know how children are.'

I did not care. At four that afternoon I was waiting by the pomegranate tree. Their car came thrusting up the steep road to the crown of the hill. There was Mr MacGregor in his khaki, Mrs MacGregor in her best afternoon dress – and William. The adults shook hands, kissed. William did not turn round and look at me. It was not possible, it was monstrous, that the force of my dream should not have had the power to touch him at all, that he knew nothing of what he must do.

Then he slowly turned his head and looked down the slope to where I stood. He did not smile. It seemed he had not seen me, for his eyes travelled past me, and back to the grown-ups. He stood to one side while they exchanged their news and greetings; and then all four laughed, and turned to look at me and my tree. It seemed for a moment they were all coming. At once, however, they went into the house, William trailing after them, frowning.

In a moment he would have gone in; the space in front of the old house would be empty. I called 'William!' I had not known I would call. My voice sounded small in the wide afternoon sunlight.

He went on as if he had not heard. Then he stopped, seemed to think, and came down the hill towards me while I anxiously examined his face. The low tangle of the gooseberry bushes was around his legs, and he swore sharply.

'Look at the pomegranate,' I said. He came to a halt beside the tree, and looked. I was searching those clear grey eyes now for a trace of that indulgence they had shown my mother over the brussels sprouts, over that first unripe pomegranate. Now all I wanted was indulgence; I abandoned everything else.

'It's full of ants,' he said at last.

'Only a little, only where it's cracked.'

He stood, frowning, chewing at his piece of grass. His lips were full and thick-skinned; and I could see the blood, dull and dark around the pale groove where the grass-stem pressed.

The pomegranate hung there, swarming with ants.

Now, I thought wildly. Now – crack now.

There was not a sound. The sun pouring down, hot and yellow, drawing up the smell of the grasses. There was, too, a faint sour smell from the fermenting juice of the pomegranate.

'It's bad,' said William, in that uncomfortable, angry voice. 'And what's that bit of dirty rag for?'

'It was breaking, the twig was breaking off – I tied it up.'

'Mad,' he remarked, aside, to the afternoon. 'Quite mad.' He was looking about him in the grass. He reached down and picked up a stick.

'No,' I cried out, as he hit at the tree. The pomegranate flew into the air and exploded in a scatter of crimson seeds, fermenting juice and black ants.

The cracked empty skin, with its white clean-looking inner skin faintly stained with juice, lay in two fragments at my feet.

He was poking sulkily with the stick at the little scarlet seeds that lay everywhere on the earth.

Then he did look at me. Those clear eyes were grave again, thoughtful, and judging. They held that warning I had seen in them before.

'That's your pomegranate,' he said at last.

'Yes,' I said.

He smiled. 'We'd better go up, if we want any tea.'

We went together up the hill to the house, and as we entered the room where the grown-ups sat over the teacups, I spoke quickly, before he could. In a bright careless voice I said: 'It was bad, after all, the ants had got at it. It should have been picked before.'

GETTING OFF THE ALTITUDE

That night of the dance, years later, when I saw Mrs Slatter come into the bedroom at midnight, not seeing me because the circle of lamplight was focused low, with a cold and terrible face I never would have believed could be hers after knowing her so long during the day-times and the visits – that night, when she had dragged herself out of the room again, still not knowing I was there, I went to the mirror to see my own face. I held the lamp as close as I could and looked into my face. For I had not known before that a person's face could be smooth and comfortable, though often sorrowful, like Molly Slatter's had been all those years, and then hard-set, in the solitude away from the dance and the people (that night they had drunk a great deal and the voices of the singing reminded me of when dogs howl at the full moon), into an old and patient stone. Yes, her face looked like white stone that the rain has trickled over and worn through the wet seasons.

My face, that night in the mirror, dusted yellow from the lamplight, with the dark watery spaces of the glass behind, was smooth and enquiring, with the pert flattered look of a girl in her first long dress and dancing with the young people for the first time. There was nothing in it, a girl's face, empty. Yet I had been crying just before, and I wished then I could go away into the dark and stay there for ever. Yet Molly Slatter's terrible face was familiar to me, as if it were her own face, her real one. I seemed to know it. And that meant that the years I had known her comfortable and warm in spite of all her troubles had been saying something else to me about her. But only now I was prepared to listen.

I left the mirror, set the lamp down on the dressing-table, and went out into the passage and looked for her among the people, and there she was in her red satin dress looking just as usual, talking to my father, her hand on the back of his chair, smiling down at him.

'It hasn't been a bad season, Mr Farquar,' she was saying, 'the rains haven't done us badly at all.'

Driving home in the car that night, my mother asked: 'What

was Molly saying to you?'

And my father said: 'Oh I don't know, I really don't know.' His voice was sad and angry.

She said: 'That dress of hers. Her evening dresses look like a cheap night-club.'

He said, troubled and sorrowful, 'Yes. Actually I said something to her.'

'Somebody should.'

'No,' he said, quick against the cold criticizing voice. 'No. It's a – pretty colour. But I said to her, There's not much *to* that dress, is there?'

'What did she say?'

'She was hurt. I was sorry I said anything.'

'H'mm,' said my mother, with a little laugh.

He turned his head from his driving, so that the car lights swung wild over the rutted track for a moment, and said direct at her: 'She's a good woman. She's a nice woman.'

But she gave another offended gulp of laughter. As a woman insists in an argument because she won't give in, even when she knows she is wrong.

As for me, I saw that dress again, with its criss-cross of narrow sweat-darkened straps over the ageing white back, and I saw Mrs Slatter's face when my father criticized her. I might have been there, I saw it so clearly. She coloured, lifted her head, lowered her lids so that the tears would not show, and she said: 'I'm sorry you feel like that, Mr Farquar.' It was with dignity. Yes. She had put on that dress in order to say something. But my father did not approve. He had said so.

She cared what my father said. They cared very much for each other. She called him Mr Farquar always, and he called her Molly; and when the Slatters came over to tea, and Mr Slatter was being brutal, there was a gentleness and a respect for her in my father's manner which made even Mr Slatter feel it and even, sometimes, repeat something he had said to his wife in a lower voice, although it was still impatient.

The first time I knew my father felt for Molly Slatter and that my mother grudged it to her was when I was perhaps seven or eight. Their house was six miles away over the veld, but ten by the road. Their house like ours was on a ridge. At the end of the dry season when the trees were low and the leaves thinning, we could see their lights flash out at sundown, low and yellow across the miles of country. My father, after coming back from seeing Mr Slatter about some farm matter, stood by our window looking at their lights, and my mother watched him. Then he said: 'Perhaps she should stand up to him? No, that's *not* it. She does, in her way. But Lord, he's a tough customer, Slatter.'

My mother said, her head low over her sewing: 'She married him.'

He let his eyes swing around at her, startled. Then he laughed. 'That's right, she married him.'

'*Well?*'

'Oh come off it, old girl,' he said almost gay, laughing and hard. Then, still laughing angrily he went over and kissed her on the cheek.

'I like Molly,' she said, defensive. 'I like her. She hasn't got what you might call conversation but I like her.'

'Living with Slatter, I daresay she's got used to keeping her mouth shut.'

When Molly Slatter came over to spend the day with my mother the two women talked eagerly for hours about household things. Then, when my father came in for tea or dinner, there was a lock of sympathies and my mother looked ironical while he went to sit by Mrs Slatter, even if only for a minute, saying: 'Well, Molly? Everything all right with you?'

'I'm very well, thank you, Mr Farquar, and so are the children.'

Most people were frightened of Mr Slatter. There were four Slatter boys, and when the old man was in a temper and waving the whip he always had with him, they ran off into the bush and stayed there until he had cooled down. All the natives on their farm were afraid of him. Once when he knew their houseboy had stolen some soap he tied him to a tree in the garden without food and water all of one day, and then through the night, and beat him with his whip every time he went past, until the boy confessed. And once, when he had hit a farm-boy, and the boy complained to the police, Mr Slatter tied the boy to his horse and rode it at a gallop to the police station twelve miles off and made the boy run beside, and told him if he complained to the police again he would kill him. Then he paid the ten-shilling fine and made the boy run beside the horse all the way back again.

I was so frightened of him that I could feel myself begin

trembling when I saw his car turning to come up the drive from the farm lands.

He was a square fair man, with small sandy-lashed blue eyes, and small puffed cracked lips, and red ugly hands. He used to come up the wide red shining steps of the veranda, grinning slightly, looking at us. Then he would take a handful of tow-hair from the heads of whichever of his sons were nearest, one in each fist, and tighten his fists slowly, not saying a word, while they stood grinning back and their eyes filled slowly. He would grin over their heads at Molly Slatter, while she sat silent, saying nothing. Then, one or other of the boys would let out a sound of pain, and Mr Slatter showed his small discoloured teeth in a grin of triumphant good humour and let them go. Then he stamped off in his big farm boots into the house.

Mrs Slatter would say to her sons: 'Don't cry. Your father doesn't know his own strength. Don't cry.' And she went on sewing, composed and pale.

Once at the station, the Slatter car and ours were drawn up side by side outside the store. Mrs Slatter was sitting in the front seat, beside the driver's seat. In our car my father drove and my mother was beside him. We children were in the back seats. Mr Slatter came out of the bar with Mrs Pritt and stood on the store veranda talking to her. He stood before her, legs apart, in his way of standing, head back on his shoulders, eyes narrowed, grinning, red fists loose at his sides, and talked on for something like half an hour. Meanwhile Mrs Pritt let her weight slump on to one hip and lolled in front of him. She wore a tight shrill green dress, so short it showed the balls of her thin knees.

And my father leaned out of our car window though we had all our stores in and might very well leave for home now, and talked steadily and gently to Mrs Slatter, who was quiet, not looking at her husband, but making conversation with my father and across him to my mother. And so they went on talking until Mr Slatter left Mrs Pritt, and slammed himself into the driver's seat and started the car.

I did not like Mrs Pritt and I knew neither of my parents did. She was a thin wiry tall woman with black short jumpy hair. She had a sharp knowing face and a sudden laugh like the scream of a hen caught by the leg. Her voice was always loud, and she laughed a great deal.

But seeing Mr Slatter with her was enough to know that they fitted. She was not gentle and kindly like Mrs Slatter. She was as tough in her own way as Mr Slatter. And long before I ever heard it said I knew well enough that, as my mother said primly, they liked each other. I asked her, meaning her to tell the truth, Why does Mr Slatter always go over when Mr Pritt is away, and she said: I expect Mr Slatter likes her.

In our district, with thirty or forty families on the farms spread over a hundred square miles or so, nothing happened privately. That day at the station I must have been ten years old, eleven, but it was not the first or the last time I heard the talk between my parents:

My father: 'I daresay it could make things easier for Molly.'

She, then: 'Do you?'

'But if he's got to have an affair, he might at least not push it down our throats, for Molly's sake.'

And she: 'Does he have to have an affair?'

She said the word, affair, with difficulty. It was not her language. Nor, and that was what she was protesting against, my father's. For they were both conventional and religious people. Yet at moments of crisis, at moments of scandal and irregularity, my father spoke this other language, cool and detached, as if he were born to it.

'A man like Slatter,' he said thoughtfully, as if talking to another man, 'it's obvious. And Emmy Pritt. Yes. Obviously, obviously! But it depends on how Molly takes it. Because if she doesn't take it the right way, she could make it hell for herself.'

'*Take it the right way*,' said my mother, with bright protesting eyes, and my father did not answer.

I used to stay with Mrs Slatter sometimes in the holidays. I went across-country over the kaffir paths, walking or on my bicycle, with some clothes in a small suitcase.

The boys were, from having to stand up to Mr Slatter, tough and indifferent boys, and went about the farm in a closed gang. They did man's work, driving tractors and superintending the gangs of boys before they were in their 'teens. I stayed with Mrs Slatter. She cooked a good deal, and sewed and gardened. Most of the day she sat on the veranda sewing. We did not talk much. She used to make her own dresses, cotton prints and pastel linens, like all the women of the district wore. She made Mr Slatter's khaki farm shirts and the boys' shirts. Once she made herself a petticoat that was too small for her to get into, and Mr Slatter saw her struggling with it in front of the mirror, and he said: 'What size do you think *you* are, Bluebell?' in the same way he would say, as we sat down to table, 'What have you been doing with your lily-white hands today, Primrose?' To which she would reply, pleasantly, as if he had really asked a question: 'I've made some cakes.' Or: 'I got some salt meat from the butcher at the station today fresh out of the pickle.' About the petticoat she said, 'Yes, I must have been putting on more weight than I knew.'

When I was twelve or thereabouts, I noticed that the boys had turned against their mother, not in the way of being brutal to her, but they spoke to her as their father did, calling her Bluebell, or the Fat Woman at the Fair. It was odd to hear them, because it was as if they said simply, Mum, or Mother. Not once did I hear her lose her temper with them. I could see she had determined to herself not to make them any part of what she had against Mr Slatter. I knew she was pleased to have me there, during that time, with the five men coming in only for meals.

One evening during a long stay, the boys as usual had gone off to their rooms to play when supper was done, and Mr Slatter said to his wife: 'I'm off. I'll be back tomorrow for breakfast.' He went out into the dark and the wet. It was raining hard that night. The window panes were streaked with rain and shaking with the wind. Mrs Slatter looked across at me and said – and this was the first time it had been mentioned how often he went off after dinner, coming back as the sun rose, or sometimes not for two or three days: 'You must remember something. There are some men, like Mr Slatter, who've got more energy than they know what to do with. Do you know how he started? When I met him and we were courting he was a butcher's boy at the corner. And now he's worth as much as any man in the district.'

'Yes,' I said, understanding for the first time that she was very proud of him.

She waited for me to say something more, and then said: 'Yes, we have all kinds of ideas when we're young. But Mr Slatter's a man that does not know his own strength. There are some things he doesn't understand, and it all comes from that. He never understands that other people aren't as strong as he is.'

We were sitting in the big living-room. It had a stone floor with rugs and skins on it. A boot clattered on the stone and we looked up and there was Mr Slatter. His teeth were showing. He wore his big black boots, shining now from the wet, and his black oilskin glistened. 'The bossboy says the river's up,' he said. 'I won't get across tonight.' He took off his oilskin there, scattering wet on Mrs Slatter's polished stone floor, tugged off his boots, and reached out through the door to hang his oilskin in the passage and set his boots under it, and came back.

There were two rivers between the Slatters' farm and the Pritts' farm, twelve miles off, and when the water came down they could be impassable for hours.

'So I don't know my own strength?' he said to her, direct, and it was a soft voice, more frightening than I had ever heard from him, for he bared grinning teeth as usual, and his big fists hung at his sides.

'No,' she said steadily, 'I don't think you do.' She did not lift her eyes, but stayed quiet in the corner of the sofa under the lamp. 'We aren't alone,' she added quickly, and now she did look warningly at him.

He turned his head and looked towards me. I made fast for the door. I heard her say, 'Please, I'm sorry about the river. But leave me alone, please.'

'So you're sorry about the river.'

'Yes.'

'And I don't know my own strength?'

I shut the door. But it was a door that was never shut, and it swung open again and I ran down the passage away from it, as he said: 'So that's why you keep your bedroom door locked, Lady Godiva, is that it?'

And she screamed out: 'Ah, leave me alone. I don't care what you do. I don't care now. But you aren't going to make use of me. *I won't let you make use of me.*'

It was a big house, rooms sprawling everywhere. The boys had two rooms and a playroom off at one end of a long stone passage. Dairies and larders and kitchen opened off the passage. Then a dining-room and some offices and a study. Then the living-room. And another passage off at an angle, with

the room where I slept and beside it Mrs Slatter's big bedroom with the double bed and after that a room they called
the workroom, but it was an ordinary room and Mr Slatter's
things were in it, with a bed.

I had not thought before that they did not share a bedroom.
I knew no married people in the district who had separate
rooms and that is why I had not thought about the small room
where Mr Slatter slept.

Soon after I had shut the door on myself, I heard them
come along the passage outside, I heard voices in the room
next door. Her voice was pleading, his loud, and he was laughing a lot.

In the morning at breakfast I looked at Mrs Slatter but she
was not taking any notice of us children. She was pale. She
was helping Mr Slatter to his breakfast. He always had three
or four eggs on thick slats of bacon, and then slice after slice of
toast, and half a dozen cups of tea as black as it would come
out of the pot. She had some toast and a cup of tea and
watched him eat. When he went out to the farm work he kissed
her, and she blushed.

When we were on the veranda after breakfast, sewing, she
said to me, apologetically and pink-cheeked: 'I hope you won't
think anything about last night. Married people often quarrel.
It doesn't mean anything.'

My parents did not quarrel. At least, I had not thought of
them as quarrelling. But because of what she said I tried to
remember times when they disagreed and perhaps raised their
voices and then afterwards laughed and kissed each other.
Yes, I thought, it is true that married people quarrel, but that
doesn't mean they aren't happy together.

That night after supper when the boys had gone to their
room Mr Slatter said, 'The rivers are down, I'm off.' Mrs
Slatter, sitting quiet under the lamp, kept her eyes down,
and said nothing. He stood there staring at her and she said:
'Well, you know what that means, don't you?'

He simply went out, and we heard the lorry start up and the
headlights swung up against the window-panes a minute, so
that they dazzled up gold and hard, and went black again.

Mrs Slatter said nothing, so that my feeling that something awful had happened slowly faded. Then she began talking about her childhood in London. She was a shop assistant
before she met Mr Slatter. She often spoke of her family,

and the street she lived in, so I wondered if she were homesick, but she never went back to London so perhaps she was
not homesick at all.

Soon after that Emmy Pritt got ill. She was not the sort of
woman one thought of as being ill. She had some kind of
operation, and they all said she needed a holiday, she needed to
get off the altitude. Our part of Central Africa was high, nearly
four thousand feet, and we all knew that when a person got run-
down they needed a rest from the altitude in the air at sea-
level. Mrs Pritt went down to the Cape, and soon after Mr and
Mrs Slatter went too, with the four children, and they all had a
holiday together at the same hotel.

When they came back, the Slatters brought a farm assistant
with them. Mr Slatter could not manage the farm-work, he
said. I heard my father say that Slatter was taking things a
bit far; he was over at the Pritts every weekend from Friday
night to Monday morning and nearly every night from after
supper until morning. Slatter, he said, might be as strong
as a herd of bulls, but no one could go on like that; and in
any case, one should have a sense of proportion. Mr Pritt was
never mentioned, though it was not for years that I thought
to consider what this might mean. We used to see him about
the station, or at gymkhanas. He was an ordinary man, not like
a farmer, as we knew farmers, men who could do anything;
he might have been anybody, or an office person. He was
ordinary in height, thinnish, with his pale hair leaving his
narrow forehead high and bony. He was an accountant as
well. People used to say that Charlie Slatter helped Emmy
Pritt run their farm, and most of the time Mr Pritt was off
staying at neighbouring farms doing their accounts.

The new assistant was Mr Andrews, and as Mrs Slatter said
to my mother when she came over for tea, he was a gentleman.
He had been educated at Cambridge in England. He came of
a hard-up family, though, for he had only a few hundred
pounds capital of his own. He would be an assistant for two
years and then start his own farm.

For a time I did not go to stay with Mrs Slatter. Once or
twice I asked if she had said anything to my mother about
my coming, and she said in a dry voice, meaning to discourage
me, 'No, she hasn't said anything.' I understood when I heard
my father say: 'Well, it might not be such a bad thing. For
one thing he's a nice lad, and for another it might make

Slatter see things differently.' And another time: 'Perhaps Slatter would give Molly a divorce? After all, he practically lives at the Pritts! And then Molly could have some sort of life at last.'

'But the boy's not twenty-five,' said my mother. And she was really shocked, as distinct from her obstinate little voice when she felt him to be wrong-headed or loose in his talk – a threat of some kind. 'And what about the children? Four children!'

My father said nothing to this, but after some minutes he came off some track of thought with: 'I hope Molly's taking it sensibly. I do hope she is. Because she could be laying up merry hell for herself if she's not.'

I saw George Andrews at a gymkhana standing at the rail with Mrs Slatter. Although he was an Englishman he was already brown, and his clothes were loosened up and easy, as our men's clothes were. So there was nothing to dislike about him on that score. He was rather short, not fat, but broad, and you could see he would be fat. He was healthy-looking above all, with a clear reddish face the sun had laid a brown glisten over, and very clear blue eyes, and his hair was thick and short, glistening like fur. I wanted to like him and so I did. I saw the way he leaned beside Mrs Slatter, with her dust-coat over his arm, holding out his programme for her to mark. I could understand that she would like a gentleman who would open doors for her and stand up when she came into the room, after Mr Slatter. I could see she was proud to be with him. And so I liked him though I did not like his mouth; his lips were pink and wettish. I did not look at his mouth again for a long time. And because I liked him I was annoyed with my father when he said, after that gymkhana, 'Well, I don't know. I don't think I like it after all. He's a bit of a young pup, Cambridge or no Cambridge.'

Six months after George Andrews came to the district there was a dance for the young people at the Slatters'. It was the first dance. The older boys were eighteen and seventeen and they had girls. The two younger boys were fifteen and thirteen and they despised girls. I was fifteen then, and all these boys were too young for me, and the girls of the two older boys were nearly twenty. There were about sixteen of us, and the married people thirty or forty, as usual. The married people sat in the living-room and danced in it, and we

were on the verandas. Mr Slatter was dancing with Emmy
Pritt, and sometimes another woman, and Mrs Slatter was
busy being hostess and dancing with George Andrews. I was
still in a short dress and unhappy because I was in love with
one of the assistants from the farm between the rivers, and I
knew very well that until I had a long dress he would not see
me. I went into Mrs Slatter's bedroom latish because it seemed
the only room empty, and I looked out of the window at the
dark wet night. It was the rainy season and we had driven over
the swollen noisy river and all the way the rain-water was
sluicing under our tyres. It was still raining and the lamplight
gilded streams of rain so that as I turned my head slightly
this way and that, the black and the gold rods shifted before
me, and I thought (and I had never thought so simply before
about these things): 'How do they manage? With all these big
boys in the house? And they never go to bed before eleven
or half-past these days, I bet, and with Mr Slatter coming
home unexpectedly from Emmy Pritt – it must be difficult. I
suppose he has to wait until everyone's asleep. It must be
horrible, wondering all the time if the boys have noticed something . . .' I turned from the window and looked from it into the
big low-ceilinged comfortable room with its big low bed
covered over with pink roses, the pillows propped high in
pink frilled covers, and although I had been in that room
during visits for years of my life, it seemed strange to me, and
ugly. I loved Mrs Slatter. Of all the women in the district she
was the kindest, and she had always been good to me. But
at that moment I hated her and I despised her.

I started to leave the bedroom, but at the door I stopped,
because Mrs Slatter was in the passage, leaning against the
wall, and George Andrews had his arms around her, and his
face in her neck. She was saying, 'Please don't, George, please
don't, please, the boys might see.' And he was swallowing
her neck and saying nothing at all. She was twisting her face
and neck away and pushing him off. He staggered back from
her, as though she had pushed him hard, but it was because
he was drunk and had no balance, and he said: 'Oh come on
into your bedroom a minute. No one will know.' She said,
'No, George. Why should we have to snatch five minutes in
the middle of a dance, like—'

'Like what?' he said, grinning. I could see how the light

that came down the passage from the big room made his pink lips glisten.

She looked reproachfully at him, and he said: 'Molly, this thing is getting a bit much, you know. I have to set my alarm-clock for one in the morning, and then I'm dead-beat. I drag myself out of my bed, and then you've got your clock set for four, and God knows working for your old man doesn't leave one with much enthusiasm for bouncing about all night.' He began to walk off towards the big room where the people were dancing. She ran after him and grabbed at his arm. I retreated backwards towards Mr Slatter's room, but almost at once she had got him and turned him around and was kissing him. The people in the big room could have seen if they had been interested.

That night Mrs Slatter had on an electric blue crêpe dress with diamonds on the straps and in flower patterns on the hips. There was a deep V in front which showed her breasts swinging loose under the crêpe, though usually she wore strong corsets. And the back was cut down to the waist. As the two turned and came along, he put his hand into the front of her dress, and I saw it lift out her left breast, and his mouth was on her neck again. Her face was desperate, but that did not surprise me, because I knew she must be ashamed. I despised her, because her white long breast lying in his hand like a piece of limp floured dough, was not like Mrs Slatter who called men Mister even if she had known them twenty years, and was really very shy, and there was nothing Mr Slatter liked more than to tease her because she blushed when he used bad language. 'What did you make such a fuss for?' George Andrews was saying in a drunken sort of way. 'We can lock the door, can't we?'

'Yes, we can lock the door,' she answered in the same way, laughing.

I went back into the crowd of married people where the small children were, and sat beside my mother, and it was only five minutes before Mrs Slatter came back looking as usual, from one door, and then George Andrews, in at another.

I did not go to the Slatters' again for some months. For one thing, I was away at school, and for another people were saying that Mrs Slatter was run down and she should get off the altitude for a bit. My father was not mentioning the Slatters by this time, because he had quarrelled with my mother over them. I knew they had, because whenever Molly Slatter was mentioned, my mother tightened her mouth and changed the subject.

And so a year went by. At Christmas they had a dance again, and I had my first long dress, and I went to that dance not caring if it was at the Slatters' or anywhere else. It was my first dance as one of the young people. And so I was on the veranda dancing most of the evening, though sometimes the rain blew in on us, because it was raining again, being the full of the rainy season, and the skies were heavy and dark, with the moon shining out like a knife from the masses of the clouds and then going in again leaving the veranda with hardly light enough to see each other. Once I went down to the steps to say goodbye to some neighbours who were going home early because they had a new baby, and coming back up the steps there was Mr Slatter and he had Mrs Slatter by the arm. 'Come here, Lady Godiva,' he said. 'Give us a kiss.'

'Oh go along,' she said, sounding good-humoured. 'Go along with you and leave me in peace.'

He was quite drunk, but not very. He twisted her arm around. It looked like a slight twist but she came up sudden against him, in a bent-back curve, her hips and legs against him, and he held her there. Her face was sick, and she half-screamed: 'You don't know your own strength.' But he did not slacken the grip, and she stayed there, and the big sky was filtering a little stormy moonlight and I could just see their faces, and I could see his grinning teeth. 'Your bloody pride, Lady Godiva,' he said, 'who do you think you're doing in, who do you think is the loser over your bloody locked door?' She said nothing and her eyes were shut. 'And now you've frozen out George too? What's the matter, isn't *he* good enough for you either?' He gave her arm a wrench, and she gasped, but then shut her lips again, and he said: 'So now you're all alone in your tidy bed, telling yourself fairy stories in the dark, Sister Theresa, the little flower.'

He let her go suddenly, and she staggered, so he put out his other hand to steady her, and held her until she was steady. It seemed odd to me that he should care that she shouldn't fall to the ground, and that he should put his hand like that to stop her falling.

And so I left them and went back on to the veranda. I was

dancing all the night with the assistant from the farm between the rivers. I was right about the long dress. All those months, at the station or at gymkhanas, he had never seen me at all. But that night he saw me, and I was wanting him to kiss me. But when he did I slapped his face. Because then I knew that he was drunk. I had not thought he might be drunk, though it was natural he was, since everybody was. But the way he kissed me was not at all what I had been thinking. 'I beg your pardon I'm sure,' he said, and I walked past him into the passage and then into the living-room. But there were so many people and my eyes were stinging, so I went through into the other passage, and there, just like last year, as if the whole year had never happened, were Mrs Slatter and George Andrews. I did not want to see it, not the way I felt.

'And why not?' he was saying, biting into her neck.

'Oh George, that was all ended months ago, months ago!'

'Oh come on, Moll, I don't know what I've done, you never bothered to explain.'

'No.' And then, crying out, *'Mind my arm.'*

'What's the matter with your arm?'

'I fell and sprained it.'

So he let go of her, and said: 'Well, thanks for the nice interlude, thanks anyway, old girl.' I knew that he had been meaning to hurt her, because I could feel what he said hurting me. He went off into the living-room by himself, and she went off after him, but to talk to someone else, and I went into her bedroom. It was empty. The lamp was on a low table by the bed, turned down, and the sky through the windows was black and wet and hardly any light came from it.

Then Mrs Slatter came in and sat on the bed and put her head in her hands. I did not move.

'Oh my God!' she said. 'Oh my God, my God!' Her voice was strange to me. The gentleness was not in it, though it was soft, but it was soft from breathlessness.

'Oh my God!' she said, after a long long silence. She took up one of the pillows from the bed, and wrapped her arms around it, and laid her head down on it. It was quiet in this room, although from the big room came the sound of singing, a noise like howling, because people were drunk, or part-drunk, and it had the melancholy savage sound of people singing when they are drunk. An awful sound, like animals howling.

Then she put down the pillow, tidily, in its proper place, and swayed backwards and forwards and said: 'Oh God, make me old soon, make me old. I can't stand this, I can't stand this any longer.'

And again the silence, with the howling sound of the singing outside, the footsteps of the people who were dancing scraping on the cement of the veranda.

'I can't go on living,' said Mrs Slatter, into the dark above the small glow of lamplight. She bent herself up again, double, as if she were hurt physically, her hands gripped around her ankles, holding herself together, and she sat crunched up, her face looking straight in front at the wall, level with the lamp-light. So now I could see her face. I did not know that face. It was stone, white stone, but her eyes gleamed out of it black, and with a flicker in them. And her black shining hair that was not grey at all yet had loosened and hung in streaks around the white stone face.

'I can't stand it,' she said again. The voice she used was strange to me. She might have been talking to someone. For a moment I even thought she had seen me and was talking to me, explaining herself to me. And then, slowly, she let herself unclench and she went out into the dance again.

I took up the lamp and held it as close as I could to the mirror and bent in and looked at my face. But there was nothing to my face.

Next day I told my father I had heard Mrs Slatter say she could not go on living. He said, 'Oh Lord, I hope it's not because of what I said about her dress,' but I said no, it was before he said he didn't like the dress. 'Then if she was upset,' he said, 'I expect what I said made her feel even worse.' And then: 'Oh poor woman, poor woman!' He went into the house and called my mother and they talked it over. Then he got on to the telephone and I heard him asking Mrs Slatter to drop in next time she was going past to the station. And it seemed she was going in that morning, and before lunchtime she was on our veranda talking to my father. My mother was not there, although my father had not asked her in so many words not to be there. As for me I went to the back of the veranda where I could hear what they said.

'Look, Molly,' he said, 'we are old friends. You're looking like hell these days. Why don't you tell me what's wrong? You can say anything to me, you know.'

After quite a time she said: 'Mr Farquar, there are some things you can't say to anybody. Nobody.'

'Ah, Molly,' he said, 'if there's one thing I've learned and I learned it early on, when I was a young man and I had a bad time, it's this. Everybody's got something terrible, Molly. Everybody has something awful they have to live with. We all live together and we see each other all the time, and none of us knows what awful thing the other person might be living with.'

And then she said: 'But, Mr Farquar, I don't think that's true. I know people who don't seem to have anything private to make them unhappy.'

'How do you know, Molly? How do you know?'

'Take Mr Slatter,' she said. 'He's a man who does as he likes. But he doesn't know his own strength. And that's why he never seems to understand how other people feel.'

'But how do you know, Molly? You could live next to someone for fifty years and still not know. Perhaps he's got something that gives him hell when he's alone, like all the rest of us?'

'No, I don't think so, Mr Farquar.'

'Molly,' he said, appealing suddenly, and very exasperated. 'You're too hard on yourself, Molly.'

She didn't say anything.

He said: 'Listen, why don't you get away for a while, get yourself down to the sea, this altitude drives us all quietly crazy. You get down off the altitude for a bit.'

She still said nothing, and he lowered his voice, and I could imagine how my mother's face would have gone stiff and cold had she heard what he said: 'And have a good time while you're there. Have a good time and let go a bit.'

'But, Mr Farquar, I don't want a good time.' The words, a good time, she used as if they could have nothing to do with her.

'If we can't have what we want in this world, then we should take what we can get.'

'It wouldn't be right,' she said at last slowly. 'I know people have different ideas, and I don't want to press mine on anyone.'

'But *Molly* –' he began, exasperated, or so it sounded, and then he was silent.

From where I sat I could hear the grass chair creaking: she

was getting out of it. 'I'll take your advice,' she said. 'I'll get down to the sea and I'll take the children with me. The two younger ones.'

'To hell with the kids for once. Take your old man with you and see that Emmy Pritt doesn't go with you this time.'

'Mr Farquar,' she said, 'if Mr Slatter wants Emmy Pritt, he can have her. He can have either one or the other of us. But not both. If I took him to the sea he would be over at her place ten minutes after we got back.'

'Ah, Molly, you women can be hell. Have some pity on him for once.'

'Pity? Mr Slatter's a man who needs nobody's pity. But thank you for your good advice, Mr Farquar. You are always very kind, you and Mrs Farquar.'

And she said goodbye to my father, and when I came forward she kissed me and asked me to come and see her soon, and she went to the station to get the stores.

And so Mrs Slatter went on living. George Andrews bought his own farm and married and the wedding was at the Slatters'. Later on Emmy Pritt got sick again and had another operation and died. It was a cancer. Mr Slatter was ill for the first time in his life from grief, and Mrs Slatter took him to the sea, by themselves, leaving the children, because they were grown-up anyway. For this was years later, and Mrs Slatter's hair had gone grey and she was fat and old, as I had heard her say she wanted to be.

A ROAD TO THE BIG CITY

The train left at midnight, not at six. Jansen's flare of temper at the clerk's mistake died before he turned from the counter: he did not really mind. For a week he had been with rich friends, in a vacuum of wealth, politely seeing the town through their eyes. Now, for six hours, he was free to let the dry and nervous air of Johannesburg strike him direct. He went into the station buffet. It was a bare place, with shiny brown walls and tables arranged regularly. He sat before a cup of strong orange-coloured tea, and because he was in the arrested, dreamy frame of mind of the uncommitted traveller, he was the spectator at a play which could not hold his attention. He was about to leave, in order to move by himself through the streets, among the people, trying to feel what they were in this city, what they had which did not exist, perhaps, in other big cities – for he believed that in every place there dwelt a daemon which expressed itself through the eyes and voices of those who lived there – when he heard someone ask: Is this place free? He turned quickly, for there was a quality in the voice which could not be mistaken. Two girls stood beside him, and the one who had spoken sat down without waiting for his response: there were many empty tables in the room. She wore a tight short black dress, several brass chains, and high shiny black shoes. She was a tall broad girl with colourless hair ridged tightly round her head, but given a bright surface so that it glinted like metal. She immediately lit a cigarette and said to her companion: 'Sit down for God's sake.' The other girl shyly slid into the chair next to Jansen, averting her face as he gazed at her, which he could not help doing: she was so different from what he expected. Plump, childish, with dull hair bobbing in fat rolls on her neck, she wore a flowered and flounced dress and flat white sandals on bare and sunburned feet. Her face had the jolly friendliness of a little dog. Both girls showed Dutch ancestry in the broad blunt planes of cheek and forehead; both had small blue eyes, though one pair was surrounded by sandy lashes, and the other by black varnished fringes.

The waitress came for an order. Jansen was too curious about the young girl to move away. 'What will you have?' he asked. 'Brandy,' said the older one at once. 'Two brandies,' she added, with another impatient look at her sister – there could be no doubt that they were sisters.

'I haven't never drunk brandy,' said the younger with a giggle of surprise. 'Except when Mom gave me some sherry at Christmas.' She blushed as the older said despairingly, half under her breath: 'Oh God preserve me from it!'

'I came to Johannesburg this morning,' said the little one to Jansen confidingly. 'But Lilla has been here earning a living for a year.'

'My God!' said Lilla again. 'What did I tell you? Didn't you hear what I told you?' Then, making the best of it, she smiled professionally at Jansen and said: 'Green! You wouldn't believe it if I told you. I was green when I came, but compared with Marie . . .' She laughed angrily.

'Have you been to Joburg before this day?' asked Marie in her confiding way.

'You are passing through,' stated Lilla, with a glance at Marie. 'You can tell easy if you know how to look.'

'You're quite right,' said Jansen.

'Leaving tomorrow perhaps?' asked Lilla.

'Tonight,' said Jansen.

Instantly Lilla's eyes left Jansen, and began to rove about her, resting on one man's face and then the next. 'Midnight,' said Jansen, in order to see her expression change.

'There's plenty time,' she said, smiling.

'Lilla promised I could go to the bioscope,' said Marie, her eyes becoming large. She looked around the station buffet, and because of her way of looking, Jansen tried to see it differently. He could not. It remained for him a bare, brownish, dirty sort of place, full of badly-dressed and dull people. He felt as one does with a child whose eyes widen with terror or delight at the sight of an old woman muttering down the street, or a flowering tree. What hunched black crone from a fairy tale, what celestial tree does the child see? Marie was smiling with charmed amazement.

'Very well,' said Jansen, 'let's go to the flicks.'

For a moment Lilla calculated, her hard blue glance moving from Jansen to Marie. 'You take Marie,' she suggested, direct to Jansen, ignoring her sister. 'She's green, but she's learning.'

Marie half-rose, with a terrified look. 'You can't leave me,' she said.

'Oh my God!' said Lilla resignedly. 'Oh all right. Sit down baby. But I've a friend to see. I told you.'

'But I only just came.'

'All right, all right. Sit down I said. He won't bite you.'

'Where do you come from?' asked Jansen.

Marie said a name he had never heard.

'It's not far from Bloemfontein,' explained Lilla.

'I went to Bloemfontein once,' said Marie, offering Jansen this experience. 'The bioscope there is big. Not like near home.'

'What is home like?'

'But it's small,' said Marie.

'What does your father do?'

'He works on the railway,' Lilla said quickly.

'He's a ganger,' said Marie, and Lilla rolled her eyes up and sighed.

Jansen had seen the gangers' cottages, the frail little shacks along the railway lines, miles from any place, where the washing flapped whitely on the lines over patches of garden, and the children ran out to wave to the train that passed shrieking from one wonderful fabled town to the next.

'Mom is old-fashioned,' said Marie. She said the word old-fashioned carefully; it was not hers, but Lilla's; she was tasting it in the way she sipped at the brandy, trying it out, determined to like it. But the emotion was all her own; all the frustration of years was in her, ready to explode into joy. 'She doesn't want us to be in Joburg. She says it is wrong for girls.'

'Did you run away?' asked Jansen.

Wonder filled the child's face. 'How did you guess I ran away?' She said, with a warm admiring smile at Lilla: 'My sister sent me the money. I didn't have none at all. I was alone with Mom and Dad and my brothers are working on the copper mines.'

'I see.' Jansen saw the lonely girl in the little house by the railway lines, helping with the chickens and the cooking, staring hopelessly at the fashion papers, watching the trains pass, too old now to run out and wave and shout, but staring at the fortunate people at the windows with grudging envy, and reading Lilla's letters week after week: 'I have a job in an office. I have a new dress. My young man said to me.' He looked over the table at the two fine young South African women, with their broad and capable look, their strong bodies, their health, and he thought: Well, it happens every day. He glanced at his watch and Marie said at once: 'There's time for the bioscope, isn't there?'

'You and your bioscope,' said Lilla. 'I'll take you tomorrow afternoon.' She rose, said to Jansen in an off-hand way: 'Coming?' and went to the door. Jansen hesitated, then followed Marie's uncertain but friendly smile.

The three went into the street. Not far away shone a large white building with film stars kissing between thin borders of coloured shining lights. Streams of smart people went up the noble marble steps where splendid men in uniform welcomed them. Jansen, watching Marie's face, was able to see it like that. Lilla laughed and said: 'We're going home, Marie. The pictures aren't anything much. There's better things to do than pictures.' She winked at Jansen.

They went to a two-roomed flat in a suburb. It was over a grocery store called Mac's Golden Emporium. It had tinned peaches, dried fruit, dressed dolls and rolls of cotton stuffs in the window. The flat had new furniture in it. There was a sideboard with bottles and a radio. The radio played: 'Or would you like to swing on a star, carry moonbeams home in a jar, and be better off than you are ...'

'I like the words,' said Marie to Jansen, listening to them with soft delight. Lilla said: 'Excuse me, but I have to phone my friend,' and went out.

Marie said: 'Have a drink.' She said it carefully. She poured brandy, the tip of her tongue held between her teeth, and she spilled the water. She carried the glass to Jansen, and smiled in unconscious triumph as she set it down by him. Then she said: 'Wait,' and went into the bedroom. Jansen adjusted himself on the juicy upholstery of a big chair. He was annoyed to find himself here. What for? What was the good of it? He looked at himself in the glass over a sideboard. He saw a middle-aged gentleman, with a worn indulgent face, dressed in a grey suit and sitting uncomfortably in a very ugly chair. But what did Marie see when she looked at him? She came back soon, with a pair of black shiny shoes on her broad feet, and a tight red dress, and a pretty face painted over her own blunt honest face. She sat herself down opposite him, as she had seen Lilla sit, adjusting the poise of her head and shoulders. But she forgot her legs, which lay loosely in front of her, like a schoolgirl's.

'Lilla said I could wear her dresses,' she said, lingering over her sister's generosity. 'She said today I could live here until I earned enough to get my own flat. She said I'd soon have enough.' She caught her breath. 'Mom would be mad.'

'I expect she would,' said Jansen drily; and saw Marie react away from him. She spread her red skirts and faced him politely, waiting for him to make her evening.

Lilla came in, turned her calculating, good-humoured eye from her sister to Jansen, smiled, and said: 'I'm going out a little. Oh, keep your hair on. I'll be back soon. My friend is taking me for a walk.'

The friend came in and took Lilla's arm, a large, handsome sunburned man who smiled with a good-time smile at Marie. She responded with such a passion of admiration in her eyes that Jansen understood at once what she did not see when she looked at himself. 'My, my,' said this young man with easy warmth to Marie. 'You're a fast learner, I can see that.'

'We'll be back,' said Lilla to Marie. 'Remember what I said.' Then, to Jansen, like a saleswoman: 'She's not bad. Anyhow she can't get herself into any trouble here at home.' The young man slipped his arm around her, and reached for a glass off the sideboard with his free hand. He poured brandy, humming with the radio: 'In a shady nook, by a babbling brook . . .' He threw back his head, poured the brandy down, smiled broadly at Jansen and Marie, winked and said: 'Be seeing you. Don't forget to wind up the clock and put the cat out.' Outside on the landing he and Lilla sang: 'Carry moonbeams *home* in a jar, be better *off* than you are . . .' They sang their way down to the street. A car door slammed, an engine roared. Marie darted to the window, and said bitterly: 'They've gone to the pictures.'

'I don't think so,' said Jansen. She came back, frowning, preoccupied with responsibility. 'Would you like another drink?' she asked, remembering what Lilla had told her. Jansen shook his head, and sat still for a moment, weighted with inertia. Then he said: 'Marie, I want you to listen to me.' She leaned forward dutifully, ready to listen. But this was not as she had gazed at the other man, the warm, generous, laughing, singing young man. Jansen found many words ready on his tongue, disliked them, and blurted: 'Marie, I wish you'd let me send you back home tonight.' Her face dulled. 'No, Marie, you really must listen.' She listened politely, from behind her dull resistance. He used words carefully, out of the delicacy of his compassion, and saw how they faded into meaninglessness in the space between him and Marie. Then he grew brutal and desperate, because he had to reach her. He said: 'This sort of life isn't as much fun as it looks'; and 'Thousands of girls all over the world choose the easy way because they're stupid, and afterwards they're sorry.' She dropped her lids, looked at her feet in her new high shoes, and shut herself off from him. He used the words whore and prostitute; but she had never heard them except as swearwords, and did not connect them with herself. She began repeating, over and over again: 'My sister's a typist; she's got a job in an office.'

He said angrily: 'Do you think she can afford to live like this on a typist's pay?'

'Her gentleman friend gives her things, he's generous, she told me so,' said Marie doubtfully.

'How old are you, Marie?'

'Eighteen,' she said, turning her broad freckled wrist, where Lilla's bracelet caught the light.

'When you're twenty-five you'll be out on the streets picking up any man you see, taking them to hotels . . .'

At the word 'hotel' her eyes widened; he remembered she had never been in a hotel; they were something lovely on the cinema screen.

'When you're thirty you'll be an old woman.'

'Lilla said she'd look after me. She promised me faithfully,' said Marie, in terror at his coldness. But what he was saying meant nothing to her, nothing at all. He saw that she probably did not know what the word prostitute meant; that the things Lilla had told her meant only lessons in how to enjoy the delights of this city.

He said: 'Do you know what I'm here for? Your sister expects you to take off your clothes and get into bed and . . .' He stopped. Her eyes were wide open, fastened on him, not in fear, but in the anxious preoccupation of a little girl who is worried she is not behaving properly. Her hands had moved to the buckle of her belt, and she was undoing it.

Jansen got up, and without speaking he gathered clothes that were obviously hers from off the furniture, from off the floor. He went into the bedroom and found a suitcase and put her things into it. 'I'm putting you on to the train tonight,' he said.

'My sister won't let you,' she cried out. 'She'll stop you.'

'Your sister's a bad girl,' said Jansen, and saw, to his surprise, that Marie's face showed fear at last. Those two words, 'bad girl' had more effect than all his urgent lecturing.

'You shouldn't say such things,' said Marie, beginning to cry. 'You shouldn't never say someone's a bad girl.' They were her mother's words, obviously, and had hit her hard, where she could be reached. She stood listless in the middle of the floor, weeping, making no resistance. He tucked her arm inside his, and led her downstairs. 'You'll marry a nice man soon, Marie,' he promised. 'You won't always have to live by the railway lines.'

'I don't never meet no men, except Dad,' she said, beginning to tug at his arm again.

He held her tight until they were in a taxi. There she sat crouched on the edge of the seat, watching the promised city sweep past. At the station, keeping a firm hold on her, he bought her a ticket and gave her five pounds, and put her into a compartment and said: 'I know you hate me. One day you'll know I'm right and you'll be glad.' She smiled weakly, and huddled herself into her seat, like a cold little animal, staring sadly out of the window.

He left her, running, to catch his own train which already stood waiting on the next platform.

As it drew out of the station he saw Marie waddling desperately on her tall heels along the platform, casting scared glances over her shoulder. Their eyes met; she gave him an apologetic smile, and ran on. With the pound notes clutched loosely in her hand she was struggling her way through the crowds back to the lights, the love, the joyous streets of the promised city.

PLANTS AND GIRLS

There was a boy who lived in a small house in a small town in the centre of Africa.

Until he was about twelve, this house had been the last in the street, so that he walked straight from the garden, across a railway line, and into the veld. He spent most of his time wandering by himself through the vleis and the kopjes. Then the town began to grow, so that in the space of a year a new suburb of smart little houses lay between him and the grass and trees. He watched this happening with a feeling of surprised anger. But he did not go through the raw new streets to the vlei where the river ran and the little animals moved. He was a lethargic boy, and it seemed to him as if some spell had been put on him, imprisoning him for ever in the town. Now he would walk through the new streets, looking down at the hard glittering tarmac, thinking of the living earth imprisoned beneath it. Where the veld trees had been allowed to stay, he stood gazing, thinking how they drew their strength through the layers of rubble and broken brick, direct from the breathing soil and from the invisibly running underground rivers. He would stand there, staring and it would seem to him that he could see those fresh, subtly-running streams of water moving this way and that beneath the tarmac, and he stretched out his fingers like roots towards the earth. People passing looked away uncomfortably. Children called out: 'Moony, moony, mooning again!' Particularly the children from the house opposite laughed and teased him. They were a large noisy family, solid in the healthy strength of their numbers. He could hardly distinguish one from another: he felt that the house opposite was filled like a box with plump, joyous, brown-eyed people whose noisy cheerful voices frightened him.

He was a lanky, thin-boned youth whose face was tall and unfinished-looking, and his eyes were enormous, blue, wide, staring, with the brilliance of distance in them.

His mother, when he returned to the house, would say tartly: 'Why don't you go over and play with the children?

Why don't you go into the bush like you used to? Why don't you ...'

He was devoted to his mother. He would say vaguely: 'Oh I don't know,' and kick stones about in the dust, staring away over the house at the sky, knowing that she was watching him through the window as she sewed, and that she was pleased to have him there, in spite of her tart complaining voice. Or he would go into the room where she sat sewing, and sit near her, in silence, for hours. If his father came into the room he began to fidget, and soon went away. His father spoke angrily about his laziness and his unnatural behaviour.

He made the mother fetch a doctor to examine the boy. It was from this time that Frederick took the words 'not normal' as his inheritance. He was not normal; well, he accepted it. They made a fact of something he had always known because of the way people looked at him and spoke to him. He was neither surprised nor dismayed at what he was. And when his mother wept over him, after the doctor left, he scarcely heard the noise of her tears: he smiled at her with the warm childish grin that no one else had ever seen, for he knew he could always depend on her.

His father's presence was a fact he accepted. On the surface they made an easy trio, like an ordinary family. At meals they talked like ordinary people. In the evenings his father sometimes read to him, for Frederick found it hard to read, although he was now half-way through his 'teens; but there were moments when the old man fell silent, staring in unconcealable revulsion at this son he had made; and Frederick would let his eyes slide uncomfortably away, but in the manner of a person who is embarrassed at someone else's shortcomings. His mother accepted him; he accepted himself; that was enough.

When his father died he was sorry, and cried with his fists in his eyes like a baby. At the graveside the neighbours looked at this great shambling child with his colourless locks of hair and the big red fists rubbing at his eyes, and felt relieved at the normal outburst of grief. But afterwards it was he and his mother alone in the small suburban house, and they never spoke of the dead father who had vanished entirely from their lives, leaving nothing behind him. She lived for him, waiting for his return from school, or from his rambles around the streets; and she never spoke of the fact that he was in a class with children five years his junior, that he was always alone at week-ends and holidays, never with other children.

He was a good son. He took her tea in the mornings at the time the sun rose; and watched her crinkled old face light up from the pillow as he set down the tray by her knees. But he did not stay with her then. He went out again quickly, shutting the door, his eyes turned from the soft, elderly white shoulders, which were not, for him, his mother. This is how he saw her: in her dumpy flowered apron, her brown sinewy arms setting food before him, her round spectacles shining, her warm face smiling. Yet he did not think of her as an old lady. Perhaps he did not see her at all. He would sometimes put out his great lank hand and stroke her apron. Once he went secretly into her bedroom and took her hairbrush off the dressing-table and brushed the apron which was lying on the bed; and he put the apron on, and laughed out loud at the sight of himself in the mirror.

Later, when he was seventeen, a very tall awkward youth with the strange-lit blue eyes, too old to be put to bed with a story after supper, he wandered about by himself through that area of ugly new houses that seemed to change under the soft brightness of the moon into a shadowy beauty. He walked for hours, or stood still gazing dimly about him at the deep starry sky, or at the soft shapes of trees. There was a big veld tree that stood a short way from their gate in a space between two street lamps, so that there was a well of shadow beneath it which attracted him very much. He stood beneath the tree, listening to the wind moving gently in the leaves, feeling it stir his hair like fingers. He would move slowly in to the tree until his long fingers met the rough bark, and he stroked the tree curiously, learning it, thinking: under this roughness and hardness moves the sap, like rivers under the earth. He came to spend his evenings there, instead of walking among the houses and looking in with puzzled unenvious eyes through the windows at the other kind of people. One evening an extra-ordinarily violent spasm shook him, so that he found himself locked about that harsh strong trunk, embracing it violently, his arms and thighs knotted about it, sobbing and muttering angry words. Afterwards he slowly went home, entering the small brightly-lit room shamedly; and his great blue eyes sought his mother's, and he was surprised that she did not say anything, but smiled at him as usual. Always there was this assurance from her; and as time went past, and each night he returned to the tree, caressing and stroking it, murmuring words of love, he would come home simply, smiling his wide childish smile, waiting for her to smile back, pleased with him.

But opposite was still that other house full of people; the children were growing up; and one evening when he was leaning against the tree in deep shadow, his arm loosely about it, as if around a tender friend, someone stopped outside the space of shadow and peered in saying: 'Why, Moony, what are you doing here by yourself?' It was one of the girls from that house, and when he did not reply she came towards him, finally putting out her hand to touch his arm. The touch struck cruelly through him and he moved away, and she said with a jolly laugh: 'What's the matter? I won't eat you.' She pulled him out into the yellowy light from the street lamp and examined him. She was a fattish, untidy, bright girl, one of the middle children, full of affection for everything in the world; and this odd silent youth standing there quite still between her hands affected her with amused astonishment, so that she said: 'Well, you are a funny boy, aren't you?' She did not know what to do with him, so at last she took him home over the street. He had never been inside her house before, and it was like a foreign country. There were so many people, so much noise and laughter and the wireless was shouting out words and music. He was silent and smiling in this world which had nothing to do with himself.

His passive smile piqued the girl, and later when he got up saying: 'My mother's waiting for me,' she replied, 'Well, at any rate you can take me to the pictures tomorrow.'

He had never taken a girl out; had never been to the pictures save with his parents, as a child is taken; and he smiled as at a ridiculous idea. But next evening she came and made him go with her.

'What's the matter, Moony?' she asked, taking his arm. 'Don't you like me? Why don't you take girls out? Why do you always stay around your mother? You aren't a baby any longer.'

These words he listened to smiling; they did not make him angry; because she could not understand that they had nothing to do with him.

He sat in the cinema beside the girl and waited for it to

be over. He would not have been in the least surprised if the building and the screen and the girl had vanished, leaving him lying under a tree with not a house in sight, nothing but the veld, the long grasses, the trees, the birds and the little animals. Afterwards they walked home, and he listened to her chattering scolding voice without replying. He did not mind being with her; but he forgot her as soon as she had gone in at her gate; and wandered back across the street to his own gate, and looked at the tree standing in its gulf of shadow with the moonlight on its branches, and took two steps towards it and stopped again; and finally turned with a bolting movement, as if in fear, and shambled quickly in to his mother. She glanced up at him with a tight suspicious face, and he knew she was angry, though she did not speak. Soon he went to bed, unable to bear this unspoken anger. He slept badly and dreamed of the tree. And next night he went to it as soon as it was dark, and stood holding the heavy dark trunk in his arms.

The girl from opposite was persistent. Soon he knew, because of the opposition of his mother, that he had a girl, as ordinary young men have girls.

Why did she want him? Perhaps it was just curiosity. She had been brought up in all that noise and warm quarrelling and laughter, and so Frederick, who neither wanted her nor did not want her, attracted her. She scolded him and pleaded with him: Don't you love me? Don't you want to marry me?

At this he gave her his rambling confused grin. The word marriage made him want to laugh. It was ridiculous. But to her there was nothing ridiculous in it. In her home, marriages took place between boys and girls, and there were always festivals and love-making and new babies.

Now he would take her in his arms beside the tree outside the gate, embracing her as he had embraced the tree, forgetting her entirely, murmuring strangely over her head among the shadows. She hated it and she loved it; for her, it was like being hypnotized. She scolded him, stayed away, returned; and yet he would not say he would marry her.

This went on for some time; though for Frederick it was not a question of time. He did not mind having her in his arms under the tree, but he could not marry her. He was driven, night after night, to the silent love-making, with the branches of the tree between him and the moon, and afterwards he went straight to his room, so as not to face his mother.

Then she got ill. Instead of going with the girl at night, he stayed at home, taking his mother drinks, silently sitting beside her, putting wet handkerchiefs on her forehead. In the mornings the girl looked at him over the hedge and said: 'Baby! Baby!'

'But my mother's sick,' he said, finding these words with difficulty from the dullness of his mind. At this she only laughed. Finally she left him. It was like a tight string snapping from him, so that he reeled back into his own house with his mother. He watched the girl going in and out of her house with her sisters, her brothers, her friends, her young men; at nights he watched her dancing on the veranda to the gramophone. But she never looked back at him. His mother was still an invalid and kept to her chair, and he understood she was now getting old, but it did not come into his head that she might die. He looked after her. Before going off to the office at the railways, where he arranged luggage under the supervision of another clerk, he would lift his mother from her bed, turn away from her while she painfully dressed herself, support her into a chair by the window, fetch her food, and leave her for the day. At night he returned directly to her from work, and sat beside her until it was time to sleep. Sometimes, when the desire for the shadowy street outside became too strong, he would go out for a little time and stand beside his tree. He listened to the wind moving in the branches and he thought: It's an old tree, it's too old. If a leaf fell in the darkness he thought: The leaves are falling, it's dying, it's too old to live.

When his mother at last died, he could not understand that she was dead. He stood at her graveside in the efficient cared-for cemetery of this new town, with its antiseptic look because of the neatness of the rows of graves and the fresh clean sunlight, and gazed down at the oblong hole in the red earth, where the spades had smoothed the steep sides into shares of glistening hardness, and saw the precisely-fitting black box at the bottom of the hole, and lifted his head to stare painfully at the neighbours, among whom was the girl from opposite, although he did not see her.

He went home to the empty house that was full of his mother. He left everything as it was. He did not expand his life to fill the space she had used. He was still a child in the house, while her chair stood empty, and her bed had pillows stacked on it, and her clothes hanging over the foot.

There was very little money. His affairs were managed by a man at the bank in whose custody he had been left, and he was told how much he could spend. That margin was like a safety-line around his life; and he liked taking his small notebook where he wrote down every penny he spent at each month's-end to the man at the bank.

He lived on, knowing that his mother was dead, but only because people had said she was. After a time he was driven by his pain down to the cemetery. The grave was a mound of red earth. The flowers of the funeral had died long ago. There was a small headstone of granite. A bougainvillaea creeper had been planted on the grave, which spread its glossy green branches over the stone, in layers of dark shining green and clusters of bleeding purple flowers. The first time he visited the cemetery he stood staring for a long time. Later he would sit by the headstone, fingering the leaves of the plant. Slowly he came to understand that his mother lay underneath where he sat. He saw her folded in the earth, her rough brown forearms crossed comfortably on her breast, her flowered apron pulled down to her fat knees, her spectacles glinting, her wrinkled old face closed in sleep. And he fingered the smooth hard leaves, noting the tiny working veins, thinking: They feed on her. The thought filled him with panic and drove him from the grave. Yet he returned again and again, to sit under the pressure of the heavy yellow sunlight, on the rough warm stone, looking at the red and purple flowers, feeling the leaves between his fingers.

One day, at the grave, he broke off a branch of the bougainvillaea plant and returned with it to the house, where he set it in a vase by his bed. He sat beside it, touching and smoothing the leaves. Slowly the branch lost its colour and the clusters of flowers grew limp. A spray of stiff dead pale leaves stood up out of the vase, and his eyes rested on it, brilliant, vague, spectral, while his face contracted with pain and with wonder.

During the long solitary evenings he began again to stand at his gate, under the stars, looking about him in the darkness. The big tree had been cut down; all the wild trees in that street were gone, because of the danger from the strong old roots to the bricks of the foundations of the houses. The authorities had planted new saplings, domestic and educated trees like bauhinea and jacaranda. Immediately outside his gate, where the old tree had been, was one of these saplings. It grew quickly; one season it was a tiny plant in a little leaning shed of grass; the next it was as high as his head. There was an evening that he went to it, leaning his forehead against it, not thinking, his hands sliding gently and unsurely up and down the long slim trunk. This taut supple thing was nothing he had known; it was strange to him; it was too slight and weak and there was no shadow around it. And yet he stood there night after night, unconscious of the windows about him where people might be looking out, unconscious of passers-by, feeling and fumbling at the tree, letting his eyes stray past to the sky, or to the lines of bushy little saplings along the road, or to the dusty crowding hedges.

One evening he heard a bright scornful voice say: 'What do you think you're doing?' and he knew it was the girl from opposite. But the girl from opposite had married long ago, and was now an untidy handsome matron with children of her own; she had left him so far behind that she could now nod at him with careless kindness, as if to say: 'Well, well, so you're still there, are you?'

He peered and gawked at this girl in his intense ugly way that was yet attractive because of his enormous lit eyes. Then, for him, the young and vigorous creature who was staring at him with such painful curiosity became the girl from opposite. She was in fact the other girl's sister, perhaps ten years her junior. She was the youngest of that large pulsing family, who were all married and gone, and she was the only one who had known loneliness. When people said with the troubled callousness, the necessary callousness which protects society against its rotten wood: 'He's never been the same since the death of his mother, he's quite crazy now,' she felt, not merely an embarrassed and fundamentally indifferent pity, but a sudden throb of sympathy. She had been watching Frederick for a long time. She was ready to defend him against people who said, troubled by this attraction of the sick for the healthy: 'For God's sake what do you see in him, can't you do better than that?'

As before, he did as she wanted. He would accompany her to the pictures. He would come out of his house at her call. He went walking with her through the dark streets at night. And before parting from her he took her into his arms against the sapling that swayed and slipped under their weight, and kissed her with a cold persistence that filled her with horror and with desire, so that she ran away from him sobbing, saying she would never see him again, and returned inevitably the next evening. She never entered his house; she was afraid of the invisibly present old woman. He seemed not to mind what she did. She was driven wild because she knew that if she did not seek him out, the knowledge of loss would never enter him; he would merely return to the lithe young tree, mumbling fierce thick reproachful words to it in the darkness.

As he grew to understand that she would always return no matter how she strove and protested, he would fold her against him, not hearing her cries, and as she grew still with chilled fear, she would hear through the darkness a dark sibilant whispering: 'Your hair, your hair, your teeth, your bones.' His fingers pressed and probed into her flesh. 'Here is the bone, under is nothing only bone,' and the long urgent fingers fought to defeat the soft envelope of flesh, fought to make it disappear, so that he could grasp the bones of her arms, the joint of her shoulder; and when he had pressed and probed and always found the flesh elastic against his hands, pain flooded along her as the teeth closed in on her neck, or while his fist suddenly drove inwards, under her ribs, as if the tension of flesh were not there. In the morning she would be bruised. She avoided the eyes of her family and covered up the bruises. She was learning, through this black and savage initiation, a curious strength. She could feel the bones standing erect through her body, a branching undefeatable tree of strength; and when the hands closed in on her, stopping the blood, half-choking her, the stubborn half-conscious thought remained: You can't do it; you can't do it, I'm too strong.

Because of the way people looked in at them, through the darkness, as they leaned and struggled against the tree, she made him go inside the hedge of the small neglected garden, and there they lay together on the lawn, for hour after hour, with the cold high moon standing over them, sucking the warmth from their flesh, so they embraced in a cold lethal ecstasy of pain, knowing only the cold greenish light, feeling the bones of their bodies cleave and knock together while he grasped her so close that she could scarcely draw each breath.

One night she fainted, and she came to herself to find him still clasping her, in a cold strong clasp, his teeth bared against her throat, so that a suffocating black pressure came over her brain in wave after wave, and she fought against him, making him tighten his grip and press her into the soil, and she felt the rough grasses driving up into her flesh.

A flame of self-preservation burnt up into her brain, and she fought until he came to himself and his grip loosened. She said: 'I won't. I won't let you. I won't come back again.' He lay still, breathing like a deep sleeper. She did not know if he had heard her. She repeated hurriedly, already uncertain, 'I won't let you.' He got up and staggered away from her, and she was afraid because of the destructive light in the great eyes that glinted at her in the moonlight.

She ran away and locked herself in her bedroom. For several days she did not return. She watched him from her window as he strode huntedly up and down the street, lurking around the young tree, sometimes shaking it so that the leaves came spinning down around him. She knew she must return, and one evening she drifted across the street, and came on him standing under the lithe young tree that held its fine glinting leaves like a spray of tinted water upwards in the moonlight over the fine slender trunk.

This time he reached out and grasped her, and carried her inside to the lawn. She murmured helplessly, in a dim panic, 'You mustn't, I won't.'

She saw the hazy brilliant stars surge up behind his black head, saw the greenish moonlight pour down the thin hollows of his cheeks, saw the great crazy eyes immediately above hers. The cages of their ribs ground together, and she heard: 'Your hair, dead hair, bones, bones, bones.'

The bared desperate teeth came down on her throat, and she arched back as the stars swam and went out.

When people glanced over the hedge in the strong early sunlight of next morning they saw him half-lying over the girl, whose body was marked by blood and by soil and he was murmuring: 'Your hair, your leaves, your branches, your rivers.'

FLIGHT

Above the old man's head was the dovecote, a tall wire-netted shelf on stilts, full of strutting, preening birds. The sunlight broke on their grey breasts into small rainbows. His ears were lulled by their crooning, his hands stretched up towards his favourite, a homing pigeon, a young plump-bodied bird which stood still when it saw him and cocked a shrewd bright eye.

'Pretty, pretty, pretty,' he said, as he grasped the bird and drew it down, feeling the cold coral claws tighten around his finger. Content, he rested the bird lightly on his chest, and leaned against a tree, gazing out beyond the dovecote into the landscape of a late afternoon. In folds and hollows of sunlight and shade, the dark red soil, which was broken into great dusty clods, stretched wide to a tall horizon. Trees marked the course of the valley; a stream of rich green grass the road.

His eyes travelled homewards along this road until he saw his grand-daughter swinging on the gate underneath a frangipani tree. Her hair fell down her back in a wave of sunlight, and her long bare legs repeated the angles of the frangipani stems, bare, shining-brown stems among patterns of pale blossoms.

She was gazing past the pink flowers, past the railway cottage where they lived, along the road to the village.

His mood shifted. He deliberately held out his wrist for the bird to take flight, and caught it again at the moment it spread its wings. He felt the plump shape strive and strain under his fingers; and, in a sudden access of troubled spite, shut the bird into a small box and fastened the bolt. 'Now you stay there,' he muttered; and turned his back on the shelf of birds. He moved warily along the hedge, stalking his grand-daughter, who was now looped over the gate, her head loose on her arms, singing. The light happy sound mingled with the crooning of the birds, and his anger mounted.

'Hey!' he shouted; saw her jump, look back, and abandon the gate. Her eyes veiled themselves, and she said in a pert neutral voice: 'Hullo, Grandad.' Politely she moved towards him, after a lingering backward glance at the road.

'Waiting for Steven, hey?' he said, his fingers curling like claws into his palm.

'Any objection?' she asked lightly, refusing to look at him.

He confronted her, his eyes narrowed, shoulders hunched, tight in a hard knot of pain which included the preening birds, the sunlight, the flowers. He said: 'Think you're old enough to go courting, hey?'

The girl tossed her head at the old-fashioned phrase and sulked, 'Oh, Grandad!'

'Think you want to leave home, hey? Think you can go running around the fields at night?'

Her smile made him see her, as he had every evening of this warm end-of-summer month, swinging hand in hand along the road to the village with that red-handed, red-throated, violent-bodied youth, the son of the postmaster. Misery went to his head and he shouted angrily: 'I'll tell your mother!'

'Tell away!' she said, laughing, and went back to the gate.

He heard her singing, for him to hear:

'I've got you under my skin,
I've got you deep in the heart of ...'

'Rubbish,' he shouted. 'Rubbish. Impudent little bit of rubbish!'

Growling under his breath he turned towards the dovecote, which was his refuge from the house he shared with his daughter and her husband and their children. But now the house would be empty. Gone all the young girls with their laughter and their squabbling and their teasing. He would be left, uncherished and alone, with that square-fronted, calmeyed woman, his daughter.

He stooped, muttering, before the dovecote, resenting the absorbed cooing birds.

From the gate the girl shouted: 'Go and tell! Go on, what are you waiting for?'

Obstinately he made his way to the house, with quick, pathetic persistent glances of appeal back at her. But she never looked around. Her defiant but anxious young body stung him into love and repentance. He stopped. 'But I never meant ...' he muttered, waiting for her to turn and run to him. 'I didn't mean ...'

She did not turn. She had forgotten him. Along the road

came the young man Steven, with something in his hand. A present for her? The old man stiffened as he watched the gate swing back, and the couple embrace. In the brittle shadows of the frangipani tree his grand-daughter, his darling, lay in the arms of the postmaster's son, and her hair flowed back over his shoulder.

'I see you!' shouted the old man spitefully. They did not move. He stumped into the little whitewashed house, hearing the wooden veranda creak angrily under his feet. His daughter was sewing in the front room, threading a needle held to the light.

He stopped again, looking back into the garden. The couple were now sauntering among the bushes, laughing. As he watched he saw the girl escape from the youth with a sudden mischievous movement, and run off through the flowers with him in pursuit. He heard shouts, laughter, a scream, silence.

'But it's not like that at all,' he muttered miserably. 'It's not like that. Why can't you see? Running and giggling, and kissing and kissing. You'll come to something quite different.'

He looked at his daughter with sardonic hatred, hating himself. They were caught and finished, both of them, but the girl was still running free.

'Can't you *see*?' he demanded of his invisible grand-daughter, who was at that moment lying in the thick green grass with the postmaster's son.

His daughter looked at him and her eyebrows went up in tired forbearance.

'Put your birds to bed?' she asked, humouring him.

'Lucy,' he said urgently. 'Lucy ...'

'Well, what is it now?'

'She's in the garden with Steven.'

'Now you just sit down and have your tea.'

He stumped his feet alternatively, thump, thump, on the hollow wooden floor and shouted: 'She'll marry him. I'm telling you, she'll be marrying him next!'

His daughter rose swiftly, brought him a cup, set him a plate.

'I don't want any tea. I don't want it, I tell you.'

'Now, now,' she crooned. 'What's wrong with it? Why not?'

'She's eighteen. Eighteen!'

'I was married at seventeen and I never regretted it.'

'Liar,' he said. 'Liar. Then you should regret it. Why do you make your girls marry? It's you who do it. What do you do it for? Why?'

'The other three have done fine. They've three fine husbands. Why not Alice?'

'She's the last,' he mourned. 'Can't we keep her a bit longer?'

'Come, now, dad. She'll be down the road, that's all. She'll be here every day to see you.'

'But it's not the same.' He thought of the other three girls, transformed inside a few months from charming petulant spoiled children into serious young matrons.

'You never did like it when we married,' she said. 'Why not? Every time, it's the same. When I got married you made me feel like it was something wrong. And my girls the same. You get them all crying and miserable the way you go on. Leave Alice alone. She's happy.' She sighed, letting her eyes linger on the sunlit garden. 'She'll marry next month. There's no reason to wait.'

'You've said they can marry?' he said incredulously.

'Yes, dad, why not?' she said coldly, and took up her sewing.

His eyes stung, and he went out on to the veranda. Wet spread down over his chin and he took out a handkerchief and mopped his whole face. The garden was empty.

From around the corner came the young couple; but their faces were no longer set against him. On the wrist of the postmaster's son balanced a young pigeon, the light gleaming on its breast.

'For me?' said the old man, letting the drops shake off his chin. 'For me?'

'Do you like it?' The girl grabbed his hand and swung on it. 'It's for you, Grandad. Steven brought it for you.' They hung about him, affectionate, concerned, trying to charm away his wet eyes and his misery. They took his arms and directed him to the shelf of birds, one on each side, enclosing him, petting him, saying wordlessly that nothing would be changed, nothing could change, and that they would be with him always. The bird was proof of it, they said, from their lying happy eyes, as they thrust it on him. 'There, Grandad, it's yours. It's for you.'

They watched him as he held it on his wrist, stroking its soft, sun-warmed back, watching the wings lift and balance.

'You must shut it up for a bit,' said the girl intimately. 'Until it knows this is its home.'

'Teach your grandmother to suck eggs,' growled the old man.

Released by his half-deliberate anger, they fell back, laughing at him. 'We're glad you like it.' They moved off, now serious and full of purpose, to the gate, where they hung, backs to him, talking quietly. More than anything could, their grown-up seriousness shut him out, making him alone; also, it quietened him, took the sting out of their tumbling like puppies on the grass. They had forgotten him again. Well, so they should, the old man reassured himself, feeling his throat clotted with tears, his lips trembling. He held the new bird to his face, for the caress of its silken feathers. Then he shut it in a box and took out his favourite.

'*Now* you can go,' he said aloud. He held it poised, ready for flight, while he looked down the garden towards the boy and the girl. Then, clenched in the pain of loss, he lifted the bird on his wrist, and watched it soar. A whirr and a spatter of wings, and a cloud of birds rose into the evening from the dovecote.

At the gate Alice and Steven forgot their talk and watched the birds.

On the veranda, that woman, his daughter, stood gazing, her eyes shaded with a hand that still held her sewing.

It seemed to the old man that the whole afternoon had stilled to watch his gesture of self-command, that even the leaves of the trees had stopped shaking.

Dry-eyed and calm, he let his hands fall to his sides and stood erect, staring up into the sky.

The cloud of shining silver birds flew up and up, with a shrill cleaving of wings, over the dark ploughed land and the darker belts of trees and the bright folds of grass, until they floated high in the sunlight, like a cloud of motes of dust.

They wheeled in a wide circle, tilting their wings so there was flash after flash of light, and one after another they dropped from the sunshine of the upper sky to shadow, one after another, returning to the shadowed earth over trees and grass and field, returning to the valley and the shelter of night.

The garden was all a fluster and a flurry of returning birds. Then silence, and the sky was empty.

The old man turned, slowly, taking his time; he lifted his eyes to smile proudly down the garden at his grand-daughter. She was staring at him. She did not smile. She was wide-eyed, and pale in the cold shadow, and he saw the tears run shivering off her face.

THE SUN BETWEEN THEIR FEET

The road from the back of the station went to the Roman Catholic Mission, which was a dead-end, being in the middle of a Native Reserve. It was a poor mission, with only one lorry, so the road was always deserted, a track of sand between long or short grasses. The station itself was busy with trains and people, and the good country in front was settled thick with white farmers, but all the country behind the station was unused because it was granite boulders, outcrops, and sand. The scrub cattle from the Reserve strayed there. There were no human beings. From the track it seemed the hills of boulders were so steep and laced with vines and weed there would be no place to go between them. But you could force your way in, and there it became clear that in the past people had made use of this wilderness. For one thing there were the remains of earth and rock defences built by the Mashona against the Matabele when they came raiding after cattle and women before Rhodes put an end to all that.* For another, the under-surfaces of the great boulders were covered with Bushmen paintings. After a hundred yards or so of clambering and squeezing there came a flattish sandy stretch before the boulders erupted again. In this space, at the time of the raiding, the women and the cattle would have been kept while the men held the surrounding defences. From this space, at the time of the Bushmen, small hunting-men took coloured clays, and earths, and plant juices for their pictures.

It had rained last night and the low grass was still wet around my ankles and the early sun had not dried the sand. There was a sharp upjut of rock in the middle of the space. The rock was damp, and I could feel the wet heat being dragged up past my bare legs.

Sitting low here, the encircling piles of boulders seemed like mountains, heightening the sky on tall horizons. The rocks were dark grey, but stained with lichens. The trees between

* Since writing this I have understood that this version of history is not necessarily the true one. Some Mashona authorities dispute it.

the boulders were meagre, and several were lightning-struck, no more than black skeletons. This was hungry country, growing sand and thin grass and rocks and heat. The sun came down hard between heat-conserving rocks. After an hour of sun the sand between the grasses showed a clean, dry glistening surface, and a dark wet underneath.

The Reserve cattle must have moved here since the rains last night, for there were a score of fresh cow pats laid on the grass. Big blue flies swore and tumbled over them, breaking the crust the sun had baked. The air was heavy and sweet. The buzzing of the flies, the tiny sucking sound of the heat, the cooing of the pigeons, made a morning silence.

Hot, and silent; and save for the flies, no movement anywhere, for what winds there were blew outside this sheltered space.

But soon there was new movement. Where the flies had broken the crust of the nearest dung-clot, two beetles were at work. They were small, dusty, black, round-bodied beetles. One had set his back legs over a bit of dung and was heaving and levering at it. The other, with a fast rolling movement, the same that a hen makes settling roused feathers over eggs, was using his body to form the ball even before it was heaved clear of the main lump of matter. As soon as the piece was freed, both beetles assaulted it with legs and bodies, modelling fast, frantic with creation, seizing it between their back legs, spinning it, rolling it under them, both tugging and pushing it through the thick encumbering grass stems that rose over them like forest trees until at last the ball rolled away from them into a plain, or glade, or inch-wide space of sand. The two beetles scuttled about among the stems, looking for their property. They were on the point of starting again on the mother-pile of muck, when one of them saw the ball lying free in the open, and both ran after it.

All over the grassy space around the cow pats, dung-beetles were at work, the blowflies hustled and buzzed, and by night all the new cow-stomach-worked grass would be lifted away, rolled away, to feed flies, beetles and new earth. That is, unless it rained hard again, when everything would be scattered by rods of rain.

But there was no sign of rain yet. The sky was the clear slow blue of African mornings after night-storms. My two beetles had the sky on their side. They had all day.

The book says that dung-beetles form a ball of dung, lay their eggs in it, search for a gentle slope, roll the ball up it, and then allow it to roll down again so that in the process of rolling 'the pellet becomes compacted'.

Why must the pellet be compacted? Presumably so that the blows of sun and rain do not beat it to fragments. Why this complicated business of rolling up and rolling down?

Well, it is not for us to criticize the processes of nature; so I sat on top of the jutting rock, and watched the beetles rolling the ball towards it. In a few minutes of work they had reached it, and had hurled themselves and the dung-ball at its foot. Their momentum took them a few inches up the slope, then they slipped, and ball and beetles rolled back to the flat again.

I got down off the rock, and sat in the grass behind them to view the ascent through their eyes.

The rock was about four feet long and three feet high. It was a jutting slab of granite, wooded and lichened, its edges blunted by rain and by wind. The beetles, hugging their ball between legs and bellies, looked up to a savage mountain, whose first slopes were an easy foot-assisting invitation. They rolled their ball, which was now crusted with dirt, to a small ridge under the foothills, and began, this time with slow care, to hitch it up from ridge to ridge, from one crust of lichen to the next. One beetle above, one below, they cherished their ball upwards. Soon they met the obstruction that had defeated them before: a sudden upswelling in the mountain wall. This time, one remained below the ball, holding its weight on its back legs, while the other scouted off sideways to find an easier path. It returned, gripped the ball with its legs, and the two beetles resumed their difficult, sideways scrambling progress, up around the swell in the rock into a small valley which led, or so it seemed, into the second great stage of the ascent. But this valley was a snare, for there was a crevasse across it. The mountain was riven. Heat and cold had split it to its base, and the narrow crack sloped down to a mountain lake full of warm fresh water over a bed of wind-gathered leaves and grass. The dung-ball slipped over the edge of the crevasse into the gulf, and rolled gently into the lake where it was supported at its edge by a small fringe of lichen. The beetles flung themselves after it. One straddling desperate legs from a raft of reed to the shore, held the ball from plunging into the depths of the lake. The other, gripping fast with its front legs to a thick bed of weed on shore, grappled the ball with its back legs, and together they heaved and shoved that precious dung out of the water and back into the ravine. But now the mountain walls rose high on either side, and the ball lay between them. The beetles remained still a moment. The dirt had been washed from the dung, and it was smooth and slippery.

They consulted. Again one remained on guard while the other scouted, returning to report that if they rolled the ball clear along the bottom of the ravine, this would in due course narrow, and they could, by use of legs and shoulders and backs, lift the ball up the crack to a new height on the mountain and, by crossing another dangerous shoulder, attain a gentle weed-roughed slope that led to the summit. This they tried. But on the dangerous shoulder there was a disaster. The lake-slippery ball left their grasp and plunged down the mountain-side to the ground, to the point they had started from half an hour before. The two beetles flung themselves after it, and again they began their slow difficult climb. Again their dung-ball fell into the crevasse, rolled down into the lake, and again they rescued it, at the cost of infinite resource and patience, again they pushed and pulled it up the ravine, again they manoeuvred it up the crack, again they tried to roll it around the mountain's sharp shoulder, and again it fell back to the foot of the mountain, and they plunged after it.

'The dung-beetle, *Scarabaeus* or *Aleuchus sacer*, lays its eggs in a ball of dung, then chooses a gentle slope, and compacts the pellet by pushing it uphill backwards with its hind legs and allowing it to roll down, eventually reaching its place of deposit.'

I continued to sit in the low, hot grass, feeling the sun first on my back, then hard down on my shoulders, and then direct from above on my head. The air was dry now, all the moisture from the night had gone up into the air. Clouds were packing the lower skies. Even the small pool in the rock was evaporating. Above it the air quivered with steam. When, for the third time, the beetles lost their ball in the mountain lake, it was no lake, but a spongy marsh, and getting it out involved no danger or difficulty. Now the ball was sticky, had lost its shape, and was crusted with bits of leaf and grass.

At the fourth attempt, when the ball rolled down to the starting point and the beetles bundled after it, it was past midday, my head ached with heat, and I took a large leaf, slipped it under the ball of dung and the beetles, and lifted this unit away to one side, away from the impossible and destructive mountain.

But when I slid the leaf from under them, they rested a moment in the new patch of territory, scouted this way and that among the grass-stems, found their position, and at once rolled their ball back to the foot of the mountain where they prepared another ascent.

Meanwhile, the cow pats on the grass had been dismantled by flies and other dung-beetles. Nothing remained but small grassy fragments, or dusty brown stains on the lifting stems. The buzzing of the flies was silenced. The pigeons were stilled by the heat. Far away thunder rolled, and sometimes there was the shriek of a train at the station or the puffing and clanging of shunting engines.

The beetles again got the ball up into the ravine, and this time it rolled down, not into a marsh, but into a damp bed of leaves. There they rested awhile in a steam of heat.

Sacred beetles, these, the sacred beetles of the Egyptians, holding the symbol of the sun between their busy stupid feet. Busy, silly beetles, mothering their ball of dung again and again up a mountain when a few minutes' march to one side would take them clear of it.

Again I lifted them, dung and beetles, away from the precipice, to a clear place where they had the choice of a dozen suitable gentle slopes, but they rolled their ball patiently back to the mountain's foot.

'The slope is chosen,' says the book, 'by a beautiful instinct, so that the ball of dung comes to rest in a spot suitable for the hatching of the new generation of sacred insect.'

The sun had now rolled past midday position and was shining on to my face. Sweat scattered off me. The air snapped with heat. The sky where the sun would go down was banked high with darkening cloud. Those beetles would have to hurry not to get drowned.

They continued to roll the dung up the mountain, rescue it from the dried bed of the mountain lake, and force it up to the exposed dry shoulder. It rolled down and they plunged after it. Again and again and again, while the ball became a ragged drying structure of fragmented grass clotted with dung. The afternoon passed. The sun was low in my eyes. I could hardly see the beetles or the dung because of the glare from a black pack of clouds which were red-rimmed from the lowering sun behind. The red streaming rays came down and the black beetles and their dung-ball on the mountain-side seemed dissolved in sizzling light.

It was raining away on the far hills. The drumming of the rain and the drumming of the thunder came closer. I could see the skirmishing side-lances of an army of rain pass half a mile away beyond the rocks. A few great shining drops fell here, and hissed on burning sand and on the burning mountain-side. The beetles laboured on.

The sun dropped behind the piled boulders and now this glade rested in a cool, spent light, the black trees and black boulders standing around it, waiting for the rain and for the night. The beetles were again on the mountain. They had the ball tight between their legs, they clung on to the lichens, they clung on to rock-wall and their treasure with the desperation of stupidity.

Now the hard red glare was gone it was possible to see them clearly. It was difficult to imagine the perfect shining globe the ball had been – it was now nothing more than a bit of refuse. There was a clang of thunder. The grasses hissed and swung as a bolt of wind came fast from the sky. The wind hit the ball of dung, it fell apart into a small puff of dusty grass, and the beetles ran scurrying over the surface of the rock looking for it.

Now the rain came marching towards us, it reached the boulders in a grey envelopment of wet. The big shining drops, outrunners of the rain-army, reached the beetles' mountain and one, two! the drops hit the beetles smack, and they fell off the rock into the already seething wet grasses at its foot.

I ran out of the glade with the rain sniping at my heels and my shoulders, thinking of the beetles lying under the precipice up which, tomorrow, after the rain had stopped, and the cattle had come grazing, and the sun had come out, they would again labour and heave a fresh ball of dung.

THE STORY OF TWO DOGS

Getting a new dog turned out to be more difficult than we thought, and for reasons rooted deep in the nature of our family. For what, on the face of it, could have been easier to find a puppy once it had been decided: 'Jock needs a companion, otherwise he'll spend his time with those dirty kaffir dogs in the compound'? All the farms in the district had dogs who bred puppies of the most desirable sort. All the farm compounds owned miserable beasts kept hungry so that they would be good hunters for their meat-starved masters; though often enough puppies born to the cage-ribbed bitches from this world of mud huts were reared in white houses and turned out well. Jacob, our builder, heard we wanted another dog, and came up with a lively puppy on the end of a bit of rope. But we tactfully refused. The thin flea-bitten little object was not good enough for Jock, my mother said; though we children were only too ready to take it in.

Jock was a mongrel himself, a mixture of Alsatian, Rhodesian Ridgeback, and some other breed – terrier? – that gave him ears too cocky and small above a long melancholy face. In short, he was nothing to boast of, outwardly: his qualities were all intrinsic or bestowed on him by my mother who had given this animal her heart when my brother went off to boarding-school.

In theory Jock was my brother's dog. Yet why give a dog to a boy at that moment when he departs for school and will be away from home two-thirds of the year? In fact my brother's dog was his substitute; and my poor mother, whose children were always away being educated, because we were farmers, and farmers' children had no choice but to go to the cities for their schooling – my poor mother caressed Jock's too-small intelligent ears and crooned: 'There, Jock! There, old boy! There, good dog, yes, you're a *good* dog, Jock, you're such a *good* dog ...' While my father said, uncomfortably: 'For goodness' sake, old girl, you'll ruin him, that isn't a house-pet, he's not a lap-dog, he's a farm dog.' To which my mother said nothing, but her face put on a most familiar

look of misunderstood suffering, and she bent it down close so
that the flickering red tongue just touched her cheek, and she
sang to him: 'Poor old Jock then, yes, you're a poor old dog,
you're not a rough farm dog, you're a good dog, and you're
not strong, no, you're delicate.'

At this last word my brother protested; my father protested; and so did I. All of us, in our different ways, had refused
to be 'delicate'; had escaped from being 'delicate' and we
wished to rescue a perfectly strong and healthy young dog
from being forced into invalidism, as we all, at different times,
had been. Also, of course, we all (and we knew it and felt
guilty about it) were secretly pleased that Jock was now absorb-
ing the force of my mother's pathetic need for something
'delicate' to nurse and protect.

Yet there was something in the whole business that was a
reproach to us. When my mother bent her sad face over the
animal, stroking him with her beautiful white hands on which
the rings had grown too large, and said: 'There, good dog,
yes Jock, you're such a gentleman—' well, there was something
in all this that made us, my father, my brother and myself,
need to explode with fury, or to take Jock away and make
him run over the farm like the tough young brute he was, or
to go away ourselves for ever so that we didn't have to hear
the awful yearning intensity in her voice. Because it was
entirely our fault that note was in her voice at all; if we had
allowed ourselves to be delicate, and good, or even gentlemen
and ladies, there would have been no need for Jock to sit between my mother's knees, his loyal noble head on her lap,
while she caressed and yearned and suffered.

It was my father who decided there must be another dog,
and for the expressed reason that otherwise Jock would be
turned into a 'sissy'. (At this word, reminder of a hundred
earlier battles, my brother flushed, looked sulky, and went
right out of the room.) My mother would not hear of another
dog until Jock started sneaking off to the farm compound to
play with the kaffir dogs. 'Oh you bad dog, Jock,' she said
sorrowfully, 'playing with those nasty dirty dogs, how could
you, Jock!' And he would playfully, but in an agony of remorse,
snap and lick at her face, while she bent the whole force
of her inevitably betrayed self over him, crooning: 'How
could you, oh how could you, Jock?'

So there must be a new puppy. And since Jock was (at

heart, despite his temporary lapse) noble and generous and above all well bred, his companion must also possess these qualities. And which dog, where in the world, could possibly be good enough? My mother turned down a dozen puppies; but Jock was still going off to the compound, slinking back to gaze soulfully into her eyes. This new puppy was to be my dog. I decided this: if my brother owned a dog, then it was only fair that I should. But my lack of force in claiming this puppy was because I was in the grip of abstract justice only. The fact was I didn't want a good, noble and well-bred dog. I didn't know what I did want, but the idea of such a dog bored me. So I was content to let my mother turn down puppies, provided she kept her terrible maternal energy on Jock, and away from me.

Then the family went off for one of our long visits in another part of the country, driving from farm to farm to stop a night, or a day, or for a meal with friends. To the last place we were invited for the week-end. A distant cousin of my father, 'A Norfolk man' (my father was from Essex), had married a woman who had nursed in the war (First World War) with my mother. They now lived in a small brick and iron house surrounded by granite kopjes that erupted everywhere from thick bush. They were as isolated as any people I've known, eighty miles from the nearest railway station. As my father said, they were 'not suited', for they quarrelled or sent each other to Coventry all the week-end. However, it was not until much later that I thought about the pathos of these two people, living alone on a minute pension in the middle of the bush, and 'not suited'; for that week-end I was in love.

It was night when we arrived, about eight in the evening, an almost full moon floated heavy and yellow above a stark granite-bouldered kopje. The bush around was black and low and silent, except that the crickets made a small incessant din. The car drew up outside a brick box-like structure whose iron roof glinted off moonlight. As the engine stopped, the sound of crickets swelled up, the moonlight's cold came in for a breath of fragrance to our faces, and there was the sound of a mad wild yapping. Behold, around the corner of the house came a small black wriggling object that hurled itself towards the car, changed course almost on touching it, and hurtled off again, yapping in a high delirious yammering which while it faded behind the house, continued faintly, our ears, or at least mine, straining after it.

'Take no notice of that puppy,' said our host, the man from Norfolk. 'It's been stark staring mad with the moon every night this last week.'

We went into the house, were fed, were looked after; I was put to bed so that the grown-ups could talk freely. All the time came the mad high yapping. In my tiny bedroom I looked out on to a space of flat white sand that reflected the moon between the house and the farm buildings, and there hurtled a mad wild puppy, crazy with joy of life, or moonlight, weaving back and forth, round and round, snapping at its own black shadow and tripping over its own clumsy feet — like a drunken moth around a candle-flame, or like ... Like nothing I've ever seen or heard of since.

The moon, large and remote and soft, stood up over the trees, the empty white sand, the house which had unhappy human beings in it, and a mad little dog yapping and beating its course of drunken joyous delirium. That, of course, was my puppy; and when Mr Barnes came out from the house saying: 'Now, now, come now, you lunatic animal ...' finally almost throwing himself on the crazy creature, to lift it in his arms still yapping and wriggling and flapping around like a fish, so that he could carry it to the packing-case that was its kennel, I was already saying, as anguished as a mother watching a stranger handle her child: careful now, careful, that's my dog.

Next day, after breakfast, I visited the packing-case. Its white wood oozed out resin that smelled tangy in hot sunlight, and its front was open and spilling out soft yellow straw. On the straw a large beautiful black dog lay with her head on outstretched forepaws. Beside her a brindled pup lay on its fat back, its four paws sprawled every-which-way, its eyes rolled up, as ecstatic with heat and food and laziness as it had been the night before from the joy of movement. A crust of mealie-porridge was drying on its shining black lips that were drawn slightly back to show perfect milk teeth. His mother kept her eyes on him, but her pride was dimmed with sleep and heat.

I went inside to announce my spiritual ownership of the puppy. They were all around the breakfast table. The man from Norfolk was swapping boyhood reminiscences (shared in place, not time) with my father. His wife, her eyes still red from the weeping that had followed a night-quarrel, was gossiping with my mother about the various London hospitals where they ministered to the wounded of the war they had (apparently so enjoyably) shared.

My mother at once said: 'Oh my dear, no, not that puppy, didn't you see him last night? We'll never train him.'

The man from Norfolk said I could have him with pleasure.

My father said he didn't see what was wrong with the dog, if a dog was healthy that was all that mattered: my mother lowered her eyes forlornly, and sat silent.

The man from Norfolk's wife said she couldn't bear to part with the silly little thing, goodness knows there was little enough pleasure in her life.

The atmosphere of people at loggerheads being familiar to me, it was not necessary for me to know *why* they disagreed, or in what ways, or what criticisms they were going to make about my puppy. I only knew that inner logics would in due course work themselves out and the puppy would be mine. I left the four people to talk about their differences through a small puppy, and went to worship the animal, who was now sitting in a patch of shade beside the sweet-wood-smelling packing-case, its dark brindled coat glistening, with dark wet patches on it from its mother's ministering tongue. His own pink tongue absurdly stuck out between white teeth, as if he had been too careless or lazy to withdraw it into its proper place under his equally pink wet palate. His brown buttony beautiful eyes ... but enough, he was an ordinary mongrel puppy.

Later I went back to the house to find out how the battle balanced: my mother had obviously won my father over, for he said he thought it was wiser not to have that puppy, 'bad blood tells, you know'.

The bad blood was from the father, whose history delighted my fourteen-year-old imagination. This district being bush, scarcely populated, full of wild animals, even leopards and lions, the four policemen at the police station had a tougher task than in places nearer town; and they had bought half a dozen large dogs to (*a*) terrorize possible burglars around the police station itself, and (*b*) surround themselves with an aura of controlled animal savagery. For the dogs were trained to kill if necessary. One of these dogs, a big Ridgeback, had 'gone wild'. He had slipped his tether at the station and taken to the bush, living by himself on small buck, hares, birds, even

stealing farmers' chickens. This dog, whose proud lonely
shape had been a familiar one to farmers for years, on moonlit
nights, or in grey dawns and dusks, standing aloof from
human warmth and friendship, had taken Stella, my puppy's
mother, off with him for a week of sport and hunting. She
simply went away with him one morning; the Barneses had
seen her go; had called after her; she had not even looked back.
A week later she returned home at dawn and gave a low whine
outside their bedroom window, saying: I'm home; and they
woke to see their errant Stella standing erect in the paling
moonlight, her nose pointed outwards and away from them
towards a great powerful dog who seemed to signal to her
with his slightly moving tail before fading into the bush. Mr
Barnes fired some futile shots after him. Then they both
scolded Stella who in due time produced seven puppies, in all
combinations of black, brown and gold. She was no pure-
bred herself, though of course her owners thought she was, or
ought to be, being their dog. The night the puppies were born,
the man from Norfolk and his wife heard a sad wail or cry,
and arose from their beds to see the wild police dog bending
his head in at the packing-case door. All the bush was flooded
with a pinkish-gold dawn light, and the dog looked as if he
had an aureole of gold around him. Stella was half-wailing,
half-growling her welcome, or protest, or fear at his great
powerful reappearance and his thrusting muzzle so close to her
seven helpless pups. They called out, and he turned his outlaw's head to the window where they stood side by side in
striped pyjamas and embroidered pink silk. He put back his
head and howled, he howled, a mad wild sound that gave
them gooseflesh, so they said; but I did not understand it until
years later when Bill the puppy 'went wild' and I saw him
that day on the ant-heap howling his pain of longing to an
empty listening world.

The father of her puppies did not come near Stella again;
but a month later he was shot dead at another farm, fifty
miles away, coming out of a chicken-run with a fine white Leg-
horn in his mouth; and by that time she had only one pup left,
they had drowned the rest. It was bad blood, they said, no
point in preserving it, they had only left her that one child out
of pity.

I said not a word as they told this cautionary tale, merely
preserved the obstinate calm of someone who knows she will

get her own way. Was right on my side? It was. Was I owed a dog? I was. Should anybody but myself choose my dog? No, but ... Very well then, I had chosen. I chose this dog. I chose it. Too late, I *had* chosen it.

Three days and three nights we spent at the Barnes' place. The days were hot and slow and full of sluggish emotions; and the two dogs slept in the packing-case. At nights, the four people stayed in the living-room, a small brick place heated unendurably by the paraffin lamp whose oily yellow glow attracted moths and beetles in a perpetual whirling halo of small moving bodies. They talked, and I listened for the mad far yapping, and then I crept out in the cold moonlight. On the last night of our stay the moon was full, a great perfect white ball, its history marked on a face that seemed close enough to touch as it floated over the dark cricket-singing bush. And there on the white sand yapped and danced the crazy puppy, while his mother, the big beautiful animal, sat and watched, her intelligent yellow eyes slightly anxious as her muzzle followed the erratic movements of her child, the child of her dead mate from the bush. I crept up beside Stella, sat on the still-warm cement beside her, put my arm around her soft furry neck, and my head beside her alert moving head. I adjusted my breathing so that my rib-cage moved up and down beside hers, so as to be closer to the warmth of her barrelly furry chest, and together we turned our eyes from the great staring floating moon to the tiny black hurtling puppy who shot in circles from near us, so near he nearly crashed into us, to two hundred yards away where he just missed the wheels of the farm wagon. We watched, and I felt the chill of moonlight deepen on Stella's fur, and on my own silk skin, while our ribs moved gently up and down together, and we waited until the man from Norfolk came to first shout, then yell, fling himself on the mad little dog and shut him up in the wooden box where yellow bars of moonlight fell into black dog-smelling shadow. 'There now, Stella girl, you go with your puppy,' said the man, bending to pat her head as she obediently went inside. She used her soft nose to push her puppy over. He was so exhausted that he fell and lay, his four legs stretched out and quivering like a shot dog's, his breath squeezed in and out of him in small regular wheezy pants like whines. And so I left them, Stella and her puppy, to go to my bed in the little brick house which seemed literally crammed with hateful emotions. I went to sleep, thinking of the hurtling little dog, now at last asleep with exhaustion, his nose pushed against his mother's breathing black side, the slits of yellow moonlight moving over him through boards of fragrant wood.

We took him away next morning, having first locked Stella in a room so that she could not see us go.

It was a three-hundred-mile drive, and all the way Bill yapped and panted and yawned and wriggled idiotically on his back on the lap of whoever held him, his eyes rolled up, his big paws lolling. He was a full-time charge for myself and my mother, and, after the city, my brother, whose holidays were starting. He, at first sight of the second dog, reverted to the role of Jock's master, and dismissed my animal as altogether less valuable material. My mother, by now Bill's slave, agreed with him, but invited him to admire the adorable wrinkles on the puppy's forehead. My father demanded irritably that both dogs should be 'thoroughly trained'.

Meanwhile, as the nightmare journey proceeded, it was noticeable that my mother talked more and more about Jock, guiltily, as if she had betrayed him. 'Poor little Jock, what will he say?'

Jock was, in fact, a handsome young dog. More Alsatian than anything, he was a low-standing, thick-coated animal of a warm gold colour, with a vestigial 'ridge' along his spine, rather wolf-like or fox-like, if one looked at him frontways, with his sharp cocked ears. And he was definitely not 'little'. There was something dignified about him from the moment he was out of puppyhood, even when he was being scolded by my mother for his visits to the compound.

The meeting, prepared for by us all with trepidation, went off in a way which was a credit to everyone, but particularly Jock, who regained my mother's heart at a stroke. The puppy was released from the car and carried to where Jock sat, noble and restrained as usual, waiting for us to greet him. Bill at once began weaving and yapping around the rocky space in front of the house. Then he saw Jock, bounded up to him, stepped a couple of feet away, sat down on his fat backside and yelped excitedly. Jock began a yawning, snapping movement of his head, making it go from side to side in half-snarling, half-laughing protest, while the puppy crept closer, right up, jumping at the older dog's lifted wrinkling muzzle.

Jock did not move away; he forced himself to remain still, because he could see us all watching. At last he lifted up his paw, pushed Bill over with it, pinned him down, examined him, then sniffed and licked him. He had accepted him, and Bill had found a substitute for his mother who was presumably mourning his loss. We were able to leave the child (as my mother kept calling him) in Jock's infinitely patient care. 'You are such a good dog, Jock,' she said, overcome by this scene, and the other touching scenes that followed, all marked by Jock's extraordinary forbearance for what was, and even I had to admit it, an intolerably destructive little dog.

Training became urgent. But this was not at all easy, due, like the business of getting a new puppy, to the inner nature of the family.

To take only one difficulty: dogs must be trained by their masters, they must owe allegiance to one person. And who was Jock to obey? And Bill: I was his master, in theory. In practice, Jock was. Was I to take over from Jock? But even to state it is to expose its absurdity: I adored the graceless puppy, and why did I need a well-trained dog? Trained for *what*?

A watchdog? But all our dogs were watchdogs. 'Natives' – such was the article of faith, were by nature scared of dogs, yet everyone repeated stories about thieves poisoning fierce dogs or making friends with them. So apparently no one really believed that watchdogs were any use. Yet every farm had its watchdog.

Throughout my childhood I used to lie in bed, the bush not fifty yards away all around the house, listening to the cry of the night-jar, the owls, the frogs and the crickets; to the tom-toms from the compound; to the mysterious rustling in the thatch over my head, or the long grass it had been cut from down the hill; to all the thousand noises of the night on the veld; and every one of these noises was marked also by the house dogs, who would bark and sniff and investigate and growl at all these; and also at starlight on the polished surface of a leaf, at the moon lifting itself over the mountains, at a branch cracking behind the house, at the first rim of hot red showing above the horizon – in short at anything and everything. Watchdogs, in my experience, were never asleep; but they were not so much a guard against thieves (we never had any thieves that I can remember) as a kind of instrument designed to measure or record the rustlings and movements of the African night that seemed to have an enormous life of its own, but a collective life; so that the falling of a stone, or a star shooting through the Milky Way, the grunt of a wild pig, and the wind rustling in the mealie-field were all evidences and aspects of the same truth.

How did one 'train' a watchdog? Presumably to respond only to the slinking approach of a human, black or white. What use is a watchdog otherwise? But even now, the most powerful memory of my childhood is of lying awake listening to the sobbing howl of a dog at the inexplicable appearance of the yellow face of the moon; of creeping to the window to see the long muzzle of a dog pointed black against a great bowl of stars. We needed no moon calendar with those dogs, who were like traffic in London: to sleep at all, one had to learn not to hear them. And if one did not hear them, one would not hear the stiff warning growl that (presumably) would greet a marauder.

At first Jock and Bill were locked up in the dining-room at night. But there were so many stirrings and yappings and rushings from window to window after the rising sun or moon, or the black shadows which moved across whitewashed walls from the branches of the trees in the garden, that soon we could no longer stand the lack of sleep, and they were turned out on to the veranda. With many hopeful injunctions from my mother that they were to be 'good dogs': which meant that they should ignore their real natures and sleep from sundown to sun-up. Even then, when Bill was just out of puppyhood, they might be missing altogether in the early mornings. They would come guiltily up the road from the lands at breakfast-time, their coats full of grass seeds, and we knew they had rushed down into the bush after an owl, or a grazing animal, and, finding themselves farther from home than they had expected in a strange nocturnal world, had begun nosing and sniffing and exploring in practice for their days of wildness soon to come.

So they weren't watchdogs. Hunting-dogs perhaps? My brother undertook to train them, and we went through a long absurd period of 'down, Jock,' 'to heel, Bill,' while sticks of barley-sugar balanced on noses, and paws were offered to be shaken by human hands, etc., etc. Through all this Jock suffered, bravely, but saying so clearly with every part of him that he would do anything to please my mother – he would send her glances half proud and half apologetic all the time my brother drilled him, that after an hour of training my brother would retreat, muttering that it was too hot, and Jock bounded off to lay his head on my mother's lap. As for Bill he never achieved anything. Never did he sit still with the golden lumps on his nose, he ate them at once. Never did he stay to heel. Never did he remember what he was supposed to do with his paw when one of us offered him a hand. The truth was, I understood then, watching the training sessions, that Bill was stupid. I pretended of course that he despised being trained, he found it humiliating; and that Jock's readiness to go through with the silly business showed his lack of spirit. But, alas, there was no getting around it, Bill simply wasn't very bright.

Meanwhile he had ceased to be a fat charmer; he had become a lean young dog, good-looking, with his dark brindled coat, and his big head that had a touch of Newfoundland. He had a look of puppy about him still. For just as Jock seemed born elderly, had respectable white hairs on his chin from the start; so Bill kept something young in him; he was a young dog until he died.

The training sessions did not last long. Now my brother said the dogs would be trained on the job: this to pacify my father, who kept saying that they were a disgrace and 'not worth their salt'.

There began a new régime, my brother, myself, and the two dogs. We set forth each morning, first, my brother, earnest with responsibility, his rifle swinging in his hand, at his heels the two dogs. Behind this time-honoured unit, myself, the girl, with no useful part to play in the serious masculine business, but necessary to provide admiration. This was a very old role for me indeed: to walk away on one side of the scene, a small fierce girl, hungry to be part of it, but knowing she never would be, above all because the heart that had been put to pump away all her life under her ribs was not only critical and intransigent, but one which longed so bitterly to melt into loving acceptance. An uncomfortable combination, as she knew even then – yet I could not remove the sulky smile from my face. And it *was* absurd: there was my brother, so intent and serious, with Jock the good dog, just behind him, and there was Bill the bad dog, intermittently behind him, but more often than not sneaking off to enjoy some side-path. And there was myself, unwillingly following, my weight shifting from hip to hip, bored and showing it.

I knew the route too well. Before we reached the sullen thickets of the bush where game birds were to be found, there was a long walk up the back of the kopje through a luxuriant pawpaw grove, then through sweet potato vines that tangled our ankles, and tripped us, then past a rubbish heap whose sweet rotten smell was expressed in a heave of glittering black flies, then the bush itself. Here it was all dull green stunted trees, miles and miles of the smallish, flattish, msasa trees in their second growth: they had all been cut for mine furnaces at some time. And over the flat ugly bush a large overbearing blue sky.

We were on our way to get food. So we kept saying. Whatever we shot would be eaten by 'the house', or by the house's servants, or by 'the compound'. But we were hunting according to a newer law than the need for food, and we knew it, and that was why we were always a bit apologetic about these expeditions, and why we so often chose to return empty-handed. We were hunting because my brother had been given a new and efficient rifle that would bring down (infallibly, if my brother shot) birds, large and small; and small animals; and very often large game like koodoo and sable. We were hunting because we owned a gun. And because we owned a gun, we should have hunting-dogs, it made the business less ugly for some reason.

We were on our way to the Great Vlei, as distinct from the Big Vlei, which was five miles in the other direction. The Big Vlei was burnt-out and eroded, and the water-holes usually dried up early. We did not like going there. But to reach the Great Vlei, which was beautiful, we had to go through the ugly bush 'at the back of the kopje'. These ritual names for parts of the farm seemed rather to be names for regions in our minds. 'Going to the Great Vlei' had a fairytale quality about it, because of having to pass through the region of sour ugly frightening bush first. For it did frighten us, always, and without reason: we felt it was hostile to us and we walked through it quickly, knowing that we were earning by this danger the water-running peace of the Great Vlei. It was only partly on our farm; the boundary between it and the next farm ran invisibly down its centre, drawn by the eye from this outcrop to that big tree to that pothole to that ant-heap. It was a grassy valley with trees standing tall and spreading on either side of the water-course which was a half-mile width of intense greenness broken by sky-reflecting brown pools. This was old bush, these trees had never been cut: the Great Vlei had the inevitable look of natural bush – that no branch, no shrub, no patch of thorn, no outcrop, could have been in any other place or stood at any other angle.

The potholes here were always full. The water was stained clear brown, and the mud bottom had a small movement of creatures, while over the brown ripples skimmed blue jays and humming-birds and all kinds of vivid flashing birds we did not know the names of. Along the lush verges lolled pink and white water-lilies on their water-gemmed leaves.

This paradise was where the dogs were to be trained.

During the first holidays, long ones of six weeks, my brother was indefatigable, and we set off every morning after breakfast. In the Great Vlei I sat on a pool's edge under a thorn tree, and day-dreamed to the tune of the ripples my swinging feet set moving across the water, while my brother, armed with the rifle, various sizes of stick, and lumps of sugar and biltong, put the two dogs through their paces. Sometimes, roused perhaps because the sun that fell through the green lace of the thorn was burning my shoulders, I turned to watch the three creatures, hard at work a hundred yards off on an empty patch of sand. Jock, more often than not, would be a dead dog, or his nose would be on his paws while his attentive eyes were on my brother's face. Or he would be sitting up, a dog statue, a golden dog, admirably obedient. Bill, on the other hand, was probably balancing on his spine, all four paws in the air, his throat back so that he was flat from nose to tail-tip, receiving the hot sun equally over his brindled fur. I would hear, through my own lazy thoughts: 'Good dog, Jock, yes, good dog. Idiot, Bill, fool dog, why don't you work like Jock?' And my brother, his face reddened and sweaty, would come over to flop beside me, saying: 'It's all Bill's fault, he's a bad example. And of course Jock doesn't see why he should work hard when Bill just plays all the time.' Well, it probably was my fault that the .training failed. If my earnest and undivided attention had been given, as I knew quite well was being demanded of me, to this business of the boy and the two dogs, perhaps we would have ended up with a brace of efficient and obedient animals, ever-ready to die, to go to heel, and to fetch it. Perhaps.

By next holidays, moral disintegration had set in. My father complained the dogs obeyed nobody. He demanded training, serious and unremitting. My brother and I watched our mother petting Jock and scolding Bill, and came to an unspoken agreement. We set off for the Great Vlei but once there we loafed up and down the water-holes, while the dogs did as they liked, learning the joys of freedom.

The uses of water, for instance. Jock, cautious as usual, would test a pool with his paw, before moving in to stand chest deep, his muzzle just above the ripples, licking at them with small yaps of greeting or excitement. Then he walked gently in and swam up and down and around the brown pool in the green shade of the thorn trees. Meanwhile, Bill would have found a shallow pool and be at his favourite game. Starting twenty yards from the rim of a pool, he would hurl himself, barking shrilly, across the grass, then across the pool, not so much swimming across it as bouncing across it. Out on the other side, up the side of the vlei, around in a big loop, then back, and around again ... and again and again and again. Great sheets of brown water went up into the sky above him, crashing back into the pool while he barked his exultation.

That was one game. Or they chased each other up and down the four-miles-long valley like enemies, and when one caught the other there was a growling and a snarling and a fighting that sounded genuine enough. Sometimes we went to separate them, an interference they suffered; and the moment we let them go one or another would be off, his hind-quarters pistoning, with the other in pursuit, fierce and silent. They might race a mile, two miles, before one leaped at the other's throat and brought him down. This game, too, over and over again, so that when they did go wild, we knew how they killed the wild pig and the buck they lived on.

On frivolous mornings they chased butterflies, while my brother and I dangled our feet in a pool and watched. Once, very solemnly, as it were in parody of the ridiculous business (now over, thank goodness) of 'fetch it' and 'to heel', Jock brought us in his jaws a big orange and black butterfly, the delicate wings all broken, and the orange bloom smearing his furry lips. He laid it in front of us, held the still fluttering creature flat with a paw, then lay down, his nose pointing at it. His brown eyes rolled up, wickedly hypocritical, as if to say; 'Look, a butterfly, I'm a *good* dog.' Meanwhile, Bill leaped and barked, a small brown dog hurling himself up into the great blue sky after floating coloured wings. He had taken no notice at all of Jock's captive. But we both felt that Bill was much more likely than Jock to make such a seditious comment, and in fact my brother said: 'Bill's corrupted Jock. I'm sure Jock would never go wild like this unless Bill was showing him. It's the blood coming out.' But, alas, we had no idea yet of what 'going wild' could mean. For a couple of years yet it still meant small indisciplines, and mostly Bill's.

For instance, there was the time Bill forced himself through a loose plank in the door of the store hut, and there ate and ate, eggs, cake, bread, a joint of beef, a ripening guinea-fowl, half a ham. Then he couldn't get out. In the morning he was a swollen dog, rolling on the floor and whining with the agony of his over-indulgence. 'Stupid dog, Bill, Jock would never do a thing like that, he'd be too intelligent not to know he'd swell up if he ate so much.'

Then he ate eggs out of the nest, a crime for which on a farm a dog gets shot. Very close was Bill to this fate. He had actually been seen sneaking out of the chicken-run, feathers on his nose, egg-smear on his muzzle. And there was a mess of oozing yellow and white slime over the straw of the nests. The fowls cackled and raised their feathers whenever Bill came near. First, he was beaten, by the cook, until his howls shook the farm. Then my mother blew eggs and filled them with a solution of mustard and left them in the nests. Sure enough, next morning, a yell of wild howls and shrieks: the beatings had taught him nothing. We went out to see a brown dog running and racing in agonized circles with his tongue hanging out while the sun came up red over black mountains – a splendid backdrop to a disgraceful scene. My mother took the poor inflamed jaws and washed them in warm water and said: 'Well now, Bill, you'd better learn, or it's the firing squad for you.'

He learned, but not easily. More than once my brother and I, having arisen early for the hunt, stood in front of the house in the dawn hush, the sky a high far grey above us, the edge of the mountains just reddening, the great spaces of silent bush full of the dark of the night. We sniffed at the small

sharpness of the dew, and the heavy somnolent night-smell off
the bush, felt the cold heavy air on our cheeks. We stood,
whistling very low, so that the dogs would come from wherever
they had chosen to sleep. Soon Jock would appear, yawning and sweeping his tail back and forth. No Bill — then we
saw him, sitting on his haunches just outside the chicken-
run, his nose resting in a loop of wire, his eyes closed in yearning for the warm delicious ooze of fresh egg. And we would
clap our hands over our mouths and double up with heartless
laughter that had to be muffled so as not to disturb our
parents. On the mornings when we went hunting, and took the
dogs, we knew that before we'd gone half a mile either Jock
or Bill would dash off barking into the bush; the one left would
look up from his own nosing and sniffing and rush away too.
We would hear the wild double barking fade away with the
crash and the rush of the two bodies, and often enough,
the subsidiary rushings-away of other animals who had been
asleep or resting and just waiting until we had gone away. Now
we could look for something to shoot which probably we would
never have seen at all had the dogs been there. We could settle
down for long patient stalks, circling around a grazing koodoo,
or a couple of duiker. Often enough we would lie watching
them for hours, afraid only that Jock and Bill would come
back, putting an end to this particular pleasure. I remember
once we caught a glimpse of a duiker grazing on the edge of
a farmland that was still half dark. We got on to our stomachs
and wriggled through the long grass, not able to see if the
duiker was still there. Slowly the field opened up in front
of us, a heaving mass of big black clods. We carefully raised
our heads, and there, at the edge of the clod-sea a couple of
arms-lengths away, were three little duiker, their heads turned
away from us to where the sun was about to rise. They
were three black, quite motionless silhouettes. Away over
the other side of the field, big clods became tinged with
reddish gold. The earth turned so fast towards the sun the
light came running from the tip of one clod to the next across
the field like flames leaping along the tops of long grasses in
front of a strong wind. The light reached the duikers and outlined them with warm gold. They were three glittering little
beasts on the edge of an imminent sunlight. They began to
butt each other, lifting their hind-quarters and bringing down
their hind-feet in clicking leaps like dancers. They tossed

their sharp little horns and made short half-angry rushes at each other. The sun was up. Three little buck danced on the edge of the deep green bush where we lay hidden, and there was a weak sunlight warming their gold hides. The sun separated itself from the line of the hills, and became calm and big and yellow; a warm yellow colour filled the world; the little buck stopped dancing, and walked slowly off, frisking their white tails and tossing their pretty heads, into the bush.

We would never have seen them at all, if the dogs hadn't been miles away.

In fact, all they were good for was their indiscipline. If we wanted to be sure of something to eat, we tied ropes to the dogs' collars until we actually heard the small clink-clink-clink of guinea-fowl running through the bush. Then we untied them. The dogs were at once off after the birds who rose clumsily into the air, looking like flying shawls that sailed along, just above grass level, with the dogs' jaws snapping underneath them. All they wanted was to land unobserved in the long grass, but they were always forced to rise painfully into the trees, on their weak wings. Sometimes, if it was a large flock, a dozen trees might be dotted with the small black shapes of guinea-fowl outlined against dawn or evening skies. They watched the barking dogs, took no notice of us. My brother or I – for even I could hardly miss in such conditions – planted our feet wide for balance, took aim at a chosen bird and shot. The carcase fell into the worrying jaws beneath. Meanwhile, a second bird would be chosen and shot. With the two birds tied together by their feet, and the rifle justified by utility, proudly swinging, we would saunter back to the house through the sun-scented bush of our enchanted childhood. The dogs, for politeness' sake, escorted us part of the way home, then went off hunting on their own. Guinea-fowl were very tame sport for them, by then.

It had come to this, that if we actually wished to shoot something, or to watch animals, or even to take a walk through bush where every animal for miles had not been scared away, we had to lock up the dogs before we left, ignoring their whines and their howls. Even so, if let out too soon, they would follow. Once, after we had walked six miles or so, a leisurely morning's trek towards the mountains, the dogs arrived, panting, happy, their pink wet tongues hot on our knees and forearms, saying how delighted they were to have found us. They licked and wagged for a few moments – then off they went, they vanished, and did not come home until evening. We were worried. We had not known that they went so far from the farm by themselves. We spoke of how bad it would be if they took to frequenting other farms, perhaps other chicken-runs? But it was all too late. They were too old to train. Either they had to be kept permanently on leashes, tied to trees outside the house, and for dogs like these it was not much better than being dead – either that, or they must run free and take their chances.

We got news of the dogs in letters from home and it was increasingly bad. My brother and I, at our respective boarding-schools where we were supposed to be learning discipline, order, and sound characters, read: 'The dogs went away a whole night, they only came back at lunchtime.' 'Jock and Bill have been three days and nights in the bush. They've just come home, worn out.' 'The dogs must have made a kill this time and stayed beside it like wild animals, because they came home too gorged to eat, they just drank a lot of water and fell off to sleep like babies ...' 'Mr Daly rang up yesterday to say he saw Jock and Bill hunting along the hill behind his house. They've been chasing his oxen. We've got to beat them when they get home because if they don't learn they'll get themselves shot one of these dark nights ...'

They weren't there at all when we went home for the holidays. They had already been gone for nearly a week. But, or so we flattered ourselves, they sensed our return, for back they came, trotting gently side by side up the hill in the moonlight, two low black shapes moving above the accompanying black shapes of their shadows, their eyes gleaming red as the shafts of lamplight struck them. They greeted us, my brother and I, affectionately enough, but at once went off to sleep. We told ourselves that they saw us as creatures like them, who went off on long exciting hunts: but we knew it was sentimental nonsense, designed to take the edge off the hurt we felt because our animals, *our* dogs, cared so little about us. They went away again that night or, rather, in the first dawn-light. A week later they came home. They smelled foul, they must have been chasing a skunk or a wild-cat. Their fur was matted with grass-seeds and their skin lumpy with ticks. They drank water heavily, but refused food: their breath was foetid with the smell of meat.

They lay down to sleep and remained limp while we, each taking an animal, its sleeping head heavy in our laps, removed ticks, grass-seeds, black-jacks. On Bill's forepaw was a hard ridge which I thought was an old scar. He sleep-whimpered when I touched it. It was a noose of plaited grass, used by Africans to snare birds. Luckily it had snapped off. 'Yes,' said my father, 'that's how they'll both end, both of them, they'll die in a trap, and serve them both right, they won't get any sympathy from me!'

We were frightened into locking them up for a day; but we could not stand their misery, and let them out again.

We were always springing game-traps of all kinds. For the big buck – the sable, the eland, the koodoo, the Africans bent a sapling across a path, held it by light string, and fixed on it a noose of heavy wire cut from a fence. For the smaller buck there were low traps with nooses of fine baling wire or plaited tree fibre. And at the corners of the cultivated fields or at the edges of water-holes, where the birds and hares came down to feed, were always a myriad tiny tracks under the grass, and often across every track hung a small noose of plaited grass. Sometimes we spent whole days destroying these snares.

In order to keep the dogs amused, we took to walking miles every day. We were exhausted, but they were not, and simply went off at night as well. Then we rode bicycles as fast as we could along the rough farm tracks, with the dogs bounding easily beside us. We wore ourselves out, trying to please Jock and Bill, who, we imagined, knew what we were doing and were humouring us. But we stuck at it. Once, at the end of a glade, we saw the skeleton of a large animal hanging from a noose. Some African had forgotten to visit his traps. We showed the skeleton to Jock and Bill, and talked and warned and threatened, almost in tears because human speech was not dog's speech. They sniffed around the bones, yapped a few times up into our faces – out of politeness, we felt; and were off again into the bush.

At school we heard that they were almost completely wild. Sometimes they came home for a meal, or a day's sleep, 'treating the house,' my mother complained, 'like a hotel.'

Then fate struck, in the shape of a buck-trap.

One night, very late, we heard whining, and went out to greet them. They were crawling towards the front door, almost on their bellies. Their ribs stuck out, their coats stared, their eyes shone unhealthily. They fell on the food we gave them; they were starved. Then on Jock's neck, which was bent over the food-bowl, showed the explanation: a thick strand of wire. It was not solid wire, but made of a dozen twisted strands, and had been chewed through, near the collar. We examined Bill's mouth: chewing the wire through must have taken a long time, days perhaps: his gums and lips were scarred and bleeding, and his teeth were worn down to stumps, like an old dog's teeth. If the wire had not been stranded, Jock would have died in the trap. As it was, he felt ill, his lungs were strained, since he had been half-strangled with the wire. And Bill could no longer chew properly, he ate uncomfortably, like an old person. They stayed at home for weeks, reformed dogs, barked around the house at night, and ate regular meals.

Then they went off again, but came home more often than they had. Jock's lungs weren't right: he would lie out in the sun, gasping and wheezing, as if trying to rest them. As for Bill, he could only eat soft food. How, then, did they manage when they were hunting?

One afternoon we were shooting, miles from home, and we saw them. First we heard the familiar excited yapping coming towards us, about two miles off. We were in a large vlei, full of tall whitish grass which swayed and bent along a fast regular line: a shape showed, it was duiker, hard to see until it was close because it was reddish brown in colour, and the vlei had plenty of the pinkish feathery grass that turns a soft intense red in strong light. Being near sunset, the pale grass was on the verge of being invisible, like wires of white light; and the pink grass flamed and glowed; and the fur of the little buck shone red. It swerved suddenly. Had it seen us? No, it was because of Jock who had made a quick manoeuvring turn from where he had been lying in the pink grass to watch the buck. Behind it was Bill, pistoning along like a machine. Jock, who could no longer run fast, had turned the buck into Bill's jaws. We saw Bill bound at the little creature's throat, bring it down and hold it until Jock came in to kill it: his own teeth were useless now.

We walked over to greet them, but with restraint, for these two growling snarling creatures seemed not to know us, they raised eyes glazed with savagery, as they tore at the dead buck. Or rather, as Jock tore at it. Before we went away we saw

Jock pushing over lumps of hot steaming meat towards Bill, who otherwise would have gone hungry.

They were really a team now; neither could function without the other. So we thought.

But soon Jock lay watching the bush, and when Bill came, he licked his ears and face as if he had reverted to the role of Bill's mother.

Once I heard Bill barking and went to see. The telephone line ran through a vlei near the house to the farm over the hill. The wires hummed and sang and twanged. Bill was underneath the wires which were a good fifteen feet over his head, jumping and barking at them: he was playing, out of exuberance, as he had done when a small puppy. But now it made me sad, seeing the strong dog playing all alone, while his friend lay quiet in the sun, wheezing from damaged lungs.

And what did Bill live on, in the bush? Rats, birds' eggs, lizards, anything *soft* enough? That was painful, too, thinking of the powerful hunters in the days of their glory.

Soon we got telephone calls from neighbours: Bill dropped in, he finished off the food in our dog's bowl ... Bill seemed hungry, so we fed him ... Your dog Bill is looking very thin, isn't he? ... Bill was around our chicken-run — I'm sorry, but if he goes for the eggs, then ...

Bill had puppies with a pedigree bitch fifteen miles off: her owners were annoyed: Bill was not good enough for them, and besides there was the question of his 'bad blood'. All the puppies were destroyed. He was hanging around the house all the time, although he had been beaten, and they had even fired shots into the air to scare him off. Was there anything we could do to keep him at home, they asked; for they were tired of having to keep their bitch tied up?

No, there was nothing we could do. Rather, there was nothing we *would* do; for when Bill came trotting up from the bush to drink deeply out of Jock's bowl, and to lie for a while nose-to-nose with Jock, well, we could have caught him and tied him up, but we did not. 'He won't last long anyway,' said my father. And my mother told Jock that he was a sensible and intelligent dog; for she again sang praises of his nature and character just as if he had never spent so many glorious years in the bush.

I went to visit the neighbour who owned Bill's mate. She was tied to a post on the veranda. All night we were disturbed by a wild, sad howling from the bush, and she whimpered and strained at her rope. In the morning I walked out into the hot silence of the bush, and called to him: Bill, Bill, it's me. Nothing, no sound. I sat on the slope of an ant-heap in the shade, and waited. Soon Bill came into view, trotting between the trees. He was very thin. He looked gaunt, stiff, wary – an old outlaw, afraid of traps. He saw me, but stopped about twenty yards off. He climbed half-way up another ant-hill and sat there in full sunlight, so I could see the harsh patches on his coat. We sat in silence, looking at each other. Then he lifted his head and howled, like the howl dogs give to the full moon, long, terrible, lonely. But it was morning, the sun calm and clear, and the bush without mystery. He sat and howled his heart out, his muzzle pointed away towards where his mate was chained. We could hear the faint whimperings she made, and the clink of her metal dish as she moved about. I couldn't stand it. It made my flesh cold, and I could see the hairs standing up on my forearm. I went over to him and sat by him and put my arm around his neck as once, so many years ago, I had put my arm around his mother that moonlit night before I stole her puppy away from her. He put his muzzle on my forearm and whimpered or rather cried. Then he lifted it and howled ... 'Oh, my God, Bill, don't do that, please don't, it's not the slightest use, please, dear Bill ...' But he went on, until suddenly he leaped up in the middle of a howl, as if his pain were too strong to contain sitting, and he sniffed at me, as if to say: That's you, is it, well, good-bye – then he turned his wild head to the bush and trotted away.

Very soon he was shot, coming out of a chicken-run early one morning with an egg in his mouth.

Jock was quite alone now. He spent his old age lying in the sun, his nose pointed out over the miles and miles of bush between our house and the mountains where he had hunted all those years with Bill. He was really an old dog, his legs were stiff, and his coat was rough, and he wheezed and gasped. Sometimes, at night, when the moon was up, he went out to howl at it, and we would say: 'He's missing Bill.' He would come back to sit at my mother's knee, resting his head so that she could stroke it. She would say: 'Poor old Jock, poor old boy, are you missing that bad dog Bill?'

Sometimes, when he lay dozing, he started up and went trotting on his stiff old legs through the house and the outhouses, anxiously sniffing everywhere and anxiously whining. Then he stood, upright, one paw raised, as he did when he was young, and gazed over the bush and softly whined. And we would say: 'He must have been dreaming he was out hunting with Bill.'

He got ill. He could hardly breathe. We carried him in our arms down the hill into the bush, and my mother stroked and patted him while my father put the gun barrel to the back of his head and shot him.

THE NEW MAN

About three miles on the track to the station a smaller overgrown road branched to the Manager's House. This house had
been built by the Rich Mitchells for their manager. Then
they decided to sell a third of their farm, with the house ready
for its owner. It stood empty a couple of years, with sacks of
grain and ox-hides in it. The case had been discussed and
adjudicated on the verandas of the district: no, Rich Mitchell
was not right to sell that part of his farm, which was badly
watered and poorish soil, except for a hundred acres or so.
At the very least he should have thrown in a couple of miles
of his long vlei with the lands adjacent to it. No wonder
Rich Mitchell was rich (they said); and when they met him
their voices had a calculated distance: 'Sold your new farm
yet, Mich?' No, he hadn't sold it, nor did he, for one year,
then another. But the rich can afford to wait. (As they said on
the verandas.)

The farm was bought by a Mr Rooyen who had already
gone broke farming down Que Que way. The Grants went
to visit, Mrs Grant in her new silk, Mr Grant grumbling
because it was the busy season. The small girl did not go, she
refused, she wanted to stay in the kitchen with old Tom the
cookboy, where she was happy, watching him make butter.

That evening, listening with half an ear to the parents' talk,
it was evident things weren't too good. Mr Rooyen hadn't a
penny of his own; he had bought the farm through the Land
Bank, and was working on an eight-hundred-pounds loan.
What it amounted to was a gamble on the first season. 'It's all
very well,' said Mr Grant, summing up with the reluctant
critical note in his voice that meant he knew he would have
to help Mr Rooyen, would do so, but found it all too much.
And, sure enough, in the dry season the Rooyen cattle were
running on Grant land and using the Grant well. But Mr
Rooyen had become 'the new man in the Manager's House'.

The first season wasn't too bad, so the small girl gathered
from the talk on the verandas, and Mr Rooyen might make out
after all. But he was very poor. Mrs Grant, when they had too

much cheese or butter, or baked, sent supplies over by the cook. In the second year Mr Grant lent Mr Rooyen two hundred pounds to tide him over. The small girl knew that the new neighbour belonged for ever to that category of people who, when parting from the Grants, would wring their hands and say in a low, half-ashamed voice: 'You've been very good to me and I'll never forget it.'

The first time she saw the new farmer, who never went anywhere, was when the Grants went into the station and gave Mr Rooyen a lift. He could not afford a car yet. He stood on the track waiting for the Grants, and behind him the road to his house was even more overgrown with bushes and grass, like a dry river-bed between the trees. He sat in the back answering Mr Grant's questions about how things were going. She did not notice him much, or rather refused to notice him, because she definitely did not like him, although he was nothing she had not known all her life. A tallish man, dressed in bush khaki, blue eyes inflamed by the sun, he was burned – not a healthy reddish brown – but a mahogany colour, because he was never out of the sun, never stopped working. This colour in a white man, the small girl already knew, meant a desperate struggling poverty and it usually preceded going broke or getting very ill. But the reason she did not like him, or that he scared her, was the violence of his grievance. The hand which lay on the back of the car seat behind Mr Grant trembled slightly; his voice trembled as he spoke of Rich Mitchell, his neighbour, who had a vlei seven miles long and would neither sell nor rent him any of it. 'It isn't right,' he kept saying. 'He doesn't make use of my end. Perhaps his cattle graze there a couple of weeks in the dry season, but that's all.' All this meant that his cattle would be running with the Grants' again when the grass was low. More: that he was appealing, through Mr Grant, for justice, to the unconstituted council of farmers who settled these matters on their verandas.

That night Mr Grant said: It's all very well! a good many times. Then he rang up Mr Matthews (Glasgow Bob) from the Glenisle Farm; and Mr Paynter (Tobacco Paynter) from Bellvue; and Mr Van Doren (The Dutchman) from Blue Hills. Their farms adjoined Rich Mitchell's.

Soon after, the Grants went into the station again. At the last minute they had remembered to ring up and ask Mr Rooyen if he wanted a lift. He did. It wasn't altogether convenient, particularly for the small girl, because two-thirds of the back seat was packed to the roof with plough parts being sent into town for repair. And beside Mrs Grant on the front seat was a great parcel full of dead chickens ready for sale to the hotel. 'It's no bother,' said Mrs Grant, to Mr Rooyen, 'the child can sit on your knee.'

The trouble was that the small girl was definitely not a child. She was pretty certain she was no longer a small girl, either. For one thing, her breasts had begun to sprout, and while this caused her more embarrassment than pleasure, she handled her body in a proud gingerly way that made it impossible, as she would have done even a season before, to snuggle in on the grown-up's lap. She got out of the car in a mood of fine proud withdrawal, not looking at Mr Rooyen as he fitted himself into the narrow space on the back seat. Then, with a clumsy fastidiousness, she perched on the very edge of his bare bony knees and supported herself with two hands on the back of the front seat. Mr Rooyen's arms were about her waist, as if she were indeed a child, and they trembled, as she had known they would – as his voice still trembled, talking about Rich Mitchell. But soon he stopped talking. The car sped forward through the heavy, red-dust-laden trees, rocking and bouncing over the dry ruts, and she was jerked back to fit against the body of Mr Rooyen, whose fierceness was that of a lonely tenderness, as she knew already, though never before in her life had she met it. She longed for the ride to be over, while she sat squeezed, pressed, suffering, in the embrace of Mr Rooyen, a couple of feet behind the Grants. She ignored, so far as was possible, with politeness; was stiff with resistance; looked at the backs of her parents' heads and marvelled at their blindness. 'If you only knew what your precious Mr Rooyen was doing to your precious daughter ...'

When it was time to come home from the station, she shed five years and became petulant and wilful: she would sit on her mother's knee, not on Mr Rooyen's. Because now the car was stacked with groceries, and it was a choice of one knee or the other. 'Why, my dear child,' said the fond Mrs Grant, pleased at this rebirth of the charming child in her daughter. But the girl sat as stiffly on her mother's knee as she had on the man's, for she felt his eyes continually returning to her, over her mother's shoulder, in need, or in fear, or in guilt.

When the car stopped at the turning to the Manager's House, she got off her mother's knee, and would not look at Mr Rooyen. Who then did something really not allowable, not in the code, for he bent, squeezed her in his great near-black hairy arms and kissed her. Her mother laughed, gay and encouraging. Mr Grant said merely: 'Good-bye, Rooyen,' as the tall forlorn fierce man walked off to his house along the grass-river road.

The girl got into the back seat, silent. Her mother had let her down, had let her new breasts down by that gay social laugh. As for her father, she looked at his profile, absorbed in the business of starting the car and setting it in motion, but the profile said nothing. She said, resentful: 'Who does he think he is, *kissing* me.' And Mrs Grant said briskly: 'My dear child, why ever not?' At which Mr Grant gave his wife a quick, grave look, but remained silent. And this comforted the girl, supported her.

She thought about Mr Rooyen. Or rather, she felt him – felt the trembling of his arms, felt as if he were calling to her. One hot morning, saying she was going for a walk, she set off to his house. When she got there she was overheated and tired and needed a drink. Of course there was no one there. The house was two small rooms, side by side under corrugated iron, with a lean-to kitchen behind. In front was a narrow brick veranda with pillars. Plants stood in painted paraffin tins, and they were dry and limp. She went into the first room. It had two old leather armchairs, a sideboard with a mirror that reflected trees and blue sky and long grass from the low window, and an eating table. The second room had an iron bed and a chest-of-drawers. She looked, long and thoughtful, at the narrow bed, and her heart was full of pity because of the lonely trembling of Mr Rooyen's arms. She went into the tiny kitchen. It had an iron Carron Dover stove, where the fire was out. A wooden table had some cold meat on it with a piece of gauze over it. The meat smelled sourish. Flies buzzed. Up the legs of the table small black ants trickled. There was no servant visible. After getting herself a glass of tepid, tasting water from the filter, she walked very slowly through the house again, taking in everything, then went home.

At supper she said, casual, 'I went to see Mr Rooyen today.'

Her father looked quickly at her mother, who dropped her eyes and crumbled bread. That meant they had discussed the incident of the kiss. 'How is he?' asked Mrs Grant, casual and bright. 'He wasn't there.' Her father said nothing.

Next day she lapsed back into her private listening world. In the afternoon she read, but the book seemed childish. She wept enjoyably, alone. At supper she looked at her parents from a long way off, and knew it was a different place where she had never been before. They were smaller, definitely. She saw them clear: the rather handsome phlegmatic man at one end of the table, brown in his khaki (but not mahogany, he could afford not to spend every second of his waking hours in the sun). And at the other end a brisk, airy, efficient woman in a tailored striped dress. The girl thought: I came out of them; and shrank away in dislike from knowing how she had. She looked at these two strange people and felt Mr Rooyen's arms call to her across three miles of veld. Before she went to bed she stood for a long time gazing at the small light from his house.

Next morning she went to his house again. She wore a new dress, which her mother had made. It was a childish dress that ignored her breasts, which is why she chose it. Not that she expected to see Mr Rooyen. She wanted to see the small, brick, ant- and fly-ridden house, walk through it, and come home again.

When she got there, there was not a sign of anyone. She fetched water in a half-paraffin tin from the kitchen and soaked the half-dead plants. Then she sat on the edge of the brick veranda with her feet in the hot dust. Quite soon Mr Rooyen came walking up through the trees from the lands. He saw her, but she could not make out what he thought. She said, girlish: 'I've watered your plants for you.'

'The boy's supposed to water them,' he said, sounding angry. He strode on to the veranda, into the room behind, and out at the back in three great paces shouting: 'Boy! Boy!'

A shouting went on, because the cook had gone to sleep under a tree. The girl watched the man run himself a glass of water from the filter, gulp it down, run another, gulp that. He came back to the veranda. Standing like a great black hot tower over her, he demanded: 'Does your father know you're here?'

She shook her head, primly. But she felt he was unfair. He would not have liked her father to know how his arms had trembled and pressed her in the car.

He returned to the room, and sat, knees sprawling apart, his arms limp, in one of the big ugly leather chairs. He looked at her steadily, his mouth tight. He had a thin mouth. The lips were burned and black from the sun, and the cracks in them showed white and unhealthy.

'Come here,' he said, softly. It was tentative and she chose not to hear it, remained sitting with her back to him. Over her shoulder she asked, one neighbour to another : 'Have you fixed up your vlei with Mr Mitchell yet?' He sat looking at her, his head lowered. His eyes were really ugly, she thought, red with sun-glare. He was an ugly man, she thought. For now she was wishing – not that she had not come – but that he had not come. Then she could have walked, secretly and delightfully, through the house, and gone, secretly. And tomorrow she could have come and watered his plants again. She imagined saying to him, meeting him by chance somewhere : 'Guess who was watering your plants all that time?'

'You're a pretty little girl,' he said. He was grinning. The grin had no relationship to the lonely hunger of his touch on her in the car. Nor was it a grin addressed to a pretty little girl – far from it. She looked at the grin, repudiating it for her future, and was glad that she wore this full, childish dress.

'Come and sit on my knee,' he tried again, in the way people had been saying through her childhood : Come and sit on my knee. She obligingly went, like a small girl, and balanced herself on a knee that felt all bone under her. His hands came out and gripped her thin arms. His face changed from the ugly grin to the look of lonely hunger. She was sitting upright, using her feet as braces on the floor to prevent herself being pulled into the trembling man's body. Unable to pull her, he leaned his face against her neck, so that she felt his eyelashes and eyebrows hairy on her skin, and he muttered : 'Maureen, Maureen, Maureen, my love.'

She stood up, smoothing down her silly dress. He opened his eyes, sat still, hands on his knees. His mouth was half-open, he breathed irregularly, and his eyes stared, not at her, but at the brick floor where tiny black ants trickled.

She sat herself on the chair opposite, tucking her dress well in around her legs. In the silence the roof cracked suddenly overhead from the heat. There was the sound of a car on the main road half a mile off. The car came nearer. Neither the girl nor the man moved. Their eyes met from time to time, frowning, serious, then moved away to the ants, to the window, anywhere. He still breathed fast. She was full of revulsion against his body, yet she remembered the heat of his face, the touch of his lashes on her neck, and his loneliness spoke to her through her dislike of him, so that she longed to assuage him. The car stopped outside the house. She saw, without surprise, that it was her father. She remained where she was as Mr Grant stepped out of the car, and came in, his eyes narrowed because of the glare and the heat under the iron roof. He nodded at his daughter, and said: 'How do you do, Rooyen?' There being only two chairs, the men were standing; but the girl knew what she had to do, so she went out on to the veranda, and sat on the hot rough brick, spreading her blue skirts wide so that air could come under them and cool her thighs.

Now the two men were sitting in the chairs.

'Like some tea, Mr Grant?'

'I could do with a cup.'

Mr Rooyen shouted: 'Tea, boy!' and a shout came back from the kitchen. The girl could hear the iron stove being banged and blown into heat. It was nearly midday and she wondered what Mr Rooyen would have for lunch. That rancid beef?

She thought: If I were Maureen I wouldn't leave him alone, I'd look after him. I suppose she's some silly woman in an office in town ... But since he loved Maureen, she became her, and heard his voice saying: Maureen, Maureen, my love. Simultaneously she held her thin brown arms into the sun and felt how they were dark dry brown, she felt the flesh melting off hard lank bones.

'I spoke to Tobacco Paynter last night on the telephone, and he said he thinks Rich Mitchell might very well be in a different frame of mind by now, he's had a couple of good seasons.'

'If a couple of good seasons could make any difference to Mr Mitchell,' came Mr Rooyen's hot, resentful voice. 'But thank you, Mr Grant. Thank you.'

'He's close,' said her father. 'Near. Canny. Careful. Those North Country people are, you know.' He laughed. Mr Rooyen laughed, too, after a pause – he was a Dutchman, and had to work out the phrase 'North Country'.

'If I were you,' said Mr Grant, 'I'd get the whole of the lands on either side of the vlei under mealies the first season. Rich has never had it under cultivation, and the soil'd go sixteen bags to the acre for the first couple of seasons.'

'Yes, I've been thinking that's what I should do.'

She heard the sounds of the tea being brought in.

Mr Rooyen said to her through the door: 'Like a cup?' but she shook her head. She was thinking that if she were Maureen she'd fix up the house for him. Her father's next remark was therefore no surprise to her.

'Thought of getting married, Rooyen?'

He said bitterly: 'Take a look at this house, Mr Grant.'

'Well, you could build on a couple of rooms for about thirty, I reckon, I'll lend you my building boy. And a wife'd get it all spick-and-span in no time.'

Soon the two men came out, and Mr Rooyen stood on the veranda as she and her father got into the car and drove off. She waved to him, politely, with a polite smile.

She waited for her father to say something, but although he gave her several doubtful looks, he did not. She said: 'Mr Rooyen's in love with a girl called Maureen.'

'Did he say so?'

'Yes, he did.'

'Well,' he said, talking to her, as was his habit, one grown person to another, 'I'd say it was time he got married.'

'Yes.'

'Everything all right?' he enquired, having worked out exactly the right words to use.

'Yes, thank you.'

'Good.'

That season Rich Mitchell leased a couple of miles of his big vlei to Mr Rooyen, with a promise of sale later. Tobacco Paynter's wife got a governess from England, called Miss Betty Blunt, and almost at once Mr Rooyen and she were engaged. Mrs Paynter complained that she could never keep a governess longer than a couple of months, they always got married, but she couldn't have been too angry about it, because she laid on a big wedding for them, and all the district was there.

The girl was asked if she would be a bridesmaid, but she very politely refused. On the track to the station there was a new signpost pointing along a well-used road which said: 'The Big Vlei Farm. C. Rooyen.'

A LETTER FROM HOME

... Ja, but that isn't why I'm writing this time. You asked about Dick. You're worrying about him? — man! but he's got a poetry Scholarship from a Texas University and he's lecturing the Texans about letters and life too in Suid Afrika, South Africa to you (forgive the hostility) and his poems are read, so they tell me, wherever the English read poetry. He's fine, man, but I thought I'd tell you about Johannes Potgieter, remember him? Remember the young poet, The Young Poet? He was around that winter you were here, don't tell me you've forgotten those big melting brown eyes and those dimples. About ten years ago (ja, time flies,) he got a type of unofficial grace-gift of a job at St — University on the strength of those poems of his, and God they were good. Not that you or any other English-speaking domkop will ever know, because they don't translate out of Afrikaans. Remember me telling you and everyone else (give me credit for that, at least, I give the devil his due, when he's a poet) what a poet he was, how blerry good he was — but several people tried to translate Hans's poems, including me, and failed. Right. *Goed*. Meanwhile, a third of the world's population or is it a fifth, or to put it another way, $X5Y59$ million people speak English (and it's increasing by six births a minute) but one million people speak Afrikaans, and though I say it in a whisper, man, only a fraction of them can read it, I mean to read it. But Hans is still a great poet. Right.

He wasn't all that happy about being a sort of unofficial Laureate at that University, it's no secret some poets don't make Laureates. At the end of seven months he produced a book of poems which had the whole God-fearing place sweating and sniffing out heresy of all kinds, sin, sex, liberalism, brother-love, etc., and so on; but, of course, in a civilized country (I say this under my breath, or I'll get the sack from my University, and I've got four daughters these days, had you forgotten?) no one would see anything in them but good poetry. Which is how Hans saw them, poor innocent soul, he was surprised at what people saw in them, and he was all upset. He didn't like being called all those names, and the good country boys from their fine farms and the smart town boys from their big houses all started looking sideways and making remarks, and our Hans, he was reduced to pap, because he's not a fighter, Hans, he was never a taker of positions on the side of justice, freedom and the rest, for to tell you the truth, I don't think he ever got round to defining them. *Goed*. He resigned, in what might be called a dignified silence, but his friends knew it was just plain cowardice or if you like incomprehension about what the fuss was over, and he went to live in Blagspruit in the Orange Free, where his Tantie Gertrude had a house. He helped her in her store. Ja, that's what he did. What did we all say to this? Well, what do you think? The inner soul of the artist (etcetera) knows what is best, and he probably *needed* the Orange Free and his Auntie's store for his development. Well, something like that. To tell the truth, we didn't say much, he simply dropped out. And time passed. Ja. Then they made me editor of *Onwards*, and thinking about our indigenous poets I remembered Johannes Potgieter, and wrote What about a poem from you? – feeling bad because when I counted up the years it was eight since I'd even thought of him, even counting those times when one says drunk at dawn: Remember Hans? Now, there was a poet ...

No reply, so I let an editorial interval elapse and wrote again, and I got a very correct letter back. Well phrased. Polite. But not just that, it took me an hour to work out the handwriting – it was in a sort of Gothic print, each letter a work of art, like a medieval manuscript. But all he said, in that beautiful black art-writing was: he was very well, he hoped I was very well, the weather was good, except the rains were late, his Tantie Gertie was dead, and he was running the store. 'Jou vriend, Johannes Potgieter.'

Right. *Goed*. I was taking a trip to Joburg so I wrote and said I'd drop in at Blagspruit on my way back and I got another Manu Script, or Missal, saying he hoped to see me, and he would prepare Esther for my coming. I thought, he's married, poor *kerel*, and it was the first time I'd thought of him as anything but a born bachelor, and I was right – because when I'd done with Joburg, not a moment too soon, and driven down to the Orange Free, and arrived on the doorstep, there was Hans, but not a sign of a wife and Esther turned out to be – but first I take pleasure in telling you that the beautiful brown-eyed poet with his noble brow and pale dimpled skin was bald, he has a tonsure, I swear it; and he's fat, sort of smooth pale fat. He's like a monk, lard-coloured and fat and smooth. Esther is the cook, or rather, his jailer. She's a Zulu, a great fat woman and I swear she put the fear of God into me before I even got into the house. Tantie Gertie's house is a square brick four-roomed shack, you know the kind, with an iron roof and verandas – well, what you'd expect in Blagspruit. And Esther stood about six feet high in a white apron and a white doekie and she held a lamp up in one great black fist and looked into my face and sighed and went off into her kitchen singing Rock of Ages. Ja, I promise you. And I looked at Hans, and all he said was : 'It's okay, man, she likes you, come in.'

She gave us a great supper of roast mutton and pumpkin fritters and samp, and then some preserved fruit. She stood over us, arms folded, as we ate, and when Johannes left some mutton fat, she said in her mellow hymn-singing voice: 'Waste not, want not, Master Johannes.' And he ate it all up. Ja. She told me I should have some more peaches for my health, but I defied her and I felt as guilty as a small kicker, and I could see Hans eyeing me down the table and wondering where I got the nerve. She lives in the *kia* at the back, one small room with four children by various fathers, but no man, because God is more than enough for her now, you can see, with all those kids and Hans to bring up the right way. Auntie's store is a Drapery and General Goods in the main street, called Gertie's Store, and Hans was running it with a Coloured man. But I heard Esther with my own ears at supper saying to his bowed bald shamed head: 'Master Johannes, I heard from the cook at the Predikant's house today that the dried peaches have got worms in them.' And Hans said: 'Okay, Esther, I'll send them up some of the new stock tomorrow.'

Right. We spent all that evening talking and he was the same old Hans, you remember how he used to sit, saying not a blerry world, smiling that sweet dimpled smile of his, listening, listening, and then he'd ask a question, remember? Well, *do* you? Because it's only just now *I'm* beginning to remember. People'd be talking about, I don't know what, the Nats or the weather or the grape-crop, anything, and just as you'd start to get nervous because he never said anything he'd lean forward and start questioning, terribly serious, earnest, about some detail, something not quite central, if you know what I mean. He'd lean forward, smiling, smiling, and he'd say: 'You really mean that, it rained all morning? It rained all *morning*, is that the truth?' That's right you'd say, a bit uneasy, and he'd say, shaking his head, God, man, it rained all morning, you say ... And then there'd be a considerable silence till things picked up again. And half an hour later he'd say: 'You really mean it, the hanepoort grapes are good this year?'

Right. We drank a good bit of brandewyn that night, but in a civilized way, you know: Would you like another little drop, Martin, Ja, just a small tot, Hans, thank you, but we got pretty pickled, and when I woke Sunday morning, I felt like death, but Esther was setting down a tray of tea by my bed, all dressed up in her Sunday hat and her black silk saying: 'Goeie môre, Master du Preez, it's nearly time for church,' and I nearly said: 'I'm not a churchgoer, Esther,' but I thought better of it, because it came to me, can it be possible, has our Hans turned a God-fearing man in Blagspruit? So I said, 'Goed, Esther, thanks for telling me, and now just get out of here so that I can get dressed.' Otherwise she'd have dressed me, I swear it. And she gave me a majestic nod, knowing that God had spoken through her to send me to church, sinner that I was and stinking of cheap *dop* from the night before.

Right. Johannes and I went to Kerk, he in a black Sunday suit, if you'd believe such a thing, and saying: 'Good morning, Mr Stein, goeie môre, Mrs Van Esslin,' a solid and respected member of the congregation and, I thought, poor *kerel*, there but for the grace of God go I, if I had to live in this god-forsaken dorp stuck in the middle of the Orange Free State. And he looked like death after the brandewyn, and so did I, and we sat there swaying and sweating in that blerry little church through a sermon an hour and a half long, while all the faithful gave us nasty curious looks. Then we had a cold lunch, Esther having been worshipping at the kaffir church down in the Location, and we slept it all off and woke covered with flies and sweating, and it was as hot as hell, which is what Blagspruit is, hell. And he'd been there ten years, man, ten years ...

Right. It is Esther's afternoon off, and Johannes says he will make us some tea, but I see he is quite lost without her, so I say, give me a glass of water, and let's get out from under

this iron, that's all I ask. He looks surprised, because his hide
is hardened to it, but off we go, through the dusty little garden
full of marigolds and zinnias, you know those sun-baked
gardens with the barbed wire fences and the gates painted
dried-blood colour in those dorps stuck in the middle of the
veld, enough to make you get drunk even to think of them, but
Johannes is sniffing at the marigolds, which stink like turps,
and he sticks an orange zinnia in his lapel, and says: 'Esther
likes gardening.' And there we go along the main street, saying good afternoon to the citizens, for a half a mile, then we're
out in the veld again, just the veld. And we wander about,
kicking up the dust and watching the sun sink, because both of
us have just one idea, which is: how soon can we decently
start sundowning?

Then there was a nasty stink on the air, and it came from
a small bird impaled on a thorn on a thorn-tree which was
a butcher-bird's cache, have you ever seen one? Every blerry
thorn had a beetle or a worm or something stuck on it, and
it made me feel pretty sick, coming on top of everything, and
I was just picking up a stone to throw at the damned thorn-
tree, to spite the butcher-bird, when I saw Hans staring at
a lower part of this tree. On a long black thorn was a great
big brown beetle, and it was waving all its six legs and its
two feelers in rhythm, trying to claw the thorn out of its
middle, or so it looked, and it was writhing and wriggling, so
that at last it fell off the thorn, which was at right angles
from the soil, and it landed on its back, still waving its legs,
trying to up itself. At which Hans bent down to look at it
for some time, his two monk's hands on his upper thighs,
his bald head sweating and glowing red in the last sunlight.
*Then he bent down, picked up the beetle and stuck it back
on the thorn.* Carefully, you understand, so that the thorn
went back into the hole it had already made, you could see he
was trying not to hurt the beetle. I just stood and gaped,
like a domkop, and I remembered for some reason how one
used to feel when he leaned forward and said, all earnest
and involved: 'You say the oranges are no good this year?
Honestly, is that really true?' Anyway, I said: 'Hans, man,
for God's sake!' and then he looked at me, and he said, reproachfully, 'The ants would have killed it, just look!' Well,
the ground was swarming with ants of one kind or another, so

there was logic in it, but I said: 'Hans, let's drink, man, let's drink.'

Well, it was Sunday, and no bars open. I took a last look at the beetle, the black thorn through its oozing middle, waving its black legs at the setting sun, and I said: 'Back home, Hans, and to hell with Esther, we're going to get drunk.'

Esther was in the kitchen, putting out cold meat and tomatoes, and I said: 'Esther, you can take the evening off.'

She said: 'Master Hans, I have had all the Sunday afternoon off talking to Sister Mary.' Hans looked helpless at me, and I said: 'Esther, I'm giving you the evening off, good night.'

And Hans said, stuttering and stammering, 'That's right, Esther, I'll give you the evening off. Good night, Esther.'

She looked at him. Then at me. Hey, what a woman; hey, what a queen, man! She said, with dignity: 'Good night, Mr Johannes; good night, Mr du Preez.' Then she wiped her hands free of evil on her white apron, and she strode off, singing All Things Bright and Beautiful, and I tell you we felt as if we weren't good enough to wash Esther's *broekies*, and that's the truth.

Goed. We got out the brandy, never mind about the cold meat and the tomatoes, and about an hour later I reached my point at last, which was, what about the poems, and the reason I'd taken so long I was scared he'd say: 'Take a look at Blagspruit, man, take a look, is this the place for poems, Martin?' But when I asked, he leaned forward and stared at me, all earnest and intent, then he turned his head carefully to the right, to see if the door into the kitchen was shut, but it wasn't; and then left at the window, and that was open too, and then past me at the door to the veranda. Then he got up on tiptoes and very carefully shut all three, and then he drew the curtains. It gave me the *skriks*, man, I can tell you. Then he went to a great old black chest and took out a Manuscript, because it was all in the beautiful black difficult writing and gave it to me to read. And I sat and slowly worked it out, letter by letter, while he sat opposite, sweating and totting, and giving fearful looks over his shoulders.

What was it? Well, I was drunk, for one thing, and Hans sitting there all frightened scared me, but it was good, it was good, I promise you. A kind of chronicle of Blagspruit it was, the lives of the citizens – well, need I elaborate, since the lives of citizens are the same everywhere in the world, but worse in Suid Afrika, and worse a million times in Blagspruit. The Manu Script gave off a stink of church and right-doing, with the sin and the evil underneath, it had a medieval stink to it, naturally enough, for what is worse than the Kerk in this our Land? – but I'm saying this to you, remember, and I never said it, but what is worse than the stink of the Kerk and the God-fearing in this our feudal land?

But the poem. As far as I can remember, because I was full as a tick, it was a sort of prose chronicle that led up to and worked into the poems, you couldn't tell where they began or ended. The prose was stiff and old-fashioned, and formal, monk's language, and the poems, too. But I knew when I read it it was the best I'd read in years – since I read those poems of his ten years before, man, not since then. And don't forget, God help me, I'm an editor now, and I read poems day and night, and when I come on something like Hans's poems that night I have nothing to say but – *Goed.*

Right. I was working away there an hour or more because of that damned black ornamental script, then I put it down and I said: 'Hans, can I ask you a question?' And he looked this way and that over his shoulder first, then leaned forward, the lamplight shining on his pate, and he asked in a low trembling sinner's voice: 'What do you want to ask me, Martin?'

I said, 'Why this complicated handwriting? What for? It's beautiful, but why this monkey's puzzle?'

And he lowered his voice and said: 'It's so that Esther can't read it.'

I said: 'And what of it, Hans? Why not? Give me some more brandewyn and tell me.'

He said: 'She's a friend of the Predikant's cook, and her sister Mary works in the Mayor's kitchen.'

I saw it all. I was drunk, so I saw it. I got up, and I said: 'Hans, you're right. You're right a thousand times. If you're going to write stuff like this, as true and as beautiful as God and all his angels, then Esther mustn't read it. But why don't you let me take this back with me and print it in *Onwards*?'

He went white and looked as if I might knife him there and

then like totsti. He grabbed the manuscript from me and held it against his fat chest, and he said: 'They mustn't see it.'

'You're right,' I said, understanding him completely.

'It's dangerous keeping it here,' he said, darting fearful looks all around.

'Yes, you're right,' I said, and I sat down with a bump in my *rimpie* chair, and I said: 'Ja, if they found that, Hans . . .'

'They'd kill me,' he said.

I saw it, completely.

I was drunk. He was drunk. We put the manuscript *boekie* on the table and we put our arms around each other and we wept for the citizens of Blagspruit. Then we lit the hurricane-lamp in the kitchen, and he took his *boekie* under his arm, and we tiptoed out into the moonlight that stank of marigolds, and out we went down the main street, all dark as the pit now because it was after twelve and the citizens were asleep, and we went staggering down a tarmac street that shone in the moon-light between low dark houses and out into the veld. There we looked sorrowfully at each other and wept some sad brandy tears, and right in front of us, the devil aiding us, was a thorn-tree. All virgin it was, its big black spikes lifted up and shining in the devil's moon. And we wept a long time more, and we tore out the pages from his manuscript and we made them into little screws of paper and we stuck them all over the thorns and when there were none left, we sat under the thorn-tree in the moonlight, the black spiky thorns making thin purplish shadows all over us and over the white sand. Then we wept for the state of our country and the state of poetry. We drank a lot more brandy, and the ants came after it and us, so we staggered back down the gleaming sleeping main street of Blagspruit, and that's all I remember until Esther was stand-ing over me with a tin tray that had a teapot, teacup, sugar and some condensed milk, and she was saying: 'Master du Preez, where is Master Hans?'

I saw the seven o'clock sun outside the window, and I re-membered everything and I sat up and I said: 'My God!'

And Esther said, 'God has not been in this house since half past five on Saturday last.' And went out.

Right. I got dressed, and went down the main street, draw-ing looks from the Monday morning citizens, all of whom had probably been watching us staggering along last night from behind their black-drawn curtains. I reached the veld and there was Hans. A wind had got up, a hot dust-devilish wind, and it blew about red dust and bits of grit, and leaves, and dead grass into the blue sky, and those pale dry bushes that leave their roots and go bouncing and twirling all over the empty sand, like dervishes, round and around, and then up and around, and there was Hans, letting out yelps and cries and shouts, and he was chasing about after screws of paper that were whirling around among the dust and stuff.

I helped him. The thorn-tree had three squirls of paper tugging and blowing from spikes of black thorn, so I collected those, and we ran after the blowing white bits that had the black beautiful script on them, and we got perhaps a third back. Then we sat under the thorn-tree, the hard, sharp black shadows over us and the sand, and we watched a dust-devil whirling columns of yellow sand and his poems up and off into the sky.

I said: 'But, Hans, you could write them down again, couldn't you? You couldn't have forgotten them, surely?'

And he said: 'But, Martin, anyone can read them now, don't you see that, man? Esther could come out here next afternoon off, and pick any one of those poems up off the earth and read it. Or suppose the predikant or the mayor got their hands on them?'

Then I understood. I promise you, it had never crossed my domkop mind until that moment. I swear it. I simply sat there sweating out guilt and brandy, and I looked at that poor madman, and then I remembered back ten years and I thought: You idiot. You fool.

Then at last I got intelligent and I said: 'But, Hans, even if Esther and the predikant and the mayor did come out here and pick up your poems, like leaves, off the bushes, they couldn't understand one word, because they are written in that *slim* black script you worked out for yourself.'

I saw his poor crazy face get more happy, and he said: 'You think so, Martin? Really? You really think so?'

I said: 'Ja, it's the truth.' And he got all happy and safe, while I thought of those poems whirling around for ever, or until the next rainstorm, around the blue sky with the dust and the bits of shining grass.

And I said: 'Anyway, at the best, only perhaps a thousand or two thousand people would understand that beautiful *boekie*. Try to look at it that way, Hans, it might make you feel better.'

By this time he looked fine, he was smiling and cheered up. Right.

We got up and dusted each other off, and I took him home to Esther. I asked him to let me take the poems we'd rescued back to publish in *Onwards* but he got desperate again and said : 'No, no, do you want to kill me? Do you want them to kill me? You're my friend, Martin, you can't do that.'

So I told Esther that she had a great man in her charge, through whom Heaven Itself spoke, and she was right to take such care of him. But she merely nodded her queenly white-doecked head and said : 'Good-bye, Master du Preez, and may God be with you.'

So I came home to Kapstaad.

A week ago I got a letter from Hans, but I didn't see at once that it was from him, it was in ordinary writing, like yours or mine, but rather unformed and wild, and it said : 'I am leaving this place. They know me now. They look at me. I'm going North to the river. Don't tell Esther. Jou vriend, Johannes Potgieter.'

    Right.

      Jou vriend,

        Martin du Preez.

HUNGER

It is dark inside the hut, and very cold. Yet around the oblong shape that is the doorway where a sack hangs, for the sake of comely decency, is a diffusing yellow glare, and through holes in the sack come fingers of yellow warmth, nudging and prodding at Jabavu's legs. 'Ugh,' he mutters, drawing up his feet and kicking at the blanket to make it stretch over him. Under Jabavu is a reed mat, and where its coolness touches him he draws back, grumbling in his sleep. Again his legs sprawl out, again the warm fingers prod him, and he is filled with a rage of resentment. He grabs at sleep, as if a thief were trying to take it from him; he wraps himself in sleep like a blanket that persists in slipping off; there is nothing he has ever wanted, nothing he will ever want again as he wants sleep at this moment. He leans greedily towards it as towards a warm drink on a cold night. He drinks it, guzzles it, and is sinking contentedly into oblivion when words come dropping through it like stones through thick water. 'Ugh!' mutters Jabavu again. He lies as still as a dead rabbit. But the words continue to fall into his ears, and although he has sworn to himself not to move, not to sit up, and hold to this sleep which they are trying to take from him, he nevertheless sits up, and his face is surly and unwilling.

His brother, Pavu, on the other side of the dead ashes of the fire which is in the middle of the mud floor, also sits up. He, too, is sulking. His face is averted and he blinks slowly as he rises to his feet, lifting the blanket with him. Yet he remains respectfully silent while his mother scolds.

'Children, your father has already been waiting for you as long as it takes to hoe a field.' This is intended to remind them of their duty, to put back into their minds what their minds have let slip – that already, earlier, they have been awakened, their father laying his hand silently first on one shoulder and then on another.

Pavu guiltily folds his blanket and lays it on the low earth mound on one side of the hut, and then stands waiting for Jabavu.

But Jabavu is leaning on his elbow by the ashen smudge of last night's fire, and he says to his scolding mother: 'Mother, you make as many words as the wind brings grains of dust.' Pavu is shocked. He would never speak any way but respectfully to his parents. But also, he is not shocked, for this is Jabavu the Big Mouth. And if the parents say with sorrow that in their day no child would speak to his parents as Big Mouth speaks, then it is true, too, that now there are many children who speak thus – and how can one be shocked by something that happens every day?

Jabavu says, breaking into a shrill whirl of words from the mother: 'Ah, mother, *shut up*!' The words 'shut up' are in English. And now Pavu is really shocked, with the whole of himself, not merely with the part of him that pays tribute to the old forms of behaviour. He says, quickly, to Jabavu: 'And now that is enough. Our father is waiting.' He is so ashamed that he lifts the sacking from the door and steps outside, blinking into the sunlight. The sun is pale bright gold, and quickly gathering heat. Pavu moves his stiff limbs in it as if it were hot water, and then stands beside his father. 'Good morning, my father,' he says; and then the old man greets him: 'Good morning, my son.'

The old man wears a brown blanket striped with red, folded over his shoulder and held with a large steel safety-pin. He carries a hoe for the fields, and the spear of his forefathers with which to kill a rabbit or buck if one should show itself. The boy has no blanket. He wears a vest that is rubbed into holes, tucked into a loincloth. He also carries a hoe.

From inside the hut come voices. The mother is still scolding. They can hear scraping sounds and the small knock of wood – she is kneeling to remove the dead ash and to build the new fire. It is as if they can see her crouching there, coaxing the new day's fire to life. And it is as if they can see Jabavu huddled on his mat, his face sullenly turned away from her while she scolds.

They look at each other, ashamed; then they look away past the little huts of the native village; they see disappearing among the trees a crowd of their friends and relatives from these huts. The other men are already on their way to the fields. It is nearly six in the morning. The father and Pavu, avoiding each other's eyes because of their shame, move off after them. Jabavu must come by himself – if he comes at all.

Once the men from this hut were first at the fields, once their fields were first hoed, first planted, first reaped. Now they were last, and it is because of Jabavu who works or does not work as he feels inclined.

Inside the hut the mother kneels at the fire, watching a small glow of flame rise inside the hollow of her sheltering hand. The warmth contents her, melts her bitterness.

'Ah, my Big Mouth, get up now,' she says with tender reproach. 'Are you going to lie there all day while your father and brother work?' She lifts her face, ready to smile forgiveness at the bad son. But Jabavu leaps from the blanket as if he had found a snake there, and roars: 'My name is Jabavu, not Big Mouth. Even my own, my given name, you take from me!' He stands there stiff, accusing, his eyes quivering with unhappy anger. And his mother slowly drops her eyes, as if guilty.

Now this is strange, for Jabavu is a hundred times in the wrong; while she has always been a proper mother, a good wife. Yet for that moment it is between these two, mother and son, as if she has done wrong and he is justly accusing her. Soon his body loses the stiffness of anger and he leans idly against the wall, watching her; and she turns towards the crescent-shaped earth shelf behind her for a pot. Jabavu watches intently. Now there is a new thought, a new need – which kind of utensil will she bring out? When he sees what it is, he quivers out a sigh of relief, and his mother hears that sigh and wonders and marvels. She has brought out not the cooking pot for the morning porridge, but the petrol tin in which she heats water for washing.

The father and Pavu, all the men of the village, will wash when they return from the fields for the first meal, or in the river by the place where they work. But Jabavu's whole being, every atom of his brain and body is concentrated on the need that she should serve him thus – should warm water especially so that he may wash in it now. And yet at other times Jabavu is careless of his cleanness.

The mother sets the half-tin on the stones in the clump of red and roaring flames, and almost at once a wisp of bluish steam curls off the rocking water. She hears Jabavu sigh again. She keeps her head lowered, wondering. She is thinking that it is as if inside Jabavu, her son, some kind of hungry animal is living, looking out of his eyes, speaking from his mouth. She loves Jabavu. She thinks of him as brave, affectionate, clever, strong, and respectful. She believes that he is all these things, that the fierce animal which has made its lair inside Jabavu is not her son. And yet her husband, her other children, and indeed the whole village call him Jabavu the Big Mouth, Jabavu the greedy, the boastful, the bad son, who will certainly one day run off to the white man's town and become one of the matsotsis, the criminal youth. Yes, that is what they say, and she knows it. There are even times when she says so herself. And yet – fifteen years ago there was a year of famine. It was not a famine as is known in other countries that this woman has never heard of, China, perhaps, or India. But it was a season of drought, and some people died, and many were hungry.

The year before the drought they sold their grain as was usual to the African store, keeping sufficient for themselves. They were given the prices that were fair for that year. The white man at that store, a Greek, stored the grain, as was his custom, for resale to these same natives when they ran short, as they often did – a shiftless lot, always ready to sell more than they should for the sake of the glittering shillings with which they could buy head-cloths or bangles or cloth. And that year, in the big markets in America and Europe there was a change of prices. The Greek sold all the maize he had to the big stores in town, and sent his men around the native villages, coaxing them to sell everything they had. He offered a little more money than they had been used to get. He was buying at half of what he could get in the city. And all would have been well if there had not been that season of drought. For the mealies wilted in the fields, the cobs struggled towards full-ness, but remained as small as a fist. There was panic in the villages and people came streaming towards the Greek store and to all the other African stores all over the country. The Greek said Yes, Yes, he had the maize, he always had the maize, but of course at the new price laid down by the Government. And of course the people did not have the money to buy this newly expensive maize.

So in the villages there was a year of hunger. That year, Jabavu's elder sister, three years old, came running playfully to her mother's teats, and found herself smacked off, like a troublesome puppy. The mother was still feeding Jabavu, who had always been a demanding, hungry child, and there was a new baby a month old. The winter was cold and dusty. The men went hunting for hares and buck, the women searched through the bush all day for greens and roots, and there was hardly any grain for the porridge. The dust filled the villages, the dust hung in sullen clouds in the air, blew into the huts and into the nostrils of the people. The little girl died – it was said because she had breathed too much dust. And the mother's breasts hung limp, and when Jabavu came tugging at her dress she smacked him off. She was sick with grief because of the death of the child, and also with fear for the baby. For now the buck and hares were scarce, they had been hunted so relentlessly, and one cannot keep life on leaves and roots. But Jabavu did not relinquish his mother's breasts so easily. At night, as she lay on her mat, the new baby beside her, Jabavu came pushing and struggling to her milk, and she woke, startled, saying: 'Ehh, but this child of mine is strong.' He was only a year old, yet she had to use all her strength to fend him off. In the dark of the hut her husband woke and lifted Jabavu, screaming and kicking, away from her, and away from the tender new baby. That baby died, but by then Jabavu had turned sullen and was fighting like a little leopard for what scraps of food there were. A little skeleton he was, with loose brown skin and enormous, frantic eyes, nosing around in the dust for fallen mealies or a scrap of sour vegetable.

This is what the mother thinks of as she crouches watching the wisps of steam curl off the water. For her Jabavu is three children, she loves him still with all the bereaved passion of that terrible year. She thinks: It was then, when he was so tiny, that Jabavu the Big Mouth was made – yes, the people called him the Big Mouth even then. Yes, it is the fault of the Long Hunger that Jabavu is as he is.

But even while she is excusing him thus, she cannot help remembering how he was as a new baby. The women used to laugh as they watched him suck. 'That one was born hungry,' they said, 'that one will make a big man!' For he was such a big child, so fierce in his sucking, always crying for food ... and again she excuses him, fondly: If he had not been so, if he had not fed his strength from the time he was born, he too would have died, like the others. And at this thought she lifts her eyes, filled with love and pride – but she lowers them again quickly. For she knows that a big lad, like Jabavu, who is nearly seventeen years old, resents it when a mother looks at

him, remembering the baby he was. Jabavu only knows what
he is, and that very confusedly. He is still leaning against the
mud wall. He does not look at his mother, but at the water
which is heating for his use. And inside there is such a storm
of anger, love, pain, and resentment: he feels so much, and all
at once, that it is as if a wind-devil had got into him. He knows
quite well that he does not behave as he ought, yet there is
no other way he can behave; he knows that among his own
people he is like a black bull in a herd of goats – yet he was
bred from them; he wants only the white man's town, yet he
knows nothing of it save what he has heard from travellers.
And suddenly into his head comes the thought: If I go to the
white man's town my mother will die of grief.

Now he looks at his mother. He does not think of her as
young, old, pretty, ugly. She is his mother, who came properly
endowed to her husband, after a proper amount of cattle had
been paid for her. She has borne five children, three of whom
live. She is a good cook and respectful to her husband. She is
a mother, as a mother should be, according to the old ideas.
Jabavu does not despise these ideas: simply, they are not for
him. There is no need to despise something from which one
is already freed. Jabavu's wife will not be like his mother: he
does not know why, but he knows it.

His mother is, in fact, according to the new ideas, not yet
thirty-five years old, a young woman who would still look
pretty in a dress such as the townswomen wear. But she wears
some cotton stuff, blue, bound around her breasts leaving her
shoulders bare, and a blue cotton skirt bunched in such a way
that the heat will not scorch her legs. She has never thought
of herself as old, young, modern or old-fashioned. Yet she,
too, knows that Jabavu's wife will not be as she is, and towards
this unknown woman her mind lifts in respectful but fearful
wonder. She thinks: Perhaps if this son of mine finds a
woman who is like him, then he will no longer be like a wild
bull among oxen ... this thought comforts her; she allows her
skirt to fall as it will, steps back from the scorching heat, and
lifts the tin off the flames. 'Now you may wash, my son,' she
says. Jabavu grabs the tin, as if it might run away from him,
and carries it outside. And then he stops and slowly sets it
down. Sullenly, as if ashamed of this new impulse, he goes
back into the hut, lifts his blanket which lies where he let it
drop, folds it and lays it on the earthen shelf. Then he rolls

his reed mat, sets it against the wall, and also rolls and places his brother's mat. He glances at his mother, who is watching him in silence, sees her soft and compassionate eyes . . . but this he cannot bear. Rage fills him; he goes out.

She is thinking: See, this is my son! How quickly and neatly he folds the blanket, sets the mats against the wall. How easily he lifts the tin of heavy water! How strong he is, and how kind! Yes, he thinks of me, and returns to tidy the hut, he is ashamed of his thoughtlessness. So she muses, telling herself again and again how kind her Jabavu is, although she knows he is not kind, and particularly not to himself; and that when a kind impulse takes him such as it has now, Jabavu behaves as if he has performed a bad deed and not a good one. She knows that if she thanks him he will shout at her. She glances through the door of the hut and sees her son, strong and powerful, his bronze skin shining with health in the new morning's sun. But his face is knotted with anger and resentment. She turns away so as not to see it.

Jabavu carries the tin of water to the shade of a big tree, strips off his loincloth and begins to wash. The comforting hot water flows over him, he likes the tingle of the strong soap: Jabavu was the first in all the village to use the white man's soap. He thinks: I, Jabavu, wash in good, warmed water, and with proper soap. Not even my father washes when he wakes . . . He sees some women walking past, and pretends he does not see them. He knows what they are thinking, but says to himself: Stupid kraal women, they don't know anything. But I know that Jabavu is like a white man, who washes when he leaves his sleep.

The women slowly go past and their faces are sorrowful. They look at the hut where his mother is kneeling to cook, and they shake their heads and speak their compassion for this poor woman, their friend and sister, who has bred such a son. But in their voices is another note of emotion, and Jabavu knows it is there, though he cannot hear them speak. Envy? Admiration? Neither of these. But it is not the first time a child like Jabavu has been bred by the villages. And these women know well that the behaviour of Jabavu can be understood only by thinking of the world of the white man. The white man has brought evil and good, things to admire and things to fear, and it is hard to know one from the other. But when an aeroplane flies far overhead like a shining beetle through the air, and when the big motor cars drive past on the road North, they think also of Jabavu and of the young people like him.

Jabavu has finished washing. He stands idle under the big tree, his back turned to the huts of the village, quite naked, covering what should not be seen of his body with his cupped hand. The yellow patches of sunlight tremble and sway on his skin. He feels the shifting warmth and begins to sing with pleasure. Then an unpleasant thought stops the singing: he has nothing to wear but the loincloth which is the garb of a kraal-boy. He owns an old pair of shorts which were too small for him years ago. They once belonged to the son of the Greek at the store when that son was ten years old.

Jabavu takes the shorts from the crotch of the tree and tries to tug them over his hips. They will not go. Suddenly they split behind. Cautiously he twists himself to see how big the tear is. His buttock is sticking out of the material. He frowns, takes a big needle such as is used for sewing grain sacks, threads it with fine strands of fibre stripped from under the bark of a tree, and begins to make a lace-work of the fibre across his behind. He does this without taking the shorts off: he stands twisted, using the needle with one hand and holding the edges of frayed material with the other. At last it is done. The shorts decently cover him. They are old, they grip him as tight as the bark of a tree grips the white wood underneath, but they are trousers and not a loincloth.

Now he carefully slides the needle back under the bark of the tree, rolls his loincloth into the crotch of the trunk, then lifts down a comb from where it is laced through a frond of leaves. He kneels before a tiny fragment of mirror that he found in a rubbish-heap behind the Greek store, and combs his thick hair. He combs until his arm is tired, but at last the parting shows clear down his scalp. He sticks the steel comb jauntily at the back of his head, like the comb of a fine cock, and looks at himself happily in the mirror. Now his hair is done like a white man's.

He lifts the tin and throws the water in a fine, gleaming curve over the bushes, watching the drops fall in a glittering shower; and an old hen, which was seeking shelter from the heat, runs away squawking. He roars with laughter, seeing that flapping old hen. Then he tosses the tin away into the bushes. It is new and glints among the green leaves. He looks at the tin, while an impulse stirs in him – that same impulse that always hurts him so, leaving him limp and confused. He is thinking that his mother, who paid a shilling for the tin in the Greek store, will not know where it is. Secretly, as if he were doing something wicked, he lifts the tin, carries it to the door of the hut and, stretching his hand carefully around the opening, sets it inside. His mother, who is stirring meal into boiling water for the porridge, does not turn around. Yet he knows that she knows what he is doing. He waits for her to turn – if she does and thanks him, then he will shout at her; already he feels the anger crowding his throat. And when she does not turn he feels even more anger, and a hot blackness rocks across his eyes. He cannot endure that anyone, not even his mother, should understand why he creeps like a thief to do a kind thing. He walks swaggering back to the shade of the tree, muttering: I am Jabavu, I am Jabavu – as if this were the answer to any sad look or reproachful words or understanding silence.

He squats under the tree, but carefully, so that his trousers may not fall completely to pieces. He looks at the village. It is a native kraal, such as one may see anywhere in Africa, a casual arrangement of round mud huts with conical grass roofs. A few are square, influenced by the angled dwelling of the white man. Beyond the kraal is a belt of trees, and beyond them, the fields. Jabavu thinks: This is my village – and immediately his thoughts leave it and go to the white man's town. Jabavu knows everything about this town, although he has never been there. When someone returns, or passes through this village, Jabavu runs to listen to the tales of the wonderful living, the adventure, the excitement. He has a very clear picture in his mind of the place. He knows the white man's house is always of brick, not of mud. He has seen such a house. The Greek at the store has a brick house, two fine rooms, with chairs in them, and tables, and beds lifted off the floor on legs. Jabavu knows the white man's town will be of such houses, many many houses, perhaps as many as will reach from where he is sitting to the big road going north that is half a mile away. His mind is bright with wonder and excitement as he imagines it, and he looks at his village with impatient dissatisfaction. The village is for the old people, it is right for them. And Jabavu can remember no time when he has not felt as he does now; it is as if he were born with the knowledge that the village was his past, not his future. Also, that he was born longing for the moment when he could go to the town. A hunger rages in him for that town. What is this hunger? Jabavu does not know. It is so strong that a voice speaks in his ear, I want, I want, as if his fingers curl graspingly in a movement. We want, as if every fibre of his body sings and shouts, I want, I want, I want . . .

He wants everything and nothing. He does not say to himself: I want a motor car, an aeroplane, a house. Jabavu is intelligent, and knows that the black man does not own such things. But he wants to be near them, to see them, touch them, perhaps serve them. When he thinks of the white man's town he sees something beautiful, richly coloured, strange. A rainbow to him means the white man's town, or a fine warm morning, or a clear night when there is a dancing. And this exciting life waits for him, Jabavu, he was born for it. He imagines a place of light and warmth and laughter, and people saying: Hau! Here is our friend Jabavu! Come, Jabavu, and sit with us.

This is what he wants to hear. He does not want to hear any longer the sorrowful voices of the old people: The Big Mouth, look at the Big Mouth, listen to the Big Mouth hatching out words again.

He wants so terribly that his body aches with wanting. He begins to day-dream. This is his dream, slipping, half-ashamed, through his mind. He sees himself walking to town, he enters the town, a black policeman greets him: 'Why, Jabavu, so there you are, I come from your village, do you remember me?' 'My friend,' answers Jabavu, 'I have heard of you from our brothers, I have been told you are now a son of the Government.' 'Yes, Jabavu, now I serve the Government. See, I have a fine uniform, and a place to sleep, and friends. I am respected both by the white people and the black. I can help you.' This son of the Government takes Jabavu to his room and gives him food – bread perhaps, white bread, such as the white man eats, and tea with milk. Jabavu has heard of such food from people returning to the village. Then the son of the Government takes Jabavu to the white man whom he serves. 'This is Jabavu,' he says, 'my friend from my village.' 'So this is Jabavu,' says the white man. 'I heard of you, my son. But no one told me how strong you were, how clever. You must put on this uniform and become a son of the Government.' Jabavu has seen such policemen, because once a year they come gathering taxes from the villages. Big men, important men, black men in uniform ... Jabavu sees himself in this uniform, and his eyes dazzle with wanting. He sees himself walking around the white man's town. Yes, Baas, no, Baas; and to his own people he is very kind. They say, Yes, that is our Jabavu, from our village, do you remember? He is our good brother, he helps us ...

Jabavu's dream has flown so high that it crashes and he blinks his eyes in waking. For he has heard things about the town which tell him this dream is nonsense. One does not become a policeman and a son of the Government so easily. One must be clever indeed and Jabavu gets up and goes to a big, flat stone, first looking around in case anyone is watching. He flips the stone over, brings from under it a roll of paper, quickly replaces the stone and sits on it. He has taken the paper off parcels of things he has bought from the Greek store. Some are all print, some have little coloured pictures, many together, making a story. The bright sheets of pictures are what he likes best.

They have taught Jabavu to read. He spreads them out on the ground and bends over them, his lips forming the words. The very first picture shows a big white man on a big black horse, with a great gun that spits red fire. 'Bang!' say the letters above. 'Bang,' says Jabavu slowly. 'B-a-n-g.' That was the first word he learned. The second picture shows a beautiful white girl, with her dress slipping off her shoulder, her mouth open. 'Help!' say the letters. 'Help,' says Jabavu, 'Help, help.' He goes on to the next. Now the big white man has caught the girl around the waist and is lifting her on to the horse. Some wicked white men with big black hats are pointing guns at the girl and the good white man. 'Hold me, honey,' say the letters. Jabavu repeats the words. He slowly works his way to the foot of the page. He knows this story by heart and loves it. But the story on the next page is not so easy. It is about some yellow men with small, screwed-up faces. They are wicked. There is another big white man who is good and carries a whip. It is that whip that troubles Jabavu, for he knows it; he was slashed himself by the Greek at the store for being cheeky. The words say: 'Grrrr, you Gooks, this'll teach you!' The white man beats the little yellow men with the whip, and Jabavu feels nothing but confusion and dismay. For in the first story he is the white man on the horse who rescues the beautiful girl from the bad men. But in this story he cannot be the white man because of the whip ... Many many hours has Jabavu spent puzzling over that story, and particularly over the words which say: 'You little yellow snakes ...' There goes the whip-lash curling over the picture, and for a long time Jabavu thought the word snake meant that whip. Then he saw the yellow men were the snakes ... And in the end, just as he has done so often before, he turns the page, giving up that difficult story, and goes on to another.

Jabavu cannot merely read the stories in pictures, but also simple print. On the rubbish heap behind the Greek store he once found a child's alphabet, or rather, half of one. It was a long time before he understood it was half only. He used to sit, hour after hour, fitting the letters in the alphabet to words like Bang! and later, to English words he already knew, from the sorrowful, admiring stories that were told about the white men. Black, white, colour, native, kaffir, mealiemeal, smell, bad, dirty, stupid, work. These were some of the words he knew how to speak before he could read them. After a long time he completed the alphabet for himself. A very long time – it took him over a year of sitting under that tree thinking and thinking while the people of the village laughed and called him lazy. Later still he tried the print without pictures. And it was so hard it was as if he had learned nothing. Months passed. Slowly, very slowly, the sheet of black letters put on meaning. Jabavu will never forget, as long as he lives, that day when he first puzzled out a whole sentence. This was the sentence: 'The African must eat beans and vegetables as well as meat and nuts to keep him healthy.' When he understood that long and difficult sentence, he rolled on the ground with pride, laughing and saying: 'The white men write that we must eat these things all the time! That's what I shall eat when I go to the white man's town.'

Some of the words he cannot understand, no matter how hard he tries. 'Any person who contravenes any provision of any of the regulations (which contain fifty clauses) is liable to a fine of £25 or three months' imprisonment.' Jabavu has spent many hours over that sentence, and it still means nothing to him. Once he walked five miles to the next village to ask a clever man who knew English what it meant. He did not know either. But he taught Jabavu a great deal of English to speak. Jabavu speaks it now quite well. And he has marked all the difficult words on the newspaper with a piece of charcoal, and will ask someone what they mean, when he finds such a person. Perhaps when a traveller returns for a visit from the town? But there is no one expected. One of the young men, the son of Jabavu's father's brother, was to have come, but he went to Johannesburg instead. Nothing has been heard of him for a year. In all, there are seven young men from this village working in the town, and two in Johannesburg at the mines. Any one of them may come next week or perhaps next year ... The hunger in Jabavu swells and mutters: When will I go, when, when, when? I am sixteen, I am a man. I can speak English, I can read the newspaper. I can understand the pictures – but at this thought he reminds himself he does not understand all the pictures. Patiently he turns back the sheet and goes to the story about the little yellow men. What have they done to be beaten with the whip? Why are some men yellow, some white, some black, some bronze, like himself? Why is there a war in the country of the little yellow men? Why are they called snakes and Gooks? Why, why, why? But Jabavu cannot frame the questions to which he needs the answers, and the frustration feeds that hunger in him. I must go to the white man's town, there I will know, there I will learn.

He thinks, half-heartedly: Perhaps I should go by myself? But it is a frightening thought, he does not have the courage. He sits loose and listless under the tree, letting his hand stir patterns in the dust, and thinks: Perhaps someone will return soon from the town and I may go back with him? Or perhaps I can persuade Pavu to come with me? But his heart stirs painfully at the thought: surely his mother and father will die of grief if both sons go at once! For their daughter left home three years before to work as a nanny at the farm twenty miles away, so that they only see her two or three times a year, and that only for a day.

But the hunger swells up until his regret for his parents is consumed by it, and he thinks: I shall speak to Pavu. I shall make him come with me.

Jabavu is still sitting under the tree thinking when the men come back from the fields, his father and brother with them. At the sight of them he at once gets up and goes to the hut. Now his hunger is for food, or rather that he should be there first and be served first.

His mother is laying the white porridge on each plate. The plates are of earthenware, made by herself, and decorated with black patterns on the red. They are beautiful, but Jabavu longs for tin plates such as he has seen in the Greek store. The spoons are of tin, and it gives him pleasure to touch them.

After she has slapped the porridge on to the plates, she carefully smooths the surfaces with the back of the spoon to make them nice and shiny. She has cooked a stew of roots and leaves from the bush, and she pours a little of this over each white mound. She sets the plates on a mat on the floor. Jabavu at once begins to eat. She looks at him; she wants to ask: Why do you not wait, as is proper, until your father is eating? She does not say it. When the father and brother come in, setting their hoes and the spear against the wall, the father looks at Jabavu, who is eating in disagreeable silence, eyes lowered, and says: 'One who is too tired to work is not too tired to eat.'

Jabavu does not reply. He has almost finished the porridge. He is thinking that there is enough for another big plateful. He is consumed with a craving to eat and eat until his belly is heavy. He hastily gulps down the last mouthfuls and pushes his plate towards his mother. She does not at once take it up to refill it, and rage surges in Jabavu, but before the words can come bubbling out of his mouth, the father, who has noticed, begins to talk. Jabavu lets his hands fall and sits listening.

The old man is tired and speaks slowly. He has said all this very often before. His family listen and yet do not listen. What he says already exists, like words on a piece of paper, to be read or not, to be listened to or not.

'What is happening to our people?' he asks, sorrowfully. 'What is happening to our children? Once, in our kraals, there was peace, there was order. Every person knew what it was they should do and how that thing should be done. The sun rose and sank, the moon changed, the dry season came, then the rains, a man was born and lived and died. We knew, then, what was good and what was evil.'

His wife, the mother, thinks: He longs so much for the old times, which he understood, that he has forgotten how one tribe harried another, he has forgotten that in this part of the country we lived in terror because of the tribes from the South. Half our lives were spent like rabbits in the kopjes, and we women used to be driven off like cattle to make wives for men of other tribes. She says nothing of what she thinks, only: 'Yes, yes, my husband, that is very true.' She lifts more porridge from the pot and lays it on his plate, although he has hardly touched his food. Jabavu sees this; his muscles tighten and his eyes, fixed on his mother, are hungry and resentful.

The old man goes on: 'And now it is as if a great storm is among our people. The men go to the towns and to the mines and farms, they learn bad ways, and when they return to us they are strangers, with no respect for their elders. The young women become prostitutes in the towns, they dress like white women, they will take any man for husband, regardless of the laws of relationship. And the white man uses us for servants, and there is no limit set to this time of bondage.'

Pavu has finished his porridge. He looks at his mother. She lays some porridge on his plate and pours vegetable relish over it. Now, having served the men who work, she serves the one who has not. She gives Jabavu what is left, which is not much, and scrapes out what is left of the relish. She does not look at him. She knows of the pain, a child's pain, that sears him because she served him last. And Jabavu does not eat it, simply because he was served last. His stomach does not want it. He sits, sullenly, and listens to his father. What the old man says is true, but there is a great deal he does not say, and can never say, because he is old and belongs to the past. Jabavu looks at his brother, sees the thoughtful, frowning face, and knows that Pavu's thoughts are his own.

'What will become of us? When I look into the future it is as if I see a night that has no end. When I hear the tales that are brought from the white man's towns my heart is dark as a valley under a raincloud. When I hear how the white man corrupts our children it is as if my head were filled with a puddle of muddy water, I cannot think of these things, they are too difficult.'

Jabavu looks at his brother and makes a small movement of his head. Pavu excuses himself politely to his father and his mother, and this politeness must be enough for both, for Jabavu says nothing at all.

The old man stretches himself on his mat in the sun for half an hour's rest before returning to the fields. The mother takes the plates and pot to wash them. The young men go out to the big tree.

'It was heavy work without you, my brother,' are the reproachful words that Jabavu hears. He has been expecting them, but he frowns, and says: 'I have been thinking.' He wants his brother to ask eagerly after these important and wonderful thoughts, but Pavu goes on: 'There is half a field to finish, and it is right that you should work with us this afternoon.'

Jabavu feels that extraordinary resentment rising in him, but he manages to shut it down. He understands that it is not reasonable to expect his brother to see the importance of the pictures on the paper and words that are printed. He says: 'I have been thinking about the white man's town.' He looks importantly at his brother, but all Pavu says is: 'Yes, we know that it will soon be time for you to leave us.'

Jabavu is indignant that his secret thoughts should be spoken of so casually. 'No one has said I must leave. Our father and mother speak all the time, until their jaws must ache with saying it, that good sons stay in the village.'

Pavu says gently, with a laugh: 'Yes, they talk like all the old people, but they know that the time will come for both of us to go.'

First Jabavu frowns and stares; then he exults: 'You will come with me!'

But Pavu lets his head droop. 'How can I come with you?' he temporizes. 'You are older, it is right that you should go. But our father cannot work the fields by himself. I may come later, perhaps.'

'There are other fathers who have sons. Our father talks of the custom, but if a custom is something that happens all the time, then it is now a custom with us that young men leave the villages and go to the city.'

Pavu hesitates. His face is puckered with distress. He wants to go to the city. Yet he is afraid. He knows Jabavu will go soon, and travelling with his big, strong, clever brother will take the fear from it.

Jabavu can see it all on his face, and suddenly he feels nervous, as if a thief were abroad. He wonders if this brother dreams and plans for the white man's city as he does; and at the thought he stretches out his arms in a movement which suggests he is keeping something for himself. He feels that his own wanting is so strong that nothing less than the whole of the white man's city will be enough for him, not even some left over for his brother! But then his arms fall and he says, cunningly: 'We will go together. We will help each other. We will not be alone in that place where travellers say a stranger may be robbed and even killed.'

He glances at Pavu, who looks as if he were listening to lovers' talk.

'It is right for brothers to be together. A man who goes alone is like a man who goes hunting alone into dangerous country. And when we are gone, our father will not need to grow so much food, for he will not have our stomachs to fill. And when our sister marries, he will have her cattle and her lobola money ...' He talks on and on, trying to keep his voice soft and persuasive, although it keeps rising on waves of passionate desire for those good things in the city. He tries to talk as a reasonable man talks of serious things, but his hands twitch and his legs will not keep still.

He is still making words while Pavu listens when the father comes out of the hut and looks across at them. Both rise and follow him to the fields. Jabavu goes because he wants to win Pavu over, for no other reason, and he talks softly to him as they wind through the trees.

There are two rough patches in the bush. Mealies grow there and between the mealies are pumpkins. The plants are straggly, the pumpkins few. Not long ago a white man came from the city in a car, and was angry when he saw these fields. He said they were farming like ignorant people, and that in other parts of the country the black people were following the advice of the white, and in consequence their crops were thick and fruitful. He said that the soil was poor because they kept too many cattle on it – but at this their ears were closed to his talk. It was well known in the villages that when the white men said they should reduce their cattle to benefit the soil, it was only because they wanted these cattle themselves. Cattle were wealth, cattle were power; it was the thought of an alien mind that one good cow is worth ten poor ones. Because of this misunderstanding over the cattle the people of this village are suspicious of everything they hear from the sons of the Government, black or white. This suspicion is a terrible burden, like a cloud on their lives. And it is being fed by every traveller from the towns. There are whispers and rumours of new leaders, new thoughts, a new anger. The young people, like Jabavu, and even Pavu, in his own fashion, listen as if this is nothing terrible, but the old people are frightened.

When the three reach the field they are to hoe, the old man makes a joke about the advice given them by the man from the city; Pavu laughs politely, Jabavu says nothing. It is part of his impatience with his life here that the father insists on the old ways of farming. He has seen the new ways in the village five miles distant. He knows that the white man is right in what he says.

He works beside Pavu and mutters: 'Our father is stupid. This field would grow twice as much if we did what the sons of the Government tell us.'

Pavu says gently: 'Quiet, he will hear. Leave him to his own knowledge. An old ox follows the path to water that he learned as a calf.'

'Ah, *shut up*,' mutters Jabavu, and he quickens his work so as to be by himself. What is the use of taking a child like this brother to the city? he is asking himself, crossly. Yet he must, for he is afraid. And he tries to make it up, to attract Pavu's attention so they may work together. And Pavu pretends not to notice, but works quietly beside the father.

Jabavu hoes as if there is a devil in him. He has finished as much as a third more than the others when the sun goes down. The father says approvingly: 'When you work, my son, you work as if you were fed only on meat.'

Pavu is silent. He is angry with Jabavu, but also he is waiting, half with longing, half with fear, for the moment when the sweet and dangerous talk begins again. And after the evening meal the brothers go out into the dark and stroll among the cooking fires, and Jabavu talks and talks. And so it is for a long time, a week passes and then a month. Sometimes Jabavu loses his temper and Pavu sulks. Then Jabavu comes back, making his words quiet and gentle. Sometimes Pavu says 'Yes,' then again he says 'No, and how can we both leave our father?' And still Jabavu the Big Mouth talks, his eyes restless and glittering, his body tense with eagerness. During this time the brothers are together more than they have been in years. They are seen under the tree at night, walking among the huts, sitting at the hut door. There are many people who say: Jabavu is talking so that his brother may go with him.

Yet Jabavu does not know that what he is doing is clear to others, since he never thinks of the others – he sees only himself and Pavu.

There comes a day when Pavu agrees, but only if they first tell their parents; he wishes this unpleasantness to be softened by at least the forms of obedience. Jabavu will not hear of it. Why? He does not know himself, but it seems to him that this flight into the new life will be joyless unless it is stolen. Besides, he is afraid that his father's sorrow will weaken Pavu's intention. He argues. Pavu argues. Then they quarrel. For a whole week there is an ugly silence between them, broken only by intervals of violent words. And the whole village is saying: 'Look – Pavu the good son is resisting the talk of Jabavu the Big Mouth.' The only person who does not know is the father, and this is perhaps because he does not wish to know anything so terrible.

On the seventh day Jabavu comes in the evening to Pavu and shows him a bundle which he has ready. In it is his comb, his scraps of paper with words and pictures, a piece of soap. 'I shall go tonight,' he says to Pavu, and Pavu replies: 'I do not believe it.' Yet he half believes it. Jabavu is fearless, and if he takes the road by himself there may never be another chance for Pavu. Pavu seats himself in the door of the hut, and his face shows the agony of his indecision. Jabavu sits near him saying, 'And now, my brother, you must surely make up your mind, for I can wait no longer.'

It is then that the mother comes and says: 'And so, my sons, you are going to the city?' She speaks sadly, and at the tone of her voice the younger brother wishes only to assure her that the thought of leaving the village has never entered his mind. But Jabavu shouts, angrily: 'Yes, yes, we are leaving. We cannot live any longer in this village where there are only children and women and old men.'

The mother glances to where the father is seated with some friends at a fire by another hut. They make dark shapes against the red fire, and the flames scatter up into the blackness. It is a dark night, good for running away. She says: 'Your father will surely die.' She thinks: He will not die, any more than the other fathers whose sons go to the towns.

Jabavu shouts: 'And so we must be shut here in this village until we die, because of the foolishness of an old man who can see nothing in the life of the white men but what is bad.'

She says, quietly: 'I cannot prevent you from leaving, my sons. But if you go, go now, for I can no longer bear to see you quarrelling and angry day after day.' And then, because her sorrow is filling her throat, she quickly lifts a pot and walks off with it, pretending she needs to fetch water for the cooking. But she does not go further than the first patch of deep shadow under the big tree. She stands there, looking into the dim and flickering lights that come from the many fires, and at the huts which show sharp and black, and at the far glow of stars. She is thinking of her daughter. When the girl left she, the mother, wept until she thought she would die. Yet now she is glad she left. She works for a kind white woman, who gives her dresses, and she hopes to marry the cook, who earns good money. The life of this daughter is something far beyond the life of the mother, who knows that if she were younger she, too, would go to the town. And yet she wishes to weep from misery and loneliness. She does not weep. Her throat aches because of the tears locked in it.

She looks at her two sons, who are talking fast and quiet, their heads close together.

Jabavu is saying: 'Now, let us go. If we do not, our mother will tell our father and he will prevent us.' Pavu rises slowly to his feet. He says: 'Ah, Jabavu, my heart is weak for this thing.'

Jabavu knows that this is the moment of final decision. He says: 'Now consider, our mother knows of our leaving and she is not angry, and we can send back money from the city to soften the old age of our parents.'

Pavu enters the hut, and from the thatch he takes his mouth-organ, and from the earthen shelf his hatchet. He is ready. They stand in the hut, looking fearfully at each other, Jabavu in his torn shorts, naked from the waist, Pavu in his loincloth and his vest with holes in it. They are thinking that they will be figures of fun when they reach the town. All the tales they have heard of the matsotsis who thieve and murder, the tales of the recruiting men for the mines, the stories of the women of these towns who are like no women they have ever met – these crowd into their seething heads and they cannot move. Then Jabavu says jauntily: 'Come now, my brother. This will not carry our feet along the road.' And they leave the hut.

They do not look at the tree where their mother is standing. They walk past like big men, swinging their arms. And then they hear quick steps, their mother runs to them and says, 'Wait, my sons.' They feel how she fumbles for their hands, and in them they feel something hard and cold. She has given

them each a shilling. 'This is for your journey. And wait –'
Now, in each hand is a little bundle, and they know she has
cooked them food for the journey and kept it for the moment.

The brother turns his face away in shame and sorrow. Then
he embraces his mother and hurries on. Jabavu is filled first
with gratitude, then with resentment – again his mother has
understood him too well, and he dislikes her for it. He is stuck
to the piece of ground where he stands. He knows if he says
one word he will weep like a little child. His mother says,
softly, out of the darkness: 'Do not let your brother come to
harm. You are headstrong and fearless and may go into danger
where he may not.' Jabavu shouts: 'My brother is my brother,
but he is also a man –' Her eyes glint softly at him from the
dark, and then he hears the apologetic words: 'And your
father, he will surely die if he does not hear word of you. You
must not do as so many of the children do – send us word
through the Native Commissioner what has happened to you.'
And Jabavu shouts: 'The Native Commissioner is for the
baboons and the ignorant. I can write letters and you will have
letters from me two – no, three times a week!' At this boast
the mother sighs, and Jabavu, although he had no intention of
doing any such thing. grabs her hand, clings to it, then gives
it a little push away from him as if it were her desire to clasp
his hand – and so he walks away, whistling, through the
shadows of the trees.

The mother watches him until she can see her sons walking
together, then waits a little, then turns towards the light of the
fires, wailing first softly, then, as her sorrow grows strength
with use, very loudly. She is wailing that her sons have left
the kraal for the wickedness of the city. This is for her husband,
and with him she will mourn bitterly, and for many days.
She saw their backs as they stole away with their bundles –
so she will say, and her voice will be filled with a bitter reproach and anguish. For she is a wife as well as a mother, and
a woman feels one thing as a mother, another as a wife, and
both may be true and heartfelt.

As for Jabavu and Pavu, they walk in silence and fear because of the darkness of the bush till on the very outskirts of
the village they see a hut that has been abandoned. They do
not like to walk at night; their plan had been to leave at dawn;
and so now they creep into this hut and lie there, sleepless,
until the light comes first grey and then yellow.

The road runs before them fifty miles to the city; they intend to reach it by night, but the cold shortens their steps. They walk, crouching their loins and shoulders against it, and their teeth are clenched so as not to confess their shivering. Around them the grass is tall and yellow, and hung with throngs of glittering diamonds that slowly grow few and then are gone, and now the sun is very hot on their bodies. They straighten, the skin of their shoulders loosens and breathes. Now they swing easily along, but in silence. Pavu turns his narrow, cautious face this way and that for new sights, new sounds. He is arming his courage to meet them, for he is afraid his thoughts have returned to the village for comfort: Now my father will be walking alone to the fields, slowly, because of the weight of grief in his legs; now my mother will be setting water to heat on the fire for the porridge ...

Jabavu walks confidently. His mind is entirely on the big city. Jabavu! he hears, look, here is Jabavu come to the town!

A roar grows in their ears, and they have to leap aside to avoid a great lorry. They land in the thick grass on hands and knees, so violently did they have to jump. They look up open-mouthed, and see the white driver leaning out and grinning at them. They do not understand that he has swerved his lorry so that they have to jump for his amusement. They do not know he is laughing now because he thinks they look very funny, crouching in the grass, staring like yokels. They stand up and watch the lorry disappearing in clouds of pale dust. The back of it is filled with black men, some of them shout, some wave and laugh. Jabavu says: 'Hau! But that was a big lorry.' His throat and chest are filled with wanting. He wants to touch the lorry, to look at the wonder of its construction, perhaps even to drive it ... There he stands, his face tense and hungry, when there is a roar, a shrill sound like the crowing of a cock – and again the brothers jump aside, this time landing on their feet, while the dust eddies and swirls about them.

They look at each other, then drop their eyes so as not to confess they do not know what to think. But they are wondering: Are those lorries trying to frighten us on purpose? But why? They do not understand. They have heard tales of how an unpleasant white man may make a fool of a black one, so that he may laugh, but that is quite different from what has just happened. They think: We were walking along, we mean no harm, and we are rather frightened, so why does he frighten us even more? But now they are walking slowly, glancing back over their shoulders so as not to be taken by surprise. And when a car or lorry comes up behind they move away on to the grass and stand waiting until it has gone. There are few cars, but many lorries, and these are filled with black men. Jabavu thinks: Soon, maybe tomorrow when I have a job, I will be carried in such a lorry ... He is so impatient for this wonderful thing to happen that he walks quickly, and once again has to make a sudden jump aside when a lorry screeches at him.

They have been walking for perhaps an hour when they overtake a man who is travelling with his wife and children. The man walks in front with a spear and an axe, the woman behind, carrying the cooking pots and a baby on her back, and another little child holds her skirt. Jabavu knows that these people are not from the town, but travelling from one village to another, and so he is not afraid of them. He greets them, the greetings are returned, and they go together, talking.

When Jabavu says he is making the long journey to the city, the man says: 'Have you never been before?' Jabavu, who cannot bear to confess his ignorance, says: 'Yes, many times,' and the reply is: 'Then there is no need to warn you against the wickedness of the place.' Jabavu is silent, regretting he has not told the truth. But it is too late, for a path leads off the road, and the family turn on to it. As they are making their good-byes, another lorry sweeps by, and the dust swirls up around them. The man looks after the lorry and shakes his head. 'Those are the lorries that carry our brothers to the mines,' he says, brushing the dust from his face and shaking it from his blanket. 'It is well you know the dangers of the road, for otherwise by now you would be in one of them, filling the mouths of honest people with dust, and laughing when they shake with fright because of the loud noise of the horn.' He has settled his blanket again over his shoulders and now he turns away, followed by his wife and children.

Jabavu and Pavu slowly walk on, and they are thinking: How often have they heard of the recruiters of the mines! Yet these stories, coming through many mouths, grow into something like the ugly pictures that flit through sleep when it is difficult and uneasy. It is hard to think of them now, with the sun shining down. And yet this companion of the road spoke with horror of these lorries? Jabavu is tempted; he thinks: This man is a village man and, like my father, he sees only the bad things. Perhaps I and my brother may travel on one of these lorries to the city? And then the fear swells up in him and so his feet are slow with indecision, and when another lorry comes sweeping past he is standing on the very edge of the road, looking after it with big eyes, as if he wishes it to stop. And when it slows, his heart beats so fast he does not know whether it is with fear, excitement, or desire. Pavu tugs at his arm and says: 'Let us run quickly,' and he replies: 'You are afraid of everything, like a child who still smells the milk of its mother.'

The white man who drives the lorry puts his head out and looks back. He looks long at Jabavu and at his brother, and then his head goes inside. Then a black man gets out of the front and walks back. He wears clothes like the white men and walks jauntily. Jabavu, seeing this smart fellow, thinks of his own torn trousers and he hugs his elbows around his hips to hide them. But the smart fellow advances, grinning, and says: 'Yes, yes – you boys there! Want a lift?'

Jabavu takes a step forward, and feels Pavu clutching his elbow from behind. He takes no notice of that clutching grip, but it is like a warning, and he stands still and plants his two feet hard in the dust like the feet of an ox who resists the yoke.

'How much?' he asks, and the smart fellow laughs and says: 'You clever boy, you! No money. Lift to town. And you can put your name on a piece of paper like a white man and travel in the big lorry and there will be a fine job for you.' He laughs and swaggers and his white teeth glisten. He is a very fine fellow indeed, and Jabavu's hunger is like a hand clutching at his heart as he thinks that he, too, will be like this man. 'Yes,' he says, eagerly, 'I can make my name, I can write and I can read, too, and with the pictures.'

'So,' says the fine fellow, laughing more than ever. 'Then you are a clever, clever boy. And your job will be a clever one, with writing in an office, with nice white man, plenty money – ten pounds, perhaps fifteen pounds a month!'

Jabavu's brain goes dark, it is as if his thoughts run into water. His eyes have a yellow dazzling in them. He finds he has taken another step forward and the fine fellow is holding out a sheet of paper covered all over with letters. Jabavu takes the paper and tries to make out the words. Some he knows, others he has never seen. He stands for a long time looking at the paper.

The fine fellow says: 'Now, you clever boy, do you want to understand that all at once? And the lorry is waiting. Now just put your cross at the foot there and come quickly to the lorry.'

Jabavu says, resentfully: 'I can make my name like a white man and I do not need to make a cross. My brother will make a cross and I will make my own name, Jabavu.' And he kneels on the ground, and puts the paper on a stone, and takes the stub of pencil that the fine fellow is holding out to him, and then thinks where to put the first letter of his name. And then he hears that the fine fellow is saying: 'Your brother is not strong enough for this work.' Jabavu, turning around, sees that Pavu's face is yellow with fear, but also very angry. He is looking with horror at Jabavu. Jabavu rests his pencil and thinks: Why is my brother not big enough? Many of us go to town when we are still children, and work. A memory comes into his head of how someone has told him that when they recruit for the mines they take only strong men with fine shoulders. He, Jabavu, has the bulky strength of a young bull – he is filled with pride: Yes, he will go to the mines, why not? But then, how can he leave his brother? He looks up at the fine fellow, who is now impatient, and showing it; he looks at the black men in the back of the lorry. He sees one of these men shake his head at him as if in warning. But others are laughing. It seems to Jabavu that it is a cruel laughter, and suddenly he gets to his feet, hands the paper back to the fine fellow, and says: 'My brother and I travel together. Also you try to cheat me. Why did you not tell me this lorry was for the mines?'

And now the fine fellow is very angry. His white teeth are hidden behind a closed mouth. His eyes flash. 'You ignorant nigger,' he says. 'You waste my time, you waste my bosses' time, I'll get the policeman to you!' He takes a big step forward and his fists are raised. Jabavu and his brother turn as if their four legs were on a single body, and they rush off into the trees. As they go they hear a roar of laughter from the men on the lorry, and they see the fine fellow going back to the lorry. He is very angry – the two brothers see that the men are laughing at him, and not at them, and they crouch in the bushes, well hidden, thinking about the meaning of these things. When the lorry has sped off into its dust, Jabavu says: 'He called us nigger, and yet his skin is like ours. That is not easy to understand.'

Pavu speaks for the first time: 'He says I was not strong enough for the work!' Jabavu looks at him in surprise. He sees that his brother is offended. 'I am fifteen years old, so the Native Commissioner has said, and for five years already I have been working for my father. And yet this man says I am not strong enough.' Jabavu sees that the fear and the anger in his brother are having a fight, and it is by no means certain which will win. He says: 'Did you understand, my brother, that this was a recruiter for the mines in Johannesburg?'

Pavu is silent. Yes, he understood it, but his pride is speaking too loudly for any other voice to be heard. Jabavu decides to say nothing. For his own thoughts are moving too fast. First he thinks: That was a fine fellow with his smart white clothes! Then he thinks: Am I mad to be thinking of the mines? For this city we are going to is hard and dangerous, yet it is small in comparison with Johannesburg, or so the travellers tell us – and now my brother who has the heart of a chicken is so wounded in his pride that he is ready not only for the small city, but for Johannesburg!

The brothers linger under the bushes, though the road is empty. The sun comes from overhead and their stomachs begin to speak of food. They open the bundles their mother has made for them and find small, flat cakes of mealie-meal, baked in the ashes. They eat the cakes, and their stomachs are only half silenced. They are a long way from proper food and the city, and yet they stay in the safety of the bushes. The sun has shifted so that it strikes on their right shoulders when they come out of the bushes. They walk slowly, and every time a lorry passes they turn their faces away as they walk through the grass at the edge of the road. Their faces are so firmly turned that it is a surprise to them when they understand that another lorry has stopped, and they peer cautiously around to see yet another fine fellow grinning at them.

'Want a nice job?' he says, smiling politely.

'We do not wish to go to the mines,' says Jabavu.

'Who said the mines?' laughs the man. 'Job in office, with pay seven pounds a month, perhaps ten, who knows?' His laughter is not the kind one may trust, and Jabavu's eyes lift from the beautiful black boots this dandy is wearing, and he is about to say 'No,' when Pavu asks, suddenly: 'And there is a job for me also?'

The fellow hesitates, and it is for as long as it would take him to say 'Yes' several times. Jabavu can see the pride strong on Pavu's face.

Then the fellow says: 'Yes, yes, there is a job for you also. In time you will grow to be as strong as your brother.' He is looking at Jabavu's shoulders and thick legs. He brings out a piece of paper and hands it to the brother, not to Jabavu. And Pavu is ashamed because he has never held a pencil and the paper feels light and difficult to him, and he clutches it between his fingers as if it might blow away. Jabavu is glowing with anger. It is he who should have been asked; he is the older, and the leader, and he can write. 'What is written on this paper?' he asks.

'The job is written on this paper,' says the fellow, as if it were of no importance.

'Before we put our names on the paper we shall see what this job is,' says Jabavu, and the fellow's eyes shift, and then he says: 'Your brother has already made his cross, so now you make your name also, otherwise you will be separated.' Jabavu looks at Pavu, who is smiling a half-proud, half-sickly smile, and he says softly: 'That was a foolish thing, my brother, the white man makes an important thing of such crosses.'

Pavu looks in fear at the paper where he has put his cross, and the fine fellow rocks on his feet with laughter and says: 'That is true. You have signed this paper, and so have agreed to work for two years at the mines, and if you do not it means a broken contract, and that is prison. And now' – this he says to Jabavu – 'you sign also, for we shall take your brother in the lorry, since he has signed the paper.'

Jabavu sees that the hand of the fine fellow is reaching out to grasp Pavu's shoulder. In one movement he butts his head into the fellow's stomach and pushes Pavu away, and then both turn and run. They run leaping through the bushes till they have run a long way. Fearful glances over their shoulders show that the fine fellow does not attempt to chase them, but stands looking after them, for the breath being shaken from his stomach has darkened his eyes. After a while they hear the lorry growl, then rumble, then purr into silence along the road.

Jabavu says, after a long time of thinking: 'It is true that when our people go to the city they change so that their own family would not know them. That man, he who told us the lies, would he have been a skellum in his own village?' Pavu does not reply, and Jabavu follows his thoughts until he begins

to laugh. 'Yet we were cleverer than he was!' he says, and as
he remembers how he butted his head into the fine fellow's
stomach he rolls on the ground with laughing. Then he sits up
again – for Pavu is not laughing, and on his face is a look that
Jabavu knows well. Pavu is still so frightened that he is trembling all over, and his face is turned away so that Jabavu may
not see it. Jabavu speaks to him as gently as a young man to a
girl. But Pavu has had enough. It is in his mind to go back
home, and Jabavu knows it. He pleads until the darkness comes
filtering through the trees and they must find a place to sleep.
They do not know this part of the country, it is more than six
hours' walking from home. They do not like to sleep in the
open where the light of their fire might be seen, but they find
some big rocks with a cleft between, and here they build a
fire and light it as their fathers did before them, and they lie
down to sleep, cold because of their naked shoulders and legs,
very hungry, and no prospect of waking to a meal of good,
warm porridge. Jabavu falls asleep thinking that when they
wake in the morning with sun falling kindly through the trees,
Pavu will have regained his courage and forgotten the recruiter. But when he wakes, Jabavu is alone. Pavu has run
away very early, as soon as the light showed, as much afraid
of Jabavu the Big Mouth's clever tongue as he is of the
recruiters. By now he will have run half-way back along the
road home. Jabavu is so angry that he exhausts himself with
dancing and shouting, and finally he quietens and wonders
whether he should run after his brother and make him turn
around. Then he says to himself it is too late, and that anyway Pavu is nothing but a frightened child and no help to a
brave man like himself. For a moment he thinks that he too
will return home, because of his very great fear of going on
to the city alone. And then he decides to go alone, and immediately: he, Jabavu, is afraid of nothing.

And yet it is not so easy to leave the sheltering trees and
take the road. He lingers there, encouraging himself, saying
that yesterday he outwitted the recruiters when so many fail.
I am Jabavu, he says, I am Jabavu, who is too clever for the
tricks of bad white men and bad black men. He thumps himself on the chest. He dances a little, kicking up the leaves and
grass until they make a little whirlpool around him. 'I am
Jabavu, the Big Mouth ...' It turns into a song.

Here is Jabavu,
Here is the Big Mouth of the clever true words.
I am coming to the city,
To the big city of the white man.
I walk alone, hau! hau!
I fear no recruiter,
I trust no one, not even my brother.
I am Jabavu, who goes alone.

And with this he leaves the bush and takes the road, and when he hears a lorry he runs into the bush and waits until it has gone past.

Because he has so often to hide in the bush his progress is very slow, and when the sun turns red that evening he has still not reached the city. Perhaps he has taken the wrong road? He does not dare ask anyone. If someone walks along the road and greets him he remains silent, for fear of a trap. He is so hungry that it can no longer be called hunger. His stomach has got tired of speaking to him of its emptiness and has become silent and sulky, while his legs tremble as if the bones inside have gone soft, and his head is big and light as if a wind has got into it. He creeps off into the bush to look for roots and leaves, and he gnaws at them, while his stomach mutters: Eh, Jabavu! So you offer me leaves after so long a fasting? Then he crouches under a tree, his head lowered, hands dangling limp, and for the first time his fear of what he might find in the big city goes through him again and again like a spear and he wishes he had not left home. Pavu will be sitting by the fire now, eating the evening meal ... The dusk settles, the trees first loom huge and black, then settle into general darkness, and from quite close Jabavu sees a glow of fire. Caution stiffens his limbs. Then he drags himself to his feet and walks towards the fire as carefully as if he were stalking a hare. From a safe distance he kneels to peer through the leaves at the fire. Three people, two men and a woman, sit by it, and they are eating. Jabavu's mouth fills with water like a tin standing in heavy rain. He spits. His heart is hammering at him. Trust no one, trust no one! Then his hunger yawns inside him and he thinks: With us it has always been that a traveller may ask for hospitality at a fire – it cannot be that everyone has become cold and unfriendly. He steps forward, his hunger pushing him, his fear dragging him back. When the three people see him, they stiffen and stare and speak together, and Jabavu understands that they are afraid he comes for harm. Then they look at his torn trousers – no longer so tight on him now, and they greet him kindly, as one from the villages. Jabavu returns the greetings and pleads: 'My brothers, I am very hungry.'

The woman at once lays out for him some white, flat cakes, and some pieces of yellowish substance, which Jabavu eats like a hungry dog, and when his sick hunger has quietened he asks what they were, and they tell him this is food from the city, he has eaten fish and buns. Jabavu now looks at them and sees that they are dressed well, they wear shoes – even the woman – they have proper shirts and trousers and the woman has a red dress with a yellow crocheted cap on her head. For a moment the fear returns: These are people from the city, perhaps skellums? His muscles tense, his eyes glare, but they speak to him, laughing, telling him they are respectable people. Jabavu is silent, for he is wondering why they travel on foot like village people, instead of by train or lorry service, as is usual for city people. Also, he is annoyed that they have so quickly understood what he is thinking. But his pride is soothed when they say: 'When people from the villages first come to the city they see a skellum in every person. But that is much wiser than trusting everyone. You do well to be cautious.'

They pack away what food is left in a square, brown case that has a shiny metal clasp. Jabavu is fascinated to see how it works, and asks if he may also move the clasp, and they smile and say he may. Then they pile more wood on the fire and they talk quietly while Jabavu listens. What they say is only half-understood by him. They are speaking of the city and of the white man, not as do the people of the villages, with voices that are sad, admiring, fearful. Nor do they speak as Jabavu feels, as of a road to an exciting new country where everything is possible. No, they measure their words, and there is a quiet bitterness that hurts Jabavu, for it says to him: What a fool you are with your big hopes and dreams.

He understands that the woman is wife to one of the men, Mr Samu, and sister to the other. This woman is like no woman he has met or heard about. When he tries to measure her difference he cannot, because of his inexperience. She wears smart clothes, but she is not a coquette, as he has heard are all the women of the towns. She is young and newly married, but she is serious and speaks as if what she says is as important as what the men say, and she does not use words like Jabavu's mother: Yes, my husband, that is true, my husband, no, my husband. She is a nurse at the hospital for women in the location at the city, and Jabavu's eyes grow big when he hears it. She is educated! She can read and write! She understands the medicine of the white man! And Mr Samu and the other are also educated. They can read, not only words like yes, no, good, bad, black, and white, but also long words like regulation and document. As they talk, words such as these fill their mouths, and Jabavu decides he will ask them what mean the words on the paper in his bundle which he has marked with charcoal. But he is ashamed to ask, and continues to listen. It is Mr Samu who speaks most, but it is all so difficult that Jabavu's brain grows heavy and he pokes the edges of the fire with a green twig, listening to the sizzle of the sap, watching the sparks snap up and fade into the dark. The stars are still and brilliant overhead. Jabavu thinks, sleepily, that the stars perhaps are the sparks from all the fires people make – they drift up and up until they come against the sky and there they must remain like flies crowding together looking for a way out . . .

He shakes himself awake and gabbles: 'Sir, will you explain to me . . .' He has taken the folded, stained piece of paper from his pocket and, kneeling, spreads it before Mr Samu, who has stopped talking and is perhaps a little cross at being interrupted so irreverently.

He reads the difficult words. He looks at Jabavu. Then, before explaining, he asks questions. How did Jabavu learn to read? Was he all by himself? He was? Why did he want to read and write? What does he think of what he reads? – Jabavu answers clumsily, afraid of the laughter of these clever people. They do not laugh. They lean on their elbows looking at him, and their eyes are soft. He tells of the torn alphabet, how he finished the alphabet himself, how he learned the words that explained the pictures, and finally the words that are by themselves without pictures. As he speaks, his tongue slips into English, out of sympathy with what he is saying, and he tells of the hours and weeks and months of years he has spent, beneath the big tree, teaching himself, wondering, asking questions.

The three clever people look at each other, and their eyes

say something Jabavu does not at once understand. And then Mrs Samu leans forward and explains what the difficult sentence means, very patiently, in simple words, and also how the newspapers are, some for white people, some for black. She explains about the story of the little yellow people, and how wicked a story it is – and it seems to Jabavu that he learns more in a few minutes from this woman about the world he lives in, than he has in all his life. He wants to say to her: Stop, let me think about what you have said, or I shall forget. But now Mr Samu interrupts, leaning forward, speaking to Jabavu. After some moments of talking, it seems to Jabavu that Mr Samu sees not only him, but many other people – his voice has lifted and grown strong, and his sentences swing up and down, as if they have been made often before, and in exactly the same way. So strong is this feeling that Jabavu looks over his shoulder to see if perhaps there are people behind him, but no, there is nothing but darkness and the trees showing a glint of starlight on their leaves.

'This is a sad and terrible time for the people of Africa,' Mr Samu is saying. 'The white man has settled like a locust over Africa, and, like the locusts in early morning, cannot take flight for the heaviness of the dew on their wings. But the dew that weights the white man is the money that he makes from our labour. The white man is stupid or clever, brave or cowardly, kind or cruel, but all, all say one thing, if they say it in different ways. They say that the black man has been chosen by God to serve as a drawer of water and a hewer of wood until the end of time; they may say that the white man protects the black from his own ignorance until that ignorance is lightened; two hundred years, five hundred, or a thousand – he will only be allowed free when he has learned to stand on his two feet like a child who lets go his mother's skirts. But whatever they say, their actions are the same. They take us, men and women, into their houses to cook, clean, and tend their children; into their factories and mines; their lives are built on our work, and yet every day and every hour of every day they insult us, call us pigs and kaffirs or children, lazy, stupid, and ignorant. Their ugly names for us are as many as leaves on that tree, and every day the white people grow more rich and the black more poor. Truly, it is an evil time, and many of our people become evil, they learn to steal and to murder, they learn the ways of easy hatred, they become the pigs the white man says they are. And yet, though it is a terrible time, we should be proud that we live now, for our children and the children of our people will look back and say: If it were not for them, those people who lived in the terrible time, and lived with courage and wisdom, our lives would be the lives of slaves. We are free because of them.'

The first part of this speech Jabavu has understood very well, for he has often heard it before. So does his father speak, so all the travellers who come from the city. He was born with such words in his ears. But now they are becoming difficult. In a different tone does the voice of Mr Samu continue, his hand is lifting and falling, he says trade union, organization, politics, committee, reaction, progress, society, patience, education. And as each new and heavy word enters Jabavu's mind he grabs at it, clutches it, examines it, tries to understand – and by that time a dozen such words have flown past his ears, and he is lost in bewilderment. He looks dazedly at Mr Samu, who is leaning forward, that hand rising and falling, his steady, intent eyes fixed on his own, and it seems to him that those eyes sink into him, searching for his secret thoughts. He turns his own away, for he wishes them to remain secret. In the kraal I was always hungry, always waiting for when I would reach the plenty of the white man's town. All my life my body has been speaking with the voices of hunger: I want, I want, I want. I want excitement and clothes and food, such as the fish and buns I have eaten tonight; I want a bicycle and the women of the town; I want, I want ... And if I listen to these clever people, straight away my life will be bound to theirs, and it will not be dancing and music and clothes and food, but work, work, work, and trouble, danger and fear. For Jabavu has only just understood that these people travel so, at night, through the bush on foot, because they are going to another town with books, which speak of such matters as committees and organization, and these books are not liked by the police.

These clever people, rich people, good people, with clothes on their bodies and nice food in their bellies, travel like village natives on foot – the hunger in Jabavu rises and says in a loud voice: No, not for Jabavu.

Mr Samu sees his face and stops. Mrs Samu says, pleasantly: 'My husband is so used to making speeches that he cannot stop himself.' The three laugh, and Jabavu laughs with them.

Then Mr Samu says it is very late and they should sleep. But first he writes on a piece of paper and gives it to Jabavu, saying: 'I have written here the name of a friend of mine, Mr Mizi, who will help you when you reach the city. He will be very impressed when you tell him you learned to read and write all by yourself in the kraal.' Jabavu thanks him and puts the paper in his bundle, and then they all four lie around the fire to sleep. The others have blankets. Jabavu is cold, and the flesh of his chest and back is tight with shivering. Even his bones seem to shiver. The lids of his eyes, weighted with sleep, fly open in protest at the cold. He puts more wood on the fire and then looks at the shape of the woman huddled under her blanket. He suddenly desires her. That's a silly woman, he thinks. She needs a man like me, not a man who talks only. But he does not believe in this thought, and when the woman moves he hastily turns his eyes away in case she sees what is in them and is angry. He looks at the brown suitcase on the other side of the fire, lying on the grass. The metal clasp glints and glimmers in the flickering red glow. It dazzles Jabavu. His lids sink. He is asleep. He dreams.

Jabavu is a policeman in a fine uniform with bright brass buttons. He walks down the road swinging a whip. He sees the three ahead of him, the woman carrying the suitcase. He runs after them, catches the woman by the shoulder and says: 'So, you have stolen that suitcase. Open it, let me see what is inside.' She is very frightened. The other two men have run away. She opens the suitcase. Inside are buns and fish, and a big black book with the name *Jabavu* written on it. Jabavu says: 'You have stolen my book. You are a thief.' He takes her to the Native Commissioner who punishes her.

Jabavu wakes. The fire has sunk low, a heap of grey with red glimmering beneath. The clasp on the suitcase no longer shines. Jabavu crawls on his belly through the grass until he reaches the suitcase. He lays his hand on it, looks around. No one has moved. He lifts it, rises soundlessly to his feet and steals away down the path into the dark. Then he runs. But he does not run far. He stops, for it is very dark and he is afraid of the dark. He asks himself suddenly: Jabavu, why have you stolen this case? They are good people who wish only to help you and they gave you food when you were sick with hunger. But his hand tightens on the case as if it spoke a different language. He stands motionless in the dark, his whole being clamorous with desire for the suitcase, while small, frightened thoughts go through his mind. It will be four or five hours before the sun comes, and all that time he will be alone in the bush. He shivers with terror. Soon his body is clenched in cold and fear. He wishes he still lies beside the fire, he wishes he had never touched the case. Kneeling in the dark, his knees painful on rough grass, he opens the case and feels inside it. There are soft, damp shapes of food, and the hard shapes of books. It is too dark to see, he can only feel. For a long time he kneels there. Then he fastens the case and creeps back until he can see the faint glow of the fire and three bodies quite still. He moves like a wild cat across the ground, lays the case down where it was, and then lies down himself. 'Jabavu is not a thief,' he says, proudly, 'Jabavu is a good boy.' He sleeps and dreams, but he does not know what he dreams, and wakes suddenly, alert, as if there were an enemy close by. A grey light is struggling through the trees, showing a heap of grey ashes and the three sleepers. Jabavu's body is aching with cold, and his skin is rough like soil. He slowly rises, remains poised for a moment in the attitude of a runner about to take the first great leap. The hunger in him is now saying: 'Get away Jabavu, quickly, before you too become like these, and live in terror of the police.' He springs away through the bushes with big, flying leaps, and the dew soaks him in clinging cold. He runs until he has reached the road, which is deserted because it is so early. Then, when the first cars and lorries come, much later, he moves a little way into the bush beside the road, and so travels out of sight. Today he will reach the city. Each time he climbs a rise he looks for it: surely it must appear, a bright dream of richness over the hill! And towards the middle of the morning he sees a house. Then another house. The houses continue, scattered, at small distances, for half an hour's walking. Then he climbs a rise, and down the other side of it he sees – but Jabavu stands still and his mouth falls open.

Ah, but it is beautiful, how beautiful is the city of the white man! Look how the houses run in patterns, the smooth grey streets making patterns between them like the marks of a clever finger. See how the houses rise, white and coloured, the sun shining on them so they dazzle. And see how big they are, why, the house of the Greek is the house of a dog compared with them. Here the houses rise as if three or four were on top of each other, and gardens lie around each with flowers of red and purple and gold, and in the gardens are stretches of water, gleaming dark, and on the water flowers are floating. And see how this city stretches down the valley and even up the other side! Jabavu walks on, his feet putting themselves down one after the other with no help from his eyes, so that he goes straying this way and that until there is a shriek of warning from a car, and once again he leaps aside and stands staring, but now there is no dust, only smooth, warm asphalt. He walks on slowly, down the slope, up the other side, and then he reaches the top of the next rise, and now he stands for a long time. For the houses continue as far as he can see in front of him, and also to either side. There is no end to the houses. A new feeling has come into him. He does not say he is afraid, but his stomach is heavy and cold. He thinks of the village, and Jabavu, who has longed for so many years for just this moment, believing he has no part in the village, now hears it saying softly to him: Jabavu, Jabavu, I made you, you belong to me, what will you do in this great and bewildering city that must surely be greater than every other city? For by now he has forgotten that this is nothing compared with Johannesburg and other cities in the South, or rather, he does not dare to remember it, it is too frightening.

The houses are now of different kinds, some big, some flimsy as the house of the Greek. There are different kinds of white men says Jabavu's brain slowly, but it is a hard idea to absorb all at once. He has thought of them, until now, as all equally rich, powerful, clever.

Jabavu says to his feet: Now walk on, walk. But his feet do not obey him. He stands there while his eyes move over the streets of houses, and they are the eyes of a small child. And then there is a slurring sound, wheels of rubber slowing, and beside him is an African policeman on a bicycle. He rests one foot on the road and looks at Jabavu. He looks at the old, torn trousers and at the unhappy face. He says, kindly: 'Have you lost your way?' He speaks in English.

At first Jabavu says no, because even at this moment it goes against the grain not to know everything. Then he says sullenly: 'Yes, I do not know where to go.'

'And you are looking for work?'

'Yes, son of the Government, I seek work.' He speaks in his own language; the policeman, who is from another district, does not understand, and Jabavu speaks again in English.

'Then you must go to the office for passes and get a pass to seek work.'

'And where is this office?'

The policeman gets off his bicycle and, taking Jabavu's arm, speaks to him a long time, thus: 'Now you must go straight on for half a mile, and then where the five roads meet turn left, and then turn again and go straight on and ...' Jabavu listens and nods and says Yes and Thank you, and the policeman bicycles away and Jabavu stands helplessly, for he has not understood. And then he walks on, and he does not know whether his legs tremble from fear or from hunger. When he met the policeman, the sun came from behind on his back, and when his legs stop of their own accord, from weakness, the sun is overhead. The houses are all around him, and white women sit on the verandas with their children, and black men work in the gardens, and he sees more in the sanitary lanes talking and laughing. Sometimes he understands what they say, and sometimes not. For in this city are people from Nyasaland and from Northern Rhodesia and from the country of the Portuguese, and not one word of their speech does he know, and he fears them. But when he hears his own tongue he knows that these people point at his torn trousers and his bundle, and laugh, saying: 'Look at the raw boy from the kraal.'

He stands where two streets cross, looking this way and that way. He has no idea where the policeman told him to go. He walks on a little, then sees a bicycle leaning against a tree. There is a basket at the back, and in it are loaves of bread and buns, such as he has eaten the night before. He looks at them, while his mouth fills with water. Suddenly his hand reaches out and takes a bun. He looks around. No one has seen. He puts the bun in his pocket and moves away. When he has left that street behind, he takes it out and walks along eating the bun. But when it is finished his stomach seems to say: What, one small bun after being empty all morning! Better that you give me nothing!

Jabavu walks on, looking for another basket on a bicycle. Several times he turns up a street after one that looks the same but it is not. It is a long time before he finds out what he wants. And now it is not easy as before. Then his hand went out by itself and took the bun, while now his mind is warning him: Be careful, Jabavu, careful! He is standing near the basket, looking around, when a white woman in her garden shouts at him over the hedge, and he runs until he has turned a corner and is in another street. There he leans against a tree, trembling. It is a narrow street, full of trees, quiet and shady. He can see no one. Then a nanny comes out of a house with her arms full of clothes, and she hangs them on a line, looking over the hedge at Jabavu. 'Hi, kraal boy, what do you want?' she shouts at him, laughing; 'look at the stupid kraal boy.' 'I am not a kraal boy,' he says, sullenly, and she says: 'Look at your trousers – ohhhhh, what can I see there!' and she goes inside, looking scornful. Jabavu remains leaning against a tree, looking at his trousers. It is true that they are nearly falling off him. But they are still decent.

There is nothing to be seen. The street seems empty. Jabavu looks at the clothes hanging on the line. There are many: dresses, shirts, trousers, vests. He thinks: That girl was cheeky ... he is shocked at what she said. Again he clasps his elbows, crouching, around his hips to cover his trousers. His eyes are on the clothes – then Jabavu has leaped over the hedge and is tugging at a pair of trousers. They will not come off the line, there is a little wooden stick holding them. He pulls, the stick falls off, he holds the trousers. They are hot and smooth, they have just been ironed. He pulls at a yellow shirt, the cloth tears under the wooden peg, but it comes free, and in a moment he has leaped back over the hedge and is running. At the turn of the street he glances back; the garden is quiet and empty, it appears no one has seen him. Jabavu walks soberly along the street, feeling the fine warm cloth of the shirt and trousers. His heart is beating, first like a small chicken tottering as it comes out of the shell, then, as it strengthens, like a strong wind banging against a wall. The violence of his heart exhausts Jabavu and he leans against a tree to rest. A policeman comes slowly past on a bicycle. He looks at Jabavu. Then he looks again, makes a wide circle and comes to rest beside him. Jabavu says nothing, he only stares.

'Where did you get those clothes?' asks the policeman.

Jabavu's brain whirls and from his mouth come words: 'I carry them for my master.'

The policeman looks at Jabavu's torn shorts and his bundle. 'Where does your master live?' he asks cunningly. Jabavu points ahead. The policeman looks where Jabavu is pointing and then at Jabavu's face. 'What is the number of your master's house?'

Again Jabavu's brain faints and comes to life. 'Number three,' he says.

'And what is the name of the street?'

And now nothing comes from Jabavu's tongue. The policeman is getting off his bicycle in order to look at Jabavu's papers, when suddenly there is a commotion in the street which Jabavu has come from. The theft has been discovered. There are voices scolding, high and shrill, it is the white mistress telling the nanny to fetch the missing clothes, the nanny is crying, and there is the word police repeated many times. The policeman hesitates, looks at Jabavu, looks back at the other street, and then Jabavu remembers the recruiter. He butts his head into the policeman's stomach, the bicycle falls over on top of him, and Jabavu leaps away and into a sanitary lane, vaults over a rubbish bin, then another, darts across a garden which is empty, then over another which is not, so that people start up and stare at him, then over into another sanitary lane and comes to rest between a rubbish bin and the wall of a lavatory. There he quickly pulls off his shorts, pulls on the trousers. They are long, grey, of fine stuff such as he has never seen. He pulls on the yellow shirt, but it is difficult, since he has never worn one, and it gets caught around the arms before he discovers the right hole in which to put his head. He stuffs the shirt, which is too small for him, inside the trousers, which are a little too long, thinking sadly of the hole in the shirt, which is due entirely to his ignorance about those little wooden pegs. He quickly pushes the torn shorts under the lid of a rubbish bin and walks up the sanitary lane, careful not to run, although his feet are itching to run. He walks until that part of the city is well left behind, and then he thinks: Now I am safe; with so many people, no one will notice grey trousers and a yellow shirt. He remembers how the policeman looked at the bundle, and he puts the soap and comb into his pockets, together with the papers, and stuffs the rag of the bundle under the low branches of a hedge. And now he is thinking: I came to this city only this morning and already I have grey trousers like a white man, and a yellow shirt, and I have eaten a bun. I have not spent the shilling my mother gave me. Truly it is possible to live well in the white man's town! And he lovingly handles the hard shape of the shilling. At this moment, for no reason that he understands, comes into his head a memory of the three he met last night, and suddenly Jabavu is muttering: Skellums! Bad people! Damn, hell, bloody. For these are words he knows of the white people's swearing, and he thinks them very wicked. He says them again and again, till he feels like a big man, and not like the little boy at whom his mother used to look, saying sorrowfully: 'Ah, Jabavu, my Big Mouth, what white man's devil has got into you!'

Jabavu swaggers himself into such a condition of pride that when a policeman stops him and asks for his pass, Jabavu cannot at once stop swaggering, but says haughtily: 'I am Jabavu.'

'So you are Jabavu,' said the policeman, at once getting in front of him. 'So, my fine, clever boy. And who is Jabavu and where is his pass?'

The madness of pride sinks in Jabavu, and he says humbly: 'I have no pass yet. I have come to seek work.'

But the policeman looks more suspicious than ever. Jabavu wears very fine clothes, although there is one small rent in the shirt, and he speaks good English. How then can he have just arrived from the kraals? So he looks at Jabavu's situpa, which is the paper that every African native must carry all the time, and he reads: Native Jabavu. District so and so. Kraal so and so. Registration Certificate No. XO78910312. He copies this down in a little book, and gives the situpa to Jabavu saying: 'Now I shall tell you the way to the Pass Office, and if by this time tomorrow you have no pass to seek work, then there will be big trouble for you.' He goes away.

Jabavu follows the streets which have been shown to him, and soon he comes to a poor part of the town, full of houses like that of the Greek, and in them are people of half-colour, such as he has heard about but never seen, who are called in this country the Coloured People. And soon he comes to a big building, which is the Pass Office, with many black people waiting in long files that lead to windows and doors in the building. Jabavu joins one of these files, thinking that they are like cattle waiting to enter the dip, and then he waits. The file moves very slowly. The man in front of him and the woman behind him do not understand his questions, until he speaks in English, and then he finds he is in the wrong file and must go to another. And now he goes politely to a policeman who is standing by to see there is no trouble or fighting, and he asks for help and is put in the right queue. And now he waits again, and because he must stand, without moving, he has time to hear the voices of his hunger, and particularly the hunger of his stomach, and soon it seems as if darkness and bright light are moving like shifting water across his brain, and his stomach says again that since he left home, three days ago, he has eaten very little, and Jabavu tries to quieten the pain in his stomach by saying I shall eat soon, I shall eat soon, but the light swirls violently across his eyes, is swallowed by heavy, nauseating blackness, and then he finds he is lying on a cold, hard floor, and there are faces bending over him, some white, some dark.

He has fainted and has been carried inside the Pass Office. The faces are kind, but Jabavu is terrified and scrambles to his feet. Arms support him, and he is helped into an inner room, which is where he must wait to be examined by a doctor before he may receive a pass to seek work. There are many other Africans there, and they have no clothes on at all. He is told to take off his clothes and everyone turns to look at him, amazed, because he clutches his arms across his chest, protecting the clothes, imagining they will be taken from him. His eyes roll in despair, and it is some time before he understands and takes them off and waits, naked, in a line with the others. He is cold because of his hunger, although outside the sun is at its hottest. One after another the Africans go up to be examined and the doctor puts a long, black thing to their chests and handles their bodies. Jabavu's whole being is crying out in protest, and there are many voices. One says: Am I an ox to be handled as that white doctor handles us? Another says, anxiously: If I had not been told that the white men have many strange and wonderful things in their medicine I would think that black thing he listens through is witchcraft. And the voice of his stomach says again and again, not at all discouraged, that he is hungry and will faint again soon if food does not come.

At last Jabavu reaches the doctor, who listens to his chest, taps him, looks in his throat and eyes and armpits and groin, and peers at the secret parts of Jabavu's body in a way that makes anger mutter in him like thunder. He wishes to kill the white doctor for touching him and looking at him so. But there is also a growing patience in him, which is the first gift of the white man's city to the black man. It is patience against anger. And when the doctor has said that Jabavu is strong as an ox and fit for work, he may go. The doctor has said, too, that Jabavu has an enlarged spleen, which means he has had malaria and will have it again, that he probably has bilharzia, and there is a suspicion of hookworm. But these are too common for comment, and what the doctor is looking for are diseases which may infect the white people if he works in their houses.

Then the doctor, as Jabavu is turning away, asks him why the blackness came into him so that he fell down, and Jabavu says simply that he is hungry. At this a policeman comes forward and asks why he is hungry. Jabavu says because he has had nothing to eat. At this the policeman says impatiently: 'Yes, yes, but have you no money?' – for if not, Jabavu will be sent to a camp where he will get a meal and shelter for that night. But Jabavu says Yes, he has a shilling. 'Then why do you not buy food?' 'Because I must keep the shilling to buy what I need.' 'And do you not need food?'

People are laughing because a man who has a shilling in his pocket allows himself to fall down to the ground with hunger, but Jabavu remains silent.

'And now you must leave here and buy yourself some food and eat it. Have you a place to sleep tonight?'

'Yes,' says Jabavu, who is afraid of this question.

The policeman then gives Jabavu a pass that allows him to seek work for a fortnight. Jabavu has put back his clothes, and now he takes from the pocket the roll of papers that includes his situpa, in order to put the new pass with them. And as he fumbles with them a piece of paper flutters to the floor. The policeman quickly bends down, picks it up and looks at it. On it is written: Mr Mizi, No. 33 Tree Road, Native Township. The policeman looks with suspicion at Jabavu. 'So Mr Mizi is a friend of yours?'

'No,' says Jabavu.

'Then why do you have a piece of paper with his name on it?'

Jabavu's tongue is locked. After another question he mutters: 'I do not know.'

'So you do not know why you have that piece of paper? You know nothing of Mr Mizi?' The policeman continues to make such sarcastic questions, and Jabavu lowers his eyes and waits patiently for him to stop. The policeman takes out a little book, makes a long note about Jabavu, tells him that it

would be wise for him to go to the camp for people newly
come to town. Jabavu again refuses, repeating that he has
friends with whom to sleep. The policeman says Yes, he can
see what his friends are – a remark which Jabavu does not
understand – and so at last he is free to leave.

Jabavu walks away from the Pass Office, very happy because
of this new pass which allows him to stay in the city. He does
not suspect that the first policeman who took his name will
hand it in to the office whose business it is, saying that Jabavu
is probably a thief, and that the policeman in the Pass Office
will give his name and number as a man who is a friend of the
dangerous agitator Mr Mizi. Yes, Jabavu is already well-known
in this city after half a day, and yet as he walks out into the
street he feels as lost and lonely as an ox that has strayed from
the herd. He stands at a corner watching the crowds of Africans streaming along the roads to the Native Township, on
foot and on bicycle, talking, laughing, singing. Jabavu thinks
he will go and find Mr Mizi. And so he joins the crowds,
walking very slowly because of the many new things there are
to see. He stares at everything, particularly at the girls, who
seem to him unbelievably beautiful in their smart dresses, and
after a time he feels as if one of them is looking at him. But
there are so many of them that he cannot keep any particular
one in his mind. And in fact many are gazing at him, because
he is very handsome in his fine yellow shirt and new trousers.
Some even call out to him, but he cannot believe it is meant
for him, and looks away.

After some time, he becomes certain that there is one girl
who has walked past him, then come back, and is now walking
past him again. He is certain because of her dress. It is bright
yellow with big red flowers on it. He stares around him and can
see no other dress like it, so it must be the same girl. For the
third time she saunters by, close on the pavement, and he sees
she has smart green shoes on her feet and wears a crocheted
cap of pink wool, and she carries a handbag like a white
woman. He is shy, looking at this smart girl, yet she is giving
him glances he cannot mistake. He asks himself, distrustfully:
Should I talk to her? Yet everyone says how immodest are
these women of the towns, I should wait until I understand
how to behave with her. Shall I smile, so that she will come
to me? But the smile will not come to his face. Does she like
me? The hunger rises in Jabavu and his eyes go dark. But she

will want money and I have only one shilling.

The girl is now walking beside him at the distance of a stretched arm. She asks softly: 'Do you like me, handsome, yes?' It is in English, and he replies: 'Yes, very much I like.'

'Then why do you frown and look so cross?'

'I do not,' says Jabavu.

'Where do you live?' – and now she is so close he can feel her dress touching him.

'I do not know,' he says, abashed.

At this she laughs and laughs, rolling her eyes about: 'You are a funny, clever man, yes that's true!' And she laughs some more, in a loud, hard way that surprises him, for it does not sound like laughter.

'Where can I find a place to sleep, for I do not wish to go to the camp run by the Native Commissioner,' he asks politely, breaking into the laughter, and she stops and looks at him in real surprise.

'You are from the country?' she asks, after a long time, looking at his clothes.

'I came today from my village, I have got a pass for looking for work, I am very hungry and I know nothing,' he says, his voice falling into a humble tone, which annoys him, for he wishes to act the big man with this girl, and now he is speaking like a child. Anger at himself makes a small, feeble movement and then lies quiet: he is too hungry and lost. As for her, she has moved away to the edge of the pavement, and there walks in silence, frowning. Then she says: 'Did you learn to speak English at a mission?'

'No,' says Jabavu, 'in my kraal.'

Again she is silent. She does not believe him. 'And where did you get that fine smart shirt and the white-man trousers just like new?'

Jabavu hesitates, then with a swagger says: 'I took them this morning from a garden as I went past.'

And now again the girl laughs, rolls her eyes, and says: 'Heh, heh, what a clever boy, he comes straight from the kraal and steals so clever!' At once she stops laughing, for she has said this to gain time; she has not believed him. She walks on, thinking. She is a member of a gang who look out for such raw country boys, steal from them, make use of them as is necessary for their work. But she spoke to him because she liked him – it was a holiday from her work. But now what should she do? For it seems that Jabavu is a member of another gang, or perhaps works by himself, and if so, her own gang should know about it.

Another glance at him shows her that he walks along with a serious face, apparently indifferent to her – she goes up to him swiftly, eyes flashing, teeth showing: 'You lie! You tell me big lie, that's the truth!'

Jabavu shrinks away – hau! but what women these are! 'I do not lie,' he says, angrily. 'It is as I have said.' And he begins to walk away from her, thinking: I was a fool to speak to her, I do not understand the ways of these girls.

And she, watching him, notices his feet, which are bare, and they have certainly never worn shoes – he is telling the truth. And in this case – she makes up her mind in a flash. A raw boy who can come to town, steal so cleverly without being caught, this is talent that can be turned to good use. She goes after him, says politely: 'Tell me how you did the stealing, it was very cunning.'

And Jabavu's vanity spurs him to tell the story exactly as it happened, while she listens thoughtfully. 'You should not be wearing those clothes now,' she says at last. 'For the white missus will have told the police, and they will be watching the boys new to town in case they have the clothes.'

Jabavu asks in surprise: 'How can they find one pair of trousers and one shirt in a city full of shirts and trousers?'

She laughs and says: 'You know nothing, there are as many police watching us as flies around porridge; you come with me, I will take those clothes and give you others, as good as those, but different.' Jabavu thanks her politely but edges away. He has understood she is a thief. And he does not think of himself as a thief – he has stolen today, but he hardly gives it that name. Rather he feels as if he has helped himself to crumbs from the rich man's table. After a pause he enquires: 'Do you know Mr Mizi of 33 Tree Road?'

For the second time she is surprised into silence; then distrust fills her, and she thinks: This man either knows nothing at all or he is very cunning. She says, sarcastically, in the same tone that the policeman in the Pass Office used: 'You have fine friends. And how should I know a great man like Mr Mizi?'

But Jabavu tells her of the encounter at night in the bush, of Mr and Mrs Samu and the others, of what they said, and how they admired him for learning to read and write by himself, and gave him Mr Mizi's name.

At last this girl believes him, and understands, and she thinks: 'Certainly I must not let him slip away. He will be of great help in our work.' And there is another thought, even more powerful: Heh! but he is handsome ...

Jabavu asks, politely: 'And do you like these people, Mr Samu and Mrs Samu and Mr Mizi?'

She laughs scornfully and with disappointment, for she wishes him only to think of her. 'You mad? You think I am mad too? Those people stupid. They call themselves leaders of the African people, they talk and talk, they write letters to the Government: Please sir, please. Give us food, give us houses, let us not carry passes all the time and the Government throws them a shilling after years of asking and they say, Thank you, sir. They are fools.' And then she sidles up to him, lays her hand inside his elbow, and says: 'Besides, they are skellums – did you not see that? You come with me, I help you.'

Jabavu feels the warm hand inside his bare arm, and she swings her hips and makes her eyes soft. 'You like me, handsome?' And Jabavu says: 'Yes, very much,' and so they walk down the road to the Native Township and she talks of the fine things there are to do, of the films and the dances and the drinking. She is careful not to talk of the stealing or of the gang, in case he should be frightened. And there is another reason: there is a man who leads the gang who frightens her. She thinks: If this new clever man likes me, I will make him marry me, I will leave the gang and work with him alone.

Because her words are one thing and what she is thinking another, there is something in her manner that confuses Jabavu, and he does not trust her; besides, that dizziness is coming back in waves, and there are moments when he does not hear what she says.

'What is the matter?' she asks at last, when he stops and closes his eyes.

'I have told you that I am hungry,' he says out of the darkness around him.

'But you must be patient,' she says lightly, for it is such a long time since she has been hungry she has forgotten how it feels. She becomes irritated when he walks slowly, and even thinks: This man is no good, he's not strong for a girl like me – and then she notices that Jabavu is staring at a bicycle with a basket on the back, and as he is reaching out his arm for the bread in the basket, she strikes down his arm.

'You crazy?' she asks in a high, scared voice, glancing around. For there are people all around them. 'I am hungry,' he says again, staring at the loaves of bread. She quickly takes some money from a place in the front of her dress, gives it to the vendor, and hands a loaf of bread to Jabavu. He begins to eat as he stands, so hungrily that people turn to stare and laugh, and she gazes at him with shocked, big eyes and says: 'You are a pig, not a smart boy for me.' And she walks away ahead of him thinking: This is nothing but a raw kraal boy. I am crazy to like him. But Jabavu does not care at all. He eats the bread and feels the strength coming back to him, and the thoughts begin to move properly through his mind. When he has finished the bread he looks for the girl but all he can see is a yellow dress far down the road, and the skirt of the dress is swinging in a way that reminds him of the mockery of her words: 'You are a pig ...' Jabavu walks fast to catch her; he comes up beside her and says: 'Thank you, my friend, for the bread. I was very hungry.' She says, without looking around, 'Pig, dog without manners.' He says: 'No, that is not true. When a man is so hungry, one cannot talk of manners.' 'Kraal boy,' she says, swinging her hips, but thinking: 'It does no harm to show him I know more than he does.' And then says Jabavu, full of bread and new strength: 'You are nothing but a bitch woman. There are many smart girls in this city, and as pretty as you.' And with this he marches off ahead of her and is looking around for another pretty girl when she runs up to him.

'Where are you going?' she asks, smiling. 'Did I not say I would help you?'

'You shall not call me kraal boy,' says Jabavu magnificently, and with real strength, since he truly does not care for her more than the others he sees about him, and so she gives him a quick, astonished look and is silent.

Now that Jabavu's stomach is filled he is looking around him with interest again, and so he asks questions continually and she answers him pleasantly. 'What are those big houses with smoke coming out?' 'They are factories.' 'What is this place full of little bits of garden with crosses and stones shaped like children with wings?' 'It is the cemetery for the white people.' So, having walked a long way, they turn off the main road into the Native Township, and the first thing Jabavu notices is that while in the city of the white people the soil lies hidden under grass and gardens or asphalt, here it billows up in thick red clouds, gives the sun a dulled and sullen face, and makes the trees look as if a swarm of locusts had passed, so still and heavy with dust are they. Also, there are now such swarms of Africans all around him that he has to make himself strong, like a rock in the middle of a swift river. And still he asks questions, and is told that this big, empty place is for playing football, and this for wrestling, and then they come to the buildings. Now these are like the house of the Greek, small, ugly, bare. But there are very many, and close together. The girl strolls along, calling out greetings in her high, shrill voice, and Jabavu notices that sometimes she is called Betty, sometimes Nada, sometimes Eliza. He asks: 'Why do you have so many names?' and she laughs and says: 'How do you know I am not many girls?' And now, and for the first time, he laughs as she does, high and hard, doubling up his body, for it seems to him a very good joke. Then he straightens and says: 'I shall call you Nada,' and she says quickly: 'My village name for a village boy!' At once he says: 'No, I like Betty,' and she presses her thighs against his and says: 'My good friends call me Betty.'

He says he wishes to see all this town now, before it grows dark, and she says it will not take long. 'The white man's town is very big and it takes many days to see it. But our town is small, though we are ten, twenty, a hundred times as many.' Then she adds: 'That is what they call justice,' and looks to see the effect of the word. But Jabavu remembers that when Mr Samu used it it sounded different, and he frowns, and seeing his frown she leads him forward, talking of something else. For if he does not understand her, she understands that what the men of light – for this is how they are called – have said to Jabavu marked his mind deeply, and she thinks: If I am not careful he will go to Mr Mizi and I will lose him and the gang will be very angry.

When they pass Mr Mizi's house, number 33 Tree Road, she makes some rude jokes about him, but Jabavu is silent, and Betty thinks: Perhaps I should let him go to Mr Mizi? For if he goes later, it may be dangerous. Yet she cannot bear to let him go, already her heart is soft and heavy for Jabavu.

She leads him through the streets very kindly and politely, answering all his questions, though their foolishness often makes her impatient. She explains that the better houses, which have two rooms and a kitchen, are for the rich Africans, and the big, strangely-shaped houses are called Nissen huts, where twenty single men sleep, and these old shacks are called the Old Bricks, and they are for those who earn only a little, and this building here is the Hall, for meetings and dances. Then they reach a big open space which is filled with people. It is the market, and policemen are everywhere, walking with whips in their hands. Jabavu is thinking that one small loaf of bread, although it was white and fine to eat, was not much for a stomach as long empty as his, and he is looking at the various foodstuffs when Betty says: 'Wait, we shall eat better than this later.' And Jabavu looks at the people who buy some groundnuts or a few cooked maize-cobs for their supper, and already feels superior to them because of what Betty says.

Soon she pulls him away, for she has lived so long here that she cannot find interest, as he does, in watching the people; and now they walk away from the centre and she says: 'Now we are going to Poland.' Her face is ready for laughter, Jabavu sees it is a joke and asks: 'And what is the joke in Poland?'

She says, quickly, before her laughter gets too strong: 'In the war of the white people that has just finished, there was a country called Poland, and there was a terrible fight, with many bombs, and so now we call where we are going Poland because of the fights and the trouble there.' She lets her laughter loose, but stops when she sees Jabavu stern and silent. He is thinking: I do not want fighting and trouble. Then she says in a little, foolish voice, like a child: 'And so now we are going to Johannesburg,' and he, not wanting to appear afraid, asks: 'What is the joke in this?' She says: 'This place is also called Johannesburg because there are fights and trouble in the townships of Johannesburg.' And now she bends double with laughing, and Jabavu laughs from politeness. Then, seeing it is only politeness, she says, wishing to impress him, and with a big important sigh: 'Ah, yes, these white people, they tell us: "See how we saved you from the wicked fighting of the tribes; we have brought you peace" – and yet see how they make wars and kill so many people one cannot understand the numbers when they are written in the newspaper.' This she has heard Mr Mizi say at a meeting; and when she notices that Jabavu is impressed, she goes on proudly: 'Yes, and that is what they call civilization!' At this Jabavu asks: 'I do not understand, what is civilization?' And she says, like a teacher: 'It is how the white men live, with houses and bioscope and cowboys and food and bicycles.' 'Then I like civilization,' says Jabavu, from the pulse of his deepest hunger, and Betty laughs amiably and says: 'Heh, but you are one big fool, my friend, I like you.'

They are now in an evil-looking place where there are many tall brick shelters crowded together in rows, and shacks made of petrol tins beaten flat, or of sacks and boxes, and there is a foul smell. 'This is Poland Johannesburg,' says Betty, walking carefully in her nice shoes through the filth and ordure. And the staring and horrified eyes of Jabavu see a man lying huddled in the grass. 'Has he nowhere to sleep?' he asks, stupidly, but she pulls at his arm and says: 'Fool, leave him, he is sick with the drink.' For now he is on her territory, and afraid, she uses a more casual tone with him, she is his superior. Jabavu follows her, but his eyes cannot leave that man who looks as if he were dead. And his heart, as he follows Betty, is heavy and anxious. He does not like this place, he is scared.

But when they turn into a small house that stands a little by itself, he is reassured. The room they stand in is of bare red brick, with a bench around the walls and some chairs at one end. The floor is of red cement, and there are streamers of coloured paper festooned from nails in the rafters. There are two doors, and one of these opens and a woman appears. She is very fat, with a broad, shiny black face and small, quick eyes. She wears a white cloth bound round her head, and her dress is of clean pink cotton. She holds a nice clean little boy by one hand. She looks in enquiry at Betty, who says: 'I am bringing Jabavu, my friend, to sleep here tonight.' The woman nods and gazes at Jabavu, who smiles at her. For he likes her, and thinks: 'This is a nice woman of the old kind, decent and respectable, and that is a nice little boy.'

He goes into a room off the big one with Betty, and it is as well he does not say what he is thinking, for it is probable that she would have given him up as a fool beyond teaching, for while it is true that this woman, Mrs Kambusi, is kind in her way, and respectable in her way, it is also true that her cleverness has enabled her to run the most profitable shebeen in the city for many years, and only once has she been taken to the courts, and that in the capacity of a witness. She has four children, by different fathers, and the three elder children have been sent by this wise and clever woman far away to Roman school where they will grow up educated with no knowledge of this place where the money comes for their schooling. And the little boy will be going next year also, before he is old enough to understand what Mrs Kambusi does. Later she intends that the children will go to England and become doctors and lawyers. For she is very, very rich.

The room where he stands makes Jabavu feel cramped and restless. It is so small that there is room for one narrow bed – a bed on legs, with a space around it for walking. Some dresses hang on a nail on the wall from wooden sticks. Betty sits on the bed and looks provocatively at Jabavu. But he remains still, rolling his eyes at the low ceiling and the narrow walls, while he thinks: My fathers! But how can I live in boxes like a chicken!

Seeing his absence of mind, she says softly: 'Perhaps you would like to eat now?' and his eyes return to her and he says: 'Thanks, I am still very hungry.'

'I will tell Mrs Kambusi,' she says, in a soft, meek voice that he does not altogether like, and goes out. After a little while she calls him to follow her, so he leaves the tiny room, crosses the big one, and goes through the second doorway into a room which makes him stare in admiration. It has a table with a real cloth on it, and many chairs around the table, and a big stove after the fashion of the white man. Never has Jabavu sat on a chair, but he does so now, and thinks: Soon I, too, will have such chairs for the comfort of my body.

Mrs Kambusi is busy at the stove, and wonderful smells come from the pots on it. Betty puts knives and forks on the table, and Jabavu wonders how he will dare to use them without appearing ignorant. The little boy sits opposite and gazes with big, solemn eyes, and Jabavu feels inferior even to this child, who understands chairs and forks and knives.

When the food is ready, they eat. Jabavu makes his thick fingers handle the difficult knife and fork as he sees the others do, and his discomfort is soon forgotten in his delight at this delicious new food. There is fish again, which comes all the way from the big lakes in Nyasaland, and there are vegetables in a thick and savoury liquid, and there are sweet, soft cakes

with pink sugar on them. Jabavu eats and eats until his
stomach is heavy and comfortable, and then he sees that Mrs
Kambusi is watching him. 'You have been very hungry,' she
observes pleasantly, speaking in his own tongue. It seems to
Jabavu that he has not heard it for many months, instead of
only three days, and he says gratefully: 'Ah, my friend, you
are one of my people.'

'I was,' says Mrs Kambusi, with a smile that has a certain
quality, and again discomfort fills him. There is a hardness
in her, and yet the hardness is not meant as cruelty against
him. Her eyes are quick and shrewd, like black sparks, and she
says: 'Now I will give you a little lesson, listen. In the villages
we may enter and greet our brothers, and take hospitality from
them by right of blood and kinship. This is not the case here,
and every man is a stranger until he has proved himself a
friend. And every woman too,' she adds, glancing at Betty.

'This I have heard, my mother,' says Jabavu, gratefully.

'What have I been telling you? I am not your mother.'

'And yet,' says Jabavu, 'I come to the city and who sets
food before me but a woman from my own people?'

And changing to English she says, quietly: 'You will pay for
your food, also, you come here as Betty's friend and not as my
friend.'

Jabavu's spirits are chilled by this coldness, and because he
has no money for the food. Then he sees again the clever eyes
of this woman, and knows this is meant as kindness.

Speaking in their mutual tongue she continues: 'And now
listen to me. This girl here, whose name I will not say so that
she does not know we are speaking of her, has told me your
story. She has told me of your meeting with the men of light
in the bush at night, and how they took a liking to you and
gave you the name of their friend here – I will not say the
name, for the people who are friends of the girl who sits here
trying to understand what we say do not like the men of light.
You will understand why not when you have been in the city
a little longer. But what I wish to tell you is this. It is probable
that like most boys who come newly to the city you have many
fine ideas about the life, and what you will do. Yet it is a
hard life, much harder than you now know. My life has been
hard, and still is, though I have done very well because I use
my head. And if I were given the chance to begin again,
knowing what I know now, I would not lightly throw away

that piece of paper with the name written on it. It means a great deal to enter that house as a friend, to be the friend of that man – remember it.'

Jabavu listens, his eyes lowered. It seems that there are two different voices speaking inside him. One says: This is a woman of great experience, do as she says, she means you well. Another says: So! Here is another busybody giving you advice; an old woman who has forgotten the excitements of being young, who wishes you to be as quiet and sleepy as herself.

She continues, leaning forward, her eyes fixed on his: 'Now listen. When I heard you had fallen in with the men of light before you even entered the city, I asked myself what kind of good luck it was that you carry with you! And then I remembered that from their hands you had fallen into those which we now see lying on the table, twitching crossly because what we say is not understood. Your luck is very mixed, my friend. And yet it is very powerful, for many thousands of our people enter this city and know nothing of either the men of light or the men of darkness – for whom this very bad girl sitting here works – save what they hear through other mouths. But since it has fallen out that you have a choice to make, I wish to tell you, speaking now as one of your own people, and as your mother, that you are a fool if you do not leave this girl and go immediately to the house whose number you know.'

She ceases speaking, rises and says: 'And now we shall have some tea.' She pours out cups of very strong, sweet tea, and for the first time Jabavu tastes it, and it seems very good to him. He drinks it, keeping his eyes lowered for fear of seeing the eyes of Betty. For he can feel that she is angry. Also, he does not want Mrs Kambusi to see what he is thinking, which is that he does not want to leave Betty – later, perhaps, not at once. For now that his body is fed and rested his desire is reaching out for the girl. When they both rise he still keeps his eyes lowered, and so watches how Betty puts money on the table for the meal. But what money! It is four shillings each, and wonder fills him at these women who handle such sums so casually. And then a quick glance at Mrs Kambusi shows him that she watches him with a heavy, ironical look, as if she understands quite well everything in his mind. 'Thank you for what you have told me,' he says, since he does not want to lose her favour; and she replies: 'It will be time to thank me when you have profited by it,' and without looking his way again, reaches for a book, lifts her child on her knee, and so sits teaching the child from the book as the young people go out, saying goodnight.

'What did she say to you?' asks Betty, as soon as the door is closed.

'She gave me good advice about the city,' says Jabavu, and then says, wishing to be told about her: 'She is a kind and clever woman.' But Betty laughs scornfully: 'She is the biggest skellum in the city.' 'And how is that?' he asks, startled; but she flaunts her hips a little and says: 'You will see.' Jabavu does not believe her. They reach her room, and now Jabavu pushes her on to the bed and puts his arm around her so that his hand is on her breast.

'And how much?' she asks, with contempt that is meant to goad him.

Jabavu sees how her eyes are heavy, and says simply: 'You know from my own mouth that I have no money.'

She lies loosely in his arm and says laughing, to tease him: 'I want five shillings, perhaps fifteen.'

Jabavu says, scornfully: 'And perhaps fifteen pounds.'

'For you no money,' she says, sighing; and Jabavu takes her for his own pleasure, allowing hers to look after itself, until he has had enough and lies sprawled across the bed, half-naked, and thinks: This is my first day in the city, and what have I not done? Truly Mrs Kambusi is right when she says I have powerful luck with me. I have even had one of these smart town girls, and without paying. The words turn into a song.

> *Here is Jabavu in the city,*
> *He has a yellow shirt and new trousers,*
> *He has eaten food like a lion,*
> *He has filled a woman of the town with his strength.*
> *Jabavu is stronger than the city.*
> *He is stronger than a lion.*
> *He is stronger than the women of the town.*

This song moves sleepily through his mind and dies in sleep, and he wakes to find the girl sitting on the foot of the bed, looking impatiently at him and saying: 'You sleep like a chicken with the setting of the sun.' He says, lazily: 'I am tired with the journey from my kraal.'

'But I am not tired,' she says lightly, and adds: 'I shall dance tonight, if not with you, with someone else.' But Jabavu says nothing, only yawns and thinks: This girl is only a woman like any other. Now I have had her I do not care. There are many in the city.

And so after a while she says, in that sweet, humble voice: 'I was teasing you only. Now get up, lazy boy. Do you not want to see the dancing?' She adds, cunningly: 'And to see also how the clever Mrs Kambusi runs a shebeen.'

But by now Mrs Kambusi and what she has said seem unimportant to Jabavu. He yawns, gets off the bed, puts on his trousers, and then combs his hair. She watches him with bitterness and admiration. 'Kraal boy,' she says, in a soft voice, 'you have been in the city half a day, and already you behave as if you were tired of it.' This pleases him, as it was meant to do, and so he fondles her breasts a little, and then her buttocks, until she slaps him with pleasure and laughs, and so they go together into the other room. And now it is full of people sitting around the walls on the benches, while there are some men with things to make music sitting on the chairs at the end. Through the open door is the dark night, and continually more people enter.

'So this is a shebeen?' says Jabavu, doubtfully, for it looks very respectable, and she replies: 'You will see what it is.' The music begins. The band is a saxophone, a guitar, a petrol tin for a drum, a trumpet, and two tins to bang together. Jabavu does not know this music. And to begin with, the people do not dance. They sit with tin mugs in their hands, and allow their limbs to move, while their heads and shoulders begin to nod and jerk as the music enters them.

Then the other door opens and Mrs Kambusi comes in. She looks the same, clean and nice in her pink dress. She carries a very big jug in her hand, and moves around from mug to extended mug, pouring in liquor from the jug and holding out her free hand for the money. A little boy follows her. It is not her own child, who is asleep in the room next door and forbidden ever to see what happens in this room. No, this is a child whom Mrs Kambusi hires from a poor family, and his work is to run out into the darkness where there is a drum of skokian buried, to bring supplies as needed, so that if the police should come it will not be found in the house, and also to take the money and put it in a safe place under the walls.

Skokian is a wicked and dangerous drink, and it is illegal. It is made quickly, in one day, and may contain many different substances. On this night it has mealie-meal, sugar, tobacco, methylated spirits, boot polish, and yeast. Some skokian queens use magic, such as the limb of a dead person, but Mrs Kambusi does not believe in magic. She makes plenty of money without it.

When she reaches Jabavu she asks in a low voice in their language: 'And so you wish to drink?'

'Yes, my mother,' he says humbly, 'I wish to taste it.'

She says: 'Never have I drunk it, though I make it every day. But I will give you some.' She pours him out half a cup instead of filling it, and Jabavu says, in the voice of his surly, hungry, angry youth: 'I will have it full.' And she stops in the act of turning away and gives him a glare of bitter contempt. 'You are a fool,' she says. 'Clever people make this poison for fools to drink. And you are one of the fools.' But she pours out more skokian until it slops over, smiling so that no one may know how angry she is, and moves on up the line of seated men and women, making jokes and laughing, while the little boy behind her holds out a tray full of sweets and nuts and fish and cakes with the sugar on top.

Betty asks, jealously: 'What did she say to you?'

Jabavu says: 'She gives me the drink for nothing because we come from the same district.' And it is true she has forgotten to take money from Jabavu.

'She likes you,' says Betty, and he is pleased to see she is jealous. Well, he thinks, these clever town women are as simple as the village girls! And with this thought he gives a certain smile across the room to Mrs Kambusi, but he sees how Mrs Kambusi only looks contemptuous, and so Betty laughs at him. Jabavu leaps to his feet to hide his shame and begins to dance. He has always been a great dancer.

He dances invitingly around the girl, throwing out his legs, until she laughs and rises and joins him, and in a moment the room is full of people who wriggle and stamp and shout, and the air fills with dust and the roof shakes and even the walls seem to tremble. Soon Jabavu is thirsty and dives towards his mug on the bench. He takes a big mouthful – and it is as if fire entered him. He coughs and chokes while Betty laughs. 'Kraal boy,' she says, but in a soft, admiring

voice. And Jabavu, taunted, lifts the mug and drains it, and it
sinks through him, lighting his limbs and belly and brain
with madness. And now Jabavu really dances, first like a bull,
standing over the girl with his head lowered and shoulders
hunched forward, sniffing at her breasts while she shakes them
at him, and then like a cock, on the tips of his toes with his
arms held out, lifting his knees and scraping his heels, and all
the time the girl wriggles and shakes in front of him, her hips
writhing, her breasts shaking, the sweat trickling down her.
And soon Jabavu grabs her, swings her through the dancers
into the other room, and there he flings her on the bed. Afterwards they return and continue to dance.

Later Mrs Kambusi comes round with the big white jug,
and when he holds out his mug, she refills it saying, with a
bright, hard smile: 'That's right, my clever friend, drink,
drink as much as you can.' This time she holds out her hand
for money, and Betty puts money into it. He swallows it all
in one gulp, so that he staggers with the power of it, and the
room swings around him. Then he dances in the packed mass
of sweating, leaping people, he dances like a devil and there
is the light of madness on his face. Later, but he does not
know how long afterwards, there is Mrs Kambusi's voice
calling 'Police!' Betty grabs him and pulls him to the bench,
and they sit, and through a haze of drink and sickness he
sees that everyone has drained his mug empty and that the
child is quickly refilling them with lemonade. Then, at a
signal from Mrs Kambusi, three couples rise and dance, but in
a different way. When two black policemen enter the room
there is no skokian, the dancing is quiet, and the men of the
band are playing a tune that has no fire in it.

Mrs Kambusi, as calm as if she were grinding meal in her
village, is smiling at the policemen. They go round looking
at the mugs, but they know they will not find skokian for
they have raided this place often. It is almost as if old friends
enter it. But when they have finished the search for the skokian
they begin to look for people who have no passes; and it is at
this point that two men duck quickly under their arms and
out of the door, while Mrs Kambusi smiles and shrugs as if
to say: Well, is it my fault they have no passes?

When the policemen reach Jabavu he shows them the pass
for seeking work and his situpa, and they ask, When did he
come to town, and he says: 'This morning,' and they look

at each other. Then one asks: 'Where did you get those smart clothes?' Jabavu's eyes roll, his feet tense, he is about to spring towards the door in flight when Mrs Kambusi comes forward and says that she gave him the smart clothes. The policemen shrug, and one says to Jabavu: 'You have done well for one day in town.' It is said with unpleasantness, and Jabavu feels Betty's hand on his arm, saying to him: Be quiet, do not speak.

He remains silent, and when the policemen go they take with them four men and one woman who have not had the right passes. Mrs Kambusi follows them outside the door and slips a pound into the hands of each; they exchange formalities with good humour, and Mrs Kambusi returns, smiling.

For Mrs Kambusi has run this shebeen so long and so profitably not only because she is clever at arranging that the skokian and the large sums of money are never found in the house, but also because of the money she pays the police. And she makes it easy for them to leave her alone. As far as such places can be called orderly, hers is orderly. If the police are searching for a criminal they go first to the other skokian queens; and often Mrs Kambusi sends them a message: You are looking for so and so who was fighting last night? Well, you will find him in such a place. This arrangement is helpful for everybody, except perhaps the people who drink the skokian, but it is not Mrs Kambusi's fault that there are so many fools.

After a few minutes' quiet, for the sake of caution, Mrs Kambusi nods at the band, and the music changes in rhythm and the dancing goes on. But now Jabavu is no longer conscious of what he is doing. Other people see him dancing and shouting and drinking, but he remembers nothing after the police left. When he wakes he is lying on the bed, and it is midday, because the slant and colour of the light say it is. Jabavu moves his head and lets it fall back with a groan that is torn out of him. Never has he felt as he does now. Inside his head there is something heavy and loose which rolls as he moves it, and each movement sends waves of terrible sickness through him. It is as if his very flesh were dissolving, yet struggling not to dissolve, and pain moves through him like knives, and where it moves his limbs hang heavy and powerless. And so he lies, suffering and wishing himself dead, and sometimes darkness comes into his eyes then goes in a dazzle

of light, and after a long time he feels there is a heavy weight
on his arm and remembers that there is also a girl. And she,
too, lies and suffers and groans, and so they remain for a long
time. It is late afternoon when they sit up and look at each
other. The light still flickers inside their eyes, and so it is
not at once that they can see properly. Jabavu thinks: This
woman is very ugly. And she thinks the same of him, and
staggers off the bed towards the window where she leans,
swaying.

'Do you often drink this stuff?' asks Jabavu in wonder.

'You get used to it,' she says, sullenly.

'But how often?'

Instead of replying directly, she says: 'What are we to do?
There is one hall for all of us and there are thousands of us.
Into the hall only perhaps three or four hundred may go. And
there they sell bad beer, made by white men, who cannot
make our beer. And the police watch us like children. What do
you expect?'

These bitter words do not affect Jabavu at all because they
are not what she feels to be true, but are what she has heard
people say in speeches. Besides, he is lost in wonder that she
often drinks this poison and survives. He leans his head in his
hand and rocks back and forth gently, groaning. Then the
rocking makes him sick and so he keeps still. Again the time
goes past, and the dark begins to settle outside.

'Let us walk a little,' she says, 'it will relieve the sickness.'

Jabavu staggers off the bed and out into the other room,
and she follows. Mrs Kambusi, hearing them, puts her head
through her door and enquires, in a sweet, polite, contemptuous voice: 'Well, my fine friend, and how do you like
skokian?' Jabavu lowers his eyes and says: 'My mother, I shall
never take this bad drink again.' She looks at him, as if to say:
'We shall see!' and then asks: 'Do you wish to eat?' and
Jabavu shudders and says, through a wave of sickness: 'My
mother, I shall never eat again!' But the girl says: 'You know
nothing. Yes, we shall eat. It will help the sickness.'

Mrs Kambusi nods and goes back inside her door; the two
go outside to walk, moving like sick hens through the shanties
of tin and sacking, and then out to the area of bedraggled and
dirty grass.

'It is a bad drink,' she says, indifferently, 'but if you do not
drink it every day it does no harm. I have lived here now for

four years and I drink perhaps two or three times a month. I like the white man's drink, but it is against the law to buy it, for they say it may teach us bad ways, and so we have to pay much money to the coloured people who buy it for us.'

And now they feel their legs will not go any further, and they stand, while the evening wind sweeps into their faces, coming from far over the bush and the kopjes which can be seen many miles away, massed dark against the young stars. The wind is fresh, the sickness lies quiet in them and so they go back, walking slowly but more strongly. In one of the doorways of the brick sheds a man lies motionless, and now Jabavu does not need to ask what is wrong with him. Yet he halts, in an impulse to help him, for there is blood on his clothes. The girl gives him a quick, anxious look, and says: 'Are you crazy? Leave him,' and she pulls him away. Jabavu follows her, looking back at the hurt man, and he says: 'In this city it is true that we are all strangers!' His voice is low and troubled, and Betty says quickly, for she knows he is ashamed: 'And is it my fault? If we are seen near that man, people may think we hurt him ...' And then, since Jabavu still looks sullen and unhappy, she says in a changed voice, full of sadness: 'Ah, my mother! Sometimes I ask myself what it is I do here, and how my life is running away with fools and skellums. I was educated in a mission with the Roman sisters, and now what is it I am doing?' She glances at Jabavu to see how he takes her sadness, but he is not affected by it. His smile makes anger rise in her and she shouts: 'Yes, it is because men are such liars and cheats, every one. Five times a man has promised to marry me so that I may live properly in a house such as they rent to married people. Five times has this man gone away, and after I have bought him clothes and food and spent much money on him.' Jabavu walks quietly along, frowning, and she continues, viciously: 'Yes, and you too – you kraal boy, will you marry me? You have slept with me not once, but six, seven times, and in one night, and you have spent not one penny of money, though I see you have a shilling in your pocket, for I looked while you slept, and I have given you food and drink and helped you.' She has come close to him, eyes narrow and black with hate, and now Jabavu's mouth falls open with surprise, for she has opened her handbag and taken out a knife, and she moves the knife cunningly so that a pale gleam from the sky shows on it. Hau! thinks Jabavu, I have lain all night beside a woman who searches my pockets and carries a knife in her handbag. But he remains silent, while she comes so close her shoulders are against his chest and he feels the point of the knife pressing to his stomach. 'You will marry me or I kill you,' she says, and Jabavu's legs go weak. Then the courage comes to him with his contempt for her and he takes her wrist and twists it so that the knife falls to the ground. 'You are a bad girl,' he says, 'I not marry a bad girl with a knife and ugly tongue.'

And now she begins to cry while she kneels and scuffles after the knife in the dust. She rises, putting the knife carefully in her bag and she says: 'This is a bad town and the life here is bad and difficult.' Jabavu does not soften, for inside him a voice is saying the same thing, and he does not want to believe it since his hunger for the good things of the town is as strong as ever.

For the second time he sits at Mrs Kambusi's table and eats. There are potatoes fried with fat and salt, and then boiled mealies with salt and oil, and then more of the little cakes with pink sugar that he likes so much, and finally cups of the hot, sweet tea. Afterwards he says: 'What you say is true – the sickness is gone.'

'And now you are ready to drink skokian again?' asks Mrs Kambusi, politely. Jabavu glances quickly at her, for the quality of her politeness has changed. It seems to him that her eyes are very frightening, for now they are saying, in that cool, quietly bitter look: Well, my friend, you may kill yourself with skokian, you may spend your strength on this girl until you have none left, and I do not care. You may even learn sense and become one of the men of light – I do not care about that either. I simply do not care. I have seen too much. She rests her bulky body against the back of her chair, stirs her tea round and round with a fine, shiny spoon, and smiles with her cool, shrewd eyes until Jabavu rises and says: 'Let us go.' Betty also rises, pays eight shillings as she did the night before and, having said goodnight, they go out.

'Not only have I paid much money for your food,' says Betty, bitterly, 'but you sleep in my room, and your nice Mrs Kambusi, who you call your mother, charges me a fine rent for it, I can tell you.'

'And what do you do in your room?' asks Jabavu, laughing,

and Betty hits him. He holds her wrists, but with one hand, and puts his other on her breasts, and she says: 'I do not like you,' and he lets her go, laughing, and says: 'That I can see.' He goes into her room and lies on her bed as if this were his right, and she comes meekly after him and lies beside him. He is thinking, and besides even his bones are tired and aching, but she wishes to make love and begins to tease him with her hand, but he pushes it away and says: 'I wish only to sleep.' At this she rises angrily from beside him and says: 'You are a man? No, you are only a kraal boy.' This he cannot bear, so he gets up, throws her down and makes love to her until she no longer moves or speaks; and then he says, with swaggering contempt: 'Now you shut up.' But in spite of his pride in his knowledge of the nature of women it is a bad time for Jabavu, and sleep will not come. There is a fight going on inside him. He thinks of the advice Mrs Kambusi has given him, then, when it seems difficult to follow, he tells himself she is nothing but a skellum and a skokian queen. He thinks of Mr and Mrs Samu and their friend, and how they liked him and thought him clever, and just as he decides to go to them he groans with the thought of the hardness of their life. He thinks of this girl, and how she is a bad girl, without modesty or even beauty, except what the smart clothes give her, and then the pride rises in him and a song forms itself; I am Jabavu. I have the strength of a bull, I can quieten a noisy woman with my strength, I can ...

And then he remembers he has one shilling only and that he must earn some more. For Jabavu still thinks that he will do proper work for his money, he does not think of thieving. And so, though only half an hour before he made the girl sleep, he now shakes her, and she wakes reluctantly, crinkling the skin around her eyes against the glare from the unshaded yellow bulb that hangs from the roof. 'I want to know what work is paid best in this city?' he demands.

At first her face is foolish, then when she understands she laughs derisively, and says: 'You still do not know what work pays the best?' She closes her eyes and turns away from him. He shakes her again and now she is angry. 'Ah, be still, kraal boy, I will show you in the morning.'

'Which work is the most money?' he insists. And now she turns back, leans on her elbow and looks at him. Her face is bitter. It is not the truthful bitterness that can be seen on

Mrs Kambusi's face, but rather the self-pity of a woman. After a while she says: 'Well, my big fool, you can work in the white people's houses, and if you behave well and work for many years you may earn two or three pounds a month.' She laughs, because of the smallness of the sum. But Jabavu thinks it is a great deal. For a moment he remembers that the food he has eaten with Mrs Kambusi cost four shillings, but he thinks: She is a skellum after all, and probably cheats me. His confusion is really because he cannot believe that he, Jabavu, will not have what he wants simply by putting out his hand and taking it. He has dreamed so long and so passionately about this town, and the essence of a dream is that it must come disguised, smiling brightly, its dark side hidden where is written: This is what you must pay –

'And in the factories?' asks Jabavu.

'Perhaps one pound a month and your food.'

'Then tomorrow I shall go to the houses of the white men, three pounds is better than one.'

'Fool, you have to work months or years to earn three pounds.'

But Jabavu, having settled his own mind, falls asleep at once, and now she lies awake, thinking she is a fool to take up with a man from the kraals who knows nothing about the city; then she is sad, with an old sadness, because it is in her nature to love the indifference of men, and it is by no means the first time she has lain awake beside a sleeping man, thinking how he will leave her. Then she is frightened, because soon she must tell her gang about Jabavu, and there is the one man, who calls himself Jerry, clever enough to know that her interest in Jabavu is a good deal more than professional.

Finally, seeing no way out of her troubles, she drifts into the bitterness which is not her own, but learned from what others say; and she repeats that the white men are wicked and make the black live like pigs, and there is no justice, and it is not her fault she is a bad girl – and many things of this sort, until her mind loses interest in them and she falls asleep at last. She wakes in the morning to see Jabavu combing his hair, looking very handsome in the yellow shirt. She thinks, maliciously: The police will be looking for that shirt, and he will get into trouble. But it appears her desire to hurt him is not as strong as she thinks; for she pulls a suitcase from under

the bed, takes out a pink shirt, throws it at him and says:
'Wear this, otherwise you will be caught.'

Jabavu thanks her, but as if he expects such attention, then
says: 'Now you will show me where to go to find good work.'

She says: 'I will not come with you. I must earn money
for myself today. I have spent so much on you I have none
left.'

'I did not ask you to spend money on me,' says Jabavu,
cruelly, and she flashes out her knife again, threatening him
with it. But he says: 'Stop being a stupid woman. I am not
afraid of your knife.' So she begins to cry. And now Jabavu's
manhood, which has been fed with pride so much that he
feels there is nothing he cannot do, tells him that he should
comfort her, so he puts his arm around her and says: 'Do not
cry,' and, 'You are a nice girl, though foolish,' and also, 'I love
you.' And she weeps and says: 'I know about men, you will
never come back to me,' and he smiles and says: 'Perhaps I
will, perhaps not.' And saying this, he rises and goes out, and
the last thing she sees of him that morning are his white
teeth flashing in a gay smile. And so for a while she weeps,
then she grows angry, then she goes in search of Jerry and
the gang, thinking all the time of that impudent smile and
how she may speak to them so that they make Jabavu one of
the gang.

Jabavu goes from the place which is called Poland and
Johannesburg, walks through the Native Township, along the
busy road to the white man's city, and so to where the fine
houses are. And here he saunters along, choosing which house
he likes best. For his success since he came to the city has
given him such a swelled head he imagines the first he enters
will open its doors saying: Ah, here is Jabavu, I have been
waiting for you! When he has made up his mind, he walks
in through the gate and stands looking around, and an old
white woman who is cutting at some flowers with a shiny
pair of scissors says, in a sharp voice: 'What do you want?'
He says: 'I want work.' She says: 'Go to the back of the
house. What cheek!' He stands insolently in front of her, till
she shouts: 'Did you hear? Get to the back; since when do
you come to the front of a house asking for work?' And so he
walks out of the garden, cursing her to himself, listening to
how she grumbles and mutters about spoilt kaffirs, and goes to
the back of the house, where a servant tells him that here there

is no work for him. Jabavu is angry. He strolls into the sanitary lane, letting his anger make words of hatred: White bitch, filthy woman, white people all pigs. Then he goes to the back part of another house. There is a big garden here, with vegetables, a cat sitting fat and happy on a green lawn, and a baby in a basket under a tree. But there is no one to be seen. He waits, he walks about, he looks through the windows carefully, the baby coos in its basket, waving its legs and arms, and then Jabavu sees there are a row of shoes on the back veranda waiting to be cleaned. He cannot help looking at the shoes. He measures them with his eyes against his feet. He glances around – still no one in sight. He snatches up the biggest pair of shoes and goes into the sanitary lane. He cannot believe it is so easy, his flesh is prickling with fear of hearing angry voices or feet running after him. But nothing happens, so he sits down and puts on the shoes. Since he has never worn any, he does not know whether his discomfort is because they are too small or because his feet are not used to them. He walks on them and his legs make small, mincing steps of pain, but he is very proud. Now he is dressed, even his feet like a white man.

He goes to the back of another house, and this time the woman there asks him what work he knows. He says: 'Everything.' She asks him: 'Are you cook or houseboy?' And now he is silent. She asks: 'What money did you earn before?' And when he is still silent she asks to see his situpa. As soon as she looks at it, she says angrily: 'Why do you tell lies? You are a raw boy.' And so he goes out into the sanitary lane, angry and sore, but thinking of what he has learned, and when he goes to the next house and a woman asks what he knows, he puts on a humble look and says in a cringing voice that he has not worked in a white house before, but that he will learn quickly. He is thinking: I look so fine in my clothes, this woman will like a smart man like me. But she says she does not want a boy without experience. And now, as Jabavu walks away, his heart is cold and unhappy and he feels that no one in the whole world wants him. He whistles jauntily, making his fine new shoes stamp, and says he will surely find a good job with much money soon, but in the next house the woman says she will take him for rough work at twelve shillings a month. And Jabavu says he will not take twelve shillings and she hands him back his situpa and says, pleasantly enough, that he will not get more than twelve shillings without experience. Then she goes back into the house. This happens several times until in the afternoon Jabavu goes to a man chopping wood in a garden, whom he has heard speaking his own language, and he asks for advice. This man is friendly and tells him that he will not earn more than twelve or thirteen shillings a month until he has learned the work, and then, after many months, a pound. He will be given mealie-meal every day to make his porridge with, and meat once or twice a week, and he will sleep in a small room like a box at the back of the house with the other servants. Now all this Jabavu knows, for he has heard it often from people passing through the village, but he has not known it for himself; he has always thought: For me it will be different.

He thanks the friendly man and wanders on through the sanitary lanes, careful not to stop or loiter, otherwise a policeman may notice him. He is wondering: What is this experience? I, Jabavu, am the strongest of the young men in my village. I can hoe a field in half the time it takes any other; I can dance longer than anyone without tiring; all the girls like me best and smile as I go past; I came to this city two days ago and already I have clothes, and I can treat one of the clever women of the town like a servant and she loves me. I am Jabavu! I am Jabavu, come to the white man's town. He dances a little, shuffling through the leaves in the sanitary lane, but then he sees dust filming his new shoes, and so he stops. The sun will soon be sinking; he has not eaten since last night, and he wonders whether he should return to Betty. But he thinks: There are other girls, and he goes slowly through the sanitary lanes looking over the hedges into the gardens, and where there is a nanny hanging up clothes or playing with children, he looks carefully at her. He tells himself that he wants just such another girl as Betty, yet he sees one with her look of open and insolent attraction, and though he hesitates, he moves on, until at last he sees a girl standing by a white baby in a small cart on wheels, and he stops. She has a pleasant, round face, and eyes that are careful of what they say. She wears a white dress and has a dark-red cloth bound round her head. He watches her for a time and then says, in English: 'Good morning.' She does not at once answer, but looks at him first. 'Can you help me?' he asks again. Then she says: 'What can I tell you?'

From the sound of her voice he thinks she may be from his district, and he speaks to her in his language, and she answers him, smiling, and they move close and speak over the hedge. They discover that her village is not more than an hour's walking from his, and because the old traditions of hospitality are stronger than the new fear in both of them, she asks him to her room, and he goes. There, while the baby sleeps in its carriage, they talk, and Jabavu, forgetting how he has learned to speak to Betty, treats this girl as respectfully as he would one in the village.

She tells him he may sleep here tonight, having first said that she is bound to a man in Johannesburg, whom she will marry, so that Jabavu may not mistake her intention. She leaves him for a time, to help her mistress put the baby to bed. Jabavu is careful not to show himself, but sits in a corner, for Alice has said that it is against the law for him to be there, and if the police should come he must try and run away, for her mistress is kind and does not deserve trouble from the police.

Jabavu sits quietly, looking at the little room, which is the same size as Betty's and has the same brick walls and floor and tin roof, and sees that three people sleep here, for their bedding is rolled into separate corners, and he tells himself he will not be a houseboy. Soon Alice returns with food. She has cooked mealie-meal porridge, not as well as his mother would do, for that needs time, and it must be done on the mistress's stove. But there is plenty of it, and there is some jam her mistress has given her. As they eat they speak of their villages and of the life here. Alice tells him she earns a pound a month and the mistress gives her clothes and plenty of mealie-meal. She speaks with great affection of this woman, and for a time Jabavu is tempted to change his mind and find just such another for himself. But a pound a month – no, not for Jabavu, who despises Alice for being satisfied with so little. Yet he looks kindly at her and thinks her very pretty. She has stuck a candle in its own grease on the door-sill, and it gives a nice light, and her cheeks and eyes and teeth glisten. Also she has a soft, modest voice, which pleases him after the way Betty uses hers. Jabavu warms to her and feels her answering warmth for him. Soon there is a silence and Jabavu tries to approach her, but with respect, not as he would handle Betty. She allows him, and sits within his arm and tells him of the man who promised her marriage and then went to Johannesburg to earn money for the lobola. At first he wrote and sent money, but now there has been silence for a year. He has another woman now, so travellers have told her. Yet she believes he will come back, for he was a good man. 'So Johannesburg is not all bad?' asks Jabavu, thinking of the many different things he has heard. 'It seems that many like it, for they go once and then go again and again,' she says, but with reluctance, for it is not a thought she enjoys. Jabavu comforts her; she weeps a little, then he takes her, but with gentleness. Afterwards he asks her what would happen if there was a baby. She says that there are many children in the city who do not know their fathers; and then she tells him things that make him dizzy with astonishment and admiration. So that is why the white women have one or two or three children or none at all? Alice tells him of the things a woman may use, and a man may use; she says that many of the more simple people do not know of them, or fear them as witchcraft, but the wise people protect themselves against children for whom there are no fathers or homes. Then she sighs and says how much she longs for children and a husband, but Jabavu interrupts her to ask how he may obtain these things she has spoken about, and she tells him it is best to ask a kind white person to buy them, if one knows such a white person, or one may buy them from the coloured people who traffic in more things than liquor, or if one is brave enough to face a snubbing, one may go and ask in a white man's shop – there are some traders who will sell to the black people. But these things are expensive, she says, and need care in use, and . . . she continues to talk, and Jabavu learns another lesson for life in the big city, and he is grateful to her. Also he is grateful and warm to her because here is a girl who keeps her gentleness and her knowledge of what is right even in the city. In the morning he thanks her many times and says goodbye to her and to the two other men who came in to sleep in the room late at night, after visiting, and while she thanks him also, for politeness's sake, her eyes tell him that if he wished he could take the place of the man in Johannesburg. But Jabavu has already learned to be afraid of the way every woman in the city longs only for a husband, and he adds that he wishes for the early return of her promised husband so that she may be happy. He leaves her, and before he has reached the end of the sanitary lane is thinking what he should do next, while she looks after him and thinks sadly of him for many days.

It is early in the morning, the sun is newly risen, and there are few people in the streets. Jabavu walks for a long time around the houses and gardens, learning how the city is planned, but he does not ask for work. When he has understood enough of the place to find his way without asking questions at every corner he goes to the part of the town where the shops are, and examines them. Never has he imagined such richness and variety. Half of what he sees he does not understand, and he wonders how these things are used, but in spite of his wonder he never stands still before a window; he makes his legs move on even when they would rather stop, in order that the police may not notice him. And then, when he has seen windows of food and of clothes, and many other strange articles, he goes to the place where the Indian shops are for natives to buy in, and there he mixes with the crowds, listens to the gramophones playing music, and keeps his ears attentive so that he may learn from what people say, and so the afternoon slowly passes in learning and listening. When he grows hungry he watches until he sees a cart with fruit on it, he walks quickly past and takes half a dozen bananas with a skill that seems to have been born in his fingers, for he is astonished himself at their cunning. He walks down a side-street eating the bananas as if he had paid money for them, quite openly; and he is thinking what he should do next. Return to Betty? He does not like the thought. Go to Mr Mizi, as Mrs Kambusi says he should? But he shrinks from it – later, later, he thinks, when I have tasted all the excitements of the town. And in the meantime, he still owns one shilling, nothing else.

And so he begins to dream. It is strange that when he was in the village and made such dreams they were far less lofty and demanding than the one he makes now; yet, even in the ignorance of the village, he was ashamed of those small and childish dreams, while now, although he knows quite well what he is thinking is nonsense, the bright pictures moving through his mind grip him so fast he walks like a mad person, open-mouthed, his eyes glazed. He sees himself in one of the big streets where the big houses are. A white man stops him and says: I like you, I wish to help you. Come to my house.

I have a fine room which I do not use. You may live in it, and you may eat at my table and drink tea when you like. I will give you money when you need it. I have many books; you may read them all and become educated ... I am doing this because I do not agree with the colour bar and wish to help your people. When you know everything that is in the books, then you will be a man of light, just the same as Mr Mizi, whom I respect very much. Then I will give you enough money to buy a big house, and you may live in it and be a leader of the African people, like Mr Samu and Mr Mizi ...

This dream is so sweet and so strong that Jabavu at last stands under a tree, gazing at nothing, quite bewildered. Then he sees a policeman cycling slowly past and looking at him, and it does not mix well with the dream, and so he makes his feet walk on. The dream's sad and lovely colours are all around him still, and he thinks: The white people are so rich and powerful, they would not miss the money to give me a room and books to read. Then a voice says: But there are many others beside me, and Jabavu shakes himself crossly because of that voice. He cannot bear to think of others, his hunger for himself is so strong. Then he thinks: Perhaps if I go to school in the Township and tell them how I learned to read and write by myself they will take me in ... But Jabavu is too old for school, and he knows it. Slowly, slowly, the foolish sweetness of the dreaming leaves him, and he walks soberly down the road to the Township. He has no idea at all of what he will do when he gets there, but he thinks that something will happen to help him.

It is now early in the evening, about five, and it is a Saturday. There is an air of festivity and freedom, for yesterday was pay-day, and people are looking how best to spend their money. When he reaches the market he lingers there, tempted to spend his shilling on some proper food. But now it has become important to him, like a little piece of magic. It seems to him he has been in the city for a very long time, although it is only four days, and all that time the shilling has been in his pocket. He has the feeling that if he loses it he will lose his luck. Also there is another thought – it took his mother so long to save it. He wonders that in the kraal a shilling is such a lot of money, whereas here he could spend it on a few boiled mealies and a small cake. He is angry with himself because of this feeling of pity for his mother, and mutters: 'You big fool, Jabavu,' but the shilling stays in his pocket and he wanders on, thinking how he may find something to eat without asking Betty, until he reaches the Recreation Hall, which has people surging all around it.

It is too early for the Saturday dancing, and so he loiters through the crowd to see what is happening. Soon he sees Mr Samu with some others at a side door, and he goes closer with the feeling: Ah, here is someone who will help me. Mr Samu talks to a friend, in the way in which Jabavu recognizes, as if that friend is not one person but many; and Mr Samu's eyes move from one face near to him to another, and then on, always moving, as if it is with his eyes that he holds them, gathers them in, makes them one. And his eyes rest on Jabavu's face, and Jabavu smiles and steps forward – but Mr Samu, still talking, is looking at someone else. Jabavu feels as if something cold hit his stomach. He thinks, and for the first time: Mr Samu is angry because I ran away that morning; and at once he walks jauntily away, saying to himself: Well, I don't care about Mr Samu, he's nothing but a big talker, these men of light, they are just fools, saying Please, Please to the Government! Yet he has not gone a hundred yards when his feet slow, he stops, and then his feet seem to turn him around so that he must go back to the Hall. Now the people are crowding in at the big door, Mr Samu has gone inside, and Jabavu follows at the back of the crowd. By the time he has got inside the hall is full, and so he stands at the back against the wall.

On the platform are Mr Samu, the other man who was with him in the bush, and a third man, who is almost at once introduced as Mr Mizi. Jabavu's eyes, dazed with so many people all together, hardly see Mr Mizi's face, but he understands this is a man of great strength and cleverness. He stands as straight and tall as he can so that Mr Samu may see him, but Mr Samu's eyes again move past without seeing, and Jabavu thinks: But who is Mr Samu? Nothing beside Mr Mizi ... And then he looks at how these men are dressed, and sees their clothes are dark and sometimes old, sometimes even with patches on them. There is no one in this hall who has as bright and smart clothes as Jabavu himself, and so the small, unhappy child in Jabavu quietens, appeased, and he is able to stand quietly listening.

Mr Mizi is talking. His voice is powerful, and the people

on the benches sit motionless, leaning forward, and their faces
are full of longing, as if they are listening to a beautiful
story. Yet what Mr Mizi says is not at all beautiful. Jabavu
cannot understand, and asks a man near him what this meeting is. The man says that the men on the platform are the
leaders for the League for the Advancement of the African
People; that they are now discussing the laws which treat
Africans differently from the white people ... they are very
clever, he says; and can understand the laws as they are written, which it takes many years to do. Later the meeting
will be told about the management of land in the reserves,
and how the Government wishes to reduce the cattle owned
by the African people, and about the pass laws and also many
other things. Jabavu is shown a piece of paper with numbers
1, 2, 3, 4, 5, and 6, and opposite these numbers are written
words like Destocking of Cattle. He is told this piece of paper
is an Agenda.

First Mr Mizi speaks for a long time, then Mr Samu, then
Mr Mizi again, and sometimes the people in the hall seem to
growl with anger, sometimes they sigh and call out 'Shame!'
and these feelings, which are like the feelings of one person,
become Jabavu's also, and he, too, claps and sighs and calls
out 'Shame, Shame!' Yet he hardly understands what is said.
After a long time Mr Mizi rises to speak on a subject which is
called Minimum Wage, and now Jabavu understands every
word. Mr Mizi says that not long ago a member of the white
man's Parliament asked for a law which would make one
pound a month a minimum wage for African workers, but
the other members of Parliament said 'No,' it would be too
much. And now Mr Mizi says he wishes every person to sign
a petition to the members of Parliament to reconsider this cruel
decision. And when he says this, every man and woman in
the hall roars out 'Yes, yes,' and they clap so long that
Jabavu's hands grow tired. And now he is looking at those
great and wise men on the platform, and every nerve of his
body longs to be like them. He sees himself standing on a platform while hundreds of people sigh and clap and cry 'Yes,
yes!'

And suddenly, without knowing how it has happened, his
hand is raised and he has called out, 'Please, I want to speak.'
Everybody in the hall has turned to look, and they are surprised. There is complete silence in the hall. Then Mr Samu

stands up quickly and says, after a long look at Jabavu:
'Please, this is a young friend of mine, let him speak.' He
smiles and nods at Jabavu, who is filled with immense pride,
as if a great hawk carried him into the sky on its wings. He
swaggers a little as he stands. Then he speaks of how he came
from his kraal only four days ago, how he outwitted the recruiters who tried to cheat him, how he had no food and
fainted with hunger and was handled like an ox by the white
doctor, how he has searched for work ... The words flow to
Jabavu's tongue as if someone very clever stood behind his
shoulder and whispered them into his ear. Some things this
clever person does not mention, such as how he stole clothes
and shoes and food, and how he fell in with Betty and spent
the night in the shebeen. But he tells how in the white
woman's garden he had been rudely ordered to the back,
'which is the right place for niggers' – and this Jabavu tells
with great bitterness – and how he had been offered twelve
shillings a month and his food. And as Jabavu speaks the
people in the hall murmur, 'Yes, yes.'

Jabavu is still full of words when Mr Samu stands up, inter-
rupting him, saying: 'We are grateful to our young friend for
what he has said. His experiences are typical for young men
coming to town. We all know from our own lives that what
he says is true, but it does no harm to hear it again.' And
with this he quietly introduces the next subject, which is how
terrible it is that Africans must carry so many passes, and
the meeting goes on. Jabavu is upset, for he feels that it is
not right the meeting should simply go on to something else
after the ugly things he has told them. Also, he has seen that
some of the people, in turning back to the platform, have
smiled at each other, and that smile stung his pride. He
glances at the man next to him, who says nothing. Then, since
Jabavu continues to look and smile, as if wanting words, the
man says pleasantly: 'You have a big mouth, my friend.' At
this, such rage fills Jabavu that his hand lifts by itself, and very
nearly hits the man, who swiftly clasps Jabavu's wrist and
murmurs: 'Quiet, you will make big trouble for yourself. We
do not fight here.' Jabavu mutters in anguish: 'My name is
Jabavu, not Big Mouth,' and the man says: 'I did not speak
of your name, I do not know it. But in this place we do not
fight, for the men of light have trouble enough without that.'

Jabavu struggles his way towards the door, for it is as if his ears were full of mocking laughter, and Big Mouth, Big Mouth, repeated often. Yet the people are standing packed in the door and he cannot go out, though he tries so that he disturbs them, and they ask him to be quiet. And while Jabavu stands there, angry and unhappy, a man says to him: 'My friend, what you said spoke to my heart. It is very true.' And Jabavu forgets his bitterness and at once is calm and full of pride; for he cannot know that this man spoke only so as to see his face clearly, for he comes to all such meetings pretending to be like the others in order to return later to the Government office which wishes to know who of the Africans are troublemakers and seditious. Before the meeting is over, Jabavu has told this friendly man his name and his village, and how much he admires the men of light, information which is very welcome.

When Mr Samu declares the meeting closed, Jabavu slips out as quickly as he can and goes out to the other door where the speakers will come. Mr Samu smiles and nods when he sees him, and shakes his hand, and introduces him to Mr Mizi. None congratulates him on what he has said, but rather look at him like village elders who think: That child may grow up to be useful and clever if his parents are strict with him. Mr Samu says: 'Well, well, my young friend, you haven't had good luck since you came to the city, but you make a mistake if you think yours is an exceptional case.' Then, seeing Jabavu's dismayed face, he says, kindly: 'But why did you run away so early and why did you not go to Mr Mizi who is glad to help people who need help?' Jabavu hangs his head and says that he ran away so early because he wished to reach the city soon and did not want to disturb their sleep for nothing, and that he could not find Mr Mizi's house.

Mr Mizi says: 'Then come with us now, and you will find it.' Mr Mizi is a big man, strong, heavy-shouldered. If Jabavu is like a young bull, clumsy with his own strength, then Mr Mizi is like an old bull who is used to his power. His face is not one a young man may easily love, for there is no laughter in it, no easy warmth. He is stern and thoughtful and his eyes see everything. But if Jabavu does not love Mr Mizi, he admires him, and at every moment he feels more like a small boy, and as this feeling of dependence, which is one he hates and makes him angry, grows in him, he does not know whether to run away or stay where he is. He stays, however, and walks with a group of others to Mr Mizi's house.

It is a house similar to that of the Greek. Jabavu knows now that compared with the houses of the white men it is nothing, but the front room seems very fine to him. There is a big mirror on the wall, and a big table covered with soft green stuff that has thick, silky tassels dangling, and around this table, many chairs. Jabavu sits on the floor as a mark of respect, but Mrs Mizi, who is welcoming her guests, says kindly: 'My friend, sit on this chair,' and pushes it forward for him. Mrs Mizi is a tiny woman, with a merry face and eyes that dart everywhere looking for something to laugh at. It seems that there is so much laughter in Mrs Mizi that there is no room for it in Mr Mizi, while Mr Mizi thinks so much he has taken all thought from Mrs Mizi. Seeing Mrs Mizi alone it is hard to believe she should have a big, stern, clever husband; while seeing Mr Mizi, one would not think of his wife as small and laughing. Yet together they fit each other, as if they make one person.

Jabavu is so full of awe at being here that he knocks over the chair and feels he would like to die of shame, but Mrs Mizi laughs at him with such good nature that he begins to laugh too, and only stops when he sees that this gathering of friends is not only for friendship, but also for serious talking.

Seated around the table are Mr Samu and Mrs Samu and the brother, and Mr Mizi and Mrs Mizi and a young boy who is the Mizis' son. Mrs Mizi sets tea on the table, in nice white cups, and plenty of little cakes with pink sugar. The young boy drinks one cup of tea quickly, and then says he wishes to study and goes next door with a cake in his hand, while Mrs Mizi rolls up her eyes and complains that he will study himself to death. Mr Mizi, however, tells her not to be a foolish woman, and so she sits down, smiling, to listen.

Mr Mizi and Mr Samu talk. It appears that they talk to each other, yet sometimes they glance at Jabavu, for what they are saying is not just what comes into their heads, but is chosen to teach Jabavu what it is good for him to know.

Jabavu does not at once understand this, and when he does that familiar storm of resentment clouds his hearing; one voice says: I, Jabavu, treated like a small child; while the other says: These are good people, listen. So it is only in fragments that their words enter his mind, and there they form a strange and twisted idea that would surprise these wise and clever men if they could see it. But perhaps it is a weakness of such men, who spend their lives studying and thinking and saying things such as: The movement of history, or the development of society, that they forget the childhood of their own minds, when such phrases have a strange and even terrible sound.

So there sits Jabavu at the table, eating the cakes which Mrs Mizi presses on him, and his face is first sullen and unwilling, then bright and eager, and sometimes his eyes are lowered to hide what he thinks, and then they flash up, saying: Yes, yes, that is true!

Mr Mizi is saying how hard it is for the African when he first comes to the town knowing nothing save that he must leave everything he has learned in the kraal behind him. He says that such a young man must be forgiven if out of confusion he drifts into the wrong company.

And here Jabavu instinctively lifts his arms to cross them over his bright new shirt, and Mrs Mizi smiles at him and refills his cup.

Then Mr Samu says that such a young man has the choice of a short life, with money and a good time, before prison or drink or sickness overtake him, or he may work for the good of his people and ... but here Mrs Mizi lets out a yell of laughter and says: 'Yes, yes, but that may be a short life too, and prison, just as much.'

Mr Mizi smiles patiently and says that his wife likes a good joke, and there is a difference between prison for silly things like stealing, and prison for a good cause. Then he goes on to say that a young man of intelligence will soon understand that the company of the matsotsis leads only to trouble, and will devote himself to study. Further, he will soon understand that it is foolish to work as a cook or houseboy or office-boy, for such people are never more than one or two or three together, but he will go into a factory, or even to the mines, because ... But for the space of perhaps ten minutes Jabavu understands not one word, since Mr Mizi is using such phrases as the development of industry, the working class, and historical mission. When what Mr Mizi says becomes again easy to follow, it is that Jabavu must become such a worker that everyone trusts him, and at night he will study on his own or with others, for a man who wishes to lead others must not only be better than they, but also know more ... and here

Mrs Mizi giggles and says that Mr Mizi has a swelled head, and he is only a leader because he can talk louder than anyone else. At which Mr Mizi smiles fondly, and says a woman should respect her husband.

Jabavu, breaking into this flirtation between Mr Mizi and Mrs Mizi asks suddenly: 'Tell me, please, how much money will I earn in a factory?' And there is the hunger in his voice so that Mr Mizi frowns a little, and Mrs Mizi makes a little grimace and a shake of the head.

Mr Mizi says: 'Not much money. Perhaps a pound a month. But ...'

And here Mrs Mizi laughs irrepressibly and says: 'When I was a girl at the Roman school, I heard nothing but God, and how I must be good, and sin is evil, and how wicked to want to be happy in this life, and how I must think only of heaven. Then I met Mr Mizi and he told me there is no God, and I thought: Ah, now I shall have a fine, handsome man for a husband, and no Church and plenty of fun and dancing and good times. But what I find is that even though there is no God, still I have to be good and not think of dancing or a good time, but only of the time when there is a heaven on earth – sometimes I think these clever men are just as bad as the preachers.' And at this she shakes with laughter so much she puts her hand over her mouth, and she makes big eyes at her husband over her hand, and he sighs and says patiently: 'There is a certain amount of truth in what you say. There was once a time in the development of society when religion was progressive and held all the goodness of mankind, but now that goodness and hope belong to the movements of the people everywhere in the world.'

These words make no sense to Jabavu and he looks at Mrs Mizi for help, like a small child at its mother. And it is true that she knows more of what is passing through his mind than either of the two clever men or even Mrs Samu, who has none of the child left in her.

Mrs Mizi sees Jabavu's eyes, demanding love from her, and protection from the harshness of the men, and she nods and smiles at him, as if to say: Yes, I laugh, but you should listen, for they are right in what they say. And Jabavu drops his head and thinks: For the whole of my life I must work for one pound a month and study at nights and have no fine clothes or dancing ... and he feels his old hunger raging in him, saying: Run, run quickly, before it is too late.

But the men of light see so clearly what should be Jabavu's proper path that to them it seems no more needs to be said, and they go on to discuss how a leader should arrange his life, just as if Jabavu were already a leader. They say that such a man must behave so that no one may say: He is a bad man. He must be sober and law-abiding, he must be careful never to infringe even the slightest of the pass-laws, nor forget to have a light on his bicycle or be out after curfew, for – and here they smile as if it were the best of jokes – they get plenty of attention from the police as things are. If they are entrusted with money they must be able to account for every penny – 'As if,' says Mrs Mizi, giggling, 'it were money from heaven which God will ask them to account for.' And they must each have one wife only, and be faithful to her – but here Mrs Mizi says, playfully, that even without these considerations Mr Mizi would have one woman only, and so he needn't blame that on the evils of time.

At this, everyone laughs a great deal, even Mr Mizi; but they see Jabavu does not laugh at all, but sits silent, face puckered with difficult thought. And then Mr Samu tells the following story, for the proper education of Jabavu, while the voices bicker and argue inside him so loudly he can hardly hear Mr Samu's voice above them.

'Mr Mizi,' says Mr Samu, 'is an example to all who wish to lead the African people to a better life. He was once a messenger at the Office of the Native Commissioner, and even an interpreter, and so was respected and earned a good salary. Yet, because he was forbidden, as employee of the Government, to talk at meetings or even be a member of the League, he saved his money, which took him many years, until he had enough to buy a little store in the Township, and so he left his employment and became independent. Yet now he must struggle to make a living, for it would be a terrible thing for the League if a leader should be accused of charging high prices or cheating, and this means that the other stores always make more money than the store of Mr and Mrs Mizi, and so . . .'

Very late, Jabavu is asked if he will sleep there for that night, and in the morning work will be found for him in a factory. Jabavu thanks Mr Mizi, then Mr Samu, but in a low and troubled voice. He is taken to the kitchen, where the son is still sitting over his books. There is a bed in the kitchen for this son, and a mattress is put on the floor for Jabavu. Mrs Mizi says to her son: 'Now that is enough studying, go to bed,' and he rises unwillingly from his books and leaves the kitchen to wash before sleeping. And Jabavu stands awkwardly beside the mattress and watches Mrs Mizi arrange the bed-clothes of the son more comfortably; and he feels a strong desire to tell her everything, how he longs to devote him-self to becoming a man of light, while at the same time he dreads it; but he does not, for he is ashamed. Then Mrs Mizi straightens herself and looks kindly at him. She comes to him and puts her hand on his arm, saying: 'Now my son, I tell you a little secret. Mr Mizi and Mr Samu are not so alarm-ing as they sound.' Here she giggles, while she keeps giving him concerned glances, and pushes his arm once or twice as if to say: Laugh a little, then things will seem easier! But Jabavu cannot laugh. Instead, his hand goes into his pocket and he brings out the shilling, and before he knows what he is doing he has pushed it into her hand. 'Now, what is this?' she asks, astonished. 'It is a shilling. For the work.' And now he longs above all that she should take the shilling and understand what he is saying. And at once she does. She stands there, looking at the shilling in her palm, then at Jabavu, and then she nods and smiles. 'That is well, my son,' she says, in a soft voice. 'That is very well. I shall give it to Mr Mizi and tell him you have given your last shilling to the work he does.' And she again puts her two hands on his arms and presses them warmly, then bids him goodnight and goes out.

Almost at once the son comes back and, having shut the door so that his mother will not see and scold him, goes back to the books. Jabavu lies on his mattress, and his heart is warm and big with love for Mrs Mizi and her kindness, also his good intentions for the future. And then, lying warm and idle there, he sees how the son's eyes are thick and red with study-ing, how he is serious and stern, just like his father, and yet he is the same age as Jabavu, and a cold dismay enters Jabavu, in spite of his desire to live like a good man, and he cannot help thinking: And must I also be like this, working all day and then at night as well, and all this for other people? It is in the misery of his thought that he falls asleep and dreams, and although he does not know what it is he dreams, he struggles and calls out, so loudly that Mrs Mizi, who has crept to the door to make sure her son has been sensible and gone to bed, hears him and clicks her tongue in compassion. Poor boy, she thinks, poor boy ... And so goes again to her bed, praying, as is her habit before sleep, but secretly, for Mr Mizi would be angry if he knew. She prays, as she has been taught in the Mission School of the Romans, for the soul of Jabavu, who needs help in his struggle against the temptations of the shebeens and matsotsis, and she prays for her son, of whom she is rather afraid, since he is so serious all the time and has always known exactly what he intends to become.

She prays so long, sitting in her bed, that Mr Mizi wakes and says: 'Eh, now, my wife, and what is this you are doing?' And she says meekly: 'But nothing at all.' And he says gruffly: 'And now sleep; that is better for our work than praying.' And she says: 'Surely times are so bad for our people that praying can do no harm, at least.' And he says: 'You are nothing but a child – sleep.' And so she lies down, and husband and wife go to sleep in great contentment with each other and with Jabavu. Mr Mizi is already planning how he will first test Jabavu for loyalty, and then train him, and then teach him how to speak at meetings, and then ...

Jabavu wakes from a bad dream when a cold, grey glimmer is already coming through the small window. The son is lying across his bed, asleep, still dressed, he has been too tired to remove his clothes.

He rises, light as a wild-cat, and goes to the table where the books lie tumbled, and looks at them. The words on them are so long and difficult he does not know what they mean. There he stands, silently, stiffly, in the small, cold kitchen, his hands clenched, his eyes rolling this way and that, first towards the clever and serious young man, who is worn out with his studying, and then towards the window, where the morning light is coming. For a very long time does Jabavu stand there, suffering with the violence of his feelings. Ah, he does not know what to do. First he takes a step towards the window, then he moves towards his mattress as if to lie down, and all the time his hunger roars and burns in him like a fire. He hears voices saying: Jabavu, Jabavu – but he does not know whether they commend a rich man with smart clothes or a man of light with knowledge and a strong persuasive voice.

And then the storm dies in him and he is empty, all feeling gone. He tiptoes to the window, slips the catch up, and is over the sill and out. There is a small bush beneath, and he crouches behind it, looking around him. Houses and trees seem to rise from shadows of night into morning, for the sky is clear and grey, flushed pink in long streaks, and yet there are street lamps glimmering pale above dim roads. And along these narrow roads move an army of people going to work, although Jabavu had imagined everything would still be deserted. If he had known, he would never have risked running away; but now he must somehow get from the bush to the road without being seen. There he crouches, shivering with cold, watching the people go past, listening to the thudding of their feet, and then it seems to him as if one of them is looking at him. It is a young man, slim, with a narrow, alert head, and eyes which look everywhere. He is one of the matsotsis, for his clothes say so. His trousers are narrow at the bottom, his shoulders are sharp, he wears a scarf of bright red. Over this scarf, it seems, his eyes peer at the bush where Jabavu is. Yet it is impossible, for Jabavu has never seen him before. He straightens himself, pretends he has been urinating into the bush, and walks calmly out into the road. And at once the young man moves over and walks beside him. Jabavu is afraid and he does not know why, and he says nothing, keeping his eyes fixed in front of him.

'And how is the clever Mr Mizi?' inquires the strange young man at last, and Jabavu says: 'I do not know who you are.'

At this the young man laughs and says: 'My name is Jerry, so now you know me.' Jabavu's steps quicken, and Jerry's feet move faster also.

'And what will clever Mr Mizi say when he knows you climbed out of his window?' asks Jerry, in his light, unpleasant voice, and he begins to whistle softly, with a smile on his face, as if he finds his own whistling very nice.

'I did not,' says Jabavu, and his voice quivers with fear.

'Well, well. Yet last night I saw you go into the house with Mr Mizi and Mr Samu, and this morning you climb out of the window, how is that?' asks Jerry in the same light voice, and Jabavu stops in the middle of the road and asks: 'Why do you watch me?'

'I watch you for Betty,' says Jerry, gaily, and continues to whistle. Jabavu slowly goes on, and he is wishing with all his heart he is back on Mrs Mizi's mattress in the kitchen. He can see that this is very bad for him, but he does not yet know why. And so he thinks: Why am I afraid? What can this Jerry do? I must not be like a small child. And he says: 'I do not know you, I do not want to see Betty, so now go away from me.'

Jerry says, making his voice ugly and threatening: 'Betty will kill you. She told me to tell you she will come with her knife and kill you.'

And Jabavu suddenly laughs, saying truthfully: 'I am not afraid of Betty's knife. She talks too much of it.'

Jerry is quiet for a few breaths, he is looking at Jabavu in a new way. Then he, too, laughs and says: 'Quite right, my friend. She is silly girl.'

'She is very silly girl,' agrees Jabavu, heartily, and both laugh and move closer together as they walk.

'What will you do next?' asks Jerry, softly, and Jabavu answers: 'I do not know.' He stops again, thinking: If I return quickly I can climb back through the window before anyone wakes, and no one will know I climbed out. But Jerry seems to know what he is thinking, for he says: 'It is a good joke you climb out of Mr Mizi's window like a thief,' and Jabavu says quickly: 'I am not a thief.' Jerry laughs and says: 'You are a big thief, Betty told me. You are very clever she says. You steal quickly so that no one knows.' He laughs a little and says: 'And what will Mr Mizi say if I tell him how you steal?'

Jabavu asks, foolishly: 'And will you tell him?' Again Jerry laughs, but does not answer, and Jabavu walks on silently. It takes some time for the truth to come into his head, and even then it is hard to believe. Then Jerry asks, still light and gay: 'And what did Mr Mizi say when you told him you had been at the shebeen and about Betty?'

'I told him nothing,' says Jabavu, sullenly, then he understands at last why Jerry is doing this, and he says eagerly: 'I told him nothing at all, nothing, and that is the truth.'

Jerry only walks on, smiling unpleasantly. Then Jabavu says: 'And why are you afraid of Mr Mizi ...' But he cannot finish for Jerry has whipped round and glares at him: 'Who has told you I am afraid? I am not afraid of that ... skellum.' And he calls Mr Mizi names Jabavu has never heard in his life.

'Then I do not understand you,' says Jabavu, in his simplicity, and Jerry says: 'It is true you understand nothing. Mr Mizi is a dangerous man. Because the police do not like him for what he does, he is very quick to tell the police if he knows of a theft or a fight. And he is making big trouble. Last month he held a meeting in the Hall, and he spoke about crime. He said it was the duty of every African to prevent skokian drinking and fighting and stealing, and to help the police close the shebeens and clean up Poland Johannesburg.' Jerry speaks with great contempt, and Jabavu thinks suddenly: Mr Mizi does not like enjoying himself so he stops other people doing it. But he is half-ashamed of this thought; first he says to himself: Yes, it would be good if Poland Johannesburg were cleaned up, then he says, hungrily: But I like dancing very much . . .

'And so,' Jerry goes on calmly, 'we do not like Mr Mizi.'

Jabavu wishes to say that he likes Mr Mizi very much, and yet he cannot. Something stops him. He listens while Jerry talks on and on about Mr Mizi, calling him those names that are new to Jabavu, and he can think of nothing to say. And then Jerry changes his voice and asks, threateningly: 'What did you steal from Mr Mizi?'

'I steal from Mr Mizi?' says Jabavu, amazed. 'But why should I steal there?' Jerry grabs his arm, stops him, and says: 'That is rich man, he has a store, he has a good house. And you tell me you stole nothing? Then you are a fool, and I do not believe you.' Jabavu stands helpless because of his surprise while he feels Jerry's quick fingers moving as light as wind through his pockets. Then Jerry stands away from him, in complete astonishment, and unable to believe what his own fingers have told him, goes through every pocket again. For there is nothing there but a comb, a mouth-organ, and a piece of soap. 'Where have you hidden it?' asks Jerry, and Jabavu stares at him. For this is the beginning of that inability to understand each other which will one day, and not so long distant, lead to bad trouble. Jerry simply cannot believe that Jabavu let an opportunity for stealing go past; while Jabavu could no more steal from the Mizis or the Samus than he could from his parents or his brother. Then Jerry decides to put on a show of belief, and says: 'Well, I have been told they are rich. They have all the money from the League in their house.' Jabavu is silent. Jerry says: 'And did you not see where it is hidden?' Jabavu makes an unwilling movement of his shoulders and looks about for escape. They have reached a crossroads, and Jabavu stops. He is so simple that he thinks of turning to the right, on the road that leads to the city, with the idea that he may return to Alice and ask her for help. But one look at Jerry's face tells him it is not possible, so he walks beside him on the other road that leads towards Poland Johannesburg. 'Let us go and see Betty,' says Jerry. 'She is a silly girl, but she's nice too.' He looks at Jabavu to make him laugh, and Jabavu laughs in just the way he wants; and in a few moments the two young men are saying of Betty that she is like this and like that, her body is so, her breasts so, and anyone looking at the two young men as they walk along, laughing, would think they are good friends, happy to be together.

And it is true that there is a part of Jabavu that is excited at the idea he will soon be in the shebeens and with Betty, although he comforts himself that soon he will run away from Jerry and go back to the Mizis, and he even believes it.

He expects they will go to Betty's room in Mrs Kambusi's house, but they go past it and down a slope towards a small river, and up the other side, and there is an old shack of a building which looks as if it were disused. There are trees and bushes all around it, and they go quickly through these, and to the back of the place, and through a window which looks as if it were locked, but opens under pressure of Jerry's knife, which he slides up against the latch. And inside Jabavu sees not only Betty, but half a dozen others, young men and a girl; and as he stands in fear, wondering what will happen, and looking crookedly at Betty, Jerry says in a cheerful voice: 'And this is the friend Betty told you about,' and winks, but so Jabavu does not see. And they greet him, and he sits down beside them. It is an empty room which was once a store, but now has some boxes for chairs and a big packing-case in the middle where there are candles stuck in their grease, and packs of cards, and bottles of various kinds of drink. No one is drinking, but they offer Jabavu food, and he eats. Betty is quiet and polite, and yet when he looks at her eyes he knows she likes him as much as before, and this makes him uneasy, and he is altogether uncomfortable and full of fear because he does not know what they want with him. Yet as time passes he loses his fear. They seem full of laughter, and without violence. Betty's knife does not leave her handbag, and all that happens is that she comes to sit near him and says, with rolling eyes: 'Are you pleased to see me again?' and Jabavu says that he is, and it is true.

Later they go to the Township and see the film show, and Jabavu is lifted clean out of his fear into a state so delirious that he does not notice how the others look at each other and smile. For it is a film of cowboys and Indians and there is much shooting and yelling and riding about on horses, and Jabavu imagines himself shooting and yelling and prancing about on a horse as he sees it on the screen. He wishes to ask how the pictures are made, but he does not want to show his ignorance to the others who take it all for granted. Afterwards it is midday and they go back, but in ones and twos, secretly to the disused store, and play cards. And by now Jabavu has forgotten that part of himself that wishes to become like Mr Mizi and be Mrs Mizi's son. It seems natural that he should play cards and sometimes put his hand on Betty's breasts, and drink. They are drinking kaffir beer, properly made, which means it is illegal, since no African is allowed to make it in the Township for sale. And when evening comes Jabavu is drunk, but not unpleasantly so, and his scruples about being here seem unimportant and even childish, and he whispers to Betty that he wishes to come to her room. Betty glances at Jerry, and for a moment rage fills Jabavu, for he thinks that perhaps Jerry, too, sleeps with Betty when he wishes – yet this morning he knew it, for Jerry said so, and then he did not mind, he and Jerry were calling her names and a whore. Now it is all different, and he does not like to remember it. But Betty says meekly, Yes, he may come, and he goes out with her, but not before Jerry has told him to meet him next morning so that they may work together. At the word 'work' everyone laughs, and Jabavu too. Then he goes with Betty to her room, and is careful to slip in through the big room filled with dancers, at a time when Mrs Kambusi is not in it, for he is ashamed to see her, and Betty humours him in everything he does and takes him to her bed as if she has been thinking of nothing else ever since he left. Which is nearly true, but not quite; she has been made to think by Jerry, and very disagreeably indeed, of her disloyalty and folly in becoming involved with Jabavu. When she first told him he was much angrier than she had expected, although she knew he would be angry. He beat her and threatened her and questioned her so long and brutally that she lost her head, which is never very strong at any time, and told all sorts of lies so conflicting that even now Jerry does not know what is the truth.

First she said she did not know Jabavu knew Mr Mizi, then she said she thought it would be useful to have someone in the gang who could tell them at any time what Mr Mizi's plans were – but at this Jerry slapped her and she began to cry. Then she lost her head and said she intended to marry Jabavu and they would have a gang of their own – but it was not long before she was very very sorry indeed she had said that. For Jerry took out his knife, which unlike hers was meant for use and not for show, and in a few moments she was writhing with inarticulate terror. So Jerry left her, with clear and certain orders which even her foolish head could not mistake.

But Jabavu, on this evening, is thinking only that he is jealous of Jerry, and will not support that another man sleeps with Betty. And he talks so long of it that she tells him, sulkily, that he has learned nothing yet, for surely he can see by looking at Jerry that he is not interested in women at all? This subtlety of the towns is so strange to Jabavu that it is some time before he understands it, and when he does he is filled with contempt for Jerry, and from this contempt makes a resolution that it is folly to be afraid of him, and he will go to the Mizis.

In the morning Betty wakes him early and tells him he must go and meet Jerry in such and such a place; and Jabavu says he does not wish to go, but will return instead to the men of light. And at this Betty springs up and leans towards him with frightened eyes and says: 'Have you not understood that Jerry will kill you?' And Jabavu says: 'I will have reached the Mizis' house before he can kill me,' and she says: 'Do not be like a child. Jerry will not allow it.' And Jabavu says: 'I do not understand this feeling about Mr Mizi – he does not like the police either.' And she says: 'Perhaps it is because once Jerry himself stole money from Mr Samu that belonged to the League, and ...' But Jabavu laughs at this and embraces her into compliance, and whispers to her that he will go to the Mizis' and change his life and become honest, and then he will marry her. He does not mean to do this, but

Betty loves him, and between her fear of Jerry and love for Jabavu, she can only cry, lying on the bed, her face hidden. Jabavu leans over her and says that he longs only for that night so that he may see her again, a thing that he heard a cowboy say on the pictures which they all visited together, and then he kisses her long and hard, exactly as he saw a kiss done between that cowboy and the lovely girl, and with this he goes out, thinking he will go quickly to Mr Mizi's house. But almost at once he sees Jerry waiting for him behind one of the tall brick huts.

Jabavu greets Jerry as if he were not at all surprised to see him there, which does not deceive Jerry in the least, and the two young men go towards the market, which is already open for buying, although it is so early, because the sellers sleep on their places at night, and they buy some cold boiled mealies and eat them walking along the road to the city. They walk in company with many others, some on bicycles. It is now about seven in the morning. The houseboys and cooks and nannies have gone to work a good hour since, these are the workers for the factories, and Jabavu sees their ragged clothes, and how poor they are, and how much less clever than Jerry, and cannot help feeling pleased he is not one of them. So resentful is he against Mr Mizi for wanting him to go into a factory, he begins to make fun of the men of light again, and Jerry laughs and applauds, and every now and again says a little bit more to spur Jabavu on.

So begins the most bewildering, frightening and yet exciting day Jabavu has ever known. Everything that happens shocks him, makes him tremble, and yet – how can he not admire Jerry, who is so cool, so quick, so fearless? He feels like a child beside him, and this happens before they have even begun their 'work'.

For Jerry takes him first to the back room of an Indian trader. This is a shop for Africans to buy in, and they may enter it easily with all the others who move in and out and loiter on the pavements. They stand for a while in the shop, listening to a gramophone playing jazz music, and then the Indian himself looks at them in a certain way, and the two young men slip unnoticed into a side room and through that into the back room. It is heaped with every kind of thing: second-hand clothes, new clothes, watches and clocks, shoes – but there is no end to them. Jerry tells Jabavu to take off his

clothes. They both do so, and put on ordinary clothes, so that
they may look like everyone else; khaki shorts, and Jabavu's
have a patch at the back, and rather soiled white shirts. No
tie and only canvas sandals for their feet. Jabavu's feet are very
happy to be released from the thick leather shoes, yet Jabavu
mourns to part with them, even for a time.

Then Jerry takes a big basket, which has a few fresh vegetables in it, and they leave the back room, but this time
through the door into the street. Jabavu asks who the Indian
is, but Jerry says, curtly, that he is an Indian who helps them
in their work, which tells Jabavu nothing. They walk up
through the area of kaffir shops and Indian stores, and Jabavu
looks marvelling at Jerry, who seems to be quite different,
like a rather simple country boy, with a fresh and open face.
Only his eyes are still the same, quick, cunning, narrow. They
come to a street of white people's houses, and Jerry and Jabavu
go to a back door and call out that they have vegetables for
sale. A voice shouts at them to go away. Jerry glances quickly
around: there is a table on the back veranda with a pretty
cloth on it, and he whisks it off, rolls it so fast that Jabavu
can scarcely see his fingers move, and it vanishes under the
vegetables. The two walk slowly away, just like respectable
vegetable sellers. And in the next house, the white woman
buys a cabbage, and while she is fetching money from inside,
Jerry takes, through an open window, a clock and an ashtray,
and these are hidden under the vegetables. In the next house
there is nothing to be stolen, for the woman is sitting on her
back veranda knitting where she may see everything, but
in the next there is another cloth.

Then there is a moment which makes Jabavu feel very bad,
though to Jerry it is a matter for great laughter: a policeman
asks them what they carry in the basket, but Jerry tells him
a long, sad story, very confused, about how they are for the
first time in the city and cannot find their way, and so the
policeman is very kind and helps them with good advice.

When Jerry has finished laughing at the policeman, he says:
'And now we will do something hard, everything we have
done so far has been work for children.' Jabavu says he does
not want to get into trouble, but Jerry says he will kill Jabavu
if he does not do as he is told. And this troubles Jabavu
for he never knows, when Jerry laughs and speaks in such a
way, whether he means it or not. One minute he thinks:

Jerry is making a joke; the next he is trembling. Yet there are moments, when they make jokes together, when he feels Jerry likes him – altogether, he is more confused about Jerry than about anyone he has known. One may say: Betty is like this or that, Mr Mizi is like this, but about Jerry there is something difficult, shadowy, and even in the moments when Jabavu cannot help liking him.

They go into a shop for white people. It is a small shop, very crowded. There is a white man serving behind the counter, and he is busy all the time. There are several women waiting to buy. One of them has a baby in a carriage and she has put her handbag at the foot of this carriage. Jerry glances at the bag and then at Jabavu, who knows quite well what is meant. His heart goes cold, but Jerry's eyes are so frightening that he knows he must take it.

The woman is talking to a friend and swinging the carriage a little way forwards, a little back, while the baby sleeps. Jabavu feels a cold wetness running down his back, his knees are soft. But he waits for when the white man has turned to reach something down from a shelf and the woman is laughing with her friend, and he nips the bag quickly out and walks through the door with it. There Jerry takes it and slips it under the vegetables. 'Do not run,' says Jerry, quietly. His eyes are darting everywhere, though his face is calm. They walk quickly around a corner and go into another shop. In this shop they steal nothing, but buy sixpence worth of salt. Afterwards Jerry says to Jabavu, and with real admiration: 'You are very good at this work. Betty told the truth. I have seen no one before who is so good so soon after beginning.' And Jabavu cannot help feeling proud, for Jerry is not one who gives praise easily.

They leave that part of the town and do a little more stealing in another, collecting another clock, some spoons and forks, and then, but by chance, a second handbag which is left on a table in a kitchen.

And then they return to the Indian shop. There Jerry bargains with the Indian, who gives them two pounds for the various articles, and there is five pounds from the two handbags. Jerry gives Jabavu one-third of the money, but Jabavu is suddenly so angry that Jerry pretends to laugh, and says he was only joking, and gives Jabavu the half that is due to him. And then Jerry says: 'It is now two o'clock in the after-

noon. In these few hours we have each earned three pounds.
The Indian takes the risk of selling those things that were
stolen and might be recognized. We are safe. And now – what
do you think of this work?'

Jabavu says, after a pause that is a little too long, for Jerry
gives him a quick, suspicious look: 'I think it is very fine.'
Then he says timidly: 'Yet my pass for seeking work is only
for fourteen days, and some of those have gone.'

'I will show you what to do,' says Jerry, carelessly. 'It is
easy. Living here is very easy for those who use their heads.
Also, one must know when to spend money. Also, there are
other things. It is useful to have a woman who makes a friend
of each policeman. With us, there are two such women. Each
has a policeman. If there should be trouble, those two policemen would help us. Women are very important in this work.'

Jabavu thinks about this, and then says quickly: 'And is
Betty one of the women?'

Jerry, who has been waiting for this, says calmly: 'Yes,
Betty is very good for the police.' And then he says: 'Do
not be a big fool. With us, there is no jealousy. I do not
allow it. I would not have women in the gang, since they are
foolish with the work, except they are useful for the police.
And I tell you now, I will have no trouble over the policeman.
If Betty says to you: Tonight there is my policeman coming,
then you say nothing. Otherwise . . .' And Jerry slips the half
of his knife a little way from his pocket so that Jabavu may
see it. Yet he remains smiling and friendly, as if it is all a joke.
And Jabavu walks on in silence. For the first time he understands clearly that he is now one of the gang, that Jerry is his
leader, that Betty is his woman. And this state of affairs will
continue – but for how long? Is there no way of escaping? He
asks, timidly: 'How long has there been this gang?'

Jerry does not reply at once. He does not trust Jabavu yet.
But since that morning he has changed his mind about him,
for he had planned to make Jabavu steal and then see that he
got into trouble with the police in such a way that would
implicate no one else, thus removing him as a danger. Yet he
is so impressed with Jabavu's quickness and cleverness at the
'work' that he wishes to keep him. He thinks: After another
week of our good life, when he has stolen several times and
perhaps been in a fight or two, he will be too frightened to
go near Mr Mizi. He will be one of us, and in perfect safety for

us all. He says: 'I have been leader of this gang for two years. There are seven in the gang, two women, five men. The men do the stealing, as we have this morning. The women are friends of the police, they make a friend of anyone who might be dangerous. Also, they pick up kraal boys who come to the town and steal from them. We do not allow the women to go into the streets or shops for stealing, because they are no good. Also, we do not tell the women the business of the gang, because they talk and because they do foolish things.' Here there is a pause, and Jabavu knows that Jerry is thinking that he himself is doing just such a foolish thing that Betty did. But he is flattered because Jerry tells him things the women are not told. He asks: 'And I would like to know other matters: supposing one of us gets caught, what would happen then?' And Jerry replies: 'In the two years I have been leader not one has been caught. We are very careful. But if you are caught, then you will not speak of the others, otherwise something will happen you won't like.' Again he slips up the haft of his knife, and again he is smiling as if it is all a joke. When Jabavu asks another question, he says: 'That is enough for today. You will learn the business of the gang in good time.'

And Jabavu, thinking about what he has been told, understands that in fact he knows very little and that Jerry does not trust him. With this, his longing for Mr Mizi returns, and he curses himself bitterly for running away. And he thinks sadly of Mr Mizi all the way along the road, and hardly notices where they are going.

They have turned off to a row of houses where the coloured people live. The house they enter is full of people, children everywhere, and they go through to the back and enter a small, dirty room that is dark and smells bad. A coloured man is lying on a bed in a corner, and Jabavu can hear the breath wheezing through his chest before he is even inside the door. He rises, and in the dimness of the room Jabavu sees a stooping, lean man, yellow with sickness beyond his natural colour, his eyes peering through the whitish gum that is stuck around the lashes, his mouth open as the breath heaves in and out. And as soon as he sees Jerry he slaps Jerry on the shoulder, and Jerry slaps him, but too hard for the sickness, for he reels back coughing and spluttering, gripping his arms across his painful chest, but he laughs as soon as he has breath. And Jabavu wonders at this terrible laughter which comes so often with these people, for what is funny about what is happening now? Surely it is ugly and fearful that this man is so sick and the room is dirty and evil, with the dirty, ragged children running and screaming along the passages outside? Jabavu is stunned with the horror of the place, but Jerry laughs some more and calls the coloured man some rude and cheerful names, and the man calls Jerry bad names and laughs. Then they look at Jabavu and Jerry says: 'Here is another cook-boy for you,' and at this they both rock with laughter until the man begins coughing again, and at last is exhausted and leans against the wall, his eyes shut, while his chest heaves. Then he gasps out, smiling painfully: 'How much?' and Jerry begins to bargain, as Jabavu has heard him with the Indian. The coloured man, through coughing and wheezing, sticks to his point, that he wants two pounds for pretending to employ Jabavu, and that every month; but Jerry says ten shillings, and at last they agree on one pound, which Jabavu can see was understood from the first – so why these long minutes of bargaining through the ugly, hurtful coughing and smell of sickness? Then the coloured man gives Jabavu a note saying he wishes to employ him as a cook, and writes his name in Jabavu's situpa. And then, peering close, showing his broken, dirty teeth, he wheezes out: 'So you will be a good cook, hee, hee, hee . . .' And at this they go out, both young men, shutting the door behind them, and down the dim passage through the children, and so out into the fresh and lovely sunshine, which has the power of making that ugly, broken house seem quite pleasant among its bushes of hibiscus and frangipani. 'That man will die soon,' says Jabavu, in a small, dispirited voice; but all he hears from Jerry is: 'Well, he will last the month at least, and there are others who will do you this favour for a pound.'

And Jabavu's heart is so heavy with fear of the sickness and the ugliness that he thinks: I will go now, I cannot stay with these people. When Jerry tells him he must go to the Pass Office to have his employment registered, he thinks: And now I shall take this chance to run to Mr Mizi. But Jerry has no intention of letting Jabavu have any such chance. He strolls with him to the Pass Office, on the way buying a bottle of white man's whisky from another coloured man who does this illegal trade, and while Jabavu stands in the queue of waiting people at the Pass Office Jerry waits cheerfully, the bottle under his coat, and even chats with the policeman.

When at last Jabavu has had his situpa examined and the business is over, he comes back to Jerry thinking: Hau, but this Jerry is brave. He fears nothing, not even talking to a policeman while he has a bottle of whisky under his coat.

They walk together back to the Native Township, and Jerry says, laughingly: 'And now you have a job and are a very good boy.' Jabavu laughs too, as loudly as he can. Then Jerry says: 'And so your great friend Mr Mizi can be pleased with you. You are a worker and very respectable.' They both laugh again, and Jerry gives Jabavu a quick look from his cold, narrow eyes, for he is above all not a fool, and Jabavu's laughter is rather as if he wishes to cry. He is thinking how best to handle Jabavu when chance helps him, for Mrs Samu crosses their path, in her white dress and white cap, on her way to the hospital, where she is on duty. She first looks at Jabavu as if she does not know him at all; then she gives him a small, cold smile, which is the most her goodness of heart can do, and is more the goodness of Mrs Mizi's heart, who has been saying: 'Poor boy, he cannot be blamed, only pitied,' and things of that sort. Mrs Samu has much less heart than Mrs Mizi, but much more head, and it is hard to know which is most useful; but in this case she is thinking: Surely there are better things to worry about than a little skellum of a mat-sotsi? And she goes on to the hospital, thinking about a woman who has given birth to a baby who has an infection of the eyes.

But Jabavu's eyes are filled with tears and he longs to run after Mrs Samu and beg for her protection. Yet how can a woman protect him against Jerry?

Jerry begins to talk about Mrs Samu, and in a clever way. He laughs and says what hypocrites! They talk about goodness and crime, and yet Mrs Samu is Mr Samu's second wife, and Mr Samu treated his first wife so badly she died of it, and now Mrs Samu is nothing but a bitch who is always ready, why she even made advances to Jerry himself at a dance; he could have had her by pushing her over ... Then Jerry goes on to Mr Mizi and says he is a fool for trusting Mrs Mizi, whose eyes invite everybody, and there is not a soul in the Township who does not know she sleeps with Mrs Samu's brother. All these men of light are the same, their women are light, and they are like a herd of baboons, no better ...

and Jerry continues to speak thus, laughing about them, until Jabavu, remembering the coldness of Mrs Samu's smile, half-heartedly agrees, and then he makes a rude joke about Mrs Samu's uniform, which is very tight across her buttocks, and suddenly the two young men are roaring with laughter and saying women are this and that. And so they return to the others, who are not in the empty store now, for it does not do to be in one place too often, but in one of the other shebeens, which is much worse than Mrs Kambusi's. There they spend the evening, and Jabavu again drinks skokian, but with discretion, for he fears what he will feel next day. And as he drinks he notices that Jerry also drinks no more than a mouthful, but pretends to be drunk, and is watching how Jabavu drinks. Jerry is pleased because Jabavu is sensible, yet he does not altogether like it, for it is necessary for him to think that he is the only one stronger than the others. And for the first time it comes into his head that perhaps Jabavu is a little too strong, too clever, and may be a challenge to himself some day. But all these thoughts he hides behind his narrow, cold eyes, and only watches, and late that night he speaks to Jabavu as an equal, saying how they must now see that these fools get to bed without harm. Jabavu takes Betty and two of the young men to Betty's room, where they fall like logs across the floor, snoring off the skokian, and Jerry takes one girl and the other men to a place he knows, an old hut of straw on the edge of the veld.

In the morning Jerry and Jabavu wake clear-headed, leaving the others to sleep off their sickness, and they go together to the town, where they steal very well and cleverly, another clock and two pairs of shoes and a baby's pillow from under its head, and also, and most important, some trinkets which Jerry says are gold. When these things are taken by the Indian, he offers much money for them. Jerry says as they walk back to the Township: 'And on the second day we each make five pounds ...' and looks hard at Jabavu so that he may not miss what he means. And Jabavu today is easier about Mr Mizi, for he admires himself for not drinking the skokian, and for working with Jerry so cleverly that there is no difference between them.

That night they all go to the deserted store where they drink whisky, which is better than the skokian, for it does not make them sick. They play cards and eat well; and all the time Jerry watches Jabavu, and with very mixed thoughts. He sees that he does as he pleases with Betty, although never before has Betty been so humble and anxious with a man. He sees how he is careful what he drinks – and never has he seen a boy raw from the kraals learning sense so quickly with the drink. He sees how the others already, after two days, speak to Jabavu with almost the respect they have for him. And he does not like this at all. Nothing of what he is thinking does he show, and Jabavu feels more and more that Jerry is a friend. And next day they go again to the white streets and steal, and afterwards drink whisky and play cards. The next day also, and so a week passes. All that time Jerry is soft-speaking, polite, smiling; his cold, watchful eyes hooded in discretion and cunning; and Jabavu is speaking freely of what he feels. He has told of his love for Mrs Mizi, his admiration for Mr Mizi. He has spoken with the free confidence of a little child, and Jerry has listened, leading him on with a soft, sly word or a smile, until by the end of that week there is a strange way of speaking indeed. Jerry will say: 'And about the Mizis ...' And Jabavu will say: 'Ah, they are clever, they are brave.' And Jerry will say, in a soft, polite voice: 'You think that is so?' And Jabavu will say: 'Ah, my friend, those are men who think only of others.' And Jerry will say: 'You think so?' But in that soft, deadly, polite voice. And then he will talk a little, as if he does not care at all, about the Mizis or the Samus, how once they did this or that, and how they are cunning, and then state suddenly and with violence: 'Ah, what a skellum!' or 'Now that is a bitch.' And Jabavu will laugh and agree. It is as if there are two Jabavus, and one of them is brought into being by the clever tongue of Jerry. But Jabavu himself is hardly aware of it. For it may seem strange that a man can spend his time stealing and drinking and making love to a woman of the town and yet think of himself as something quite different – a man who will become a man of light, yet this is how things are with Jabavu. So confused is he, so bound up in the cycle of stealing, and then good food and drink, then more stealing, then Betty at night, that he is like a young, powerful, half-broken ox, being led to work by a string around his horns which the man hardly allows him to feel. Yet there are moments when he feels it.

There is a day when Jerry asks casually, as if he does not mind at all: 'And so you will leave us and join the men of

light?' And Jabavu says, with the simplicity of a child: 'Yes,
that is what I wish to do.' And Jerry allows himself to laugh,
and for the first time. And fear goes through Jabavu like a
knife, so that he thinks: I am a fool to speak thus to Jerry.
And yet in a moment Jerry is making jokes again and saying,
'Those skellums,' as if he is amused at the folly of the men of
light, and Jabavu laughs with him. For above all Jerry is cunning in the use of laughter with Jabavu. He leads Jabavu gently
onwards, with jokes, until he becomes serious, and in one
moment, and says: 'And so you will leave us when you are
tired of us and go to Mr Mizi?' And the seriousness makes
Jabavu's tongue stick in his mouth, so that he says nothing.
He is like the ox who has been led so softly to the edge of the
field, and now there is a pressure around the base of his
horns and he thinks: But surely this man cannot mean to
make a fool of me? And because he does not wish to understand he stands motionless, his four feet stubborn on the earth,
blinking his foolish eyes, and the man watches him, thinking:
In a moment there will be the fighting, when this stupid ox
bellows and roars and leaps into the air, not knowing it is all
useless since I am so much more clever than he is.

Jerry, however, does not think of Jabavu quite as the man
thinks of the ox. For while he is in every way more cunning
and more experienced than Jabavu, yet there is something in
Jabavu he cannot handle. There are moments when he wonders: Perhaps it would be better if I let this fool go to Mr
Mizi, why not? I shall threaten to kill him if he speaks of us
and our work ... Yet it is impossible, precisely because of this
other Jabavu which is brought into being by the jokes. Once
with the Mizis, will not Jabavu have times when he longs
for the richness and excitement of the stealing and the
shebeens and the women? And at those moments will he not
feel the need to call the matsotsis bad names, and perhaps
even tell the police? The names of all the gang, and the
coloured men who help them, and the Indian who helps them
... Jerry wishes bitterly that he had put a knife into Jabavu
long ago, when he first heard of him from Betty. Now he
cannot, because Betty loves Jabavu, and therefore is dangerous. Ah, how Jerry wishes he could kill them both ... Yet he
never kills unless it is really necessary and certainly not two
killings at once. But his hatred for Jabavu, and more particularly Betty, grows and deepens, until it is hard for him to

shut it down and appear smiling and cool and friendly.

But he does so, and gently he leads Jabavu along the path of dangerous laughter. The jokes they make are frightening, and when Jabavu is frightened by them, he has to say: 'Well, but it is a joke only.' For they speak of things which would have made him tremble only a few weeks before. First he learns to laugh at the richness of Mr Mizi, and how this clever skellum hides money in his house and so cheats all the people who trust him. Jabavu does not believe it, but he laughs, and even goes on with the joke saying: 'What fools they are,' or 'It is more profitable to run a League for the Advancement of the African People than to run a shebeen.' And when Jerry speaks of how Mrs Mizi sleeps with everyone or how Mrs Samu is in the movement only because of the young men whom she may meet, Jabavu says Mrs Samu reminds him of the advertisement in the white man's papers: Drink this and you will sleep well at night. Yet all the time Jabavu does not believe any of these things, and he sincerely admires the men of light, and wishes only to be with them.

Later Jerry tightens the leash and says: 'One day the men of light will be killed because they are such skellums,' and he makes a joke about such a killing. It takes a few days before Jabavu is ready to laugh, but at last it seems unimportant and a joke only, and he laughs. And then Jerry speaks of Betty and says how once he killed a woman who had become dangerous, and he laughs and says a stupid woman is as bad as a dangerous one, and it would be a good idea to kill Betty. Many days pass before Jabavu laughs, and this is because the idea of Betty being dead makes his heart leap with joy. For Betty has become a burden on his nights so that he dreads them. All night she will wake him, saying: 'And now marry me and we will run away to another town,' or 'Let us kill Jerry, and you may be leader of this gang,' or 'Do you love me? Do you love me? Do you love me?' – and Jabavu thinks of the women of the old kind who do not talk of love day and night: women with dignity; but at last he laughs. The two young men laugh together, reeling across the road, sometimes, as they speak of Betty, and of women and how they are this and that, until things have changed so that Jabavu laughs easily when Jerry speaks of killing Betty, or any other member of the gang, and they speak with contempt of the others, how they are fools and not clever in the work, and the only two with any sense are Jerry and Jabavu.

Yet underneath the friendship both are very frightened, and both know that something must happen soon, and they watch each other, sideways, and hate each other, and Jabavu thinks all the time of how he may run to Mr Mizi, while Jerry dreams at night of the police and prison, and often of killing, Jabavu mostly, but Betty too, for his dislike of Betty is becoming like a fever. Sometimes, when he sees how Betty rubs her body against Jabavu, or kisses him, like the cinema, and in front of the others, and how she never takes her eyes away from Jabavu, his hand goes secretly to the knife and fingers it, itching with the need to kill.

The gang itself is confused, for it is as if they have two leaders. Betty stays always beside Jabavu, and her deference towards him influences the others. Also, Jerry has owed his leadership to the fact that he is always clearheaded, never drunk, stronger than anyone else. But now he is not stronger than Jabavu. It is as if some fast-working yeast of dissolution were in the gang, and Jerry names this yeast Mr Mizi.

There comes a day when he decides to get rid of Jabavu finally one way or the other, although he is so clever with the stealing.

First he speaks persuasively of the mines in Johannesburg, saying how good the life is there, and how much money for people like themselves. But Jabavu listens indifferently, saying: 'Yes,' and 'Is that so?' For why should a man make the dangerous and difficult journey south to the richness of the City of Gold when life is rich where he is? So Jerry drops that plan and tries another. It is a dangerous one, and he knows it. He wishes to make a last attempt to weaken Jabavu by skokian. And for six nights he leads them to the shebeens, although usually he discourages his gang from drinking the bad stuff because it muffles their will and their thinking. On the first night things are as usual, the rest drink, but Jerry and Jabavu do not. On the second it is the same. On the third, Jerry challenges Jabavu to a contest and Jabavu first refuses, then consents. For he has reached a state of mind which he by no means understands – it is as if he is ceasing to care what happens. So Jabavu and Jerry drink, and it is Jerry who succumbs first. He wakes on the fourth afternoon to find his gang playing cards, while Jabavu sits against a wall, staring at nothing, already recovered. And now Jerry is filled with

hatred against Jabavu such as he has never known before.
For Jabavu's sake he has drunk himself stupid, so that he has
lain for hours weak and out of his mind, even while his gang
play cards and probably laugh at him. It is as if Jabavu is now
the leader and not himself. As for Jabavu, his unhappiness
has reached a point where something very strange is happening
to him. It is as if very slowly he, the real Jabavu, is moving
away from the thief and the skellum who drinks and steals,
and watches with calm interest, not caring. He thinks there is
no hope for him now. Never can he return to Mr Mizi; never
can he be a man of light. There is no future. And so he stares
at himself and waits, while a dark grey cloud of misery settles
on him.

Jerry comes to him, concealing what he is thinking, and sits
by him and congratulates him on having a stronger head. He
flatters Jabavu, and then makes jokes at the expense of the
others which they cannot hear. Jabavu assents without interest.
Then he begins calling Betty names, and then all women
names, for it is in these moments, when they are hating
women, that they are most nearly good friends. Jabavu joins
in the game, indifferently at first, and then with more will.
And soon they are laughing together, and Jerry congratulates himself on his cunning. Betty does not like this, and
comes to them, and is pushed aside by both, and returns
to the others, filled with bitterness, calling them names. And
Jerry says how Betty is a dangerous woman, and then tells
how once before he killed a girl in the gang who fell in love
with a policeman she was supposed to be keeping sweet and
friendly. He tells Jabavu this partly to frighten him, partly
to see how he will react now at the thought of Betty being
killed. And into Jabavu's mind again flickers the thought
how pleasant if Betty were no longer there, always boring
him with her demands and her complaints, but he pushes it
away. And when Jerry sees him frown he swiftly changes the
joke into that other about how funny it would be to rob Mr
Mizi. Jabavu sits silent, and for the first time he begins to
understand about laughter and jokes, how it is that people
laugh most at what they fear, and how a joke is sometimes
more like a plan for what will some day be the truth. And he
thinks : Perhaps all this time Jerry really was planning to kill,
and even to rob Mr Mizi? And the thought of his own foolishness is so terrible that the misery, which has lifted in the

moment of comradeship with Jerry, returns, and he leans silent against the wall, and nothing matters. But this is better for Jerry than he knows, for when he suggests they go to the shebeens, Jabavu rises at once. On that fourth night Jabavu drinks skokian and for the first time willingly, and with pleasure, since he came to the Township and drank it at Mrs Kambusi's. Jerry does not drink, but watches, and he feels an immense relief. Now, he thinks, Jabavu will take to skokian like the others, and that will make him weak like the others, and Jerry will lead him like the rest.

On the fifth day Jabavu sleeps till late, and wakes as it grows dark, and finds that the others are already talking about going to the shebeen. But the sickness in him rises at the thought and he says he will not go to the shebeen, but will stay while the others go. And with this he turns his face to the wall, and although Jerry jokes with him and cajoles and jokes, he does not move. But Jerry cannot tell the others that he wishes them to go to the shebeen only for the sake of Jabavu, and so he has to go with them, cursing and bitter, for Jabavu remains in the disused store. So the next day is the sixth, and by now the gang are sodden and sick and stupid with the skokian, and Jerry can hardly control them. And Jabavu is bored and calm and sits in his place against the wall, looking at his thoughts, which must be so sad and dark, for his face is heavy with them. Jerry thinks: It was in such a mood that he agreed to drink the night before last, and woos Jabavu to drink again, and Jabavu does. That is the sixth night. Jabavu gets drunk as before, with the others, while Jerry does not. And on the seventh day Jerry thinks: Now this will be the last. If Jabavu does not come willingly to the shebeen tonight, I will give up this plan and try another.

On that seventh day Jerry is truly desperate, though it does not show on his face. There he sits against the wall, while his hands deal out the cards and gather them in, and his eyes watch those cards as if nothing else interested them. Yet from time to time they glance quickly at Jabavu, who is sitting, without moving, opposite him. The others are still not conscious, but are lying on the floor, groaning and complaining in thick voices.

Betty is lying close by Jerry, in a loose, disgusting heap, and he looks at her and hates her. He is full of hate. He is thinking that two months ago he was running the most profitable gang in the Township, there was no danger, the police were controlled sufficiently, there seemed no reason why it should not all go on for a long time. Yet all at once Betty takes a liking to this Jabavu, and now it is at an end, the gang restless, Jabavu dreaming of Mr Mizi, and nothing is clear or certain.

It is Betty's fault – he hates her. It is Jabavu's fault – ah, how he hates Jabavu! It is Mr Mizi's fault – if he could he would kill Mr Mizi, for truly he hates Mr Mizi more than anyone in the world. But to kill Mr Mizi would be foolish – for that matter, to kill anyone is foolish, unless there is need for it. He must not kill needlessly. But his mind is filled with thoughts of killing, and he keeps looking at Betty, rolling drunkenly by him, and wishing he could kill her for starting all this trouble, and as the cards go flick! flick! flick! each sharp small noise seems to him like the sound of a knife.

Then all at once Jerry takes a tight hold of himself and says: I am crazy. What is this? Never in all my life have I done a thing without thought or cause, and now I sit here without a plan, waiting for something to happen – this man Jabavu has surely made me mad!

He looks across at Jabavu and asks, pleasantly: 'Will you come to the shebeen tonight for some fun, hey?'

But Jabavu says: 'No, I shall not go. That is four times I have drunk the skokian and now what I say is true. I shall never drink it again.'

Jerry shrugs, and lets his eyes drop. So! he thinks. Well, that has failed. Yet it succeeded in the past. But if it has failed, then I must now think and decide what to do – there must be a way, there is always a way. But what? Then he thinks: Well, and why do I sit here? Before there was just such a matter, when things got too difficult, but that was in another town, and I left that town and came here. It is easy. I can go south to another city. There are always fools, and always work for people like myself. And then, just as this plan is becoming welcome in his mind, he is stung by a foolish vanity: And so I should leave this city, where I have contacts, and know sufficient police, and have an organization, simply because of this fool Jabavu? I shall not.

And so he sits, dealing the cards, while these thoughts go through his mind, and his face shows nothing, and his anger and fear and spiteful vanity seethe inside him. Something will happen, he thinks. Something. Wait.

He waits, and soon it grows dark. Through the dirty window-panes comes a flare of reddish light from the sunset which makes blotches and pools of dark red on the floor. Jerry looks at it. Blood, he thinks, and an immense longing fills him. Without thinking, he slides up his knife a little, lovingly fingering the haft of it. He sees that Jabavu is looking at him, and suddenly Jabavu shudders. An immense satisfaction fills Jerry. Ah, how he loves that shudder. He slides up the knife a little further and says: 'You have not yet learned to be afraid of this as you should.' Jabavu looks at the knife, then at Jerry, then drops his eyes. 'I am afraid,' says Jabavu, simply, and Jerry lets the knife slide back. For a moment the thought slides into him: This is nothing but madness. Then it goes again.

Jerry's own feet are now lying in a pool of reddish light from the window, and he quickly moves them back, rises, takes candles from the top of the wall where they lie hidden, sticks them in their grease on the packing-cases, and lights them. The reddish light has gone. Now the room is lit by the warm yellow glow of candles, showing packing-cases, bottles stacked in corners, the huddled bodies of the drunken, and sheets of spider web across the rafters. It is the familiar scene of companionship in drink and gambling, and the violent longing to kill sinks inside Jerry. Again he thinks: I must make a plan, not wait for something to happen. And then, one after another, the bodies move, groaning, and sit up, holding their heads. Then they begin to laugh weakly. When Betty heaves herself up from the floor she sees she is some way from Jabavu, and she crawls back to him and falls across his knees, but he quietly pushes her aside. And this sight, for some reason, fills Jerry with irritation. But he suppresses it and thinks: I must make these stupid fools sensible, and wait until they have come out of the skokian, and then: Then I shall make a plan.

He fills a large tin with fresh tea from the kettle that boils on the fire he has made on the floor, and gives mugs of it to everyone, including Jabavu, who simply sets it down without touching it. This annoys Jerry, but he says nothing. The others drink, and it helps their sickness, and they sit up, still holding their heads.

'I want to go to the shebeen,' says Betty, rocking sideways, back and forth, 'I want to go to the shebeen.' And the others, taking up her voice without thought, say: 'Yes, yes, the shebeen.' Jerry whips round, glaring at them. Then he holds down his irritation. And as easily as the desire came into them, it goes. They forget about the shebeen, and drink their tea. Jerry makes more, even stronger, and refills their mugs. They drink. Jabavu watches this scene as if it were a long way from him. He remarks, in a quiet voice: 'Tea is not strong enough to silence the anger of the skokian. I know. The times I have drunk it, it was as if my body wanted to fall to pieces. Yet they have drunk it each night for a week.' Jerry stands near Jabavu, and his face is twitching. Into him has come again that violent need to kill; and yet again he stops it. He thinks: Better if I leave all these fools now . . . But this sensible thought is drowned by a flood of rising vanity. He thinks: *I* can make them do what I want. Always they do as I say.

He says calmly: 'Better if you each take a piece of bread and eat it.' In a low voice to Jabavu he says: 'Shut up. If you speak again I will kill you.' Jabavu makes that indifferent movement of his shoulders and continues to watch. There is a blank look in the darkness of his eyes that frightens Jerry.

Betty staggers to her feet and walks, knees rocking, to the wall where a mirror is hanging on a nail. But before she gets there she says: 'I want to go to the shebeen.' Again the others repeat the words, and they rise, planting their feet firmly so as not to fall down.

Jerry shouts: 'Shut up. You will not go to the shebeen tonight.'

Betty laughs, in a high, weak way, and says: 'Yes, the shebeen. Yes, yes, I want that badly, to go to the shebeen . . .' The words having started to make themselves, they are likely to continue, and Jerry takes her by her shoulders and shakes her. 'Shut up,' he says. 'Did you hear what I said?'

And Betty laughs, and sways, and puts her arms around him and says: 'Nice Jerry, handsome Jerry, oh, please, Jerry . . .' She is speaking in a voice like a child trying to get its way. Jerry, who has stood rigid under her touch, eyes fixed and black with anger, shakes her again and flings her off. She goes staggering backwards till she reaches the other wall, and there she sprawls, laughing and laughing, till she straightens again and goes staggering forward towards Jerry, and the others see what she is doing, and it seems very funny to them and they go with her, so that in a moment Jerry is surrounded by them, and they put their arms around his neck and pat his shoulders, and all say, in high, childish voices, laughing as if laughter in them is a kind of a spring, bubbling up and up and forcing its way out of their lips: 'Nice Jerry, yes, handsome, please, clever Jerry.'

And Jerry snaps out: 'Shut up. Get back. I'll kill you all . . .'

His voice surprises them into silence for one moment. It is high, jerky, crazy. And his face twitches and his lips quiver. They stand there around him, looking at him, then at each other, blinking their eyes so that the cloud of skokian may clear, then all move back and sit down, save Betty, who stands in front of him. Her mouth stretched in such a way across her face that it might be either laughter or the sound of weeping that will come from it, but it is laughter again, and with a high, cackling sound, just like a hen, she rocks forward, and for the third time her arms go around Jerry and she begins pressing her body against his. Jerry stands quite still. The others, watching, see nothing but that Betty is hugging and squeezing him, with her body and her arms, while she laughs and laughs. Then she stops laughing and her hands loosen and then fall and swing by her side. Jerry holds her with his hand across her back. They set up a yell of laughter because it seems to them very funny. Betty is making some sort of funny joke, and so they must laugh.

But Jerry, in a flush of anger and hatred such as he has never known before, has slipped his knife into Betty, and the movement gave him such joy as he has not felt in all his life. And so he stands, holding Betty, while for a moment he does not think at all. And then the madness of anger and joy vanishes and he thinks: I am truly mad. To kill a person, and for nothing, and in anger . . . He stands holding her, trying to make a plan quickly, and then he sees how Jabavu, just beside him on the floor, is looking up, blinking his eyes in slow wonder, and at once the plan comes to him. He allows himself to stagger a little, as if Betty's weight is too much, then he falls sideways, with Betty, across Jabavu, and there he makes a scuffling movement and rolls away.

Jabavu, feeling a warm wetness come from Betty, thinks: He has killed her and now he will say I killed her. He stands up slowly, and Jerry shouts: 'Jabavu has killed her, look, he has killed Betty because he was jealous.'

Jabavu does not speak. The thought in his mind is one that shocks him. It is an immense relief that Betty is dead. He had not known how tired he was of this woman, how she weighed on him, knowing that he would never be able to shake her off. And now she lies dead in front of him.

'I did not kill her,' he says. 'I did not.'

The others are standing and staring, like so many chickens. Jerry is shouting: 'That skellum – he has killed Betty.'

Then Jabavu says: 'But I did not.'

Their eyes go first to Jerry, and they believe him, then they go to Jabavu, and they believe him.

Jerry stops saying it. He understands they are too stupid to hold any thoughts in their heads longer than a moment.

He seats himself on a packing-case and looks at Betty, while he thinks fast and hard.

Jabavu, after a long, long silence while he looks at Betty, seats himself on another. A feeling of despair is growing so strong in him that his limbs will hardly move. He thinks: And now there is nothing left. Jerry will say I killed her; there is no one who will believe me. And – but here is that terrible thought – I was pleased he killed her. Pleased. I am pleased now. And from here his mind goes darkly into the knowledge: It is just. It is a punishment. And he sits there, passive, while his hands dangle loosely and his eyes go blank.

Slowly the others seat themselves on the floor, huddling together for comfort in this killing they do not understand. All they know is that Betty is dead, and their goggling, empty eyes are fixed on Jerry, waiting for him to do something.

And Jerry, after sorting out his various plans, lets his tense body ease, and tries to put quietness and confidence into his eyes. First he must get rid of the body. Then it will be time to think of the next thing.

He turns to Jabavu and says, in a light, friendly voice: 'Help me put this stupid girl outside into the grass.'

Jabavu does not move. Jerry repeats the words, and still Jabavu is motionless. Jerry gets up, stands in front of him, and orders him. Jabavu slowly lifts his eyes and then shakes his head.

And now Jerry comes close to Jabavu, his back to the others, and in his hand he holds his knife, and this knife he presses very lightly against Jabavu. 'Do you think I'm afraid to kill you too?' he asks, so low only Jabavu can hear. The others cannot see the knife, only that Jerry and Jabavu are thinking how to dispose of Betty. They begin to cry a little, whimpering.

Jabavu shakes his head again. Then he looks down, feeling the pressure of the knife. Its point is at his flesh, he can feel a slight cold stinging. And into his mind comes the angry thought: He is cutting my smart coat. His eyes narrow, and he says furiously: 'You are cutting my coat.'

He's mad, thinks Jerry, but it is the moment of weakness that he knows and understands. And now, using every scrap of his will, he narrows his eyes, stares down into Jabavu's empty eyes, and says: 'Come now, and do as I say.'

And Jabavu slowly rises and, at a sign from Jerry, lifts Betty's feet. Jerry takes the shoulders. They carry her to the door, and then Jerry says, shouting loudly so that it will be strong enough to get inside the fog of drink: 'Put out the candles.' No one moves. Then Jerry shouts again, and the young man who sleeps at night with Jerry gets up and slowly pinches out the candles. The room is now all darkness and there is a whimper of fear, but Jerry says: 'You will not light the candles. Otherwise the police will get you. I am coming back.' The whimper stops. They can hear hard, frightened breathing, but no one moves. And now they move from the blackness of the room to the blackness of the night. Jerry puts down the body and locks the door, and then goes to the window and wedges it with stones. Then he comes back and lifts the shoulders of the body. It is very heavy and it rolls between their gripping hands. Jerry says not a word, and Jabavu is also silent. They carry her a long way, through grass and bushes, never on the paths, and throw her at last into a deep ditch just behind one of the shebeens. She will not be found until morning, and then it will be the people who have been drinking in the shebeen who will be suspected, not Jerry or Jabavu. Then they run very quickly back to the disused store, and as they enter they hear the others wailing and keening in their terror of the darkness and their muddled understanding. A window-pane has been smashed where someone tried to get out, but the wedged stones held the frame. They are crowded in a bunch against the wall, with no sense or courage in them. Jerry lights the candles and says: 'Shut up!' He shouts it again, and they are quiet. 'Sit down!' he shouts, and they sit. He also sits against the wall, takes up his cards, and pretends to play.

Jabavu is looking down at his coat. It is soaked with blood. Also, as he pulls the cloth over his chest, there is a small cut, where the point of the knife pressed. He is asking himself why he is so stupid as to mind about a coat. What does a coat matter? Yet, even at that moment, Jerry nods at a hook on the wall, where there hang several coats and jackets, and Jabavu goes to the hook, takes down a fine blue jacket, and then looks again at Jerry. And now their eyes stare hard across the space between them. Jabavu's eyes drop. Jerry says: 'Take off your shirt and your vest.' Jabavu does so. Jerry says: 'Put on the vest and shirt you will find among the others in that packing-case.' Jabavu goes as if he has no will, to the packing-case, finds a vest and shirt that will fit him, puts them on, and puts on the blue jacket. Now Jerry quickly rises, strips off his own jacket and shirt, which have blood on them, wipes his knife carefully on them, and then gives the bundle to Jabavu.

'Take my things out with yours and bury them in the ground,' he says. Again the two pairs of eyes stare at each other, and Jabavu's eyes drop. He takes all the bloodied things and goes out. He makes his way in the darkness to a place where the bushes grow close, and then he digs, using a sharp stick. He buries the clothes, and then goes back to the store. And as he enters he knows that Jerry has been talking, talking, talking to the others, explaining how he, Jabavu, killed Betty. And he can see from the way their frightened eyes look at him that they believe it.

But it is as if in burying the soiled and cut clothes he also buried his weakness towards Jerry. He says quickly: 'I did not kill Betty,' and with this he goes to the wall and seats himself, and gives himself up to whatever may happen. For he does not care. Most deeply he does not care. And Jerry, seeing this deep lassitude, misunderstands it entirely. He thinks: Now I can do what I like with this one. Perhaps it was a good thing I killed that stupid woman. For at last Jabavu will do as I tell him.

But he ignores Jabavu, whom he thinks is safe, and goes to the others and tries to calm them. They are weeping and crying out, and sometimes they call out for skokian as a remedy for the fear of this terrible night. But Jerry speaks firmly to them, and makes more strong tea, and gives each a piece of bread and makes them eat it, and finally tells them to sleep. But they cannot. They huddle in a group, talking about the police, and how they will all be blamed for the murder, until at last Jerry makes them drink some tea in which he has put some stuff he bought from an Indian, which is to make people sleep. Soon every one is lying again on the floor, but this time in a sleep which will heal them and drive away the sickness of the long skokian drinking.

For all the long hours of the night they lie, groaning sometimes, sometimes calling out, making thick, frightened words. And Jerry sits and plays cards and watches Jabavu, who does not move.

Jerry is now full of confidence. He makes plans, examines them, alters them; all night his mind is busy, and all the fear and weakness has gone. He decides that killing Betty was the only clever thing he has ever done without planning it.

The night struggles on in the flick of playing cards and groans from the sleepers. The light comes grey through the dirty window, then rose and gold as the sun rises, then strengthens to a steady, warm yellow. And when the day is truly there, Jerry kicks the sleepers awake, but so that when they sit up they will not know they have been kicked.

They sit up, to see Jerry playing cards and Jabavu slumped against the wall, staring. And into each mind comes a wild, confused memory of murder and fighting, and they look at each other and see that the memory shows in every face. Then they look towards Jerry for an explanation. But Jerry is looking at Jabavu. And they remember that Jabavu has killed Betty, and their faces turn greyish and their breath comes with difficulty. Yet they are no longer stupid with skokian, only weak and tired and frightened. Jerry has no fear at all that he may not be able to handle them. When they are properly awake and he can see the knowledge in their faces he begins to talk. He explains, in a quiet and off-hand way, what happened last night, saying that Jabavu has killed Betty, and Jabavu says nothing at all.

It is only the silence of Jabavu that upsets Jerry for he has not expected it. But he is so confident that he takes no notice. He explains that according to the rules of the gang, if suspicion should fall on them, Jabavu must give himself up to the police, saying nothing of the others. But if the trouble should pass, they must all keep silence and continue as if nothing has happened. Jerry speaks so lightly that they are reassured, and one slips out to buy some bread and some milk for tea, and they eat and drink together, even laughing when Jerry makes a joke. The laughter is not very deep, but it helps them. And all this time Jabavu sits against the wall, apart, saying nothing.

Jerry has now made his plans. They are very simple. If the police shows signs that day of finding out who killed Betty, he will quickly slip away, go to people he knows who will help him, and travel south, with papers that have a different name, leaving all the trouble behind him. But he has very little money left, after the week of drinking. Perhaps five shillings. His friends may give him a little more. Jerry does not like to think of going all the way to Johannesburg with so little. He wants some more. If the police do not know on whom to put the blame, Jerry will stay here, in this store, with Jabavu and the others, until the evening. And then – but now the plan is so audacious that Jerry laughs inside himself, longing to tell the others, because it is such a good joke. Jerry plans nothing else than to go to Mr Mizi's house, take the money that will be there, and with it run away to the south. He believes that there is money in the house, and a great deal. When he robbed Mr Samu, five years ago, and in another town, he took nine-teen pounds. Mr Samu had the money in a big tin that once held tobacco, and it was in the grass roof of a hut. Jerry believes that he has only to go to Mr Mizi's house to find enough money to take him in luxury and safety, with plenty of funds for bribery, to Johannesburg. And he will take Jabavu with him. Jabavu is now safe, sullen, and too afraid to tell Mr Mizi. Also, he must know where the money is.

It is all very simple. As soon as Jabavu has given the money to Jerry, Jerry will tell him to go back to the others and wait for his return. They will wait. It will be some days before they understand he has tricked them, and by then he will be in Johannesburg.

Towards midday, Jerry brings out the last bottle of whisky and gives everyone a little of it. Jabavu refuses, with a small shake of his head. Jerry ignores him. So much the better.

But he takes care that all the group are sitting playing cards, drinking a little whisky, and that they have plenty to eat. He wishes them to like him and trust him before explaining his plan, which might frighten them in their condition of being softened by the drinking and the murder.

In the middle of the afternoon he slips out again and mingles with the people of the market, where he hears much talk of the killing. The police have questioned a lot of people, but no one has been arrested. This will be a case like so many others – yet another of the matsotsis killed in a brawl, and no one cares much about that. The newspapers will print a paragraph; perhaps a preacher will make a sermon. Mr Mizi might make another speech about the corruption of the African people through poverty. At this last idea Jerry laughs to himself and returns to the others in a very good humour indeed.

He tells them that everything will be safe, and then speaks of Mr Mizi, half as part of his plan, but partly because of the pleasure it gives him. He gives a fine imitation of Mr Mizi making a speech about corruption and degradation. Jabavu does not stir through this, or even lift his eyes. Then Jerry makes a lot of jokes about Mrs Mizi and Mrs Samu and how they are immoral, and everyone laughs except Jabavu.

And everyone, including Jerry, misunderstands this silence of Jabavu. They think that he is afraid, and above all afraid of them because they know he has killed Betty, for now they all believe it; they even believe they saw it.

They do not understand that what is happening in Jabavu is something very old. His mind is darkening in despair, in accepting of what destiny has willed for him, and is turning towards death. This feeling of destiny, of fate, is very strong in the life of the tribe where guilt and responsibility for evil is decided by the old ways of magic. Perhaps if these young people had not lived so long in the white man's city they might understand what they see now in Jabavu. Even Jerry does not, although there are moments when this long silence annoys him. He would like to see Jabavu a little more afraid, and respectful.

Late in the afternoon Jerry takes his last five shillings, gives it to the girl who worked with Betty, and who is more troubled than the rest, and tells her that because of her cleverness she is the one chosen again to go to the market and buy food. She is pleased, and returns in half an hour with bread and cold boiled mealies, saying that people are no longer speaking of the murder. Jerry urges them all to eat. It is very important that they must be full and comfortable, and when they are, he speaks of his plan. 'And now I must tell you a good joke,' he says, laughing already. 'Tonight we shall rob from the house of Mr Mizi; he is very rich. And Jabavu will do the stealing with me.'

For a second there is uncertainty. Then they look at each other, see Jabavu's heavy eyes, lifted painfully towards them, and then they roll on the floor with laughing and do not stop for a long time. But Jerry is looking at Jabavu. He decides to taunt him a little: 'You kraal nigger,' he says. 'You're scared.'

Jabavu sighs, but does not move, and panic moves through Jerry. Why does Jabavu not cry out, protest, show fear?

He decides to wait for a show of strength until the moment itself. As the others cease laughing and look at him for the next good joke he makes a grimace towards Jabavu, inviting their complicity, and they grin and look at each other. He lights the candles, and makes them come together in a small, lit space around a packing-case, with Jabavu outside in the shadow, and there they all play cards, with much noise and laughter, and Jerry coaxes their excitement into the cards so that their attention is not on Jabavu. And all the time he is thinking of every detail of the plan, and his mind is set hard on his purpose.

At midnight, with a wink at the others, he gets up and goes to Jabavu. He is sweating with the effort of his will. 'It is time,' he says, lightly, and fixes his eyes on Jabavu. Jabavu does not lift his eyes, or move. Jerry kneels, very swiftly, and exactly as he did the night before, keeping his back to the others, he presses the tip of his knife lightly against Jabavu's chest. He stares hard, hard at Jabavu, and he whispers: 'I am cutting the coat.' He narrows his eyes, forcing their pressure at Jabavu, and says again: 'I am cutting the coat, soon the knife will go into you.' Jabavu lifts his eyes. 'Get up,' says Jerry, and Jabavu rises like a drugged man. Jerry is a little dizzy with the relief of that victory, but resting his hand against the wall he turns and says to the others: 'And now listen to what I shall tell you. We two go now to Mr Mizi's house. Blow the candles out and wait in the darkness — no, you may keep one candle, but set it on the floor so that no sign of light may show. I know that there is a great sum of money hidden in Mr Mizi's house. This we shall bring back. If there is trouble, I shall go quickly to one of our friends. There I shall stay perhaps one day, perhaps two. Jabavu will return here. If I am not here by tomorrow morning, then you may leave here one by one, not together. Do not work together for a few days, and do not go near the shebeens, and I forbid you to touch skokian again until I say. I shall tell you when it is safe for us to meet again. But all this is if there is trouble, and there is no need for it. Jabavu and I will be back in three-quarters of an hour with the money. Then we shall share it out between us. It will mean there is no need to work for a week, and by that time the police will have forgotten the murder.'

For the first time Jabavu speaks. 'Mr Mizi is not rich and he has no money in his house.' Jerry frowns, and then swiftly draws Jabavu after him into the darkness. The candles flicker out in the room behind. There is dark everywhere, the trees are swinging in a fast, cool wind, mounds of thick cloud move across the sky, showing damp, weak stars between. It is a good night for stealing.

Jerry thinks: 'Why does he say that? It is strange.' But what is strange is that in all these weeks Jerry has believed Jabavu is lying about the money, and Jabavu has never understood that Jerry truly thinks there is money.

'Come,' says Jerry, quietly. 'It will be over soon. And now, as we go, think of what you saw in the Mizis' house, and where the money will be hidden.'

Suddenly across Jabavu's mind flickers a picture, then another. He sees how on that evening Mr Mizi went to the corner of the room, lifted a piece of plank from the flooring, and leaned down into the dark hole underneath to bring up books. That is where he keeps books which the police might take away from him. But following this picture comes another, which he has not seen at all, but which his mind creates. He sees Mr Mizi reaching up a large tin filled with rolls of paper money. Yes, Jerry is very clever, for the old hunger in Jabavu raises its head and almost speaks. Then the pictures vanish from his mind, and the hunger with them. He plods along beside Jerry, thinking only: We are going to Mr Mizi. Somehow I will speak to him when we get there. He will help me. Jerry says, in a loud voice: 'Don't stamp so loud, you fool.' Jabavu does not change the way he walks. Jerry glances all around him through the dark, thinking nervously: Surely Jabavu is not mad? Or perhaps he has some drug I know nothing of? For his behaviour is very strange. Then he comforts himself: See how the killing of Betty turned out well, although it was not meant. See how this night is so good for stealing, although I did not choose it. My luck is very strong. Everything will be all right ... And so he does not again tell Jabavu about walking quietly, for the wind is swishing the branches back and forth and raising swirls of dust and leaves around their feet. It is very dark. The lights are out in the houses, for now they are walking in the respectable part of the city where people rise early for work and so must sleep early. Then Jabavu stumbles over a stone and there is a big noise, and Jerry whips out his knife and nudges Jabavu with his elbow until he turns and looks. 'I'll stick this into you if you call out or run away,' he says, softly, but Jabavu says nothing. He is thinking that Jerry is very strange indeed. Why does he go to Mr Mizi for money? Why does he take him, Jabavu? Perhaps the killing of Betty hurt his mind and he has gone crazy? And then Jabavu thinks: Yet it is not so strange. He made jokes about killing Betty and then he killed her, and he made jokes about stealing from Mr Mizi and now we are doing that too ... And so Jabavu plods on, through the noise of the wind and the blackness that is full of dust and moving leaves, and his head is empty and he does not feel. Only he is very heavy in his limbs, for he is tired with so little sleep, and then the nights of dancing and the skokian, and above all, he is tired from the despair, which tells him all the time: There is nothing for you, you will die, Jabavu. You will die. Words of a song form themselves, a sad, slow song, as for someone who has died. 'Eh, but see Jabavu, there he goes, the big thief. The knife has spoken, and it says: See the murderer, Jabavu, he who creeps through the dark to rob his friend. See Jabavu, whose hands are red with blood. Eh, Jabavu, but now we are coming for you. We are coming, Jabavu, there is no escape from us ...'

Under the street lights, but at great distances, since there are few lamps in the Native Township, are shed small patches of yellow glimmer. Jabavu blunders straight into such a patch of light. 'Be careful, fool,' says Jerry, in a violent, frightened voice. He drags Jabavu aside, and then stops. He is thinking: Perhaps this man is mad? How, otherwise, could he behave like this? How can I take a mad fool on a dangerous job like this? Perhaps I had better not go to the house ... Then he looks at Jabavu, who is standing quiet and patient beside him, and he thinks: No, it is simply that he is so afraid of me. So he goes on walking, gripping Jabavu by the wrist.

Then Jabavu laughs out loud and says: 'I can see the Mizis' house, and there is a light in the window.'

'Shut up,' says Jerry, and Jabavu goes on: 'The men of light study, at night. There are things you know nothing of.'

Jerry slams his hand over Jabavu's mouth, and Jabavu bites the hand. Jerry jerks it away and for a moment stands trembling with the desire to slip his knife sweetly home between Jabavu's ribs. But he keeps himself tight and controlled. He stands there, quietly shaking his bitten hand, looking at the light in the Mizis' house. Now he can almost see the money, and the desire for it grows strong in him. He cannot bear to stop now, to turn back, to change the plan. It is so easy simply to go forward, the money will be his inside five minutes, then he will give Jabavu the slip and in another fifteen minutes he will be in the house of that friend who will shelter him safely till morning. It is all so easy, so easy. And to go back difficult and, above all, shameful. So he shuts his teeth close and promises himself: You wait, my fine kraal nigger. In a moment I'll have got the money, and you might be caught. And even if you're not, what will you do without me? You'll go back to the gang, and without me they're like a lot of chickens, and you'll be in trouble with the police inside a week. The thought gives him great pleasure, so strong he nearly laughs, and in good humour he takes Jabavu's wrist and pulls him forward.

They walk until they are ten paces from the window, just beyond where the light falls dimly, showing the ground, rough and broken, and the bush under the window standing dense and black. The damp and windy dark is loud in their ears. They can see how Mr Mizi's son lies sprawled on his bed, still dressed. He has fallen asleep with a book in his hand.

Jerry thinks rapidly, then he says: 'You will climb quickly in at the window. Do not try to be clever. I can throw a knife as well as I can use it close, so . . .' He wriggles it lightly against the cloth of Jabavu's coat and with what exultation feels Jabavu move away! It is strange that Jabavu has no fear for himself, but it hurts him even now to imagine his jacket cut and spoilt. He has moved away instinctively, almost with irritation, as if a fly were pestering him, yet he moved, and he hears Jerry's voice, now strong and confident: 'You will keep away from the door into the other room. You will stand against the wall, with your back to it, and reach out your arm sideways and switch the light off. You needn't think you can be clever, for I shall keep my torch on you, so ...' And he switches on the tiny torch he has in the palm of his hand, that sends a single, strong beam of light, as narrow as a pencil. He switches it off and grips his teeth tight, against the desire to curse, because the blood where Jabavu bit him is making the torch slippery. 'Then I shall come into the room and tie that fool on the bed quickly, and then you will show me the money.'

Jabavu is silent, and then he says: 'But this money. I have told you there is no money. Why do you really come to this house?'

Jerry grips his arm and says: 'It's time to stop joking.'

Jabavu says: 'Sometimes I said that there was money, but it was when we were making jokes. Surely you understood ...' He stops, thinking about the nature of those jokes. Then he thinks: It does not matter, for when I am inside I shall call the Mizis.

Jerry says: 'And how could there not be money? Where does he keep the money for the League? Did you not see the place where such people keep what is forbidden? When I took money from Mr Samu it was in such a place ...' But Jabavu has pulled his arm free and is walking forward through the light to the window, making no effort to quieten his steps. Jerry hisses after him: 'Quiet, quiet, you fool.'

Then Jabavu pushes his heavy shoulder against the window so that it slides up with a bang, and he climbs in. Behind him Jerry is dancing and swearing with rage. For a second he wavers with the thought of running away. Then it is as if he sees a big tin full of money, and he flings himself across the lit space after Jabavu and climbs in at the window.

The two young men have climbed in at a window filled with light, and made a great deal of noise. The boy on the bed stirs, but Jerry has leaned over him, tangled his eyes in a cloth and stuffed into his mouth a handkerchief into which is kneaded some wet dough, while in the same movement he has knelt on his legs. He ties him with some thick string and in a moment the boy cannot move or see or cry out. But when Jabavu sees Mr Mizi's son lying tied up on the bed, something inside him moves and speaks, the heavy load of fatalistic indifference lifts, and he raises his voice and shouts: 'Mr Mizi,

Mrs Mizi!' It is the voice of a terrified child, for his terror of Jerry has returned. Jerry whips round, cursing, and lifts his arm with the knife in it. Jabavu jumps forward and grabs his wrist. The two stand swaying together under the light, their arms straining for the knife, when there is a noise in the room behind. Jerry springs aside, very quickly, so that Jabavu staggers, and then he jumps away and out of the window. As the door opens Jabavu is staggering back against the door with the knife in his hand.

It is Mr Mizi and Mrs Mizi, and when they see him Mr Mizi leaps forward and grips his arms to his body with his own, and Jabavu says: 'No, no, I am your friend.'

Mr Mizi speaks over his shoulder to Mrs Mizi: 'Leave that boy. Give me some cloth to tie this one with.' For Mrs Mizi is moaning with fear over her son who is lying helpless and half suffocated under the cloth. And Jabavu stands limp under Mr Mizi's hands and says: 'I am not a thief, I called you, but believe me, Mr Mizi, I wanted to warn you.' Mr Mizi is too angry to listen. He grips Jabavu's wrists and watches Mrs Mizi let her son loose.

Then Mrs Mizi turns to Jabavu and says, half crying: 'We helped you, you came to our house, and now you steal from us.'

'No, no, Mrs Mizi, it is not so, I will tell you.'

'You will tell the police,' says Mr Mizi roughly. And Jabavu, looking at the hard, angry face of Mr Mizi, feels that he has been betrayed. Somewhere inside him that well of despair slowly begins to fill again.

The boy who is now sitting on the bed holding his jaw, which has been wrenched with the big lump of dough, says: 'Why did you do it? Have we harmed you?'

Jabavu says: 'It was not I, it was the other.'

But the son has had cloth wound over his eyes before he even opened them, and has seen nothing.

Then Mr Mizi looks at the knife lying on the ground and says: 'You are a murderer as well as a thief.' There is blood on the floor. Jabavu says: 'No, the blood must be from Jerry's hand, which I bit.' Already his voice is sullen.

Mrs Mizi says, with contempt: 'You think we are fools. Twice you have run away. Once from Mr and Mrs Samu when they helped you in the bush. Then from us, when we helped you. All these weeks you have been with the matsotsis, and now you come here with a knife and expect us to say nothing when you tie our son and fill his mouth with uncooked bread?'

Jabavu goes quite limp in Mr Mizi's grip. He says, simply: 'You do not believe me.' Despair goes through his veins like a dark poison. For the second time that despair takes the people with him by surprise. Mr Mizi lets go his grip and Mrs Mizi, who is crying bitterly, says: 'And a knife, Jabavu, a knife!'

Mr Mizi picks up the knife, sees there is no blood on it, looks at the blood on the floor, and says: 'One thing is true. The blood does not come from a knife wound.' But Jabavu's eyes are on the floor, and his face is heavy and indifferent.

Then the police come, all at once, some climbing through the window, some from the front of the house. The police put handcuffs on Jabavu and take a statement from Mr Mizi. Mrs Mizi is still crying and fluttering around her son.

Only once does Jabavu speak. He says: 'I am not a thief. I came here to tell you. I wish to live honestly.'

And at this the policemen laugh and say that Jabavu, after only a few weeks in the Township, is known as one of the cleverest thieves and a member of the worst gang. And now, because of him, they will all be caught and put into prison.

Jabavu hears this with indifference. He looks at Mrs Mizi, and it is with the bitter look of a child whose mother has betrayed him. Then he looks at Mr Mizi, and it is the same look. They look in a puzzled way at Jabavu. But Mr Mizi is thinking: All my life I try to live in such a way to keep out of sight of the police, and now this little fool is going to make me waste time in the courts and get a name for being in trouble.

Jabavu is taken to the police van, and is driven to the prison. There he lies that night, and sleeps with the dark, dreamless sleep of a man who has gone beyond hope. The Mizis have betrayed him. There is nothing left.

In the morning he expects to be taken to the court, but he is transferred to another cell in the prison. He thinks this must be very serious indeed, for it is a cell to himself, a small brick room with a stone floor and a window high up with bars.

A day passes, then another. The warders speak to him and he does not answer. Then a policeman comes to ask him questions, and Jabavu does not say a word. The policeman is first patient, then impatient, and finally threatening. He says the police know everything and Jabavu will gain nothing by keeping quiet. But Jabavu is silent because he does not care. He wishes only the policeman would go away, which at last he does.

They bring him food and water, but he does not eat or drink unless he is told to do so, and then he eats or drinks automatically, but is likely to forget, and sit immobile, with a piece of bread or the mug in his hand. And he sleeps and sleeps as if his soul is drugging itself so that he may slip easily into death. He does not think of death, but it is there with him, in his cell, like a big, black shadow.

And so a week passes, though Jabavu does not know it.

On the eighth day the door opens and a white preacher comes in. Jabavu is asleep, but the warder kicks him till he wakes, then gives him a shake so that he stands up, and finally he sits when the preacher tells him to sit. He does not look at the preacher.

This man is a Mr Tennent from the Church of England, who visits the prisoners once a week. He is a tall man, lean, grey, stooping. He moves slowly, speaks slowly, and gives an impression of distrusting even the words he chooses to use.

He is a deeply doubting man, as are so many of his persuasion. Perhaps, if he were from another church, that which the Africans call the Romans, he would enter this cell in a different way. Sin is this, a soul is that, there would be definite things to say, and his words would have the ring of faith which does not change with changing life.

But Mr Tennent's church allows him much latitude in belief. Also, he has been working with the poorer Africans of this city for many years, and he sees Jabavu rather as Mr Mizi sees him. First, there is an economic process, and caught in it like a leaf in a whirlpool, there is Jabavu. He believes that to call a child like Jabavu sinful is lack of charity. On the other hand, a man who believes in God, if not the devil, must put the blame on something or someone – and what or who should it be? He does not know. His view of Jabavu robs him of comfort, even for himself.

This man, who comes to the prison every week, hates this work from the bottom of his heart because he does not trust himself. He enters Jabavu's cell taking himself to task for lack of sympathy, and at the first glance towards Jabavu he hardens himself. He has often seen such prisoners weeping

like children and calling on their mothers, a sign which is
deeply distasteful to him because he is English and despises
such shows of emotion. He has seen them stubborn and indifferent and bitter. This is bad, but better than the weeping. He has also, and very often, seen them as Jabavu is,
silent, motionless, their eyes lacking sight. It is a condition he
dislikes more than any other, because it is foreign to his own
being. He has seen prisoners condemned to death as Jabavu
is today; they are dead long before the noose goes round their
neck. But Jabavu is not going to be hanged, his offence is
comparatively light, and so this despair is altogether irrational,
and Mr Tennent knows by experience that he is not equipped
to deal with it.

He seats himself on an uncomfortable chair that the warder
has brought in, and wonders why he finds it hard to speak
of God. Jabavu is not a Christian, as can be seen from his
papers, but should that prevent a man of God from speaking
of Him? After a long silence he says: 'I can see that you are
very unhappy. I should like to help you.'

The words are flat and thin and weak, and Jabavu does not
move.

'You are in great trouble. But if you spoke of it, it might
ease you.'

Not a sound from Jabavu, and his eyes do not move.

For the hundredth time Mr Tennent thinks that it would
be better if he resigned from this work and let one of his
colleagues do it who do not think of better housing and bigger
wages rather than of God. But he continues in his mild,
patient voice: 'Perhaps things are better than you think. You
seem to be too unhappy for the trouble you are in. There will
be only light charges against you. Housebreaking and being
without proper employment, and that is not so serious.'

Jabavu remains motionless.

'There has been such a long delay in the case because
of the number of people involved in it. Your accomplice, the
man they call Jerry, has been denounced by his gang as the
person who incited you to rob the Mizis' house.'

At the name Mizi, Jabavu stirs slightly, then remains still.

'Jerry will be charged with organizing the robbery, for
carrying a knife, and for being in the city without proper employment. The police suspect he has been involved in many
other things, but nothing can be proved. He will get a fairly

heavy sentence – that is to say, he will if he is caught. They think he is on his way to Johannesburg. When they catch him he will be put in prison. They have also caught a coloured man who has been giving Africans, you among them, false employment. But this man is very ill in hospital and not expected to live. As regards the other members of the gang, the police will charge them with being without proper employment, but that is all. There has been such a cloud of lies and counter-charges that it has been a very difficult case for the police. But you must remember it is your first offence and you are very young, and things will not go badly for you.'

Silence from Jabavu. Then Mr Tennent thinks: Why should I comfort this boy as if he were innocent? The police tell me they know him to have been involved with all kinds of wickedness, even if they cannot prove it. He changes his voice and says, sternly: 'I am not saying the fact that you were known to be a member of a gang will not influence your sentence. You will have to pay the penalty for breaking the law. It is thought you may get a year in prison . . .'

He stops, for he can see that if he said ten years it would be the same to Jabavu. He remains silent for some time, thinking, for he has a choice to make which is not easy. That morning Mr Mizi came to his house and asked him if he intended to visit the prison. When he said Yes, Mr Mizi asked him if he would take a letter to Jabavu. Now, it is against the rules to take letters to prisoners. Mr Tennent has never broken the law. Also, he dislikes Mr Mizi because he dislikes all politics and politicians. He thinks Mr Mizi is nothing but a loud-voiced, phrase-making demagogue out for power and self-glory. Yet he cannot disapprove of Mr Mizi entirely, who asks nothing for his people but what he, Mr Tennent, sincerely believes to be just. At first he refused to take the letter, then he stiffly said Yes, he would try . . . The letter is in his pocket now.

At last he takes the letter from his pocket and says: 'I have a letter for you.' Jabavu still does not move.

'You have friends waiting to help you,' he says, loudly, trying to make his words pierce Jabavu's apathy. Jabavu lifts his eyes. After a long pause he says: 'What friends?'

It gives Mr Tennent a shock to hear his voice, after such a silence. 'It is from Mr Mizi,' he says stiffly.

Jabavu snatches it, scrambles up and stands under the light

that falls from the small, high window. He tears off the envelope, and it falls to the floor. Mr Tennent picks it up and says: 'I'm not really supposed to give you letters,' and understands that his voice sounds angry. And this is unjust, for it is his own responsibility that he agreed. He does not like injustice, and he controls his voice and says: 'Read it quickly and then give it back to me. That is what Mr Mizi asked.'

Jabavu is staring at the letter. It begins: 'My son . . .' And at this the tears begin to roll down his cheeks. And Mr Tennent is embarrassed and put out, and he thinks: 'Now we are going to have one of these unpleasant displays, I suppose.' Then he chides himself again for lacking Christian charity, and turns his back so as not to be offended by Jabavu's tears. Also it is necessary to watch the door in case the warder should come in too soon.

Jabavu reads:

I wish to tell you that I believe you told the truth when you said you came unwillingly to my house, and that you wished to warn us. What I do not understand is what you expected us to do then. For certain members of the gang have come to me saying that you told them you expected me to find you employment and look after you. They came to me thinking I would then defend them to the police. This I shall not do. I have no time for criminals. If I do not understand this case, neither does anyone else. For a whole week the police have been interviewing these people and their accomplices, and very little can be proved, except that the brain was the man Jerry, and that he used some kind of pressure on you. They appear to be afraid of him, and also of you, for it seems to me there are things you might tell the police if you wished.

And now you must try to understand what I am going to say. I am writing only because Mrs Mizi persuaded me to write. I tell you honestly I have no sympathy with you . . .

And here Jabavu lets the paper fall, and the coldness begins to creep around his heart. But Mr Tennent, tense and nervous at the door, says: 'Quickly, Jabavu. Read it quickly.'

And so Jabavu continues to read, and slowly the coldness dissolves, leaving behind it a feeling he does not understand, but it is not a bad feeling.

Mrs Mizi tells me I think too much from the head and too little from the heart. She says you are nothing but a child. This may be so, but you do not behave like a child, and so I shall speak to you as a man and expect you to act like one. Mrs Mizi wishes me to go to the Court and say we know you, and that you were led astray by evil companions, and that you are good at heart. Mrs Mizi uses words like good and evil with ease, and perhaps it is because of her mission education, but as for me, I distrust them, and I shall leave them to the Reverend Mr Tennent, who I hope will bring you this letter.

I know only this, that you are very intelligent and gifted and that you could make good use of your gifts if you wanted. I know also that until now you have acted as if the world owes you a good time for nothing. But we are living in a very difficult time, when there is much suffering, and I can see no reason why you should be different from everyone else. Now, I shall have to come to Court as a witness, because it was my house that was broken into. But I shall not say I knew you before, save casually, as I know hundreds of people – and this is true, Jabavu . . .

Once again the paper drops, and a feeling of resentment surges through Jabavu. For harder than any other will be this lesson for Jabavu, that he is one of many others and not something special and apart from them.

He hears Mr Tennent's urgent voice: 'Go on, Jabavu, you can think about it afterwards.' And he continues:

Our opponents take every opportunity to blacken us and our movement, and they would be delighted if I said I was a friend of a man whom everyone knows is a criminal even if they cannot prove it. So far, and with great effort, I have kept a very good character with the police as an ordinary citizen. They know I do not thieve or lie or cheat. I am what they call respectable. I do not propose to change this for your sake. Also in my capacity as leader of our people, I have a bad character, so if I spoke for you, it would have a double meaning for the police. Already they have been asking questions which make it clear that they think you are one of us, have been working with us, and I have denied it absolutely. Also, it is true that you have not.

And now, my son, like my wife, Mrs Mizi, you will think

I am a hard man, but you must remember I speak for hundreds of people, who trust me, and I cannot harm them for the sake of one very foolish boy. When you are in Court I will speak sternly, and I will not look at you. Also, I shall leave Mrs Mizi at home, for I fear her goodness of heart. You will be in prison for perhaps a year, and your sentence will be shortened if you behave well. It will be a hard time for you. You will be with other criminals who may tempt you to return to the life, you will do very hard work, and you will have bad food. But if there are opportunities for study, take them. Do not attract attention to yourself in any way. Do not speak of me. When you come out of prison come to see me, but secretly, and I will help you, not because of what you are, but because your respect for me was respect for what I stand for, which is bigger than either of us. While you are in prison, think of the hundreds and thousands of our people who are in prison in Africa, voluntarily, for the sake of freedom and justice, in that way you will not be alone, for in a difficult and round-about way I believe you to be one of them.

I greet you on behalf of myself and Mrs Mizi and our son, and Mr Samu and Mrs Samu, and others who are waiting to trust you. But this time, Jabavu, you must trust us. We greet you . . .

Jabavu lets the paper drop and stands staring. The word that has meant most to him of all the many words written hastily on that paper is *We*. We, says Jabavu. We, Us. Peace flows into him.

For in the tribe and the kraal, the life of his fathers was built on the word *we*. Yet it was never for him. And between then and now has been a harsh and ugly time when there was only the word I, I; I – as cruel and sharp as a knife. The word *we* has been offered to him again, accepting all his goodness and his badness, demanding everything he can offer. *We*, thinks Jabavu, We . . . And for the first time that hunger in him, which has raged like a beast all his life, wells up, unrefused, and streams gently into the word *We*.

There are steps outside clattering on the stone.

Mr Tennent says: 'Give me the letter.' Jabavu hands it to him and it slides quickly into Mr Tennent's pocket. 'I will give it back to Mr Mizi and say you have read it.'

'Tell him I have read it with all my understanding, and that

I thank him and will do what he says and he may trust me. Tell him I am no longer a child, but a man, and that his judgment is just, and it is right I should be punished.'

Mr Tennent looks in surprise at Jabavu and thinks, bitterly, that he, the man of God, is a failure; that an intemperate and godless agitator may talk of justice and of good and evil, and reach Jabavu where he is afraid to use these terms. But he says, with scrupulous kindness: 'I shall visit you in prison, Jabavu. But do not tell the warder or the police I brought you that letter.'

Jabavu thanks him and says: 'You are kind, sir.'

Mr Tennent smiles his dry, doubting smile, and goes out, and the warder locks the door.

Jabavu seats himself on the floor, his legs stretched out. He no longer sees the grey walls of the cell, he does not even think of the Court or of the prison afterwards.

We, says Jabavu over and over again, *We*. And it is as if in his empty hands are the warm hands of brothers.

THIS WAS THE OLD CHIEF'S COUNTRY
Volume One of Doris Lessing's Collected African Stories

All Doris Lessing's stories and short novels are being collected
in four volumes. This first volume comprises her collection of
African stories entitled *This Was the Old Chief's Country*,
together with three of the short novels from *Five*, the book which
won the Somerset Maugham Award in 1954. In her preface,
Doris Lessing writes: 'All the stories here are set in a society
which is more short-lived than most . . . But looking round the
world now, there isn't a way of living anywhere that doesn't
change and dissolve like clouds as you watch.'

'Mrs Lessing stands out sharply as one of the finest chroniclers
of this period in history'
Saturday Review

'Her sense of setting is so immediate, the touch and taste of her
continent is so strong, that Africa seems to become the universe'
Newsweek

£1.50

THE GOLDEN NOTEBOOK

Somewhere between emancipation and liberation were Free
Women – women without husbands following marital collapse.
The Golden Notebook is a story of Free Women, and has been
variously seen as the 'bible' of Women's Liberation, as a political
tract and as a story of mental breakdown. It is a book in which
men and women will go on finding themselves and their battles
for generations.

'One of the most serious, intelligent and honest writers of the
whole post-war generation'
Sunday Times

£1.35

MARTHA QUEST

Book One in the *Children of Violence* series

Martha is a young girl living on a farm in Africa, feeling her way through the torments of adolescence and early womanhood to marriage. She is a romantic idealist in revolt against the puritan snobbery of her parents, trying to live life to the full with every nerve, emotion and instinct bared to experience. For her this is a time of solitary reading, daydreams, dancing – and the first disturbing encounters with sex.

'Extraordinarily impressive'
New York Times

95p

A PROPER MARRIAGE

Book Two in the *Children of Violence* series

The war clouds are gathering over Europe, and for Martha Quest, the first passionate flush of marriage is beginning to fade. Sensuality becomes dulled by habit, marriage becomes motherhood, and, with the outbreak of war, Martha's political consciousness begins to dawn. The barriers between her and the frightening world outside finally dissolve.

£1.00

A RIPPLE FROM THE STORM

Book Three in the *Children of Violence* series

The outstanding continuation of the story of Martha Quest, Doris Lessing's most brilliantly portrayed representative of modern womanhood – passionate, wilful, uneasy in her emancipation. As the reader follows Martha through her emotional entanglements and her deepening involvement with politics, a magnificent panorama of twentieth-century life emerges, compassionate yet uncompromising in the fierce integrity of the author's vision.

'Not even Osborne or Amis can have much to teach author Doris Lessing'
Time

95p

LANDLOCKED

Book Four in the *Children of Violence* series

The whole world seems to have the post-war blues in the aftermath of World War II, and Martha Quest is no exception. Increasingly disillusioned with the Communist faith she once so fervently embraced, tiring of her neurotic lover Thomas, Martha embodies the plight of liberated twentieth-century womanhood. Doris Lessing portrays Martha and her crumbling world with an insight and compassion unmatched by any other living author.

'She never puts a foot wrong . . . for sheer poise I don't think there's been an author to touch her since Jane Austen'
John Wain, *The Observer*

95p

THE FOUR-GATED CITY

Book Five in the *Children of Violence* series

The Four-Gated City is the concluding volume in Doris Lessing's epic novel-sequence. It gives us Martha Quest in the Britain of the CND marches, 'Swinging' London, permissiveness and maybe social anarchy. But the author is not content to leave us there – we are taken a few years forward into a post third-world-war world where the mutated fruits of humanity's stupidity are beginning to show their eerie presence.

'Staggering'
New York Times

'A powerful, prophetic, mysterious work, a truly extraordinary novel'
Saturday Review

'A brilliant and disturbing book'
The Times

'The supreme achievement of a writer whom I regard as quite simply beyond my – or anyone else's – criticism'
Mervyn Jones, *Tribune*

£1.50

The Golden Notebook	£1.35	☐
The Black Madonna	80p	☐
Winter in July	95p	☐
Briefing for a Descent into Hell	75p	☐
The Habit of Loving	75p	☐
A Man and Two Women	75p	☐
Going Home (non-fiction)	95p	☐
Five	95p	☐

'Children of Violence' Series

Martha Quest	95p	☐
A Proper Marriage	£1.00	☐
A Ripple from the Storm	95p	☐
Landlocked	95p	☐
The Four-Gated City	£1.50	☐

Collected Stories

This Was the Old Chief's Country	£1.50	☐

All these books are available at your local bookshop or newsagent, or can be ordered direct from the publisher. Just tick the titles you want and fill in the form below.

Name ....

Address ....

....

Write to Panther Cash Sales, PO Box 11, Falmouth, Cornwall TR10 9EN

Please enclose remittance to the value of the cover price plus:

UK: 22p for the first book plus 10p per copy for each additional book ordered to a maximum charge of 82p.

BFPO and EIRE: 22p for the first book plus 10p per copy for the next 6 books, therafter 3p per book.

OVERSEAS: 30p for the first book and 10p for each additional book.

Granada Publishing reserve the right to show new retail prices on covers which may differ from those previously advertised in the text or elsewhere.